CARRION SAINTS

HIYODORI

Contents

Part Three
Artificial Immortals

Part Four
A Saint and a Devil

Part Five
Carrion City

Part Six
The Scenic Route to the End of the World

PART ONE

The Woman in the Hills

1

Crow often got mistaken for a man or a monster.

It had happened just now, in fact, here in a small countryside tea shop where anxious locals sold a drink made from translucent rose-pink beetles. The tea was light brown and tasted unremarkable, but emanated a faintly troubling scent.

"Here you go, sir," the server had said when handing Crow her cup.

Crow smiled and nodded. It was easiest to let people think whatever they wanted. The next time she came this far east might be decades or centuries later. By then every human in this shop would be dead, and perhaps the shop itself would have vanished together with them.

A long time had passed since the beginning of the end of the world. Which was both a time and a place. The end of the world meant this dragged-out twilight era of mortal civilization, a terminal fading. It also meant the shrinking physical boundaries of land and sea alike. Ships could only go so far across the ocean before meeting with certain ruin.

Even high-flying aerial creatures knew better than to try passing that point of no return. There were obscure liminal areas where the continent itself crumbled away into impassable nothingness. Or so poets claimed.

There were no real cities left anymore. Not like there used to be. A massively concentrated human population tended to attract a massive number of monsters. Crow rather liked what remained: these quiet, scattered towns and settlements. Though she did look back with nostalgia on the great lost cities that used to stretch as far as the eye could see.

She wasn't sure why people in this era took her for a man. She favored loose-fitting, light-colored clothing (in defiance of her name). Around humans, she usually wore a pair of small tinted sunglasses. She had black hair scraped back into a short ponytail.

She also had wings. She could reduce them to the size of sparrow wings and shift them anywhere on her body—to enfold her wrist like a watchband, for instance. At the moment, they grew from the nape of her neck, shrunken down to furl around her throat in the shape of an eccentric high collar.

If anyone asked, she'd tell them she was a woman. They often changed their minds after hearing her speak. But they rarely asked or cared. She was above all else a monster-slaying saint, except for the times when she'd been termed a monster herself. Immortals like Crow had little control over what humans decided to call them.

Anyway, she couldn't keep up with changing fashions. Even in a single isolated region, the gender coding of clothing could flip around in a matter of decades. Green used to be considered masculine, the green of rugged forest and untamed wilderness. Fifty years later, that same green became incurably feminine: delicate springtime growth, budding fertility. And nowadays? No idea.

Crow sat for a long time in the tea shop. She sipped her beetle drink very slowly. Yellowing curtains fluttered in the breeze from open windows. Small botanical sketches hung on the nearest wall: painstaking studies of snakeroot and ashwort.

On her way into the village, she'd spotted a dilapidated shrine to the God of the End, who assumed many different forms and went by many different names, and who was most often depicted taking a nap. A personable deity, one who would receive immense gratitude for doing nothing whatsoever. The villagers had festooned the god's bed with radish leaves.

It was the first season of long radishes, as they called it here. Warm and sunny, but not yet hot enough for humans to sweat while sitting still. The second season of radishes would come closer to winter.

She'd gotten worried looks when she first walked in. A few residents—those with keen magic perception—instantly recognized her as an immortal. Others shied away after glimpsing the eyes behind her sunglasses, or the miniaturized wings folded about her neck. Word would spread quickly in a village like this one.

She couldn't blame them. A lone immortal was often bad news. Humans had no way to distinguish monsters from saints at a glance.

Before anyone took her order, the tea shop owner had lumbered over. He drew himself up with the portly dignity of a walrus.

"I'm a saint," Crow said, although any clever monster could have made the same claim.

"You have a companion?"

"No."

"Looking for one?"

"Not yet." She tilted her head to indicate the area northeast of the tea shop and the village. Hilly, uninhabited land. "No human companion of mine should have to face that."

His wariness ebbed. He knew what she meant.

The tension in the room eased once she'd gotten the shopkeeper's unspoken seal of approval. Now adolescents huddled in a shady corner, playing mancala with colorful dried beans. Crow listened to the clinking of beans filling up the wooden game board, and then she listened to the murmurs of those around her.

There were two types of humans here: locals and outsiders. Her cultural knowledge was far out of date, but she found it easy to tell the difference. Locals mostly wore neat tabards and pants gathered at the ankle, all in lovely shades of pink and rose and blushing lavender. Their beetles were good for dye as well as for tea.

Also, the locals made no sound when they walked. Nor did they make much mention of the primary topic favored by outsiders: a great evil lurking near this very town. A monster called—rather unimaginative-ly—the Woman in the Hills.

The largest table was occupied by a hunting party who had come to slay said Woman in the Hills. Crow finished her beetle tea and went up to them.

The clinking from the mancala players grew quieter. Crow was not the only one here with a penchant for eavesdropping.

The hunters seemed friendly enough. Only their apparent leader refused to speak with her. He was an astonishingly low-contrast man. His hair and skin and sunken eyes were all the same sandy hue.

Crow asked if they knew what the Woman in the Hills could do.

"We aren't fools," said the oldest in the group. "She bewitches you with her voice."

"With her magic," Crow said.

"We've heard all the stories. Earplugs won't stop her. Not to worry— we've got a secret weapon."

He clapped the faded man on the back. Other party members told Crow that the faded man was a bard (the least cheery bard she'd ever seen) and that he carried a cursed flute. He could play a song of absolute silence. Not only that, he'd previously fought the Woman in the Hills with a different party. He knew what she was really like. He knew her weaknesses.

"A monster of that caliber, and you lived?" Crow said neutrally.

The older hunter grinned at her. "Impressive, isn't he?"

Crow wished them luck. The faded man, still saying nothing, stared fixedly at her sunglasses until the whole party left.

She ran into some difficulty when she attempted to pay for her drink. The coins she'd brought, which had been issued by a now-fallen regional city-state, were several centuries out of date. The metal had little intrinsic value.

Even so, the shopkeeper was not averse to taking her money. Other locals drifted over from the fringes and launched into a lengthy debate over what her coins might be worth. Crow gave a handful to the mancala players, who promptly used them to start a new game.

"I can take a look at your roof," she said to the shopkeeper. "I've been complimented on my repairs."

He laughed. "No greater honor than to get our roof patched by a saint. Don't bother. It's already in good shape."

"You knew I was an immortal from the start," Crow said curiously.

"We live in the shadow of the Woman in the Hills. We know an immortal when we see one."

His fellow locals had also been quick to peek around the sides of her sunglasses. Like all corporeal immortals, she had red eyes—in her case, a color akin to tart hibiscus tea. But most other immortals were less adept at passing for human. Out of the hunting party, only the bard had regarded her with open suspicion. Why hadn't he spoken up?

"How can I pay for my tea?" Crow asked again. "You can't do much with those coins."

He took a kitchen cloth printed with acorns and dabbed at his brow. "There's one thing ... but it's worth far more than a single cup of tea."

"I was planning to go see the Woman in the Hills regardless," she assured him.

"When?"

Mortals were always particular about when.

"In a few..." She started to say *weeks*, then caught the expression on his face. "In a few days. I'll let the other hunters have a try first. They seemed very confident."

"They'll die."

"The bard didn't think I was human. But he didn't ask me to help him. That flute of his must be a remarkable artifact."

A shrug. "Many hunters come bearing legendary artifacts. So far, none have made any difference."

"Did he really fight your monster before?"

"He's not lying," the shopkeeper said. "That bard did come through here about a year ago, with a different party. Back then he had bright orange hair. He was very outgoing. His own grandmother wouldn't recognize him now."

Other locals, listening in, nodded emphatically. Crow was the only outsider left in the shop.

"I'm impressed that you remembered him, then."

"We're used to seeing people like that. The Woman in the Hills always leaves one survivor. Just one."

"As a form of mercy?" Crow inquired, although that couldn't possibly be the case.

"They go back out in the world," the shopkeeper said heavily. "They escape with their lives. Then they come back to her. They always come back, a few months or years later. They return with deadened faces, bringing eager new companions. They tell stories of secret ways to kill the Woman in the Hills. They tell stories about the treasure buried under her tree."

"There are enormous bounties on her head," Crow said.

"That's what they all claim. But who's promised to pay those bounties? Not us. We don't have that kind of money."

The shopkeeper invited her to go out on the terrace with him and drink more beetle tea. On the house, he said.

The awning had a few holes, but it offered plenty of shade. Crow found a large woody beetle leg floating in her new cup of tea. This was apparently very rare—a sign of good fortune to come. The shopkeeper's fleshy face brightened.

He asked if there were anything else he could provide for her. He made no mention of cost. She slid her slim trunk out from beneath her chair. She didn't need an inn; she just needed a place to stash her things (what little she had). He gladly offered to put her trunk in storage.

In a nearby grassy square, young men and women practiced a noisy dance that involved a lot of shouting and brandishing arm-length white radishes. The shopkeeper explained that their radish dance would be performed at the next harvest festival. It had been performed at local harvest festivals for over a hundred years. Crow made polite noises. No such tradition had existed the last time she'd come through here.

"You called her our monster," the shopkeeper said at last.

"I'm sorry," Crow offered. "Was that rude?" She was used to putting her foot in her mouth. It could hardly be avoided when you missed out on decades or eons of local cultural context.

He shook his head. "She *is* our local monster. She defends her territory. For her own sake, not to protect us. But we've been kept safe from other monsters for as long as anyone can remember."

"There must be a price," Crow said.

"There used to be."

"There must still be a price."

"My great-grandfather told me that the Woman in the Hills took her prey from this village, long ago." He gazed intently at the beetle leg in Crow's cup. "We brought her gifts. Human sacrifices. In exchange she gave us good luck and abundant harvests. For generation after generation.

"Eventually she made them drag the mayor up in front of her. She demanded answers. Why did they keep willingly sending her their beloved sons and daughters? Why had they just accepted the fact that all such sacrifices need to come from them? 'Where's the satisfaction,' she demanded, 'in killing a soft child barely old enough to have an ego? Where's the satisfaction in taking a sacrifice who doesn't even know how to fight?'

"The mayor bowed on the ground before her and begged her to take sacrifices from outside the village instead. At that point, what else could he tell her? 'Thank you,' she said. 'Goodness. All you had to do was ask. There are rules to this, you know. I'm a monster. I can't turn down a proper sacrifice. But there isn't much pleasure to be found in preying on you people, let me tell you.'"

After that, the shopkeeper concluded, she began luring in strangers.

"Like the bard and his hunters."

"We welcome all visitors," he said without emotion. "We feed them. If they ask about the Woman in the Hills, we tell them what we know. We neither encourage nor discourage them. They're generous with their money and supplies. They expect to come into enormous riches as soon as they slay her."

"This town seems to want for nothing."

"This town is where ambitious hunters come to die. No one marks their graves. No one collects their bones."

Locals had tiptoed around the hunting party, soundlessly crossing the tea shop. Despite his bulk, the shopkeeper was the quietest and most careful of them all. So graceful that you could almost forget he was there.

"If I slay your monster, you may no longer have bountiful harvests," Crow said. "You may no longer be protected from disease and disaster. Not to mention other monsters."

"But no matter what we tell you—you came to slay her. Didn't you?"

"Yes," Crow admitted. "Yes, that's true."

"Then, please—go to her soon. Before she kills the men who just left my shop."

He must have seen off countless other groups. Like the hunting party that confronted the Woman in the Hills back when the faded bard still had bright orange hair.

Maybe the shopkeeper had warned some of them that they were going to be eaten. Maybe he had told them to forget tall tales about treasure and bounties, to turn back while they still could. Maybe he hadn't said a word. Ominous warnings had a way of making would-be heroes even more determined to launch doomed assaults on abominable monsters.

The difference between now and all those other times was that an immortal saint had come to town.

"All right." Crow extracted the beetle leg from her tea and laid it gently on the edge of her saucer. "I'll go kill her today."

2

TODAY THE SKY was blue streaked through with red and purple. There had been times, people said, when the sky used to be less exciting. But no one could remember such a time. Not even Crow.

She went to a stand of trees at the far end of the settlement. Along the way, she saw—and smelled—numerous dark earthy sheds for farming beetles. Farther off lay a field of tall taro plants, bowing under the weight of their own huge leaves. An old woman popped her head out from among the rows of taro as if she'd been lurking there for relief from the sun.

Someone had left a number of long white radishes propped up in a nearby stream, perhaps to keep them cool. They were as tall and thick as Crow's calves, though much paler.

She knelt among damp mossy roots to speak with tiny soil-dwelling isopods. She was secretly proud of the fact that she'd always gotten along well with the isopod community. They never spoke to humans, and hardly ever said a word to immortals. This time, they hardly said a word to her, either. They'd been put off by the scent of beetle tea on her breath.

Isopods were not closely related to beetles. But she could understand their reluctance. She apologized at length, and eventually the isopods told her where the hunters were. They hadn't gone far yet.

She plucked a dark feather from the folded-down wings that cupped her neck like a pair of choking hands. The feather grew in her fingers until it looked as though it might have fallen from a soaring black eagle.

She returned quickly to the village and thrust her feather at the tea shop owner.

"Hang it out of the reach of children," she said. "If you ever need rescuing, break it to summon me."

He held the feather across his palms as if it were a sword bequeathed by a queen. "A crow feather," he said. "I've heard of you."

"I'm not the only saint who's ever had wings."

"Arrows fletched with your feathers fly true."

"Don't put it on an arrow. Save it for when you really need it."

Crow hadn't dallied for long. But when she went back to the slender running stream, the bathing radishes had vanished. Some hardworking farmer must have carted them away.

Her roots spread far, the isopods warned. *You might be too late.*

Crow sighed. Nothing for it. She sent her wings sliding down to anchor themselves in the musculature of her back. They found their way out through long slashes cut in her tunic. They swelled so large that they could have wrapped her entire body in a makeshift cocoon.

Her wings only beat once. A soundless motion, an eruption of tension—magic held and held and held and finally released like spilling water.

In that single wingbeat, she ported to the hunters' current location.

She tried to, at any rate.

She'd made it deep into the hills. The human settlement lay far out of sight. It was as silent here as a ghost town in the middle of a desert. Butterflies fluttered nervously to and fro—so many of them that, off in the distance, they looked like swarming midges.

No sign of any hunters. No sign of anyone at all. Her wings sheepishly folded themselves down to more modest dimensions. She hadn't used porting magic in several decades. She had never in her life ventured all the way to the heart of these hills. Some inaccuracy was only to be expected.

While she was sometimes capable of porting across great distances with a flick of her wings, there were also benefits to taking things slowly. Especially when entering enemy territory.

Besides, the hunting party wouldn't appreciate her popping up out of nowhere to snatch away their glory. Would it be better to turn back and let them have a fair chance? She'd been raised by humans, but the older she got, the more difficult it became to view them as anything other than children. She worked hard to compensate for this tendency. Perhaps too hard. She had no god to tell her if she was being overly hands-off.

Crow kept going, now on foot. The land was not at all elevated, but the atmosphere felt as thin as a naked mountaintop. Like a place where you could see the far edge of the world bending out of sight. The hollowed-out air susurrated against her skin, a million tiny insect wings. That was the presence of the Woman in the Hills. Her roots ran far and deep indeed.

Strange wet-looking snakes slithered beneath yellow gorse. The colors in the sky had stopped moving: it was stiller than a painting. The disembodied scent of magnolia blossoms grew with each step.

Hills was something of a misnomer. The earth formed grassy mounds like natural barrows, as neatly spaced as a well-regulated graveyard. From the perspective of an aerial in flight, the land would look like a body pimpled with a deadly contagious pox. The mounds weren't much taller than Crow herself.

The thinner the air got, the heavier her trepidation. She should have come faster. She shouldn't have gone back to give the shopkeeper her feather. In truth, there had been no time to spare.

Overhead, the sun refused to budge. No clouds drew shut across the sky like curtains. No trees showed themselves anywhere on the horizon. No greenery grew higher than Crow's hip. The entire world might have been made of undulating barrows.

Dimness closed in around her as if evening had arrived early.

Abruptly—though she had not ported—she stood at the edge of a wide clearing. The hills stopped. A vast magnolia tree cast dense shade across flat root-packed dirt. Nothing grew beneath it except a fuzz of silver-gray moss and foamy rot-eating fungi.

The monster's aura pumped in the air like a throbbing pulse. There was a hideous vitality to it. Crow knew then that she would be very lucky to find any of the human hunters left alive.

She plucked another feather from her left wing. In her hand, it transformed into a sleek obsidian blade.

She stepped beneath the tree's branches. It felt like stepping into an enormous subterranean cavern. The temperature dropped, and the floral scent thickened. The blossoms were a confused mix of colors, some deep purple-red and some as creamy white as the local radishes—as if the tree didn't know what type of magnolia it was supposed to be. Perhaps it didn't much care.

Roots pulsated beneath the soil like busy arteries. People lay tangled in the thickest roots closest to the corpulent trunk. She counted each of the hunters she'd met at the tea shop, and then some. They were as gray as the pitiful moss underfoot. The faded man was the grayest of all, as if he'd been dead for a long time now. His flute had been unceremoniously snapped in two.

Pity stirred in Crow: the current of an old, old river.

"Help," said a strangled voice. A woman's voice. Crow hadn't seen any women among the hunters.

"Help me." With only the tiniest shift in timbre, it sounded like the voice of a young boy.

"Carrie..."

No one, mortal or immortal, had called Crow by that nickname in decades.

"I'm hurt," he said. "Carrie, please help."

Nonexistent light danced madly along the length of Crow's obsidian blade. "I'm going to kill you now," she said to the tree. This was the same tone she'd used when requesting a drink at the tea shop.

"Behind you!" cried the voice, that familiar voice she'd followed faithfully from the moment the boy learned to speak to the moment he died a hero.

She whirled like a machine.

A human body had crawled out of the earth like a revenant. It dragged itself toward her on its elbows. Vegetal roots stretched from its lower back and hips and calves, ends still anchored deep below the soil. As if the body were a bloated exotic tuber.

It was not the body of a warrior. It carried no weapons. It was just another one of this tree's long-dead victims. Crow's blade remained still.

The voice tipped back towards female, though it could nevertheless have been the voice of a boy. "I can't believe you fell for that."

"I didn't fall for—"

"But you did," said the Woman in the Hills. "You listened to me."

"It won't happen again," Crow said evenly.

"Yes, it will. Again and again. Why don't you have a promised companion? Why'd you come to me alone?"

"I wouldn't bring my companion here like a sacrificial goat for you to devour."

"Hah! How chivalrous. A companion would've offered you a token veneer of mental protection. Instead, you came naked. You gave me a way in. All I need is a tiny, tiny crack. You trod on my earth, and you filled your lungs with my scent. You let me barge inside your head.

"Let's see—what else did he say before he died? *Carrie, one day we'll save the world.* His mother called you Carrie, too, didn't she?

"Did you think I needed to drink your blood or bite you or split you open to best you? No, no. This is my territory. You came here with your own wings and your own feet, and without a companion. You're a fool, Carrie. And I couldn't be happier."

The body's head looked up. Then it detached itself without fanfare, scuttling past Crow on little fast-moving roots like crab legs.

She stabbed rapidly at the fleeing head. There was no reason she should have missed. Yet the head slipped out of reach. It scampered up the haggard tree and settled on a broken branch, as pompous as the sculpted bust of an emperor.

Some said the Woman in the Hills was a magnolia tree. Some said she was nothing but a severed human head.

The truth seemed to lie somewhere between the two. The tree was part of her, rooting her to the land. She never made physical appearances in the nearby village; she just invaded people's dreams. Customers at the tea shop had told Crow of how she appeared in their sleep like the ghost of a meddling granny.

"How unexciting it would be if you poisoned your entire household by accident!" she'd said to one woebegone homesteader, telling him off for his basement full of botulism. He'd had no choice but to take her word for it.

Only the tea shop owner harbored qualms about the status quo. The other villagers always took her word for it, even in half-remembered dreams. "She looks out for us," they said. "She hasn't harvested any of our children since the beginning of the end of the world."

That phrase was a catch-all way to refer to a very long time ago. Longer than any human would care to calculate. Longer than Crow herself had walked this world.

Crow raised her sword and drew closer to the Woman in the Hills.

The monster's head looked human, minus the fact that it lacked a body. It was handsome and androgynous, as open to interpretation as her changeable voice. If she weren't known as the Woman in the Hills, most hunters would probably have thought she was a beautiful man. Or else that she encompassed every gender, or none whatsoever. Tufted eyebrows—one slashed in half by a dashing scar—lent her an expression of innocent surprise.

Crow had never seen a monster or a saint with a lasting scar.

The head opened her mouth and let out a perfect imitation of a mockingbird's elaborate song.

"Are you done showing off?" Crow asked, far more politely than the monster deserved.

"Never. Want to hear from your boy again? Nailed his voice in one try, didn't I?"

Crow was close enough to lower her shadowy sword and cleave this chattering head in half like a melon. It would be smooth, almost silent, a death blow dealt more with magic than with physical force.

An alien discomfort curled in her gut. Only after she'd brought her blade down, only after it had sliced without resistance through a human-shaped cranium and a human-shaped brain—only then did she grasp the source of her unease. The Woman in the Hills had never been afraid. She'd watched Crow with avaricious eyes. Those eyes were dark enough to seem brown-black but were in fact a deep red. The opaque color of ancient wine. She didn't so much as blink when the blade descended on her.

Because it had not descended at all. There was fog in Crow's mind, and illusions infiltrating her flesh.

"That trick will only work once," she said.

"Amazing!" cried the head. "Look at you shake off hallucinations like morning dew. A beautiful sight. You have a strong sense of purpose, and you remember it well. That boy gave you one last mission, and you'll do anything to carry it out. Seems like just yesterday that he was still alive, doesn't it? Decades pass in the blink of an eye. He was like your own child—no, that can't be right. He was a human boy. In terms of lifespan, he was more like your goldfish."

"You can read my heart," said Crow, "but you can't understand it."

This time, no illusion deceived her into thinking she'd moved when she hadn't. As she cut toward the Woman in the Hills, rogue branches and roots shot out of the tree and the ground, an ever-sprouting protective hydra. She let go of her sword. It flew on its own to chop a path through writhing wood. She barely had to put any magic in it at all.

Her feet were steady on the moss-glazed ground. Her wings flicked open absentmindedly to parry spear-like twists of sap-scented growth. The spears drilled at her back without ever making it past her feathers.

"You're weak," Crow said. She wasn't trying to rattle the Woman in the Hills. She was simply too startled not to speak. "You're the weakest of the Four Great Adversaries. I don't know why we saved you for last."

The head scrambled up to higher branches, running on the root-like nubs that grew from its severed neck.

"I do have an outsize reputation," the head admitted. "Look, I never submitted an application to be termed a Great Adversary of humanity. It's mortals who wanted there to be four of us. We have no other connection—we never gathered together to hold a conference. The fourth could've been any other monster. It never had to be me."

Crow glanced at the lifeless and colorless bodies that lay strewn at the base of the magnolia tree, half-submerged. As wild branches attacked her, the bodies had begun melting away into sapwood and bark. Crow herself had yet to receive a single scratch, though the tireless branches lashed out faster than rattlesnakes. Her sword and wings had moved in a blur, without effort or thought.

She ported to hover among the upper branches, at eye level with the frantically retreating head. Her sword flew back to her hand.

She'd braced herself to face an army of magical thralls. Perhaps the Woman in the Hills had already sucked all her old immortal minions dry. At least she hadn't tried to fend Crow off by puppeting human corpses. That would have been rather insulting to everyone involved.

She readied her blade to split the woman's forehead. This time, she would cleave through every last useless illusion.

"Stop," the woman said.

Crow's body stopped moving, and so did her sword.

She didn't understand. The monster had spoken in her own voice, not in an imitation of the boy who Crow had once known and raised and ushered gently to his death. Stealing his voice wouldn't have tripped her up again, anyway. She was armed with enough magic to ram past layer after layer of misdirection and cheap tricks.

Yet the cool voice of the monster ran down through her like a tingling waterfall. She was relaxed—so relaxed as to become absent from her own body. As if she were on her fiftieth year of meditating on a windy mountaintop, scoured utterly clean, empty inside and out.

It occurred to her that the monster had not made any serious attempts at self-defense. The frenetic undulating roots and mutant wooden spikes had all been for show. A dramatic distraction, easily batted aside.

The monster read Crow's mind like a prophet poking at entrails. "You're quite right about me. I'm as weak as a worm. Just a frail little thing, a pretty decapitated head stuck to a flowering tree. Your magic is to mine as the sun is to a lamp. But can't you see? My unique talents are perfectly fitted to your unique vulnerabilities. As if someone made us for each other. Yes, you were right to save me for last, but don't think I'm not extremely irritated about it! You kept me waiting for ages.

"Now," she said, "let's go down and talk at ground level. I feel silly perching here like a bird."

That voice flowed in Crow with more certainty than her own immortal blood. Fighting that current would be like sticking her hand in a river and trying to hold it back with open fingers.

She reached up and took hold of the severed head. She tried to make herself choke it—although it clearly wasn't kept alive by breathing—but her hands would not tighten. On the underside of the chopped-off neck, stubs of some unnatural growth writhed like delighted insect legs against her cradling palms.

Crow's wings unfurled, and she glided down to earth. She found herself holding the head up to face her. Large petals fell from the spreading tree above, some white as a mushroom and some the dark purple of a bruise.

"Just as you've heard of me, Carrie, I've heard a thing or two about you," said the Woman in the Hills. "You still need a proper name for me, don't you? Don't want you calling me Woman, that's for sure. Think of me as Magnolia. Yes—that should do. It's as good a name as any."

3

Magnolia instructed Crow to put her sword away. It had been floating around them, too meek to break into the conversation. Now it crumbled into a shower of glittering dust.

"Quit that," Magnolia said dismissively.

Crow had been attempting to use a finger to bore a hole in her temple. She didn't need special weapons to fatally damage a human-shaped head.

Her finger withdrew as Magnolia's voice washed over her. What on earth had rendered her so pliant? The monster herself had admitted that Crow was superior in every other realm of magic and combat.

Such total control couldn't possibly be sustainable. Would the effects wear off over time? Act quick enough, and she might succeed in annihilating her own hearing, or gagging Magnolia's mouth. But she didn't think she took in that voice with her ears alone, or that breaking Magnolia's jaw would be sufficient to stop it.

"You have unusually violent fantasies for a saint," said Magnolia.

"You killed twelve hunters today." Crow was surprised to find herself capable of speech.

"Why wouldn't I let you talk?" Magnolia asked. "I love talking. It's my only hobby, and I don't get to do nearly enough of it. Humans are never in a very talkative mood, especially once you start killing them. I could point out that they came here with every intention of killing me first, but for some reason no one seems to view that as an adequate excuse. Why are the powerful expected to show mercy? Why shouldn't I do to them what they hoped to do to me? Why should I spare them just because I can? How wasteful.

"You might ask yourself the same question. If you observed the vast discrepancy in our magic—if you had noted that I was a braggadocious small fry, unworthy to be deemed anyone's Great Adversary—why, you might have chosen to spare me." She wore a shark-like smile. "If you'd shown mercy, perhaps I too would have let you walk away."

"No," Crow said. "You never had any intention of letting me go."

"Hm? Can you read minds, too?"

"You can command my movements. You can't make me think I brought it on myself."

"I could, actually, but that would be as sad as holding a conversation with a hand puppet, and I don't even have hands. Oh—you've got a hair clip in your pocket," Magnolia added suddenly. "Rarely use it, do you? Get these bangs out of my face. No, not like that. Don't be sloppy. Make me look good."

Much against her will, Crow did.

Magnolia's hair was the dark hue of heartwood. None of it quite reached the cut-off edge of her neck. She wore teardrop earrings: light-catching beads like fallen amber. She had a tiny mole near her lower lip, and a few others dotted by her eye.

As Crow pushed her hair around, an angry scar revealed itself like a third eye burnt across her forehead. Some sort of twisted cosmetic choice?

An immortal might come in the form of a butterfly or a chimera or an intangible phrase of music or a disembodied human head. Her state of severance could very well be her complete and total self—not a sign of loss, not an unhealed wound. These extraneous marks on her face might have nothing to do with the fact that she lacked a body below the neck. Crow had been through an untold number of battles, but she'd never kept any of her scars for good. It was in an immortal's nature to heal.

Crow used the clip to pull half her bangs over to one side, which was stylish enough to be deemed suitable. At least according to the incomprehensible standards of a sentient severed head.

"You're a cold fish, aren't you?" Magnolia commented.

"I don't know what you mean."

"Shouldn't you be beating your breast in humiliation right about now? Shouldn't you swear horrific vengeance on all my ancestors and descendants?"

"Do you have ancestors or descendants?"

"It's a figure of speech."

"Would wailing in humiliation help me escape you?"

"Unfortunately not. Although it would make for an excellent show."

"You want something from me," said Crow. This monster would happily chitchat for years before getting to the point.

"Well, yes. You can't even imagine how long I've been dying for someone to get that hair out of my eyes."

"You could have grown a twig from your tree to scrape it back."

"That sounds much less fun than getting fussed over by a certified saint. Some things are worth the wait."

"What else will you make me do?" Crow asked.

"Do you really want to know?"

She could command Crow to burn down the nearest settlement. She could make Crow raze every village in the east. She could make Crow drag living humans to her massing roots, lining them up like offerings in a temple, like pale radishes soaking in a shady stream.

How many atrocities would she have to commit before Magnolia's hold on her weakened?

She couldn't destroy herself—no immortal could. But if she became a servant of evil, she would find a hero to slay her. Temporarily or forever. Like how she'd teamed up with human heroes to slay other formidable monsters across the centuries. That was how she could remain true to her own wishes, in the end, no matter what Magnolia's voice tried to force on her.

"Let's not get too far ahead of ourselves," Magnolia said cheerfully. "One step at a time. We all labor under certain restrictions. First, I'd like you to remove some of mine. You can start by cutting down my tree."

4

It was the work of several weeks—disappointingly quick. Too quick for Crow to devise a way out of this.

The bodies of the human hunters were all gone. They soaked into the earth and vanished like rainwater. Fallen magnolia petals melted away together with them. There were never enough left to completely carpet the ground.

Crow had warned the hunters about Magnolia's voice. To think that she'd required more of a warning herself. She'd meant to come prepared—she'd gone on a long magical fast. For four decades, she'd used barely any magic.

She'd arrived here at the height of her power. But it wouldn't make sense to unleash her full power on this one solitary monster. Would you drown an entire coastal city to depose its king? Would you fire cannonballs to kill a rabbit? Humans might. They rushed through their short lives without any sense of proportion. Crow knew better.

Magnolia had turned out to be a small-time monster, her influence limited to this obscure stretch of eastern wilderness. She'd masterfully manipulated rumors to make herself seem like some towering figure of unconquerable evil. In reality, she didn't even have enough magic to craft herself a full body of flesh.

Crow should have been able to shatter the chains of her voice with sheer magical muscle alone. Yet here they were: she'd been faithfully working to grant Magnolia's wish for almost a month now. And she wasn't any closer to escaping.

Being immortals, neither of them required sleep or physical food or hydration. Crow never stopped digging up and reeling in the wide-spreading roots of the now-fallen tree, which seemed to multiply as she worked. Meanwhile, Magnolia never stopped chattering.

"You still seem confused," Magnolia said.

A few dead branches of the tree had rolled over to her and scraped together a generous pile of petals. She bounced her head atop the pile like a child bouncing on a mattress.

Crow didn't respond. Much to her disappointment, the magic of obedience on her never flagged. It seemed so insubstantial. Yet she couldn't shrug it off like a mere illusion. Magnolia's commanding voice had wormed its way into the deepest part of her through a fatal crack, a weakness that Crow herself had never noticed, and that no other magic-user had ever observed or exploited. Yes, she was still very confused. She couldn't understand how Magnolia had gotten so entrenched in her.

"You're much more powerful than me." Magnolia needed no encouragement to keep talking. "If you're a dragon, then I'm a worm—et cetera. But the real difference between us is that you're an all-rounder. You've fought every other Great Adversary. You've fought human armies, too. You've lived embedded with farmers and merchants and artisans and poets. In every case, you made yourself useful. You couldn't do that if you were only good at one type of magic."

She stopped bouncing. "Me, on the other hand—I'm only good at one thing. All my other magic? Pitiful. The thing is, the one type of magic I'm good at—I've absolutely perfected it. It doesn't matter that I'm weaker than you in every other sense. It doesn't matter, because I can make you my servant."

Thanks to Crow's labors, the clearing had utterly changed. Sunlight fell straight down from a color-streaked sky. The hacked-up trunk looked like the besieged wreckage of a wooden castle. A tangle of denuded roots soared taller than the surrounding hills. Flower-spattered branches splayed out across scarred ground.

A clear liquid, reminiscent of brain fluid, leaked out from the cup-shaped blossoms. Peculiar songbirds—bare-faced, like vultures—darted down to drink it before the dawn light grew too strong.

"I can't have been the first visiting immortal with enough magic to uproot your tree," Crow said at last.

"I made low-level monsters hack away at the trunk for centuries on end, to no avail. Two steps forward, two steps back. Very frustrating. Maybe you're the one who deserves to be called a Great Adversary—you're certainly great at destroying things. And you seem to enjoy it."

"I'm only an adversary to monsters."

"Spoken like a true saint."

"I enjoyed it," Crow added, "because I hoped it might hurt you." There had been a certain catharsis in slashing her way through the deep-rooted magic that bound Magnolia to the hills, a magic like a stake that went all the way down to the burning heart of the earth.

"Too bad," said Magnolia. "It felt wonderful. Like a snake shedding old skin." In the morning light, the carcass of the once-eternal magnolia tree began to flicker in and out of sight like a dragonfly's wings.

"You must have lured higher-level monsters and saints," Crow said.

"That I did."

"You could've found someone else to free you ages ago."

"Do you think I didn't try? Cutting my tree down and unearthing its roots might have seemed easy enough to you, Carrie. It wasn't easy for anyone else. At one point I even got humans to help. They sawed away at my trunk until all the skin came off their hands, until ligaments started tearing. It would never have worked. I just wanted to see if they would fail in the same way as monster and saints.

"You're hopelessly weak to me—but as my thrall, you're more effective than any other being to ever set foot in my clearing. Naturally I'd want the strongest servant I could get. And I knew you'd be stronger than anyone else I've ever encountered."

Her confidence was bewildering. "We've never met before."

"Of course not. But you knew where to find me. You're the Saint of the Carrion Crow—slayer of humanity's adversaries, champion of the weak, guardian to generation after generation of grateful mortals. I've never cared much about being called a Great Adversary. It gave me a little ray of hope, though. You wiped out each of the others. My fearsome peers. Surely one day you'd come to kill me, too. Even if every other immortal failed to dig me out of here, there was still a chance you might succeed.

"As long as I knew you were somewhere out there, I couldn't give up. I couldn't resign myself to being forever bound to the land. You certainly took your sweet time, but I suppose I'll forgive that. You can make it up to me now that you're here."

Crow had lived too long to react on reflex. She let Magnolia's words wash past her, provoking nothing. Internally, she tried to test the boundaries of Magnolia's ability to command her, but she couldn't even get a firm grip on the bars of her cage. She couldn't use magic or willpower to extract herself. It would be like trying to punch a virus out of her blood with bare fists.

She'd learned more about Magnolia in the time she'd spent demolishing that looming tree. For example: the tree was not an outside restraint, a sacred being planted to trap this dreadful monster in place. It was very much a part of Magnolia herself—who, as she grew in years and honed her magic, had found herself increasingly root-bound to these desolate hills.

All monsters suffered from some manner of congenital limitation. They called it a compulsion. Other immortals might free them, but nature forbade them from freeing themselves. Land-bound monsters were tied to their unique territory from birth, as if by an umbilical cord that they could never sever with their own claws.

Magnolia's grand tree had been the cord magically tying her to the heart of the hills. She'd forced Crow to sever it, liberating her for the first time in her life.

"I came to slay you," Crow said.

"Well, now you can do penance for it. Come sit with me."

A conveniently shaped stump rose from the moss-silvered ground, shedding petals as it grew. The hulk of the ruined tree had already dissolved and scattered like scraps of fog.

Magnolia ordered Crow to examine the underside of her neck.

The plant-like growths that she used as primitive limbs had fully retracted. The wound at the bottom of her neck was neither bloody nor thick with scars. It wasn't entirely solid, for that matter: it felt like looking at a rift exposing the loneliest reaches of deep space, winking with distant stars. Or like lifting a rock to see insects writhing in wet loam. Pale leeches clung to the bizarre starry surface where her neck came to an end. Each split off into an irregular number of hungry pulsating heads.

"These parasites have been driving me crazy," Magnolia announced. "You wouldn't believe how badly it itches. Pluck them off."

Crow's fingers reluctantly went to work. The worms stretched gummily, snapping with a horrid wet spatter like being spit on. Crow tasted bile.

"Is this necessary?" she asked.

"Alas, I can only command beings with language and reason. I was once mauled by a bear. Nearly died from it. Not an experience I would care to repeat. Have you ever been killed by a bear?"

"No."

"They were much bigger, back in the day. It could fit my entire head in its mouth like an apple."

Crow peeled off the final metaphysical leech. It turned to a twist of sickly green smoke as she lobbed it aside.

"Wow," said Magnolia. "You really did it."

"You ordered me to."

"I thought you'd complain more. Do you have an affinity for parasites?" She snorted. "I'm rather more surprised that you just up and believed me. You really think I've been suffering from these for centuries? I let them come hitch a ride while you sawed away at my tree. Of course I can command animals."

Crow contemplated the head in her hands. Bangs pulled back with Crow's own clip. Sooty brows and lashes. A sprinkling of moles like an obscure constellation. An expression of fearless glee.

She had the strength to crush that mischievous head between her palms as if juicing a grapefruit. It didn't matter. The invasive magic in her blood would stop her before she applied enough pressure to cause serious pain.

Yet nothing stopped her from standing up calmly, lifting the head, and hurling it like a trebuchet into far-off hills.

5

MAGNOLIA SOARED OFF with a combination of shrieking laughter and dog-like yelps. She landed far enough away that Crow could no longer make out what she said. Unfortunately, she found herself hiking off to go fetch Magnolia anyway. The commands that moved her were not solely reliant on sound.

She discovered Magnolia atop one of the tallest grassy mounds, resting there like a beheaded criminal. A warning to restless citizens.

"That was fun," Magnolia said. "Did you think you could get away?"

"You let me throw you."

"You really are gullible. Don't feel too bad about it, though. In my experience, it's the very strongest heroes who tend to be the most gullible. They've never had to bow and scrape and use their wits to survive. Different skill sets shine in different situations.

"Now reach back," she said—without a feigned pause for breath—"and tear off your wings."

Tiger-striped butterflies danced over the crown of her head. An intense warm scent rose from the weeds and grass and prickly tangles of wildflowers. As if these earthen mounds were secret ovens baking something beyond mortal or immortal comprehension.

Magnolia smiled.

"My wings," Crow said. She said it without panic. Even now, even as she knew herself to be wholly at Magnolia's mercy, her sense of their respective magical power was still too unbalanced.

"Your wings," Magnolia agreed. "I want them gone."

"They'll grow back."

"Eventually, yes."

"But losing them will weaken me."

"So?"

"I thought—"

"Hm?"

"I thought you wanted a powerful servant."

"Don't misunderstand me. I'm not *greedy*," Magnolia said soulfully. "I wanted you to free me from the land, and you did. At the moment, I don't have any grand designs for world domination—and so, having been freed, I don't need such a supremely powerful immortal at my beck and call. Not anymore.

"You came to kill me, and you still very much want to kill me, and perhaps I would be a tad more comfortable if you didn't throb quite so forcefully with all that deadly magic. Besides, from a scientific standpoint, I'm curious about how much you can do without your wings. Let's find out. Stop stalling. You're not very good at it."

She studied Crow with wine-dark eyes. Her tone stayed bright and chipper throughout.

Crow mechanically reached back and took hold of her shrunken-down wings. Their roots slid around frantically beneath her skin. But they never quite fled out of reach. They were the size of pigeon wings when she ripped them out together with a single sharp exhalation. Blood smacked tall blades of grass. It freckled Magnolia's face. The tip of her tongue darted out to taste the corner of her mouth—a snake-like flash of pink.

Crow stood there on top of the natural barrow with her own small bloody wings gripped in both hands. She stood there dully, her back alight more with the violation of it than with straightforward physical pain. It reminded her of being caned. She couldn't remember why she'd ever been caned—it must have happened so very long ago. Something in her reeled, dizzy and heartsick. It gave her the sense that the earth was reeling, rather than her own body; that everything was spinning into irredeemable chaos, and she alone remained as still as a broken rock.

"Stop bleeding everywhere," Magnolia said briskly. "This isn't my territory anymore, strictly speaking. But for old time's sake, I'd prefer to keep it clean."

Crow's blood had the iridescent sheen of oil on water. Like the sky, it didn't quite seem to know what color it ought to be. She stopped the hot trickle creeping down her back with difficulty. Her magic felt very dilute.

She'd seen humans lose limbs before. On occasion, she'd been the one to do the chopping. This was devastating in a different way—although the pain was nevertheless considerable, and unfamiliar. It had been a long time since anyone or anything had seriously hurt her.

Magnolia regarded her critically. "You don't bleed enough, actually."

"You just told me to—"

"I'm talking about before you stopped it. You've gotten lazy. The blood would have come out differently if you were a mortal with big holes in your torso. Can you really pride yourself on passing for human if you don't keep up your act when injured, too? In any case—if you had doubts about my ability to make you do anything I want, I expect that's cleared it up."

Crow stared at the broken wings in her fists. She had to dig deep to uncover her anger, as if drilling past bedrock to find the earth's hidden heat. That anger was even less familiar than the sensation of her own body betraying her, the horror of mutilation, the mind-obliterating tyranny of physical pain.

"You didn't have to kill the hunters," she said slowly.

Magnolia looked downright startled. "What? Who?"

"The hunters who came to slay you."

"There are always hunters coming to slay me."

"On the day we met. Nearly a month ago. The twelve fresh dead below your tree."

A long silence lay over the low hills.

"Are you sure you haven't gotten me mixed up with someone else?" Magnolia asked.

"The gray bard," Crow said.

"A bard? I've had entire marching bands surround me in an attempt to drown out my voice. But I can't recall seeing any bards in the past couple of—"

"He had a flute."

"...Ohhhhhhhh. That bard. Look, he was very short-lived. You can't expect me to remember every hunter who comes after me. Do you remember every biting fly you smack?"

"You'd seen him before. You spared him, once."

"Did the villagers tell you that? Then I suppose I did," she said carelessly. "What about it?"

"You had no reason to kill any of them."

Magnolia blinked.

"The twelve hunters," Crow repeated. She'd been clutching her wings so hard that her hands had gone numb. Her blood on the sod below had rapidly turned a rotten-looking black.

"By the time they reached you, you could already feel me on your territory. You knew I was coming. It was me you wanted—me and my magic, to tear up your tree. To break your bond with the land. You could have sent them away without killing them. Did you even need to feed? Only one of them had a magic core. You shouldn't have—"

Magnolia burst out laughing.

A gnarled sprout grew from the base of her neck, bending and twisting as it pushed her up high enough to look down on Crow. She was like a wooden serpent with the head of a woman—sun behind her, face shadowed. Long roots anchored her, slipping beneath the skin and plump soil of the vulnerable hill.

"That's what you're all worked up about?" she said to Crow in seeming amazement. "Not the fact that I made you tear off your wings. Not the fact that I taunted you with your dearly beloved Arion." She slipped once more into a flawless imitation of his voice. "You care more about a bunch of fortune-seeking hunters? Did you even know their names?"

Crow pointed one severed wing at her as if it could be used as a weapon. "Get Arion out of your mouth."

Magnolia's voice reverted, but her merriment remained unabated. "They were quite earnestly trying to kill me. I respected their efforts, and answered in kind. Where's the harm in that? No one's come looking for them in all these weeks. I don't suppose they've been missed. It hasn't affected any of the locals."

Crow stuffed her gory wings under one arm. She raked her hair back, getting blood everywhere. The sky was a striated mix of pink and white.

"Lives aren't valuable because they're missed," she said tonelessly. "Mortals aren't like us. They can't—"

"You think I'm an innocent?" Magnolia said, wide-eyed. "You think I don't understand that I've crushed your bard's one precious life? Not to worry. I understand humans better than most other immortals ever have or ever will. Better than you do, friend, despite your centuries of cultural immersion."

Crow said nothing. Her blood smelled like chemicals burning.

"We immortals know the meaning of death. Temporary death and permanent death, You could kill me for good yourself—right here on this hilltop. If only I would let you. I can feel how much you want to maul me. Is it normal for a saint to be so bloodthirsty?"

She sounded genuinely curious. The wind made ghostly sounds as it filtered through crevices in the contorted wooden stem below her neck. This monster that gazed down in imitation of a mythical tree-snake—it still exuded the scent of sweet magnolia. Like a far-off fire bell clanging, Crow felt a distant urge to murder everything living in sight.

Yes. If she could, she would raise her small bloody wings and sandwich the sides of the monster's face. She would crack that skull, and she would feel nothing but ecstatic relief.

Not all immortals were remotely human in shape. Not all immortals used human language. Crow had previously encountered one that took the form of a neverending tornado. She found it difficult to ascribe real malice to anything that lacked a fleshly body or a face.

Monsters without malice towards humans—even those without any conscious awareness of humanity's existence—could be just as deadly as cunning predators like Magnolia. But a mindless tornado could not simply choose to stop being a tornado.

Magnolia, on the other hand, seemed to possess a rational mind. She could think and communicate. She could peer inside the brains of those who approached her, feeding off their memories, parroting the voices of loved ones. She could toy with them and lead them astray. She could feed them to her roots like fertilizer. Or she could let them go. She'd let the gray bard go once, over a year ago. She'd sent him off to spread the word of her horrors—and of her alleged vulnerability to a well-equipped party.

Magnolia had a choice. She was not a tornado.

Even if she didn't have a choice, Crow would still have come to kill her. Was it bloodthirsty to think of how many other men and women and children might be spared by hacking open this living head, making this sweet-scented voice fall forever silent? Someone had to do it. Only a fellow immortal could truly end her.

The silhouettes of a couple lonely aerials coursed high in the sky. One looked much like Magnolia's current form: a ribbony snake oscillating against fallow pink clouds.

"Go on," Magnolia said. "Slap me with your feathers. Give it your best shot."

An invitation, not a command.

Crow whipped her fistful of wings at Magnolia's face.

There was no impact. Her arm ground to a halt as though the air had dried up around it like a solid thing, a tomb of mud. Her muscles—from her thighs to her torso to her shoulder to her forearm—rippled and strained to no avail. The tips of a few crushed black feathers just barely brushed the delicate mole near Magnolia's mouth.

6

"WELL, YOU TRIED," Magnolia said blandly.

Her wooden stem elongated, carrying her high out of reach. It hissed as it went, as if she had a steam engine hidden inside her. She swiveled to survey her domain.

"Speaking of hunters, you have excellent timing. I see more on their way across the hills right now. Get rid of them, would you? I'll ride along to enjoy the show."

Her head broke off its crooked trunk like a ripe fruit falling. Crow reached out and caught it. Her next instinct would've been to fling it far into the distance once more, as if ridding herself of a bomb. But Magnolia smiled up at her, and that smile said *No*.

Instead she held the severed head near her shoulder. Finger-like nubs spiraled out of the ragged neck to get a death grip on her upper back. The abandoned trunk dissolved in a flurry of orange-brown leaves.

"You'll unbalance me," Crow said.

"My weight will make up for the lost weight of your wings." A pause. Then, exasperated: "Stop trying to think of ways to let those human hunters kill us both. You know it won't work. Even if it did, it's not a permanent solution—it would just be extremely unpleasant. You'll need to recruit a fellow immortal to dispatch us if you're so determined to die with me. That won't work either, though. You're too strong to let other immortals defeat you."

"I'm not so strong now," Crow said. "That's your doing."

"You did lose an enormous amount of power when you lost your wings, didn't you?"

She could hear the grin in Magnolia's voice. Tendrils reached through the wing-slits in her shirt and probed at her back. They pulled her wounds open wider. The blood deep inside was unnaturally coagulated. Crow stopped hearing the wind; her vision lost its depth. She couldn't speak, but she didn't stagger.

The tendrils retreated.

"Handle the newcomers however you like," Magnolia said. "How's that for motivation? I don't care whether you eat them or spare them, so long as you don't let them touch a hair on my head. Protect me with your immortal life. I'm quite interested to see how you deal with this. If you struggle, of course, I'll make you kill them posthaste."

Summer insects buzzed in the grass. Crow kept her mouth shut. If she argued, Magnolia might simply order her to kill them all from the start.

She leapt down off the hill. Magnolia kept clinging on. The other hills spread around them with such regularity as to give the impression of a sprawling farm field. Perhaps Magnolia had cultivated her ancient malice in these swollen earthen wombs. Crow thought again of factories, industrial ovens.

She too could sense the hunters approaching now. They'd split into two cautious groups. They must have seen Magnolia rearing up on her stem like an avant-garde scarecrow.

There was still time to flee. She could think of no better way to protect these humans than by putting as much distance as possible between them and the smiling monster that had grafted itself to her shoulder. Except that fleeing would not amuse Magnolia. Crow could not read minds, but she suspected that any attempt to run away would deeply displease her.

Magnolia might give orders to turn around and come back, to execute the humans one by one. There was enough time for Crow to flee them, but not nearly enough time for them to flee her.

She inhaled. Her wings—still clenched in rigid fingers—wove themselves into a dark sword. It was rough and broad, single-edged. It looked like a sword for a monster. Any human warrior would dislocate multiple joints if they tried to lift it.

She swung it up and rested the blunt back edge of the blade on her shoulder.

"*Excuse* me!" squawked Magnolia. She would've been cracked like an egg if she hadn't scrambled out of the way. She scooted further left, resentfully tightening her hold on Crow's trapezius.

A second later: "Oh!" she said, all recrimination forgotten. "One of them has a magic core. You can let the others go if it pleases you, but you really ought to eat him up. You'll regain your lost power in an instant."

"I'm a saint," Crow said.

"We'll see how long that lasts."

They'd begun shooting crossbow bolts. Crow wearily swatted them out of the air with magic alone. Her mangled back muscles twitched, trying to move absent wings. A high-pitched whine trembled along the sharper edge of her ugly sword.

Behind her, Magnolia made a throaty sound of displeasure.

The shooting ceased. "They think you're the Woman in the Hills," Magnolia murmured. "Hilarious. At last you've shown your true form—a two-headed beast. Are you sure you don't want to kill them? This is a bad habit of yours, I think."

"What?" Crow said, distracted. "Pacifism?"

"No. Infantilizing humans. They're very sincere in their desire to slay you. Me, rather—but we come as a package deal now. Why condescend to spare them? Why not give them the fight of their lives? It's what they want, isn't it? A glorious clash. Mortal versus immortal. Even if the best they can hope for is to put us out of commission for a generation or two. What they really need is a saint like you on their side."

"If I gave them the fight of their lives, it wouldn't be much of a fight, and there wouldn't be anything left of their lives."

She felt laughter: a quivering in the parasitic growths that sewed Magnolia's head behind her shoulder.

The hunters hadn't come to talk. Wise of them. They'd researched the Woman in the Hills. Perhaps they'd worn earplugs, even if that was widely known to offer little protection. They wouldn't listen to a word that came out of Crow's mouth.

Having given up on long-distance attacks, they rushed in on Crow from two sides. They were disciplined. About twenty in number. No shouting. Only light armor: they valued movement.

She'd hoped her hideous sword would scare them off. Now that they were in reach, it would prove largely useless. The last thing she wanted was to do was cleave these mortal bodies in two.

She whipped around and tossed the impossibly heavy-looking sword at the squad coming up behind her. It flew like a javelin, but she'd aimed for the ground at their feet. They scattered, unharmed. They would quickly regroup.

The sword vanished in a whirl of black feathers. They flew over to shield her from an axe that a very large man tried to bring down on her shoulder. He was aiming for Magnolia. Crow wished she could let him follow through.

Her dead feathers circled around her like a flock of birds, blocking polearms and maces and double-edged blades. It only took one feather to halt each blow; they could be much harder than steel. To these humans, it must have felt like striking full force at a stone wall nine feet thick. They'd be lucky not to hurt themselves, or permanently damage their weapons—but they redoubled their attacks all the same. They were correctly betting that she couldn't stay on the defensive forever.

Magnolia remained remarkably quiet. Perhaps because she kept coming within a hair's breadth of losing her eyes, nose, tongue, ears, or all of the above at once. Not that she couldn't regrow them, given sufficient time.

Crow's magic was in its rawest state. Even at her best, she'd never possessed any gift for subtle acts of manipulation. She wouldn't be able to magically put these hunters to sleep. Nor (unlike Magnolia) could she convince them that they had no interest in attacking her—that they had in truth come for an idyllic picnic surrounded by luxurious green tussocks and swarming moths.

If she hadn't ripped out her own wings, she could have deferred the issue. She could've put up enough of a fight to satisfy Magnolia, then ported the hunters three towns away. But right now she couldn't port a flea. Magnolia had quite deliberately driven her into a corner. She'd known this new party was creeping closer. She must've known since before she ordered Crow to reach back and dismember herself. She'd wanted Crow to face them at a severe disadvantage. She'd wanted to make mercy difficult.

Could you even call this mercy? Protected by swirling feathers, Crow knocked them out one by one. Some dropped and stopped moving. Some kept trying to get up, dazed, swaying, flailing at her and missing by a mile.

She felt a brimming sickness. They were so, so, so young. None over fifty, if she had to guess. She was trying not to kill them, but some might bleed out in their brains and die anyway. Some might wake so damaged that they forgot how to hold the weapons they'd mastered, how to go home, how to insert a key in a lock, how to eat porridge with a spoon. Here she was, an immortal saint with a monstrous second head sprouting from her back, and the best she could do was bash them into brutal unconsciousness.

"Behind you," Magnolia said in a curiously sweet and clear tone.

She had said it too late.

Ordinarily, Crow would never have failed to notice the swordsman who'd risen in her shadow. He was the youngest of all, hardly more than a boy, with hair in a black topknot and a clean shining face. She'd felled him before anyone else. She'd hoped he would stay down and out of the way. He reminded her of the last human boy she'd spent time with: an easy smile, a uncanny way with swords, the reckless bravery unique to youths who had yet to wrap their minds around the notion of death.

Carrie, one day we'll save the world.

Her feathers had coalesced in a clot in the air out in front of her. They were tired. With each passing second, their movements grew slower. The young hunter's sword plunged at Crow's back—at Magnolia's bolted-on head—and her feathers couldn't circle around fast enough to stop the blade in its tracks.

She felt herself move quicker than the logical limits of her human-shaped body. She spun to take the blade through the front of her right shoulder instead of the back of her left.

He would have—and should have—skewered her together with Magnolia's head.

Crow's arm swept sideways like a scythe made of flesh.

That was all it took. A slash with her bare hand. A reflexive motion as she turned to stop Magnolia from getting stabbed.

The boy's head came off. It hit the slope of the nearest hill, rolling down to an ignominious halt. His headless body tumbled forward to lean its full dead weight on Crow. A spurt of blood hit her face, hot and reeking. She eased him to the ground. Her stomach boiled with something she had no name for.

"You got his blood on me," Magnolia said.

A female hunter crawled through the grass, less stupefied than the others. She saw his head. Then she saw his body. She let out a heart-splitting cry.

Crow extracted the sword from her shoulder with a grunt. She laid it down next to the dead hunter. She turned to leave.

"Wait." Magnolia again. "Take his clothes."

Crow froze. She started to ask for an explanation. The words choked and died.

She knelt as if in a dream. Her hands—strong and capable—efficiently stripped the headless body. Undergarments and all. Magnolia snapped at her to be more careful, to stop getting everything dirty. Between the blood and the mud, that was an impossible task.

Once finished, she got back on her feet. Her floating feathers crumbled like a rain of volcanic ash. None of the hunters were capable of chasing her, or even of watching to see which way she went.

"Where are you going?" asked Magnolia, still riding her back.

"I'm going to kill you," Crow said. She held the hunter's limp wet clothes in her arms. Dangling sleeves flapped like boneless limbs as she walked, heavy with blood.

"You know you can't go against my wishes."

"One day I'll find a way to kill you. I have all the time in the world."

"That you do," Magnolia said by her ear, "but so do I."

7

CROW MADE FOR the distant edge of the sea of hills. She didn't utter another word.

"That kid you killed. He had a magic core," Magnolia said. "Did you even notice? Now it's lost—wasted—irretrievable. You have terrible instincts. You should've told me. If I'd known you were just going knock his head away without taking his core, I'd have reaped it myself. At least we got some clothes in exchange."

She was happy enough to hear herself talk. She didn't need any acknowledgment from Crow to continue.

"If word of this goes round, your reputation could take quite a hit. But you're lucky. None of them seemed to know you. They saw us, collectively, as the Woman in the Hills. They might've thought you were a dead body I'd commandeered to ride around on."

By now they were at the fringes of the forest beyond the mysterious hills.

Crow looked straight ahead. "The moment you slip up, I'll kill you faster than I killed that hunter."

"If I ever slip up that badly, then I'll deserve it."

Magnolia's head climbed higher, summiting Crow's shoulder. Her right shoulder, which had recently been run through with a dead man's sword. The wound was still there—as were the sluggish empty wing-sockets in her back. Magnolia, heedless, clawed her way up with fresh-grown hooks.

"Catch me," she said. She let go of Crow's shoulder, flinging herself forward.

Crow had no choice but to catch her. It happened more gently than she might've hoped. Magnolia looked up triumphantly; dried blood spattered her face like a birthmark. Sharp curved thorns receded stealthily into the bottom of her neck. She'd been maneuvering around Crow's torso like a climber driving in spikes.

Crow didn't care if those claws raked her flesh to ribbons. Just so long as she was the only one affected. But she didn't think Magnolia would be content to spend the rest of her eternal existence needling one lone servant out in the eastern wilderness.

"Of course not." Magnolia had read her thoughts. "I want so much more than that. I'm so used to peeking inside other people's minds—sometimes I forget that you can't look in mine. Don't you wonder what I'm thinking? I don't know how you put up with it."

Warm pinkish light glowed in summer foliage. The forest beyond the hills smelled green and humid. Magnolia was nothing but a vulnerable human head cradled in Crow's open palms. Her hair spilled down through Crow's fingers. Crow longed to crush the life out of her before she could say another word.

"I want to see everything I've missed, stuck out here in the hills. You've been around—show me the continent. Take me everywhere you've gone, and maybe I'll be satisfied enough to let you go."

"Don't lie," Crow said. "Don't dangle false rewards."

"Figured it might be more fun if you had a little something to entice you. Nothing like a dash of hope to spice up a desperate march from coast to coast. You'd rather be cynical? Go on; I won't stop you. But"—she grimaced—"my face itches like crazy. Before we embark on our epic journey, you'd better pause and clean me up. Gently, mind you. Do something about yourself, too, while you're at it. You look atrocious."

Magnolia gave her no immediate deadline. Crow spent the next several days exploring the woods, whispering to isopods, and coaxing a hidden underground stream to the surface. There was nothing much to be done for her clothes: the bloodstains would never come out. She'd already worn the same stuff nonstop for over a month. After losing so much vital power together with her wings, she'd reached the limits of her ability to purify garments with magic.

She lounged naked at the edge of the newly risen stream while her ragged outfit hung from branches to dry. The dead hunter's washed clothing hung there, too. She'd developed a taut scar where his sword had pieced her shoulder, but it would soon fade to nothing. The pitted wounds left by her ripped-out wings would take longer to fill in.

She'd never lost her wings before. She had every faith that they would return, but she had no idea when.

A three-legged corvid flew over to peck at her hanging shirt.

"Look," Magnolia said. "Your namesake."

"Mm." Crow had learned that sometimes it was best to feign a reaction. Her brethren flew off after a few sharp scolding cries.

Magnolia's head rested on a rock in the middle of the stream. Pale thready roots extended from her neck, rippling in running water like the tentacles of a jellyfish. Her eyes followed the passage of a slender-limbed fly that kept meandering from bank to bank.

"Imagine if I couldn't make bugs stay off me," she said. "I'd have been covered in bites for a millennium or more. Mosquitoes would've laid eggs in my eyes. I'd have been in a much worse mood when we met."

"Mm," Crow said again, trying to think of magic to dry her clothes faster without burning them to a crisp.

When she glanced over, Magnolia's head had rotated to face her.

Magnolia could be as mobile as any limber forest animal. The wounded end of her neck freely generated flexible roots and prehensile vines, as well as knuckle-sized wooden stubs like little hidden feet. But she preferred being hoisted around like a holy relic.

She ran her eyes from the scar near Crow's collarbone down to her stretched-out legs. "Must be nice, always having a body."

"It's mine. You can't take it."

"We'll see about that."

This was, if nothing else, a new experience. Never before had Crow lolled about, naked and unarmed, in the company of a Great Adversary. She figured that if Magnolia had the ability to outright steal her body, it would already have been stolen.

"Show me your back," Magnolia ordered.

Crow turned around before her body could do her the indignity of moving on its own. She flicked curious insects off her arms while Magnolia ogled her from behind.

She yelped when something cold and damp touched the holes where she used to have wings. Magnolia had dulled her senses—she hadn't felt it coming.

Twisting, she caught a glimpse of disturbingly long white roots vanishing inside the gummy caverns gouged in her back. The wet roots extended through flowing water and across slick rocks before rearing up in the air to meet her.

It should have been unbearable. If her body were mortal, there was no way she'd have been able to contort and look back like this, with the loss of her wings still so fresh, a contagion of pain racing through neighboring muscles. She did feel a profound wrongness, but it was more magical than physical in nature.

"Are you done?" she asked flatly.

The hairlike roots retreated, trailing down her hips. Crow suppressed a shudder and went to grab her half-dry clothes.

At first she'd hoped to delay Magnolia's grand tour across the continent for as long as she could. Many settlements were dotted so far apart that it'd be easy to thread a path to avoid them. Year after year, the human population kept dropping. But what if Magnolia insisted on being brought to points of interest where people still lived in abundance?

If she lost patience with Crow's dallying, their next encounter with hunters might end in a massacre. Crow's willpower had been locked up inside an unbreakable box. All her rage was equally hollow and useless. If Magnolia said *Kill them*, leaving no loopholes, then she would obey. She knew it.

Maybe this was why Magnolia had been utterly content to amble along at Crow's pace. She swished her roots in the stream and pontificated about historical approaches to the art of laundry while Crow grimly wrestled with indelible bloodstains. Maybe Magnolia was perfectly happy to wait until another batch of hunters caught up with them. Maybe she already had a plan for how to make the next fight more entertaining.

Would Magnolia be less dangerous in other lands? If Crow managed to conceal her—or if no one realized she was the last of the Four Great Adversaries—how would she react to the ensuing lack of hostility? Would she go out of her way to hurt people who weren't actively trying to slaughter her? How avid was her appetite for human cores?

Earlier in her immortal life, she'd had a warped sense of fairness. Generations ago, she'd been frustrated with her villagers for sacrificing their own children. Ever since, battle-ready strangers had gone to die to her instead, lured in by phantom rewards—or by their own innate heroism. Maybe she wouldn't even disagree with them. Mortals had every right to try to rid themselves of a remorseless monster. But Magnolia wasn't an oppressed mortal. She was their monster, and she'd defend her existence with every tool at her disposal.

Crow didn't ask how Magnolia planned to behave during their travels. She didn't ask what Magnolia would or wouldn't make her do. Whatever answer came in return, she couldn't trust it. Magnolia must have already seen the thoughts that ran ceaselessly through her head, turning full circle like wanderers lost in the woods.

8

"IT'S A FULL MOON, and the sky looks clear," Magnolia said that night. "Good timing. Bring me back to the hills."

Crow carried her to the top of a hill that Magnolia claimed had a particularly pleasing shape. (To Crow, it looked the same as all the others.)

She set the dark-haired head in a patch of clover. It felt like placing an irreverent gravestone.

"Leave his clothes with me."

Crow placed the hunter's clothes in front of her. She'd folded each garment as neatly as possible—as a gesture of respect to their former owner, not to Magnolia.

"The village will be having their harvest festival tonight," Magnolia told her. "Part of it, anyway. Go enjoy yourself. Don't complain about your outfit. The blood looks like black dye now. It'll be less conspicuous by torchlight."

"I don't—"

"You should be delighted for a chance to ditch me. Go to the festival. That's an order."

So Crow left her.

The hills were full of voices—insects, frogs, burrowing creatures that humans had no name for, shy flittering beings that came out at night just to sing. They weren't so shy around Crow. She'd come from far away, but they didn't see her as something foreign.

The moon hung low on the horizon, huge and pink-rimmed like dirty wet porcelain. A similar layer of filth seemed to coat the sky, but the stars were painfully bright.

Crow put on her sunglasses. She lingered at the fringes of the settlement, willing herself not to be noticed. Her feet would not carry her any further away from the festival: Magnolia's order held fast.

She'd stand out less if only she had a human companion. No one else was alone. They mingled and laughed and drank and clapped raucously after each performance of the radish dance.

The village was overflowing with outsiders; many hooted and cheered as loudly as the locals. Hunters, presumably. She didn't recognize any. Was this one last hurrah before they charged off to exterminate the Woman in the Hills? Had they been fired up by tales of the last returning party?

Not the bard's party, who'd vanished without a trace. The party that would've returned carrying a beheaded young swordsman, a naked corpse. If no others had died—and even if a few had succumbed to head injuries—they could boast of the best survival rate in living memory. Other ambitious slayers might argue that the Woman in the Hills must be growing weaker. The next group to launch an assault might stand even more of a chance.

The shopkeeper who'd given her beetle tea hustled about behind a drink stall, one towel tied around his forehead and another draped around his neck. It was hotter here than in the darkness of the hills. He didn't see Crow—she strenuously avoided his glance.

The crowd hollered in anticipation of another round of the bellowing radish dance. On a stage lit by torches, hoarse and exhausted dancers rallied to stomp bare feet and wave around giant radishes. Drummers pounded away like thunder in the distance.

A hand tugged at Crow's sleeve. She jerked, shocked. She'd been mentally keeping tabs on every human presence within a considerable radius.

Behind her, true night lay curled like a mystical beast around the perimeter of the settlement. She gaped. She didn't understand what she was seeing.

At the border of the shadows stood someone in the dead hunter's clothing.

It fit more loosely on her. Gaps in the fabric showed her shoulders. But it also looked as though the blood-darkened clothes were always meant to be worn that way.

Her skin glistened with good health. Not just her face, punctuated by those moles placed with infuriating precision, but also below her clavicle, where another exquisite little mole winked into sight like a mockery of all that was good and right. She looked as much like a pretty man as she did like a woman, slim-bodied, narrow-hipped, her hair damp and raked back off her face in a way that could only be accomplished with human fingers.

She did have human fingers. She held a whole salted cucumber on a stick. (One of the most popular festival foods. All the local children ran around with cold skewered cucumbers or orange-gold ears of corn.)

She raised the cucumber to her lips and took a hearty bite.

Crow said the first thing that came to mind. "Did you steal that?"

"I show up with this magnificent body of mine, and your only concern is for petty theft?"

It was still a struggle not to sound dumbfounded. "You're already wearing stolen clothes."

"You were the one who stole them. At best, I'm an accomplice." Magnolia waved her cucumber about in a faint imitation of the radish dance. "The locals are very welcoming. You could probably nab some freebies yourself, if you didn't feel self-righteously compelled to lurk in the shadows and cast a terrible pall over everyone's mood. Here."

She made Crow take her half-eaten cucumber. Crow held the stick and stared helplessly at the cucumber's pale bitten-off flesh.

Magnolia linked arms with her. "The moon helps my magic. I'll have you know, however, that I've already stored up thousands of years of moonlight. I can take this form whenever I like. But it demands effort, and power, and all I get in return is immeasurable beauty and charm. So I don't assume full human form for no reason."

Her scent had grown headier and more confusing, rich with the heat of a body that had a heart. Something more like summer gardenia. The tireless drums echoed in Crow's bones. So many humans here, and not a single one looked their way. Was that Magnolia's influence?

"Yes," Magnolia said. "It's all me. Hurry up and finish that cucumber. I want to try some tea."

The shopkeeper didn't recognize them. He ladled out cupfuls of chilled beetle tea—a purplish variant—and his eyes skated over Crow and Magnolia as if they were just another pair of sweaty travelers. Magnolia thanked him effusively. A few bystanders gave her hazy looks, entranced. Crow wanted to tell them all to run. She settled for dragging Magnolia away again.

Magnolia let herself be dragged. She sipped contentedly at her tea, occasionally stopping to discuss how it did or didn't remind her of other insect-based teas that had gone out of fashion over a thousand years ago. Entire species gone extinct, production methods lost to time, et cetera. Then she reminisced about spica, an old plant-derived drink that no living human had ever tasted.

Along the way, she pointed out a pile of ripe golden loquats.

"You can stop hunching your shoulders like that," she said once they'd shared a loquat and disposed of the seeds. "I won't tell you to wipe out the entire village on a whim. I've always been very good to them. They're mine, even if I plan on leaving them behind. I won't make you decapitate all those other hunters, either. For now, they're just here for the revelry. As are we."

This was not reassuring. But arguing might tempt her to change her mind.

"You're suspicious." Magnolia drained her cup and passed it to Crow. She licked gleaming traces of tea from her lips. "Know this, then. I'm going easy on you. I can force you to do anything. Anything. With just a couple soft words. But I do value you unbroken. What's the saying? You catch more flies with—"

"This is honey?" Crow said, stupefied, eyes caught on the dry brown-black stains that dyed Magnolia's clothing down to her knees. "This is your honey?"

"Why, yes. What'd you think it was?" Magnolia pushed her hair back so casually that it was like she'd always had a body. Like she knew exactly how her bare wrist looked in the feathery outer rim of torchlight. "You catch more flies with honey than with vinegar," she finished. "That's the one."

"What's your vinegar?"

Magnolia's smile stayed in place. Those hooded eyes gave her a look of languid cruelty. Like an empress lying on a velvet couch, idly sentencing political rivals to death or exile.

Crow didn't push it. She asked instead what would become of this settlement after Magnolia left.

"They'll continue to be spared from famine for another generation or two. That said, they'll suffer economically if the steady stream of aspiring slayers starts to dwindle. It'll be in their best interest to cover up the fact that I'm gone. They must've already realized that something has changed."

"Because—"

"So many hunters came back alive recently." Magnolia tugged at her stolen clothes. "Thanks to you. Those hunters won't be grateful, though. They saw you beating them down, giving out concussion after concussion. Then you punched their comrade's head off. You stripped his bleeding corpse. They must've come away convinced that the Woman in the Hills is lower than the worst kind of bandit. Or maybe they think I'm a pervert." She shook her head. "Unforgivable."

Crow would have liked to punch her head off. She would have liked to do it right here, in the light of the festival, flooded by the drunken chants of the blissful radish-worshiping crowd. If she had any ability to hurt Magnolia, she wouldn't have hesitated for a second.

Instead she ended up seated on a crooked wooden bench. Magnolia rested on her shoulder, pretending to sleep.

That gardenia scent—or was it another flower?—curled up around Crow like a cage. Her heart thudded until it beat itself sore. Her arteries ached with intolerable pressure, with what she at last recognized as unadulterated hatred. What would become of her if she could never explode?

She had fought many monsters, but she'd rarely loathed them on such a personal level. She'd been the target of enraged mortal mobs. She'd been labeled a monster herself. She'd witnessed the utmost depths of depravity in times of starvation and war. Yet she'd never felt such a coursing rush of hatred for any one human being, either, no matter how debased. It would be like hating a poorly raised hound.

"Yes," Magnolia murmured against her shoulder. "It's all wrong, isn't it? You wouldn't despise a dumb beast. You could meet the worst human to ever breathe the air of our continent, and you still wouldn't be able to scrounge up any lasting contempt. Not on a personal level. You won't pass judgment on your lessers."

Crow sat still—her captive, and her audience.

"If a panther attacked me in the woods, would you blame me for killing it?" Magnolia asked.

"You could order it to leave without violence."

"I could. Should I have to?" Still leaning on Crow, she shrugged. "However you define it, I'm far from the worst monster to ever walk these lands. I don't normally walk at all."

Crow didn't laugh.

9

MAGNOLIA WAS one of the most modern-sounding monsters that Crow had ever met. Based on some of her mutterings, though, her birth as an immortal had come long before Crow.

Certain older saints and monsters seemed centuries out of date when they spoke. The current generation of mortals might find them downright incomprehensible. That had never been much of a problem for Crow. She'd been embedded in human society throughout her life as a saint. She'd gotten used to reflecting the speech of those around her.

Sometime she used forgotten sayings, or lapsed into old-fashioned phrasing. Still, after a short stay in a new locale, she'd become functionally fluent in the contemporary vernacular—a slippery and ever-changing beast. You had to actively hold on to it so it wouldn't bolt from your grasp. Magnolia must've kept her vocabulary fresh by mining the minds of traveling hunters. Perhaps she'd left some alive for a time, forcing them to converse with her.

"How long..." Crow started to say. They were still at the village, squeezed together on a bench that had plenty of room to sit further apart.

"Hm?"

"How long were you rooted there?"

"In the clearing?" Magnolia straightened up. "Less than thirty centuries, maybe. I haven't been counting. Or—hey! Excuse you."

"What?"

"How rude. You should know to never ask a severed head her age."

"You're not severed at the moment," Crow said. "I'd be happy to change that."

"I can dispose of my body on my own, thanks."

It was close to morning. Ragged festival banners stirred in a weak breeze. The awakening sky was a smeary translucent green, the color of flourishing algae.

Immortals always understood one another. There was never any question of a language barrier—at least not between those capable of language. Unlike humans, though, immortals had no shared history or religion or culture, no unique traditions, no towering legends to explain their origin. Any myths about them came from human society.

As for immortal society, there was no such thing. They were born alone, and they lived alone—or, like Crow, with mortals. When they permanently died, it would be at the hands of a rival immortal. Thus, none would ever die alone. At least not in the sense of being unwitnessed.

Humans could deal immortals a fatal blow, too, but that sort of death wouldn't last. Some of the other Great Adversaries had risen and fallen numerous times before Crow put a permanent end to them. She had been the slayer of multiple Great Adversaries, and now she was Magnolia's drudge.

Magnolia pulled her up.

"I'm tired of being a body," she said. "Let's go. Unless you'd like to put on a show for the villagers."

They left. In the shadow of a low hill, she made Crow hold her face in both hands.

"Don't drop me," she warned. "Close your eyes. Let me have some semblance of modesty."

Crow closed her eyes. Magnolia's body was shorter than her, though not by much. Magic unraveled in the air as if all the flesh below that seamless-looking neck had shredded itself into ribbons. The weight of the head in her hands increased.

Magnolia let her open her eyes again. Nothing remained but the usual head—which Crow had held without dropping—and an abandoned pile of empty clothes. Crow tucked Magnolia under one arm and bent to retrieve them.

"This is what will happen next," said the living head in the crook of her elbow. "We start on our journey. Unless you'd rather wait around for all those new hunters to get over their hangovers. That might be just as interesting. Oh—you'd rather leave? I'm glad I'm not the only one who's raring to go. Now, I love nature and all, but don't think you'll convince me to follow you on a trip where we never see another human soul."

Crow tried anyway. "We could spend decades exploring natural landmarks. People are transient. The earth, much less so. We could chase the migratory volcanoes up north. We could chase herds of giant tardigrades."

Magnolia dismissed this. "You've never spent much time up north, have you? You've lived your whole life around mortals. I want to see where you've been."

"...Why?"

"The memories will give you more to talk about."

"All the great cities are gone now. The empire I fought for—it's vanished. You want a tour of wreckage?"

"I would expect no less," Magnolia said. "Humans are always making new wreckage."

"I'm not a travel guide."

"If I order you to become one, that's what you'll be. You can figure it out along the way. The world is wide and ever-changing, and you've witnessed a lot of it. You're my companion now, Carrie. Show me what I've missed."

You're my companion now, Carrie.

She had stolen Arion's words again, stolen them right out of Crow's head.

Magnolia might not have crisscrossed the continent in person, but she wasn't ignorant, either. She'd plumbed the brains of countless visitors from distant territories. She could've given Crow a detailed list of sights to put on their agenda.

Perhaps that would come later. Perhaps the first leg of this trip was intended as an experiment. Her main priority might be to get her bearings—and to put Crow through her paces. To test Crow's long-term effectiveness as a servant.

"Still don't know why you did it," Magnolia went on.

"Did what?"

"Came to face me without a promised companion."

"I already told you."

"That you're an idiot, and a martyr? Sounds about right. Because of that, you're stuck with me—and I'll never let you take another proper human companion. You'll never feed like a saint again. You'll have to make do with scraps from monsters. Eventually you'll become a monster yourself."

"Saints can go much longer between meals than monsters."

"Yes, you're very special. But it's already been a long time, hasn't it? Let's see—ah, now you're thinking about it. Now you're doing the math for me. Wow. Sixty-something years since you last ate a human core."

Crow had lost her previous two companions to different Great Adversaries. No force in this world could have persuaded her to make the same mistake again.

"Some saint you are," Magnolia said. "You might go about it slowly, and take inexplicable breaks, but your entire purpose is to bond with human companions. Over and over and over. I've cut you off from that. You're mine alone, for as long as I want. Where's your distress?"

Crow denied her any further reaction. She lifted the smirking head higher and strode out of the sinuous hills.

The next thing she said was: "You don't want to bid farewell to your villagers?"

"What, you think I'll never be back?"

"Not if I kill you first."

"How charming. I'd feel more threatened if you weren't carrying me around as lovingly as a prizewinning wheel of cheese."

There was nothing loving about the way she carried Magnolia's head, but Crow didn't argue the point. "They might all be dead by the time you return," she said, which was true.

"I was there before that town existed. How many successive generations do you think I've witnessed? I can hardly keep track. They're practically dead to me already. That tea master is the spitting image of his grandfather. Or was it his great-grandfather? Not that it matters. They're my people, by virtue of living on my territory, but they've only ever met me in dreams. Besides, they won't have any proof that I'm gone for good. They won't be brave enough to go looking."

"Hunters will—"

"Minor monsters will swarm the hills without me there to preemptively kill them. They'll keep visiting hunters busy for a while, I reckon."

Later, in a nondescript meadow beneath a sky full of daytime auroras, Magnolia demanded a halt.

"There." She pointed with a brown root. "The next step you take will bring us out of my territory. Not that it's really my territory anymore—not since you've unrooted me. Which I do thank you for. Couldn't have done it on my own, obviously."

Crow took the next step without further ceremony. Brown grasshoppers bounced away past masses of prickly wildflowers. The meadow looked unchanged.

For the next three weeks or so, she managed to avoid encountering any humans or human-shaped creatures. Aerials coasted in the unreachable sky, but that was nothing unusual. Nowadays, aerials far outnumbered people.

They traveled by daylight and by moonlight. One sunlit morning, they passed a mountain-sized tortoise in the middle of a decades-long slumber. Magnolia wanted Crow to wake it; Crow argued desperately on behalf of letting it be. To her surprise, Magnolia—who was grafted to her shoulder again—actually shut up and gave in.

Unlike the tortoise, neither of them slept a wink. Some immortals cycled through occasional periods of dormancy, though none required true sleep in the same way as mortal creatures. Crow had hoped against hope that Magnolia—always wielding that magic of constant control— might eventually exhaust herself to the point of dormancy.

So far, Magnolia showed no sign of flagging.

It was her wounded shoulder that Magnolia preferred to ride on. The aches were unpredictable and transient now, like echoes of thunder from a cloudless sky. Gnarled vestigial roots snaked out of Magnolia's neck-stump to circle around her back and clamp down on her upper arms. They ground against her healing scars as Magnolia looked about, facing backwards like an owl.

At other times, she turned herself to gaze straight into the side of Crow's face.

Crow didn't say *What?*, but she couldn't help thinking it.

Magnolia kept staring. "It's been ages since I last got to observe a genuine saint close up."

"What happened to the last one?"

"He wasn't powerful enough to free me from the land. So he wasn't nearly as good of a saint as you. But he had his uses."

Crow could hear the sharpness of the smile in her voice. It was night, the moon misshapen, aerials in the sky as thick as flies. She didn't ask for more details. Magnolia continued, undeterred.

"If nothing else, he was an excellent test subject. He taught me the limits of what I can and can't demand of fellow immortals. The line between what we find merely repulsive, and what's physiologically impossible. I ordered him to kill himself, but he could never go all the way. Immortals just can't do it. Curious, right? I ordered him to give up his magic core—another form of suicide, come to think of it—and he couldn't do that, either.

"Humans can make the decision to surrender their core to a saint, no matter the cost, but we immortals just aren't built for it. We aren't capable of certain choices. Maybe, deep down, I'm something of a scientist at heart ... I doubt our peers have ever thought of systematically testing it. He broke down eventually, poor thing. He became corrupted—a monster himself. Which was never my intention. I admired him much more when he still struggled to hold on to his saintly self. Even while handily dispatching endless waves of human hunters."

Crow said, by way of summary: "So you admired him more when you were torturing him."

"Why, yes. I could relate to that." She spoke as if this made all the sense in the world. "In the end he lost his mind. He would have crossed the hills to devour my village. Couldn't have that. So I devoured him instead. Take it as a cautionary tale."

"Is that why you're being careful not to break me?"

"For now," Magnolia said smoothly.

PART TWO

The Town Without a Name

10

CROW TRIED TO figure out the parameters of Magnolia's commands. How long did they last—forever, unless revoked?

Protect me with your immortal life.

Would that command resurface whenever Magnolia felt threatened? Or would she invoke it anew the next time hunters stalked them?

Everlasting commands would need to be fed by an everlasting supply of magic. Given all her talk of hoarding moonlight, Magnolia seemed to favor efficiency. Crow suspected that her orders were circumstantial; they'd expire when she no longer had an immediate use for them. And not all her directives came in the form of audible words.

Magnolia appeared amused by her efforts to understand. She left Crow's questions unanswered. She was happy to talk about anything and everything else. She never paused for breath—at least not out of actual necessity.

Crow, for her part, had never spent such a long time in the company of a monster. She'd only ever met them in battle.

People called their immortal enemies *monsters*. They called their immortal saviors *saints*. But they weren't actually separate species. All that distinguished one immortal from another was surface-level behavior. Specifically—how they behaved towards the human race. Like the difference between a wild cat and a domesticated cat. By changing their behavior, a saint could become a monster at any moment. A monster could evolve into a saint, too, though all such tales of this were apocryphal. It never happened in real life.

Humans were prone to confusing saints with monsters. To immortals, however, the difference was perfectly clear, and easily defined.

All immortals consumed magic cores. Sometimes from fellow immortals, but preferably from humans. You could harvest human magic cores the slow way, or the fast way. Saints did it the slow way, with consent. Monsters did it the fast way, by force. Either way, a core-deprived human would die. A saint would take their core as close as possible to the end of their natural life. A monster would take it as soon as hunger called—and monsters were always hungry.

A magic core given up willingly was infinitely more precious than a magic core taken by force. The longer the wait, and the closer your companionship, the greater the gift. But sainthood demanded more patience. A human who'd promised you their core might change their mind at the last moment. Or they might die in a sudden accident—and then their core would be lost for good, without a chance to reap it.

Only humans could consent to giving up magic. For immortals, such a sacrifice would go against their very nature. No immortal could willingly surrender their core. Likewise, no immortal could turn down a freely offered gift.

Crow rested Magnolia atop her own head as they forded a wide, shallow river full of singing fish. Red-winged blackbirds whistled from the banks, and slender eels slipped past her ankles. This was a time river—days would pass faster going with the current than against it. But their goal was to get to the other side, not to lose years to drifting.

"I'm starving," Magnolia said wistfully. "I'd gobble your core down if only it wouldn't destroy you. Still need someone to hold me up when crossing rivers."

"You've been well-fed."

"What makes you say that? I'm still hungry."

"You had human hunters coming at you year-round. And competing monsters, too."

"Other monsters were always a good snack, sure. But with each passing decade, they gave me a wider berth. It's not like every human is born with a core, either."

"The percentage increases every year."

The fluctuating prevalence of magic cores had confounded scholars all over the continent. Now there were fewer people, and many fewer scholars. Crow had been around long enough to observe that as the human population dropped, the proportion of those born with magic cores began to rise. As if to make up for the decrease. As if to guarantee just enough sustenance for monsters and saints alike.

Mortal magic was a lost art. In recent centuries, they'd come to view their cores solely as bargaining chips for extracting oaths of loyalty from saints. Ironically, far fewer humans had possessed magic cores back in the days of skilled mages.

"More humans have cores, yes," Magnolia agreed. "But they don't usually become slayers. Why risk turning into fuel for the fire you seek to destroy? If you've got a core, you're safest letting saints and the coreless protect you."

"There are exceptions."

"Of course. Some people with cores are just that talented, or stubborn, or determined to stamp out evil predators. But they're scarce. That's especially hard on us land-bound monsters. We can't go roaming from shore to shore in search of snacks."

Was that Magnolia's plan? For Crow to guide her from shore to shore on a journey of gathering human cores? If so, Crow would have to think of a way to lead them both straight to the bottom of the sea.

Magnolia had turned her into a luggage-carrying porter, and a reluctant bodyguard, and a prisoner. Crow could've spent all day and all night recklessly struggling against the slippery magic that bound her. But she didn't want to dash herself to pieces without anything to show for it. She was used to playing the long game. It was what made her a saint.

She'd taken the cores of myriad monsters, but only seven humans. Those seven made all the difference.

She'd had more than seven promised companions. She'd spent a lifetime, or close to it, with twenty-three different humans, one at a time. Some lived with her like family. Some treated her like an indentured servant, or a deadly chained beast. Some had seen her as a holy guardian, and some as a weapon of war.

Some, in their old age, had forgotten their original promise. They'd lost all memory of her name, her face—they mistook her for a mother or a daughter or a long-lost wife. They no longer had the presence of mind to give up anything as precious as their core.

She would go along with it, pretending to be whoever they thought she was. Then she would bid them farewell, with no compensation for the fifty or sixty or eighty years she'd spent waiting. But she'd always known that was a possibility.

This was what it meant to live as a saint. Although her success rate was, if anything, unusually low.

She knew for a fact that she'd grown more powerful than saints who'd consumed twice as many human cores as her—and in half the time.

Her patience throughout all those missed chances had somehow made her rare successes even more potent.

There had been times when the family of an aged promised companion closed ranks, refusing to let her see them. Refusing to let the reaper in. As long as this reflected her companion's own will, she would concede gracefully. She would back away.

There had been times when a monster killed one of her companions. Like Arion. There had been other times when humans banded together to kill her companion instead. Like the young empress who, crying and apologizing, had ordered Crow not to save her. She'd broken her promise to offer up her core, her promise to live a long and beautiful life and then give it all up to Crow at the end. Because of that, Crow no longer had any moral obligation to obey.

Crow had obeyed anyway. If she were human, maybe it would have occurred to her to rebel. If she were human, maybe she would have saved the empress. But the empress's killers were long dead now. So was every last witness, and all the mobs that had screamed for her neck, and the entire fallen empire, and all three or four kingdoms that followed it. Only a dedicated regional historian would have any notion of those kingdoms' names.

In all her life, Crow had outwaited every other dire predicament, every other agony of despair. She wasn't sure if she'd have the luxury of outwaiting Magnolia, but so far, she could perceive no other choice. She'd keep examining Magnolia's magic and demeanor, her personality and her pride and her quirks. There had to be a weakness somewhere. Even the best-made armor came with inconvenient gaps.

They crossed a weary old mountain range. Sad hollow voices called from peak to peak in various languages, trying to lure them off sudden edges. A rather common type of monster, one without any tangible body.

Crow was adept at letting those voices flow past her. She mused to herself that this lowly monster had some qualities in common with Magnolia. It would reflect and borrow from languages held in the minds of passersby, like a mountain lake reflecting the colors of the sky.

"Would you *shut up*?" Magnolia said.

The voices quailed, then fell silent. That command went right through Crow, too. It wasn't directed at her, but for a moment she plunged deep underwater. She was a drifting sunken thing at the very bottom of the sea. The ocean pressure equalized with her helpless compressed loathing for the creature on her back. She felt a burst of nothing at all, and it was perhaps the best feeling she'd ever had.

"Watch it!" Magnolia barked.

Crow recovered herself. She was gripping the sides of a crevice halfway up a giant rocky crag. The monstrous voices had whined at them while Crow methodically climbed the crag unaided—no ropes, no pitons, no helmet. Crow had been too focused on the mechanics of her ascent to pay the voices much heed, but Magnolia apparently had a low tolerance for the yammering of others. She'd finally snapped.

The eerie echoes seemed disinclined to ever speak again. The silence of the open mountain air made Crow feel the palpable hugeness of the space behind her, the sheer distance she might fall.

Magnolia's roots could have been of assistance, but she didn't volunteer to help, and Crow refused to ask. So she remained a lump of dead weight peeking over Crow's shoulder, getting in the way whenever Crow tried to look to her right.

Being immortals, they had no need to cart around water or food or other sundry supplies. The hunter's stolen clothes hung from Crow's waist in a sack. She'd left her trunk back at the tea shop in Magnolia's land. She could have retrieved it, but she hadn't been much interested in letting Magnolia leer at her scant belongings.

"You keep moaning," Magnolia said.

"What?"

"There. You just did it again."

They were almost at the top of the vertical rock face. Crow grunted with effort.

"See?" Magnolia said.

Crow entertained fantasies of letting go of the crag and flying out into the quiet void behind them. Of falling down, down, down, flat on her wingless back, and crushing Magnolia beneath her on a boulder. It was an extraordinarily vivid image. She hoped Magnolia could see it, too.

For all practical purposes, the rocky top of the crag was the summit of the mountain itself. Once she'd pulled them up there, Crow stopped to thoroughly stretch out her limbs.

She'd told Magnolia that she was too magically weakened to port. Which was not an outright lie. There was just no way to prove it without trying. She'd been somewhat taken aback when Magnolia didn't force her to make an attempt, but then, immortals weren't known for rushing.

A wispy golden lattice stippled the sky with a pattern like fish scales. The mountain wasn't tall enough to break the tree line, but it had brought them closer to coasting eagles. A couple leviathan-sized aerials dimmed the sun like cruiser-class airships from days of legend. Huge curved rocks—the ribcage of an ancient dead beast?—grew from another tree-furred mountain across the way.

There wasn't much on top of the crag. Perhaps a long time ago it had been a smoother plateau. Now it had degenerated into a dangerous jumble. Rock formations tilted together with treacherous cracks between them. At the center rested a cocoon taller than Crow, an unattractive thing that resembled a nest made by mud wasps.

"I see," Magnolia said appreciatively. "Not bad."

Crow was uncertain of the best way to ask her for a favor. She chafed at the fact that she needed to ask Magnolia for anything. But there was no way around it.

"Can we stay till it hatches?"

"What if I demand first dibs?"

"I'm here to slay a monster," Crow said. "Whether or not I get its core."

"Well, then. You'd better amuse me in the meantime."

But Magnolia was actually rather gifted at amusing herself. In the following days, she detached from Crow's shoulder. She generated vines and roots to rappel her head down every last vertical face of the crag. She found a flock of cabbage birds in the mountainside forest. She complained about disturbing a hidden ant hill and getting her face covered in swarming ants.

"I thought you could order insects to stay away," said Crow.

"They caught me by surprise."

"You surprised them first."

"Oh, shut it. I told them to get off me, but they can't port away with magic. They're just ants, and not the flying kind, either. They had to find a path. They were crawling all over each other, going in circles, confused. They would've gone away eventually, but I couldn't stand the tickling. I hurled myself in the nearest pond."

That explained why her hair was still wet and slicked back.

The cocoon would be ready to come open any day now. While Magnolia frolicked up and down the sides of the mountain, Crow stayed atop the crag. She waited through sun and rain, through mornings of fog when the clouded sky came down to submerge the ragged cliffs.

On their own, humans could not give any immortal a permanent death. But they could deal out a kind of death all the same. They could, if fortunate, put a marauding immortal out of commission for the rest of their own natural lives, or longer. Not their problem anymore.

Then again, a monster slain by humans might come back to seek revenge on their descendants. And some humans did care about the world they would be leaving to future generations, even if it was a world that had already been sickened beyond repair.

So if a band of humans managed to slay a monster on their own, they'd spread the word to every saint they could reach. Certain areas were so remote that few saints ever came by, but they had to keep trying.

The monster inside the mud-colored cocoon had been waiting to revive for seventy-something years. Crow, after hearing scraps of old tales, had already checked this cocoon once on her journey east to meet the Woman in the Hills. It needed another season to ripen, she'd thought. Here she was again, deep into summer. She was relieved that she hadn't returned too late.

Immortals had plenty to fear from humans, though they didn't much like to admit it. Even a temporary death was a grievous setback in terms of lost time and lost power. Crow had never been killed herself, at least not since she'd received her name. She assumed that Magnolia had never been killed, either, although it was entirely possible she'd already boasted of being murdered multiple times by humans or other mortal wildlife. Crow didn't remember half the things Magnolia told her.

The cocooned monster might have been very powerful before his mortal foes vanquished him. Perhaps almost equivalent to the Four Great Adversaries. Once reborn, he would find himself far weaker than before.

Crow could have destroyed the cocoon—and the regenerating being inside—with ease. Even Magnolia could've grown a tree through it to smash it. Or maybe she would rather strangle it with rope-like roots.

But neither of them would do anything of the sort. In this, saints and monsters were all the same: no immortal would ever attack an underdeveloped cocoon. In doing so, you could permanently kill a reviving enemy—without giving them a chance to fight back. But you wouldn't be able to properly claim their core. You could only inherit a foul shadow of their magic.

Crow had found it difficult to explain to her human companions why this felt so wrong. It went far beyond the obvious calculus: better to wait for the monster's emergence, and thus an opportunity to steal their core—higher risk, and a much higher reward. Eventually she settled for saying that immortals didn't attack cocoons for the same reasons that humans—well, most of them—couldn't even bear to think about smashing an infant to death with a hammer. In reality there was nothing comparable about these scenarios. But it was the only way she'd ever gotten anyone to understand.

People had begged Crow to smash cocoons in busy settlements. Cocoons were invulnerable to any sort of mortal assault, and so humanity remained helpless to stop the reviving monsters in their midst. They'd pleaded with saints like Crow instead, and she'd always refused. She gave them feathers to break if they needed her. She swore to come back and defeat each monster as soon as it emerged. But she wouldn't touch a closed cocoon. Even under strict orders, she hadn't been able to do it.

Only once had she ever failed to make it back in time. Immortals had a reputation for slowness, but most were capable of astonishing punctuality when they knew it might result in claiming a core. For that reason, Crow had expected to find competition awaiting atop the crag. Other monsters, if not other saints.

"Oh," Magnolia said when Crow made a comment about their peculiar solitude. "Were you bored up here? Looking for a warm-up fight? Sorry. I took them all."

"What?" Crow said blankly.

Magnolia rolled her eyes. She was perched grandly on a rock formation shaped like a flat-topped mushroom, resting in a nest of her own roots. "Bless you. What do you think I've been doing all this time? Nibbling the wingtips of cabbage birds? The mountain has been seething with monsters since long before we set foot here. They've been gathering year after year, slowly encircling the crag."

"But..."

"They're mostly weaklings. Even in your current state, you outclass them. You haven't noticed them because you've never *needed* to notice those so far below you. Just like how you've never needed to notice how many bats or sparrows live here.

"The answer is a lot, by the way. A lot of bats. A lot of sparrows. And a lot of monsters of varying degrees of corporeality. Too bad they didn't come try their luck while you strained your way up the side of the crag. The two of us were too intimidating for anything except those stupid whining echoes. A shame—I was looking forward to showing off."

"With your voice?"

"Or maybe I wouldn't have done a thing. If you seemed too proud to accept my help, I'd have let a herd of nameless monsters tear you down. So long as you kept protecting me." Magnolia grinned. "Who knows? Maybe I'm a thrill-seeker. Maybe I'd enjoy a long fall, complete with strong and capable cushioning. Might've taken too long for you to put yourself back together, though. You'd have missed the emergence of our friend up here. Speaking of which—"

The cocoon cracked.

<h1 align="center">11</h1>

Temporary death might not only come at the hands of humans. An immortal could die in a natural disaster. They could succumb to a metaphysical illness, or burn through all their magic under duress. Or they could fade from prolonged deprivation. The disembodied voices haunting these mountains might meet with that fate soon enough, unless Magnolia had already reaped their core.

The monster at the top of the mountain, however, had been killed by a heroic assembly of humans. Or so the stories claimed. He emerged from the vertical crack in his cocoon together with an outpouring of light like the first rays of the rising sun.

Freshly revived, he stood before them glistening with magic. It was dusk, and he gleamed brighter than anything else up on the crag. He was naked and unselfconscious, human in appearance except for the exaggerated silk moth antennae that grew from his head. His face was beautiful in the way of a sculpture made for a god. Beautiful but empty:

he lacked Magnolia's shining eyes, her edge of malice.

Crow felt him assessing her and Magnolia, but mostly her. He would try to take out the stronger threat first. She registered belatedly that he had a few extra arms.

Magnolia had said nothing whatsoever for a full minute running.

The monster started to speak rustily, then stopped, as if acknowledging the futility of it. He charged at Crow, a flash cutting through the growing dark.

At the last second, he veered off toward Magnolia.

Crow—without thinking, and with superhuman speed—hurled herself between them. She caught the monster. She used magic to hold him in place as if lashing herself to a mast in a storm.

He struggled without words. His fringed antennae kept palpitating against her. His body smelled like leaf matter disintegrating into fertile soil, and his magic smelled like woodsmoke. Globs of that magic oozed over her arms. With each splat, her flesh bruised and crumpled like fruit ripening past the point of rot.

She could not have described how it felt in any language she knew. But she didn't let go. They were both unarmed (despite his multiple arms continuously beating and clawing at her). She held him tighter, ignoring the damage to her own body—the decaying splotches, the too-sweet scent. The dust and rock beneath them grew wetter and wetter.

She crushed the monster until she felt the balance tip, until his defeat became total. Then his core was hers to take.

His ragged body—leaking, wrung out, unrecognizable—slipped through Crow's purpling arms and pooled on the ground like discarded clothing. He'd broken both delicate antennae as he fought to get free. His core stayed behind, floating, a luminous concentration of magic larger than a human heart.

Crow opened her mouth. The monster's core looked too big to fit, but it slipped between her lips and went down in one swallow. Nothing remained of him when she glanced at her feet. Just a few dusty trails like ash from a campfire.

The core of an immortal had no particular physical location. You couldn't cut it out like a liver. It only became accessible in a moment of utter defeat.

Humans were different. Focus your magic perception on a human with a core, and you'd see it glowing in their lower torso. A mortal surgeon could not reach it with a scalpel, but any monster could stick their claws in and rip it out. Only saints asked permission.

"Did you just *squeeze* him to death?" Magnolia said.

"There was magic involved."

"What a way to go."

The core of a single defeated monster would be far less transformative for Crow than the freely given core of a human companion. But it was enough to fill her veins with magic, to repair all the softened rotting parts of her. Her left leg had eroded down to show bone; she hadn't noticed till now. The flesh grew back, gangrene miraculously retreating, bruises shrinking to the size of freckles.

The pits in her back filled in, too. Her wings budded anew as tiny downy stubs. The sudden growth made her shoulder blades itch hotly, as if outlined in bug bites.

Beneath the irrepressible ecstasy of consuming a core came a blinding tide of regret. She should have let the monster try his chances with Magnolia. If he annihilated her, then Crow would be free, and Crow could have annihilated him next.

If Magnolia defeated him and ate his core, then nothing would have changed. Which was arguably a better outcome. By ingesting his core, Crow had accelerated her recovery from her self-inflicted wounds. She'd made herself more powerful, and in doing so, had placed more power in Magnolia's nonexistent hands. She was Magnolia's tool—a shield and a weapon. Why sharpen her own edges when doing so would result in her wielder becoming more of a menace?

Why had Crow flung herself between them?

But the answer was obvious. Even when Magnolia kept her mouth shut, Crow was always under her command. Once she got her claws in you, she could make you do anything without saying a word.

"Wrong." Magnolia had skimmed thoughts off the surface of her mind again. "I didn't make you do that. I very specifically didn't make you do anything in that one particular moment. You had full freedom of movement—and full freedom not to move at all."

Crow turned to argue. Night had closed in around the mountaintop, but they could both see well enough in the dark. Magnolia was still on her pedestal of rock. Pale vein-like roots flicked in and out from around her cut-off neck like a lizard's tongue tasting the air.

"No, I didn't command you," Magnolia continued. "I commanded him. Not in a way you could hear, of course. Doesn't take much to establish mastery over a newly revived immortal. Feels like seizing command of a nigh-empty ship."

"You—" And then, dizzyingly, Crow understood. "You commanded him to attack you. You wanted his core? You could have told me to let you take it."

"If I wanted his core, it would already be mine," Magnolia said tartly. "I did crave his core—we immortals are all the same when it comes to our primordial drives. You didn't hesitate to crush him like a python, did you? But I managed to restrain myself. I didn't make him come at me so I'd have a chance at his core. I wanted to see what you'd do about it." She smiled brilliantly. "You never disappoint."

I managed to restrain myself.

All those lower-tier monsters Magnolia had consumed while roaming the mountain. Had she devoured them to fortify her self-control? To ensure that she'd be able to cede the cocoon monster's core to Crow? She'd used him for a different purpose. She'd tricked Crow into debasing herself, leaping to defend her when no defense was demanded. Or—

"I didn't do it to save you," Crow said. "I dove at him to take his core for myself." And, she thought guiltily, because he would have been a vicious threat to humanity. Just as he was in the past. "I craved his core more than you did. I moved on pure instinct. I wouldn't have moved like that to protect you. Not without orders."

"So you say."

Magic-starved after the loss of her wings, Crow had flung herself at a morally acceptable target. That would take precedence over any instinct to defend the defenseless—which Magnolia was most definitely not. Yet Magnolia had engineered the situation in such a way as to leave a splinter of doubt. To make Crow believe she'd moved in anticipation of a command that never came. To make Crow believe she'd shielded Magnolia of her own volition.

"You think I planned it all?" Magnolia said. "Oh, please. There's not a single strategic thought in this head of mine. I'm just like you—drifting through life, trying to get by. Can you port now?"

"Might reopen my wounds," Crow said. There'd be no point in losing her temper—Magnolia would enjoy it—but she struggled to sound civil.

"Then I guess we'll have to go down the mountain the slow way."

They set off that night. Despite having proven that she could be highly mobile on her own, Magnolia rode Crow's back. She relished being carried like a prince in a palanquin.

Crow's simmering discontent hardened into a more definite shape as they (well, mostly Crow) did the work of descending.

Magnolia was unlike any immortal Crow had ever met, saints and monsters alike. Even the most predatory monsters, even those adept at using human language like a weapon—they weren't malicious towards their prey. When cornered by humans, they might babble sweet words to plead for mercy. But there was no glee in their attempts at deception. It was just a practical maneuver to dodge death and regroup.

Something about Magnolia seemed inherently more human than other immortals. More human than any of her fellow Great Adversaries. That—more so than knowledge of her past predations—was the true origin of Crow's soul-deep revulsion.

Human malice and cruelty and petty vindictiveness could be forgiven because it wouldn't last forever. In Crow's view, it could never be more than a brief passing storm. Mortals who suffered brutally and perished to the storm might see things differently. Still, give it a century, two centuries, three centuries, ten centuries—and there would be new storms to preoccupy new mortals, who barely remembered anything that came before them.

But if no one stopped her, Magnolia might keep honing her malice till the end of time, and the end of this already-faltering world. She brought together the worst of humanity and immortality: a bright twisted curiosity, a senseless sadism that could last for eternity. The sheer wrongness of that combination horrified Crow in a way that felt at once hopelessly cosmic and profoundly personal.

"So you think I'm different," Magnolia said over her shoulder.

"It's not a good thing."

"I'll be the judge of that. I like being special."

12

CROW STOPPED to rinse her clothes again as they came down out of the mountains. The itching around her wing-stubs had subsided, but the surge of excess power from the cocoon monster's core was beginning to manifest in other ways. She'd developed grape-sized cysts around the joint of her right wrist, as if her body were bursting at the seams with magic.

"I know what to do about those," Magnolia said. "There's a family in the radish village that's gotten them for generations. You take a big, heavy book, and—"

Crow smashed the cysts with her bare hand. They burst internally, flattening as they drained. For once, Magnolia seemed taken aback.

When she looked over, though, Magnolia was blinking rapidly, the cysts forgotten. She'd made herself a tall stump of petrified wood to rest on. It looked like it could've been there since before the beginning of the end of the world.

"What's wrong with your eye?" Crow said reluctantly.

"Thought you would never ask! Look at these luscious lashes I'm cursed with. Hurts like the dickens when one falls out and pokes me. Fish it out for me, would you?"

"Use a root to flick it out."

"But I want you to take care of it."

Magnolia was so totally impenitent that there was nothing more Crow could say in response. She wished she could make it hurt. But her fingers betrayed her. As always, they were terribly gentle.

Once it was over, Magnolia blinked again. Then, satisfied, she told Crow to talk up their next destination. "It better not be a goat pasture in the middle of nowhere. Get me excited."

"It's my hometown," Crow said. "In a manner of speaking."

Magnolia's eyebrows went up. "This close to the hills?"

"Wouldn't call it close."

"How much longer will we have to travel?"

"A couple months." Crow stretched the truth in hopes of dawdling.

Behind them, a noisy and narrow river rushed through a high-walled rocky canyon. Magnolia went silent while Crow shook out her clothes and got dressed. She had enough magic to spare that she could soften the fabric and modulate the worst stains to an evenness that resembled deliberate dye.

She put Magnolia on her shoulder. If Magnolia clambered up there with claws, her shirt (and skin) would end up getting shredded all over again.

"So what's it called?" Magnolia asked.

"What's what called?"

"Your hometown."

"Not sure."

"Come on."

"The names of places change over time," Crow said.

"You're technically correct, but that makes it harder to hold a conversation."

"Why should I work to make conversations with you any easier?"

Magnolia ignored this. "Humans come and go. Humans change their minds about what to call things. Us, on the other hand—we'll live for a long while to come. Let's assign this place a name. For all you know, we might still be talking about it twenty centuries from now."

"If I haven't killed you," said Crow, "and if the world hasn't ended yet."

"Don't be that way. No one likes a pessimistic immortal."

"You don't even use a name for your own place. You call it the radish village."

"So? We're discussing your town now. Not mine."

Crow gave up. "Name the town anything you want, but at least wait till you see it."

"Better stop dragging your heels, then."

She told Magnolia about her hometown in order to distract from the fact that she was indeed dragging her heels. Ages ago, it had been a tiny hamlet founded by refugees from the coast. Then it became a great city. Now it was a handful of settlements nestled around the fallen city's remains. Deadly caves tunneled below a nearby lake, and beneath the leftovers of the old city lay an even older necropolis.

"The town might not be there anymore," Crow warned. "I haven't been back in two hundred years."

"Cold of you," said Magnolia.

"By human standards. Not by ours."

"As a formerly land-bound monster, I suppose I see it differently." Magnolia paused. "You freed me from my compulsion to stay forever in the hills," she added casually. "Don't you want to be free as well?"

"Free from what? Free from you? Yes," Crow said. "Please."

"No, dingus. From your own compulsion. You've never asked a fellow saint to break your chains?"

"I don't have a compulsion."

"What, you think saints are immune?"

"Never seen any evidence otherwise."

"Believe what you like," Magnolia said. The verbal equivalent of a shrug.

They trekked across a series of interminable blue plains. At high noon, the sky above shone a verdant golden green. At night, the full moon loomed near the horizon, so impossibly huge that it looked as if it were descending to kill the world for good.

Sometimes, on a whim, Magnolia manifested the rest of her body and strolled around wearing the dead hunter's clothes, or nothing but mellow summer moonlight. Even in human form, she delighted in making Crow lift and carry her.

"You gain power by soaking up moonlight. What about sunlight?" Crow asked.

"The moon itself isn't what matters. It's about the wait for the full moon. It's about the interval. Comets work best for that. Remember the Cat Comet?"

"The what?"

"The one with four tails. Last seen over a thousand years ago."

"Oh." Crow did remember. She'd watched it with one of her earliest companions: the last human mage.

"If it ever comes back, I'll be unbeatable. I won't have to be nearly so stingy about whipping out my body. Not that I mind living as a cute little head."

"Not so little," Crow interjected. "You give me backaches."

"Only because you tense up so much when I ride you. You're like a prisoner getting dragged to the guillotine."

"I'm not like a prisoner," said Crow. "I *am* a prisoner."

"Best one I've ever had."

They came toward the end of the plains. Reduced once more to the shape of a severed head, Magnolia said: "This has been pleasant, I'll admit. I've enjoyed the chance to stretch my legs."

"Ninety percent of the time you had legs to walk on, you forced me to haul you around like a—"

"I've always been out there in nature, but the fresh air of the prairies tastes different. After all those years, it's a most invigorating change. I must say, though, I'm intrigued by your stories of your hometown. I'd like to get there a little faster."

"I haven't healed enough to port."

"Yes, yes. And you would never lie to my face, would you? No, I'm not that impatient. But I have an idea of where we can get a ride."

She directed Crow west past the rippling blue grasslands. "Even mortals used to travel by port gates and bypass tunnels, by airships and freighters and skimmers and war machines and pure human magic. And now ... well, no need to dwell on the past."

Her goal turned out to be a pile of ruins. It was overrun by primeval beasts covered in plate-sized keratinous scales. One came up to Crow and attempted to chew through her arm, which Magnolia found absolutely hilarious. Crow punched it on the nose, pried herself free, and scrambled to the top of a stony pillar. Not easy, given that her bitten arm had lost all its gripping power.

The pillar was so wide that she had trouble imagining what kind of human building it might have decorated or supported. It leaned steeply, but seemed in no immediate danger of collapsing. Rubble the color of sun-bleached bones helped bolster it from below.

The herd of primevals clustered around the base of the pillar, claws screeching on rock. Magnolia laughed while Crow humorlessly healed her dangling arm. After a few minutes, the primevals began climbing on top of one another, reaching higher and higher.

"They eat humans," Crow said.

"It was just an exploratory bite."

"I almost lost my arm."

"Don't jump to conclusions. You aren't human, are you? Maybe they only nibble on immortals."

"How'd you learn the way here?" Crow asked doggedly.

"The hunters who preceded you—some knew of it as a place to avoid. The ruins have been thoroughly picked over. There's no bounty on these charming beasts. Nothing left but risk."

"So they do eat people."

"I'm just saying, I haven't seen the evidence first-hand."

Crow shushed her before she could toss in one of her usual blithe comments about not having hands.

Together they eyed the seething mass of scaled primevals. Some licked the pillar with shockingly long blue-black tongues. Their back legs were huge and muscular. Their stacks of shriveled forearms waved in the air like the front half of a rearing caterpillar.

"These are man-eating beasts," Crow said. "And you want me to ride one to my old hometown?"

"It'll be much faster than catching a wild horse."

Crow pinched the bridge of her nose. Conversations with Magnolia often gave her the sense that something was about to start spontaneously bleeding—be it her unfortunate ears, the overburdened depths of her brain, or her hard-bitten tongue.

"There are no humans in these ruins," she said eventually.

"Well, yes. Primevals ate them all."

"How long ago?"

"An eon ago."

"Then your primevals can survive without regularly feasting on human flesh. Order them not to eat people anymore. No matter who shows up here."

"My orders won't apply to their descendants, you know. I'm not that skilled."

The pillar shook faintly as dozens of beasts—each individually much larger than a carthorse—pushed their weight at it.

"Order them," Crow repeated. Quickly—so Magnolia couldn't force her to say it—she added: "Please."

"Or what?" Magnolia asked, amused. "Or you'll kick up an enormous fuss, for as long as I let you? I'd rather like to see that, too, but I suppose today I'll keep the peace. I've had my fun. Hold me up above them."

Crow held Magnolia's head out over the edge of the pillar. Magnolia's hair tickled her wrists. She willed her fingers to loosen, to fumble, to become sweaty and helpless, just for a second—but they refused to falter. Magnolia, for her part, seemed utterly assured that Crow would never drop her.

"You will not consume us." Magnolia's voice filled the ruins like rainfall. "You will carry us wherever we wish, for as long as we wish, and you'll like it. In fact, I'll reward you."

Crow glared at the back of her head.

"All right, fine," Magnolia muttered. "Don't chew on any human beings, either," she told her bestial audience. "Living or otherwise. I know it's hard to believe, but some of them get extremely upset when you gnaw the bones of their dead."

The primevals dispersed, losing interest. Most went back to hunching down like living boulders in pools of sunlight. The sky was an unusually plain purple-blue, with only a half-hearted scattering of tawny clouds. Crow descended the pillar with relief.

"I suppose we only need one primeval to ride," Magnolia said reluctantly. "It'll be hard to choose. They're all so cute."

The paths around the ruins were littered with hard rounded stones, in some places piled knee-deep. Crow had to reach back to old, old memories to realize that those rocks were dried-up dung.

She spent a full day carrying Magnolia through the herd of primevals. When not gnashing their teeth in search of living flesh, they spent the majority of their time sleeping. When asleep, they all looked like indistinguishable brown lumps. At last Magnolia picked one curled up away from the rest.

"Young and full of wanderlust," she said. "You'll do."

The primeval blinked one eye at her. It was missing a few scales here and there. From those bare patches—and most of its joints—trailed coarse stringy fibers like the hairs of a horse's tail.

"Open your mouth," Magnolia ordered.

The primeval obeyed. Its tongue spilled out, long as a whip.

"I'm going to drip on it," she announced. "Position me above it—no, closer. Don't miss."

"Drip what?" Crow said. "Tears? Sweat? Snot?"

"Sweet nectar of the gods."

A clear dew—like tree sap, or water transpired through leaves—fell from the base of her neck. Just a few drops. Most of it entered the primeval's waiting mouth. A single bead trickled along Crow's forearm, pooling in the crease of her elbow. She had a vision of Magnolia wearing her body, fresh dew streaking irregular paths down her back. That vision cut through her senses like ice in a heat wave, and then it was gone.

The primeval's tongue retracted, making Crow wonder where on earth it all went. If she kept a tongue that size inside her, she'd have no room to speak or breathe.

"A blessing from Auntie Mag," Magnolia said fondly to the primeval.

"You won't have to eat, sleep, or drink for a very long time. Just like us!"

It nudged Magnolia with its elongated snout, almost knocking her out of Crow's hands.

"Your turn," she told Crow. "Give our friend a name."

"Dung," Crow said. She'd picked her way around heaps of it all day. At one point, she'd accidentally disturbed a head-height pyramid of dessicated egg-shaped dung—which toppled and scattered and chased her down a sloping road blocked by enormous walls of solid wreckage. Magnolia had laughed so hard that it sounded as though she were dying. If only.

"Dung," Magnolia repeated. "That's terrible."

"You think of a name, then."

"No take-backs. Dung it is." Magnolia extended a woody root to pat the primeval's flank. "Which is ironic. Having sipped from my dew—a very rare treat—our Dung won't be producing much dung of his own. If you know what I mean. Unless I give him a break to go gorge himself just for the sake of it."

Crow pretended not to hear her. At least Dung the primeval would give Magnolia someone else to talk to, even if he might never reply.

13

HUMANS WOULD NOT normally ride primevals like horses. Some varieties might be trained to pull carts, but the real extent of their domestication had been a matter of long debate. Water buffaloes were much more reliable.

Magnolia offered to grow a mat of smooth roots to use as a saddle. Crow declined for about half a week, then—steeling herself for a barrage of smug looks—finally accepted. The keratin scales of a primeval wouldn't slash up her thighs. Still, it was far from comfortable.

Dung's massive hind legs thumped the earth tirelessly, and the scenery flew by. The nearest they came to human habitation were a couple rotted-out homesteads. A journey that might have taken months ended up being reduced to a matter of weeks.

Crow still had no good answer for how to intercede if Magnolia became hostile toward human civilians, or vice versa. Her best bet would be to do something absolutely bizarre and unexpected. To startle

Magnolia out of her anger or boredom, if only for a few seconds. But Crow had never been a court jester.

She had some sense of how Magnolia would behave when it was just the two of them (with or without Dung). She just couldn't predict what would happen when they walked among humans. Would Magnolia insist on entering town in the form of a severed head? Would she force Crow to retaliate when people threw stones at her?

"I was on the fence about that," Magnolia said, unprompted, "but I think I'll take the opportunity to exercise my legs. If I collapse from exhaustion, I expect you to bring over a big leaf and fan me."

A steady drizzle fell from a mud-colored sky, deepening the brown of Dung's scales, plastering Magnolia's hair to the sides of her face. She liked to tie herself up near the highest point of Dung's neck. Maybe she thought of herself as the figurehead on the prow of a ship.

"Can you make it stop raining?" she asked Crow. A question, not a command.

"No," Crow lied.

"You dislike weather magic? Well, no matter. I didn't hire you to clear the skies."

"You didn't hire me at all. You—"

"What's that?" Magnolia said.

Dung came to an abrupt halt. Only the dense roots gripping her calves and thighs kept Crow from pitching off sideways.

A branch grew from Magnolia's left ear like a skinny knob of ginger. It crooked itself to point at the side of the rarely-used road, which—over years of semi-abandonment—had been reduced to little more than a doleful memory.

She made Crow get down and bring her over for a closer look. Next to the road was a small broken shrine, drowning in vegetation, stone pocked with old lichen in a pattern reminiscent of diseased skin.

"Hmm," Magnolia said. "That's not the God of the End. What is it, an aerial?"

Crow was briefly left speechless. The knee-height statue depicted a coiled serpent with a seemingly human head. The face was mostly a blob, eyeless, all distinguishing features worn smooth.

No one else would have looked at this and labeled it an aerial. A sea serpent, a snake, an eel, a giant worm—it could have been any of those. Why think of the sky? It didn't appear to be flying. It had no visible wings. Then again, many aerials didn't.

"Yes," Crow said at last. "That's an aerial."

"A shameful display," Magnolia muttered obscurely. "Would you like to destroy it?"

"What? No!"

"Suit yourself. Really, though—do you fancy yourself a guardian of humanity's leftovers? Talk about a losing battle. All the grandest temples and castles will crumble in the end. You can't stem the tide of decay. What's the point of protecting remnants that every living human has already forgotten?"

"There's a difference between fighting uselessly against entropy and going out of your way to smash ancient artifacts."

"Indeed. One of those options is much more cathartic than the other. Well, this marks a good turning point. Let's walk the rest of the way to town."

"It's not even in sight yet."

"Close enough," Magnolia said, as if she'd been here before. "Dung, go frolic in the wilderness while your parents take care of business. Eat fruit from abandoned orchards. Fertilize the earth with your droppings. Wallow in mudholes, if you find any. Swim through a swamp and paint yourself with algae. Get birds to groom the gaps in your scales. You'll have a grand old time without us.

"Afterward, come meet us on the opposite side of the lake. You're a good boy. You'll know when it's time. You'll sense us coming."

Dung ambled off into the mist.

Would they ever see him again? Crow knew little about the life expectancy of primevals. She had never been one to bond deeply with animals—blink, and they'd vanish forever. One past companion had bequeathed her a parrot, saying it would keep her company after he passed. The parrot did stay with her for ninety-something years. Which was longer than the average human lifespan, but not by much.

She'd made multiple visits to a giant tortoise that had lived over two hundred years in human care, way down south, although by now he was probably long gone. When she came across other mortal creatures with greater longevity—certain crocodiles and sharks and whales—she tried to make note of them. She tried to remember them, although they were highly unlikely to remember her.

"Unless there's something seriously wrong with this town of yours, Dung won't die of old age while we're parted," Magnolia said.

Heedless of the weather, she materialized the rest of her body and pulled on a few token damp garments.

"You'll get a rash if you walk around like that," Crow warned. She'd had a bad habit of mothering her human companions: reminding them to put on scarves or ponchos, or asking repeatedly about their blisters.

"Maybe," Magnolia said. "Maybe not. If I do find myself covered in rashes, you'll have to rub cream on me. Or perhaps I'll pack it all up and go back to being a head. You can wrap me in gauze and pretend I'm a coconut."

"Good idea," Crow said. Coconuts couldn't talk.

Water came into view before the town did.

The town, if you could even call it that, clung to the edge of a lake that looked as wide as the sea. Shanties and other wooden buildings rose up precariously among the stone leftovers of a sprawling dead city. The old city had half-collapsed into the lake. Or water had risen to submerge its outskirts in a single catastrophic flood. Crow couldn't quite recall the order of events.

Two hundred years later, the foundations of the place hadn't changed. Stone husks of drowned buildings wavered deep underwater. The mist and rain cleared, giving way to clean white-gold light. Giant aerial beasts in the sky traced reflected paths on the water's surface, slow and complacent.

Wooded islands clustered in the middle of the lake. Past the islands, which had peaks like minor mountains, water stretched out to touch a dubious gray horizon.

"Another shrine." Magnolia indicated a gate-like structure halfway up the largest island.

Crow didn't break stride. But she felt an invisible weight on her back. A weight very similar to the feeling of carting around Magnolia's damned head. The past lapped at her like water eating away at the shore.

She'd expected to feel stares. This was a place that would rarely get strangers. Any traders who came by would be the same people year after year, following the same isolated routes.

Normally, when she reached such a settlement, she might greet a few farmers at work, or get accosted by curious children. But soon enough, a representative would come out to inquire after her intentions.

This time, no one showed up.

The town was not devoid of people, although she spotted far more birds, especially down by the water. Swooping gulls and small black ducks, cormorants hunting side by side with egrets, and the ubiquitous three-legged crows, which maintained a relationship of bristling hostility with most other species.

As for the human population, a few women waded near where the ruins met the water. Probably harvesting clams or snails. Heaps of old discarded mollusk shells rose like sand dunes all around them.

Further inland, past a half-withered patch of sunflowers, a child tended to a flock of flightless chickens. They were luxuriously downy all the way to their toes, and as fluffy as an unshorn alpaca. Some shone a brighter white than any woolly sheep, and some looked like bunched-up black cats.

The curly-haired child glanced at Crow and Magnolia. She ducked her head dutifully. Not at all the usual attitude of a rural kid meeting strangers.

Crow couldn't take it anymore. "You're doing something," she accused. "You're making them think we belong here."

"I'm not, actually," Magnolia said. "Isn't that interesting? I haven't used a speck of magic. Not since I sent Dung off to gambol."

Crow was chagrined to find that she believed this. Usually her senses prickled with a constant awareness of Magnolia's magic. From the moment they began approaching this town on foot, Magnolia had been uncharacteristically docile.

Lacebark pines grew all over the wreckage of the hilly old city, rooting in every crevice with adequate access to dirt. Someone must have planted these over the course of the last two centuries. They didn't provide much shade, and it seemed an inefficient way to farm timber. Maybe—given the scant population, and the way their dwellings merged with the stony skeleton of the city—this gave them just enough wood to get by.

They climbed up to a square that offered a wide-open view of the lake. The slope of the city tumbled down towards the water like a rockslide frozen in time. The closest buildings around the square had completely collapsed. Only faint stone outlines remained.

A round crumbling fountain had been filled in with soil and repurposed as a community garden. It was mostly planted with practical summer vegetables. One chunk, roped off by low bamboo stakes and lovingly packed with yellow-brown sphagnum, had been set aside for growing modest orchids. They were topped with white fringed flowers shaped like egrets in flight.

There were people in the square, too. They didn't whisper to each other. They didn't tend the round garden, or admire the fruits of their labor. They stood as if they'd spent decades waiting patiently for someone to visit them.

The moment Magnolia crouched to peer at the egret flowers, everybody came to life at once. "What a handsome pair of women!" said a sun-browned old lady with her hands clasped behind her back.

"Only the handsomest," said Magnolia. "Aren't we the most exciting visitors you've ever had?"

"But of course!"

They grinned at each other. The old lady had probably been quite handsome herself, back in the day. Crow deeply regretted letting Magnolia loose on a place with a mortal population. This felt like ushering a dragon in among cattle and then locking the gate shut.

Unlike Crow, who had put on her token sunglasses, Magnolia had done nothing to conceal the dark red tint of her eyes. Unless everyone had terrible vision, they would soon realize she was an immortal. Could Crow convince them that she and Magnolia were both saints? Would anyone believe it? Two centuries later, there was no one left here to vouch for the honesty of the saint known as Carrion Crow.

Yet the confrontation she'd feared never came. She heard Magnolia asking about the shrine on the island, asking if they could borrow a rowboat.

"We don't take boats past the visible end of the ruins," said the woman with clasped hands. "We stop at the point where nothing pokes up out of the water. Go farther out, and you'll drown."

"Something pulls boats down?"

"Something does, yes."

Subsequent interrogation revealed that the locals had no idea if anyone lived on the islands. They didn't know if people dwelt on the opposite shore of the lake, either, and they didn't seem interested in finding out. Talk of the outside world made their eyes glaze over.

Magnolia asked about the town's name. Everyone she spoke to fudged their answers. They gave clearer responses when she asked whether waterbird guano made for good fertilizer.

Certain details were different from the last time Crow had stopped by. That insistence on staying away from the island shrine. The plethora of lacebark pines. The increased degradation of the old city. The local accent she heard when they spoke (although it had only shifted a little). Other parts were much the same. The voluble three-legged crows. The earnest attempts to grow egret orchids. The enthusiastic consumption of snails. The unbothered pace of their lives.

"We can leave anytime," she reminded Magnolia.

"Are you afraid I'll be bored? I'm fascinated," Magnolia said, as if that wasn't more cause for worry. "Let's stay."

"For how long?"

"Let's play it by ear."

She clapped her hands together and soulfully requested food, accommodations, and clothes. The residents snapped to attention and began murmuring to each other about how they might best fulfill her wishes.

Crow edged closer, jaw tense, and said: "Did you just—"

Magnolia gave her look of round-eyed innocence. "There wasn't any magic in my voice. You're well-traveled, aren't you? You should know better than anyone—people in small towns can be very hospitable. Even if they have little of their own to share."

"They can also be extremely suspicious of outsiders."

"We'll worry about that when the time comes."

While the adult residents conferred, the child they'd seen earlier came clambering up to the square. She carried a silky white chicken in her arms like a kitten. Behind a profusion of furry feathers, the only visible part of its face was its shy black beak.

The child came over to Magnolia and asked, with a weighty air of professional responsibility, "Want to hold her?"

"I would like nothing more." Magnolia hoisted the chicken up before Crow could say a word. It looked more like a fancy lapdog from ye olden days than any sort of barnyard animal. It let itself be cuddled without complaint.

"How sweet," Magnolia pronounced. "How affectionate. You must take very good care of them."

The child beamed.

"Call me Auntie Mag, won't you? What's your name?"

Rather than reply, the child held her arms out. Magnolia gave the chicken back. The child hugged it carefully. Her dark hair puffed up around her head much like the luxuriant down of her chickens, although hers was much curlier.

"Auntie Mag?" Crow said.

"Are you jealous? You can call me that, too." She crouched in front of the girl and her chicken and chattered nonsensically about gardening. Somehow she'd deduced that this girl was also in charge of caring for the city's sole surviving patch of sunflowers.

It felt like watching a con woman at work. Magnolia got the girl talking about how there were never any monsters here. She scarcely seemed to know what a monster was. The adults let her wander wherever she liked: they let her climb the ruins and dig around in old shell middens. She spoke as if she had never been afraid in her life, except maybe of getting her chickens snatched by a hawk. Her greatest complaint was she got tired, sometimes, of eating so much crab and crayfish.

"I wish my biggest problem in life was an abundance of fresh-caught crab," Magnolia said after the girl grew antsy and darted off, chicken in tow. "What an idyllic childhood. What a heavenly place to grow up."

14

The old woman and her husband brought Crow and Magnolia home for dinner. They had quite an audience. Other residents made all sorts of excuses to drop by (and drop off assorted dishes), and the curly-headed little girl kept peering in the nearest window.

The wide wooden bowl in front of Crow was filled with a mix of steamed mussels and ear-shaped pasta. Not ear-shaped in the usual abstract sense. These were the exact size of adult human ears. Even cooked, they retained each tell-tale fold and crenelation, the rigid curves of cartilage, the softer lobe.

The ears and mussels had been dressed with fish roe, which glinted like a scattering of jewels. They spread roe on toast, too. A host of oyster shells—repurposed as small dishes—cradled heaps of vegetables, most fermented beyond recognition.

The old woman apologized for not having snails. The latest wild batch they'd picked would need to be fed and purged for a few more days before going on anyone's table.

Magnolia praised the ear pasta. She also liked the soup flavored with ginger and wolfberries. The starring ingredient: soft-cooked meat covered in coal-black skin, from one of those fluffy and affectionate chickens.

Crow ate just enough to avoid insulting their hospitality. As evening approached, and the chorus of bullfrogs outside grew louder, she asked if anyone in this town still had her feather.

"Your feather," repeated the old man.

She removed her sunglasses and explained that she was an immortal saint. During her previous visit, she'd left a long dark feather with a pale shaft.

"Like a crow feather," she said. "A charm against evil. No matter how many years pass, I'll be called here if someone breaks it."

The old couple exchanged a look. They brought in a few friends, some even older and more bent. No one remembered her feather. They seemed afraid of having caused offense, but Crow waved it off. This was not an uncommon occurrence.

While the villagers held an emergency meeting at the head of the table, Crow leaned toward Magnolia. "Should I have given them an arm?" she said under her breath. "I could cut off an arm and make them mummify it. I can always grow it back."

"Next time, perhaps," Magnolia advised. "That would probably have a better retention rate. Why not offer them a replacement feather first?"

"Can't grow the right kind yet. My wings are fuzzy lumps."

"How inconvenient. Who did that to you?"

Crow gritted her teeth, then chomped down on another piece of ear pasta. It had a very satisfying bite to it.

The case of the lost feather remained unresolved. The bearded old man sadly led them up to a guest house surrounded by pines.

"We're most grateful," Magnolia said, "but we would've been happy to stay with you, or in any old empty shed."

"The guest house is for guests." He sounded confused.

"Do you often welcome guests?"

"The guest house is for you," he said, as if that concluded the matter.

It was dark now—dark enough that Crow insisted on escorting him back to his own dwelling. Despite the treacherous terrain of the ruined city, none of the residents carried lights. Did they usually retire to their homes right at sundown?

By the time she returned to the guest house, the voices of bullfrogs had swollen into a mighty torrent. Magnolia sat on the front step, lounging against the door like a drunkard who'd locked herself out. She had her eyes closed, though she didn't seem to be dozing.

"What?" she said shortly.

"You're blocking the way."

"Help me up."

Crow reached to help her, then realized belatedly that those words had not been backed by the propulsive force of a magical order. She tried to let go, but Magnolia—already gripping her forearm—refused to be dropped.

Magnolia hauled herself to her feet, then leaned on the door again. Her heavy-lidded eyes had an ember-like glow. She slapped her own arm, quick and sharp, to kill a bug.

"There are perks to having a body," she said, "but that doesn't mean I want to carry one around all the time. It's like constantly wearing a corset. I'm not a head missing the rest of me, you know. I really am just a head. With optional tree parts."

She gestured at herself. "Putting this thing on—and keeping it on—takes real effort. When you're used to having a whole body of your own, you don't realize how much upkeep it requires. It's a lot of work!"

"Not for immortals," Crow said, puzzled.

"Whatever. Hard work deserves compensation. Or at least appreciation. Where's my payment? No, don't answer that." She flung the door open.

Crow let a beat pass, then followed her into the guest house.

The building had been cobbled together from a mix of salvaged stone and new-cut wood. Eroded sculptures and dusty, patched-together vases lined the walls: artifacts of the old city. A vague moldy scent lingered in forgotten corners. Crow found bedding in a back room, but left it untouched.

An alcove held a small shrine. Nearby hung a long scroll, water-spotted and difficult even for Crow to make out without light. The figure painted on it was another serpentine elder aerial.

"You kept looking strangely at that older gentleman," said Magnolia. She'd dragged out a pile of bedding. She sat in it, arms around her knees, like a proud dove in a lazy nest.

"He reminded me of someone."

"Who? Your father?"

"You know we aren't born like that."

Magnolia shrugged. For all her complaints about the travails of wearing a body, she took to it like a natural.

"He has some resemblance to the first human I ever met," Crow said.

"Your first promised companion."

"It's just a coincidence. That family line died out."

"The same human faces and personalities pop up again and again over the course of history," Magnolia murmured. "I suppose you've experienced it more directly than I have, although I've met enough slayers and supplicants to notice patterns. Even among people that couldn't possibly have any direct relation. The same weak chin, the same nose, the same gait, the same smile, the same creaky voice, the same bad habits when holding a weapon. I've seen humans that I could've sworn I already killed five hundred years ago. It's not reincarnation. It's happenstance. They'll never know about their lookalikes. Not unless it was someone historically famous, and maybe not even then.

"When was the last time you heard about anyone making a daguerreotype, or sitting to have their portrait painted? A hero for the ages would be lucky to receive a single honorary sculpture. You haven't taken me to any memorials for your Arion."

"Don't speak of him," Crow said tightly.

Magnolia scratched her arm with vicious energy, then lurched upright. "I'm going out before I get eaten alive."

As the door banged shut, Crow tilted her head. Would there be fewer mosquitoes outside than inside?

It didn't seem safe to leave Magnolia to her own devices. Crow left the guest house, closing the door gently, and tracked her over to the open square. Night was mild here, though the breeze coming off the lake made it cooler than anywhere else they'd been (except for the peaks of mountains). The bullfrogs were still deafening.

Magnolia stood at the very edge of the square, treading on the stone footprint of a vanished building from the old city. Below her awaited a steep unlit drop to a path of crumbling stone stairs. She was still clad in borrowed homespun garments. Wind pulled at her neck-length hair. She rubbed her shoulders as if they pained her.

"I'm tired," she announced. "Tired and grumpy."

"I noticed."

"You still can't see why?" She thumped her shoulder again, then shot Crow a baleful look. "I told you—this body isn't really me. It's certainly not my true form. It's an accessory. A disguise. It's a pastiche of human flesh, complete with human needs. Why do you think I complained so much whenever I manifested legs and hiked on foot? When I'm like this, eating and hydrating and sleeping are actual needs."

"But you never—"

"All those other times, I didn't stay in this form long enough to wilt from sleep deprivation or thirst. I switched back once I got sick of it."

"Why can't you switch back now?" Crow asked.

"In case you haven't noticed, I'm trying not to use magic."

"Why not?"

"For reasons of my own, which are extremely deep and intelligent."

"You picked a strange time to go on a fast."

Magnolia stared at her as if she were unfathomably stupid. Crow, who had experience dealing with tetchy companions—from raging teenagers to old curmudgeons—remained unmoved. That caretaker instinct reared its head again, heedless of the fact that Magnolia deserved no such consideration.

"If you need sleep," Crow said, "and you're stuck this way, then you should sleep tonight. There's no other solution."

Magnolia shook her head. She looked out at the lake. Something glittered on its surface—starlight, or phosphorescence. The bullfrogs had gone a notch or two quieter. In the distance, chickens raised a brief evening clamor.

She hadn't issued true commands to any of the locals. She'd let striped mosquitoes land on her arms; she was still scratching the bites. Her eyes gleamed in the night, but her body was thoroughly human, vulnerable and weaponless.

If this continued—

Crow could walk out of town, and Magnolia would have no way to stop her.

Better yet—Crow could push her right off the edge of this plaza. Break her on the rubble below. Take her core. End this farcical servitude to an entity who, despite sometimes acting like a harmless annoyance, had very much earned her title as the last of the Four Great Adversaries.

Crow stepped forward, soundless.

"I know what you're thinking, even without magic." Magnolia didn't turn around. "Don't be foolish. I'm not flat-out incapable of using magic here. I'd just prefer not to. I'll use it to save my own life, if you force me. But I won't be happy. I'll be so piqued, in fact, that the very next thing I'll do is this. I'll order the locals to come kill you, and I'll order you not to fight back. I'll give you your first taste of transient death. See how you like it. Your seven precious core-gifting companions, all the magic you painstakingly inherited—how much of it will you retain when you come clawing out of your cocoon of rebirth?"

"You won't," Crow said. "You need me."

Magnolia cackled. "Make me angry enough, and you'll be surprised how much my needs can change! I can settle in for a few decades while I wait for you to revive. Maybe, the instant you break out of your cocoon, I'll tell the latest locals to make you step right back inside. Wouldn't that be rich?"

Crow had drawn close enough to breathe down her neck. Quick as a snake, she shoved Magnolia with her full immortal strength.

15

Magnolia fell. She didn't cry out. The sound of her hitting rock wasn't loud enough to cut through every other sound of the night. If the locals were shut up in their houses, they might not have heard a thing.

Crow remained still for an extra second at the edge of the drop. She had not entirely expected to succeed. She'd figured it would come down to who could act faster. Magnolia hadn't been bluffing, but she was tired and irritable, worn out by the confines of the human body she'd consigned herself to drag around like an inconvenient prop.

The sky above the lake was milky with stars.

Crow hopped down off the cliff formed by the end of the elevated square. A human jumping from this height would have broken both legs, and various other bones, but Crow made little noise as she landed on the steep uneven steps below. She straightened up slowly. Magnolia lay a little further down, a dark sprawled figure.

Her legs did look broken.

Crow picked up a brick-sized stone in one hand. These steps, which bent away from some higher street, had seen much better days. They followed a strange crooked path, like water seeking its way down a mountain.

Magnolia had struck the side of her skull. Blood, black in the shadows, coated the steps below. Crow crouched near her head, avoiding the wet parts of the stairs, and raised the rock.

Magnolia's eyes were lowered. It would've been a simple matter if only Magnolia would deign to look at her. Those eyes might shine garnet even in a darkness too thick to reveal the color of anyone's blood. If their eyes met, Crow's monster-slaying drive would kick in, and she wouldn't even have to think about her next move. The rock would come down.

Her arm froze in the air because Magnolia looked like a human shattered by a fatal fall. Her arm froze because her body remembered ancient battles, soldiers clad in heavy armor that would do absolutely no good against an immortal. Her body remembered bloodily inciting civilian riots and bloodily suppressing them, sometimes in short succession.

No one ever said that saints couldn't be sordid. No one ever said that saints couldn't be murderers. No one ever said that saints couldn't be hated. No one ever said that saints couldn't kill as many people as monsters. You could kill someone without reaping their core. Your victim would stay dead, and you would stay a saint, a pure saint who only ate cores willingly offered.

Crow had often been called a monster, rightly or wrongly. The real distinction was not in the presence or lack of compassion, or in the presence or lack of a love for humanity. Saints could be vicious. Monsters could be kind.

The only difference was that saints took magic from people slowly, and monsters took it quick.

Saints spent years—entire lifetimes—cultivating human relationships. All so the gift they received at the end would be that much greater. Saints moved heaven and earth to grant the wishes of their promised companions. Sometimes that meant trampling an enemy army. Sometimes that meant trampling people who weren't armed at all. Usually there was some kind of reason for it.

She remembered people who had pleaded with her for mercy, throats full of smoke, and people who had been too bereft to remember how to beg for their lives. She remembered arriving too late to a town she was supposed to save.

Today, she'd met a bleary old bearded man whose face echoed other long-dead men. People's quirks and cheekbones and voices and childhood habits resurfaced across generations, bobbing up like random flotsam. Everything in the world was an endless refrain. She remembered other fragile mortal bodies that had lain bleeding and unresisting on a slope or on steps, too stunned to move.

A whisper at the back of her head told her that Magnolia must know this. That was why Magnolia said nothing. That was why Magnolia refused to raise her eyes. Magnolia understood how much this would feel like hurting an actual human—a human already broken and suffering—and she would do nothing to spoil it.

Crow slammed her stone down.

Rock met rock with a crack so loud that it went through her like a spear. Magnolia had moved at the last moment. Not far. Just enough to avoid getting her skull flattened. She still didn't breathe a word of command. She still lay there—no further scrambling.

It felt as if the killing rock was welded to the stairs below, and as if Crow's hand was in turn welded to the rock. Even though, on a physical level, she could've lifted it like a feather.

Magnolia was lying mostly on her back now. Her bloody hand touched Crow's wrist, then Crow's knuckles. As if they were both holding the rock. As if they were about to use it together.

Crow knocked her away, recoiling, and raised the rock again. At last Magnolia looked her in the eye, dazed and shadowed.

"Can't move my head again," she said hoarsely. "My brains will start leaking." She sipped shallow breaths, trying not to shift her ribs.

Crow's grip faltered. She lowered her rock with a crawling sensation of disbelief. It escaped loosening fingers and crashed on one of the bloodied steps. She hardly heard it.

Magnolia had not been too slow to react. She had simply been confident that she could survive this fall. She might even have invited it. She might have staged the scene herself, standing at the edge on purpose, planning for Crow to view her as she was now, the spitting image of a wounded mortal.

She'd been certain that Crow would not deliver the decisive blow. If she turned out to be wrong, she'd use a command and save herself before the moment of final defeat. Before it went far enough for Crow to claim her core, to free it like a bird from a cage. So why did this still feel exactly like torturing a defenseless human woman?

Because her body wasn't healing. Because no magic coursed through her injuries.

Crow's thinking mind reached this conclusion long seconds after her churning unconscious. Immortals were extremely resilient against physical damage. They couldn't recover from anything and everything, but their inherent magic would try to do repairs—constantly, faithfully, without thought or effort, all the way to the end.

Crow would have assumed it was impossible to bring that natural process to a forceful stop. What mortal animal could—without any sort of chemical aid—consciously will their own blood not to clot? Self-healing magic was the product of a metaphysical system that would drive relentlessly toward survival. Even if you lost consciousness, or even if the pain of it made you wish you could die.

"How?" Crow said, stunned. "How are you doing that?"

"Lying here bleeding to death, with no feeling below my waist? It's quite easy. Much easier than trying to move. If I crawled away, would you chase me? It'd be like chasing a snail."

"How can you not..."

Her thoughts trailed off. Was Magnolia's control over her magic so total, so extreme, that she could manipulate even the aspects of it that would fight to keep her alive at all cost? Could she throttle that healing impulse because much of the damage fell below her neck—and the bulk of her body was just a disposable guise, not her true essence?

No—she'd cracked her head wide open, too.

Was this related to her specialty, her ability to issue ruthless commands? Could she magically command herself not to use magic again unless it was her only tool left to dodge death?

But if Magnolia kept languishing here, she would die anyway. She was chasing herself into a corner with every second she wasted bleeding out on the steps. Eventually she'd have to use magic regardless.

She read Crow's mind without the help of magic, saying: "I won't heal myself. But you can."

"I'm trying to kill you," Crow said.

"I do a very persuasive imitation of a dying human, don't I? It's the lack of healing that makes it convincing. That's why you hesitated. You're used to monsters assuming pitiful disguises, trying to play on people's sympathies, exaggerating their wounds. But I'm not exaggerating, and I'm not letting my own natural magic bail me out."

Her eyes were bright.

"The agony is genuine, and quite unrelenting. That's why your muscles seized up. That's why it reminds you of abusing a feeble mortal lady. In your career as a saint, how often did you become a hunter of humans? Were you ever made to hurt anyone who was already utterly helpless? Did you grab a brick and do it with your own hands back then, too? Very primitive."

"You're giving me more reasons to bash your head in," Crow said. The words fell half-formed from her lips, as if she'd become a clumsy puppeteer of her own unresponsive body.

"You won't kill me, Carrie," Magnolia croaked. "Not now. You're dying to know why I've pushed myself this far. You'll start to find out in a bit. But first you'll patch me up, yes? I'm exhausted from not screaming my head off. So to speak. Aha ... ha..."

None of these words were imbued with the power of a command. Crow healed her wounds anyway, dreamlike, feeling vaguely as though she'd been duped by a trickster in a folktale.

The backs of her shoulders ached. It was harder to mend the injuries of another immortal than it was to mend your own. Especially injuries like these—rapidly veering towards fatal. But she did it, and she scoured the blood from the dark stairs, too.

She'd wondered if Magnolia was suppressing her magic to avoid provoking some other entity in the area. Apparently Crow could wave around as much magic as she liked, though, which seemed equally liable to attract unwanted attention.

"You're not very good at this," Magnolia said.

"I can stop."

"Please do continue. Are you better at healing humans? Or beings you don't detest from the bottom of your heart?"

"I'm worse at healing humans," Crow said.

"Hard to imagine."

Once Magnolia was capable of sitting up, she put her arms out like a child and said, imperiously, "Carry me."

Crow stared down at her, marveling at her gall.

They continued to eye each other until Magnolia raised her chin haughtily and began to get up. She was halfway there when her legs buckled under her. She toppled into Crow.

"See?" she said against Crow's shirt. "You put my bones back together, but I'm still very weak. What will you do?"

Crow didn't bother sighing. She scooped Magnolia up and began ascending the stairs.

The bullfrogs had grown quieter. Or maybe she'd just gotten used to them. The scent of night-blooming flowers—cloying and peculiarly addictive—rose from Magnolia's neck.

As they passed the square again, Magnolia made her stop. Bits of white light fluttered near the filled-in fountain.

"The egrets," Magnolia said. "The egrets are flying."

Crow carried her closer. There was no one else in the unlit plaza, no sound of hidden footsteps. The frilly flowers of the small orchids had left their stems. They flapped and glided, circling Crow's shoulders. All these egrets could have been little free-roaming fragments of the moon.

The human residents might never have seen this. Wild magic often preferred to reveal itself when no one was watching. Crow and Magnolia didn't count; on the inside, they themselves were more like magical flowers than two-legged mortals.

An egret flower landed on Magnolia's lips, illuminating her scars and her dewdrop earrings with silver-white light. Her arms tightened around Crow's neck. Her sweet floral scent contrasted eerily with the austere androgyny of her face and body, her carefully placed moles like black stars.

She sneezed uproariously, ruining the moment. The flower flew away. Crow threw her over one shoulder and lugged her back to the guest house.

16

"You should sleep," Crow told her.

Magnolia was back in her nest on the floor. She sat cross-legged, hands drumming away at her ankles. "I can't sleep in front of you. You'll strangle me."

"I just failed to make the easiest kill of my life," Crow said tautly. "It would have been more than justified. And yet you live on. For now, you don't have much reason to worry."

"You should obsess less about murdering me and more about the state of this settlement."

"What about it?"

"Goodness. Where do I start? Surely you've noticed that almost no one has a core."

Crow opened her mouth to contradict this, then stopped. She flicked back through her recollections of each inhabitant they'd met. The old man and woman, their friends and relatives—all coreless.

"You know I'm right," Magnolia said. "We saw just one local human with a magic core."

"The little girl who looks after chickens."

"Bizarre, isn't it? This might have been normal thousands of years ago, but given the modern prevalence of human cores … makes you wonder. Don't think they're a secret self-selecting clan of slayers. And it's not just that. The whole city is devoid of minor monsters.

"Strangest of all—look at how they welcomed us. No pitchforks. No difficult questions. For all they knew, we could both have been ravenous beasts. You may wear those sunglasses out of some old-fashioned sense of courtesy, but let me tell you, they don't make you look especially trustworthy."

"Maybe they're not used to immortals," said Crow, "and maybe they have less to fear because they mostly lack cores. That could explain why other monsters haven't shown interest."

"They ought to be more concerned with protecting their little girl. Some monsters would kill the coreless together with their true prey, just for sport."

Magnolia said this without judgment—as if, depending on her mood, she too might take the same approach.

"Your radish village wasn't surrounded by walls, either," Crow said. "They welcomed me without brandishing weapons."

"Most of their visitors are hunters. Besides, they had me for protection. That was my territory, and I did an excellent job of defending it."

"Then—you think—"

"Shhhh." Magnolia had a finger to her lips. "Who knows what might be listening?"

"Haven't we already said too much?"

"Not quite—not yet."

"You refuse to use magic, but you never stopped talking about it."

"A lot of creatures don't understand or don't pay attention until you start discussing them in particular," Magnolia replied, unrepentant.

Crow wasn't sure she agreed, but she'd never had much experience with sneaking around other immortals. If they were a threat, they would either leave or attack her, and that was that. She wouldn't devote energy to going unnoticed unless her companion at the time requested it.

The locals' lack of hostility hadn't put her off, either. She'd been to so many different settlements with varying approaches to self-defense. She'd dwelt in walled cities and fenceless farmsteads. Naive countryside hospitality didn't strike her as being unusual to the point of suspicion. Even these days, some lucky people could go their whole lives without meeting a monster.

As she stated something to this effect, Magnolia waved her off. "You've lived with all kinds of people, sure. You don't go inside their heads—not the way I do. You can pass for human if you hide your eyes, but you aren't any good at thinking like one."

Later on, she scraped together her bedding and retreated to the back room. "I want a door between us, thank you very much," she said. "Don't attack me in my sleep."

The closed door would not offer anything in the way of meaningful protection. Crow stood facing it, listening to the small animalistic sounds of Magnolia dramatically fluffing her floor bed.

There were better things she could do than wait around for Magnolia to fall asleep. Now might be a good time to explore the area. If a powerful immortal had already established territory here, where would they lurk? Higher up in the old city, where no humans lived? Deep under the lake?

Minutes passed. As she pondered the possibilities, the interior door creaked open. Magnolia emerged, grumpy, holding a pillow like a hostage.

"I can't sleep."

"Isn't your body worn out?"

"It is! But sleep won't come to me."

"I was about to go out," said Crow.

"Don't. Talk to me."

"I could search for—"

Magnolia grabbed her sleeve. "Don't speak of it."

Crow's long life of dutiful companionship was working against her. She'd always attempted to be agreeable, even when human fears and passions confused her. She'd been overly conditioned to go with the flow. That was the only way she could explain how the two of them ended up sitting nonchalantly on the clay-tiled roof of the guest house.

"Moonlight makes everything better," Magnolia said with satisfaction. "You should've taken the opportunity to go borrow liquor from our hosts."

"It's not called borrowing if you can't return it."

Magnolia cupped her hands as though filling them with moonlight and starlight. She brought them to her face and took a sip of nothingness.

"What?" she said, catching Crow staring. "You want some?"

"I won't drink from your hands."

The roof tiles were curved and deep grey, rendered colorless in the night. The house was not tall, but its elevated position gave them a view of the square where fluttering egret orchids still wheeled (unseen by mortals), and the shore where the old city ran headlong into the lake, and the islands without a single light on them.

"Have you ever wondered what we are?" Magnolia asked.

This question felt like a trap.

"You haven't thought much about it, have you?"

"No," Crow said warily.

"Humans are extremely curious, you know. They wonder more about our origins than we do. We aren't much inclined to question our own existence. I suppose that's the key to enjoying a life of indefinite length. What about the beginning of the end of the world?"

"That was before our time."

Magnolia snapped her fingers. "That's what every immortal says. No one dwells on it. But I have an idea of how it all went down. I was in the hills for a very long time, and my roots went very deep. I invaded the minds of other beings, and I invaded the—well, I went deep enough to brush up against the memories of the land itself."

"And now you're going to sermonize about it," Crow said dryly.

"No, no, that's a lecture for another night. But I'm glad you realize that we immortals haven't been around forever. We only started showing up once the world was doomed—which happened through an act of purely human magic. Did you know that? Bet you didn't.

"I had my roots, infinite time to kill, and an interest in communing with the land. A genuine interest in learning more about why, after a certain point in history, this world started spawning us out of nowhere. Most other immortals lack that burning desire to seek, to know."

She sipped from empty hands again. Phantom liquid glistened momentarily on her lower lip. Her hanging earrings twitched; they resembled suspended beads of water. If she were partaking in magic right now, it was a magic that existed wholly outside her. Like those snowy egret flowers, smaller than butterflies.

"Picture a dead body left in a forest," she said. "All kinds of creatures will pop up to digest it, some seemingly out of nowhere. Maggots and flies, microorganisms and fungi and your precious isopods. I'll grant that there's at least one forest out there where nothing ever decays in the usual sense. But that's the exception to the rule, and it lies across the sea. My point stands. All those little critters that emerge to diligently process decaying flesh—that's us."

"We're maggots?" Crow said.

"Think of us as undertakers, if it suits you. We began emerging—or being birthed—as thoughtlessly as flies that swarm toward open wounds. We came into being after the world was already set on a trajectory toward certain death. An extremely slow death—it's practically geological in scale—but still. We're preparing a body for a funeral. We're nibbling away at its prodigious flesh. We're reverse midwives, guiding the world gently through its final days. Simply by gathering and stealing and eating cores.

"What happens to magic after we consume it? It becomes ours, yes, but couldn't there be some greater significance to the act of digestion? Why does our survival hinge on it? Couldn't our drive to ingest and integrate magic be part of a much larger natural process—a movement beyond our understanding? Like maggots wriggling in a corpse without any comprehension of the cycle of mortal life, or of all the other maggots that have ever wriggled in other corpses, in this world or much stranger ones."

"I have no idea what you're talking about," Crow said honestly.

Magnolia lay flat on her back on the undulating tiles, some of which bore deep cracks. "That's the opening argument of my unified theory of the end of the world."

"Just the opening?"

"Yes, and don't you forget it."

"If you know so much," Crow said, "and you've seen so much through the eyes of others, and you can order around anyone you meet—why did you wait so long to leave the hills?"

"You may have found it a simple matter to sever me from the land, but don't make the mistake of thinking that what's simple for you would be simple for others." Magnolia patted the central roof ridge as if stroking the spine of an obedient pet. Its stacked tiles no longer ran perfectly straight.

"It really did take me that long to lure you in. Of all the Great Adversaries, you just had to put me off for last."

"You could've gotten another saint to—"

"You know I tried."

"You could have called a monster of equivalent strength."

"What do you think I am, some kind of god? My sphere of influence doesn't encompass the entire continent. They have to come to me before I can make them listen." She sat up, elbows on her knees. "I couldn't beat any immortal in a fair fight, without my commands. I'd lose to some experienced humans, too. Of course, no need to beat them if I can just tell them to submit. Haha. But that isn't nearly as easy as I make it seem."

"It isn't?"

Magnolia turned toward her, earrings swinging, and said: "The fact is, you have an overinflated opinion of my capabilities. Which I suppose is understandable. It's like you were made for me. Any other immortal of your caliber—it would've been a life-and-death battle to bend them to my will. The struggle would've lasted years and years. A protracted stalemate, one with few signs of hope."

And yet Magnolia had asserted mastery over Crow in an instant. In retrospect, it felt as though there had been no struggle whatsoever.

"Are you saying that I'm ... uniquely mentally weak?"

"I'm not insulting you," Magnolia answered, as breezy as ever. "You have a different set of vulnerabilities. You're just very unlucky, to be honest. Your only real weak spot aligns perfectly with my only real strength. It would've been different if you came to me with a promised companion in tow, but you made the mistake of coming to see me alone. That sealed your fate."

The roof tiles were comfortingly hard and cool and colorless, as if they had never known sunlight. Aerials glided through the night sky like leviathans in black water. A thought came to Crow, an obscure prickling hint of sensation beyond a thick veil of numbness: she had gone stargazing with humans, but never with another immortal.

"I'm not surprised," Magnolia said (after harassing Crow until she spoke her mind). "We aren't like humans or rabbits. We won't die of solitude. Humans have to scramble early on to get socialized—they've got to run around like little rats before they run out of time. Their lives are just that short. We, on the other hand, are born on our own, and we can only die permanently at the hands of another immortal. It's natural to be standoffish. Every peer is a potential competitor, or potential prey."

Magnolia's conversational stamina made her a wild outlier among immortals. Most were less chatty than Crow. Monsters might become voluble when surrounded by humans; they might lie and tell stories. But they'd clam up when Crow came after them. They knew talking wouldn't get them anywhere.

She'd never had more than a distant working relationship with a fellow saint, either. Their paths might briefly intersect when their human patrons allied or clashed. Never for any other reason.

Magnolia, yawning, made Crow help her down off the roof. After she barricaded herself in the back room for another attempt at sleep, Crow quietly left.

In the shadow of lacebark pines, she wondered how far away she could get without porting. How many miles would need to lie between them before Magnolia's hold on her began to weaken? If Magnolia used magic again, how quickly would she catch up? Was she perhaps incapable of porting, even with her millennia of moonlight?

Fleeing might work—so long as Magnolia wasn't just pretending to sleep. But that would mean abandoning the town to Magnolia's whims. If she woke up to find herself alone, how would she treat the residents?

It's your fault, she'd would say matter-of-factly, if they ever met again. *What'd you think I would do if you ran?*

Crow, returning to the guest house, gazed once more with bemusement at the door between them. Magnolia knew it would make no difference if Crow decided to wring her neck in her sleep.

She touched the door and convinced it to let her through. She slipped past, ghostlike, and found Magnolia sound asleep in a coil of bedding. With her eyes closed and her face wrought in a rictus of displeasure, she looked even more human than she had when awake.

That frown made it seem as if someone had already placed hands on her neck. As if she were holding her breath, waiting for murder.

Crow leaned closer. The gardenia scent was softer now, and less certain. Eager strength filled her fingers. Impatient magic fizzed in her joints. She would not regret any incidental enjoyment she might derive from holding Magnolia down while she choked.

She leaned close enough to see the delicate moles on Magnolia's face and neck scurry around like black insects, like egret flowers taking flight while mortals slept. She reared back.

The moles settled back into their original arrangement, as if they'd never moved at all.

Magnolia opened one claret eye and said, "Oh. Is it already time for my strangling?"

Crow leapt away. She leapt all the way past the still-closed door, dissolving through it like mist and re-forming on the opposite side. Her skeleton felt altogether too tight. Her wing-nubs seared like hot coals. Magnolia's room remained quiet; no one came out in pursuit.

17

CROW DIDN'T try to kill Magnolia again that night, and she didn't leave town. There was something off about this place, something that had little to do with either Magnolia or Crow herself. Magnolia seemed vaguely interested in intervening—for her own reasons, with no thought for how it might affect those who lived on the carapace of the lost city.

Around sunrise, Crow heard chickens. She let herself in Magnolia's room again.

The heaps of bedding on the floor were empty. Summer spiders jumped around in otherwise untouched corners. Magnolia might have climbed out through the open window—but to what end?

There was no one in the square. The egret flowers had flown in to roost motionless on their stems. Crow made her way down to the shore formed by the tops of dead city buildings, passing a startling profusion of shoulder-height wild lilies. The shadows of aerials and water birds scudded across the lake.

The chickens never stopped crying. She conversed with a couple gray-haired residents. Some had tools in hand—a spade, a fishing rod—and yet they wandered back and forth in front of empty houses as if they'd forgotten what they were supposed to be doing. No one had seen Magnolia.

She asked them their names. Few managed to cough up a coherent answer. There were parts of the world where giving your real name to an outsider simply wasn't done. But this area had never been one of them.

She tried asking an old man at the water's edge. He looked at her oddly. It was the same man who had shown them to the guest house last night. He too seemed to have lost track of whether he'd wandered over here to check fishing nets, or to savor the morning air.

"Haida," he said.

"Haida?"

"My name. You asked."

"Oh."

Haida had a big, venerable nose with bristly hairs fit for a potato brush. He hadn't seen Magnolia anywhere, either.

"The chickens." Crow gestured. "Are they always this loud in the morning?" She could still hear them, a distant cacophony beneath the nearer squawks of ducks, geese, and gulls.

Haida blinked rheumy eyes. "...No."

His speech reminded her of the way wounded soldiers would fumble for words. But there was little tension in his face. White beard, jaundiced eyes, earthy skin—all remained calm.

Crow's gut stayed calm, too. But a premonition in her magic churned like a whirlpool.

"The girl is gone," he said. "They miss her."

The curly-haired girl who'd walked around carrying chickens. The girl who tended to withering sunflowers. The only human in this entire settlement who had a core.

"Is she hurt?" Crow asked, thrown off by his lack of urgency. "What happened?"

"She's gone."

"She vanished? But when?"

"In the night. When else?"

She pictured Magnolia stealing out to find the girl like a fox stalking a flightless chicken. That was a very real possibility. She should have fought harder to kill Magnolia when she had a chance. What if it had all been a cunning ploy—every meaningful look, every allusion to a greater mystery enveloping these people who no longer knew their own names?

Magnolia would manipulate her sympathies and then eat the little girl anyway. And Crow, after finally killing her, would have to consume that wretched soul full of human victims. Even if it turned her stomach, even if the acid taste of unquenchable rage had flayed her gullet, even if she had taken every wrong turn and arrived too late to save anyone.

But there were other possibilities she had to account for, too.

When she glanced at the mountainous shape of the rising city, motionless figures stood scattered at lonely intervals. One person further down the shoreline, on the roof of a tilted building. One person on bone-white steps winding up toward higher parts of town. One person in front of a palatial mansion with only two standing walls, and rows of columns leading nowhere.

"The missing girl," she said to Haida. "Does she have a name?"

"Rinlin," he replied, briefly sour-faced. He made it sound impious to speak the names of the vanished.

"I'll find her."

Haida stared as if to say *No one asked you to do anything.*

Magnolia might have kidnapped Rinlin to kill her and take her core.

Or Rinlin herself was the local monster in disguise.

Or another monster lurked here, preying on the human population, and now on Magnolia. If this were the case, then Crow owed the local monster her thanks. But she wouldn't leave it to keep feasting off the land like a tick.

She told Haida that she wanted to go to the islands in the lake.

He shook his head. "No one will lend you a boat."

If a monster had hidden itself in the air of the city, or below the lake, then it was very good at hiding indeed. She'd have to take painful shortcuts to avoid a long and fruitless hunt. If Rinlin wasn't dead already, she certainly would be by the time Crow tracked her down the slow way.

"You saw the orchids flying," Haida said suddenly.

"You saw them, too?" she asked, startled.

"They used to mean something. Not sure what."

Some had called them aerial orchids, Crow remembered. They were grown in dedicated plots near the island shrine.

On summer nights, they would fly down into the open shrine in the dark. They would go all the way up to the altar and dance around for hours.

"Face the other way," she said.

Haida obeyed, turning his back to her and to the clear water where ethereal fish darted out of sunken stone dwellings. Something had made the people of the lake very suggestible.

The stumps of her wings began to itch again. She clenched her teeth and ported to the largest island.

It could have been worse. She knew where she was going. She had been here many times before. Yet she scarcely recognized it.

At least up until two hundred years ago, people had still made regular trips to the islands. The forests had been partially groomed for human use, with wide walkable paths touched by splatters of sunlight.

There used to be bridges from island to island, along with diligently maintained docks. In some seasons, a floating bridge went all the way from the main island to the carcass of the lakeside city. Families of caretakers lived in the woods, tending to ancient shrines. They passed down stories to explain how the lake had formed, how the city had fallen, and how a legendary saint had once been born here.

Gone—all gone. The sole sign of the past was the huge open gate without any paint, the one visible from the city shoreline. Everything around it grew shriveled, as if intimidated by its height. Beyond the gate, no slivers of sunlight penetrated the canopy. She couldn't name a single color in the sky. The trees looked like alien species, and beneath them it felt as cold and dank as a midsummer cave.

Wetness ran down her back. Her fragile wings must've torn open when she wrenched her magic to get here. A few minutes past the gate, she turned about, borrowed clothing snagging on the waist-high rustling underbrush. Given the lack of light, this vegetation seemed preternaturally dense. She couldn't detect the sound of lake water lapping.

Three-legged crows perched on branches all around her, as if they'd been frozen here for centuries, as if they'd known she would one day materialize in this exact spot. Or maybe they'd been drawn by her blood.

She needed to find the shrine. The original shrine.

Would it still be accessible? The island had been abandoned for some unknowable length of time. The forest had swallowed and fully digested every last manmade trail and sign, every wooden building where four or five generations of caretakers used to live together in all seasons. Only the symbolic stone gate remained, standing alone.

She forged ahead, relying more on instinct than on memory. The blood trickling under her clothes began to feel like cold sweat. The crows shouted at irregular intervals that seemed calculated to startle, and the trees presented a dense unchanging face.

She stopped and knelt, parting the underbrush. Needlessly sharp leaves opened swift shallow cuts on her hands. Ignoring the stinging, she put her face down near the soil and asked the local isopods if she were going the right direction.

As individuals, none of them had ever spoken with her before. As a population, they remembered her far more clearly than the humans dwelling by the shore.

Keep going, they said. *You have always known the way.*

With the isopods' encouragement, Crow stopped thinking. She pressed on through the clinging undergrowth until she began to stumble over statues. Some leaned against trees. Some had fallen off their pedestals. They were all bare stone now, without a hint left of colorful paint. Mold and lichen and furry moss stained their long serpentine coils.

Up ahead, the ground cover gave way to bare earth. It was as though someone had used fire to carve out a cavernous green-walled hollow inside the forest. There was no reason for all the aggressive chest-high ferns to have beaten a sudden retreat. But this place had always been like that. Nothing grew here.

As she stepped forward, she felt the pricking of ticks and other clinging creatures detaching from her en masse, leaping backwards into the brush.

It was oppressively quiet.

She faced a stone entrance flanked by more heavy serpentine carvings. Some rocks had tumbled out of place, but the whole structure was devoid of crevice-seeking vines and roots. No lichen speckled the crushing curves of the serpent's body.

The entrance was partly clogged with matted layers of brown leaves and silt and all sorts of rotting matter, which merged to form a thickly scented mulch. Hidden animal bones crunched underfoot as she walked inside. It felt like walking into a stone oven made for giants.

At the back of the oven-shaped maw, she descended the wide stone steps that led down to the main body of the shrine. The stairs were expansive enough to accommodate streams of pilgrims going in both directions, but today Crow was the only visitor.

Once upon a time, the shrine had been adorned with textile hangings and bamboo screens and ropes of rice straw and everlasting flames. No trace of them remained. The air tasted unpleasantly hollow. If she couldn't see in the dark, she wouldn't have been able to proceed any further.

She used to wonder why they'd built a shrine to aerials deep underground—out of fear, or misplaced humility? Was it supposed to double as a shelter if the sky started falling?

There was still an altar housed at the far end of the shrine. She looked just long enough to see that it lay empty. Her wing-nubs felt like red-hot knives in her back. The pain mounted and mounted until she turned and soundlessly vomited into centuries-old dust. It had nothing to do with her stomach, but past a certain point, the body could only choose from a limited set of reactions.

She waited to make sure she could stand without staggering. Then she explored the shrine from end to end, keeping her eyes averted from the empty altar.

There had been a time when people worshipped Crow here. No—not Crow herself. Something she used to be. There was a certain power she could mine by returning to this spot, like how Magnolia mined magical strength by basking in the silence of a full moon. There was a certain power that could be derived from this reflexive pain, a pain that had made her throw up three times now. An odd thing to do with a body that never ate much to begin with.

She needed to boost her magic in order to locate Rinlin and Magnolia. Coming here was the only way she could accomplish that in short order.

She was also looking for the old feather she'd given to the people of two hundred years ago. They might have placed it in this shrine for safekeeping. She couldn't grow new feathers yet, but if she found one she'd shed in times past, she could use it.

Her search didn't take long. The shrine was bare. Almost unnaturally so: was two hundred years in darkness really long enough to eradicate every last thread of every last decorative hanging? Hadn't there been metal artifacts, too?

The naked rock made it feel more than ever like a cold empty oven, a womb that would never let her go. She glanced away from the familiar altar. No feather. She'd have to go in unarmed. The wing-blades in the backs of her shoulders kept burning, digging deeper.

She focused instead on seeking Rinlin and Magnolia. She cast out a wide net of magic.

They weren't anywhere on the islands. They weren't drowning in lake water. They weren't in the caves below the lake, or hidden high up in one of the city's crumbling guard towers. They were far from all the other residents.

They were in the necropolis. Way on the opposite side of the city. And they weren't alone. She could port there—but once she arrived, would she be in any state to fight? The slashes on her hands had only just begun to heal.

Even in this, Crow had any semblance of choice stolen out from under her. As she steeled herself, magic yanked at her ankles like a drowning current.

18

ALL THE AIR had been siphoned out of her lungs. Her back screamed as if it had been split by a whip. She took in the new scenery around her with a bitter burst of understanding.

Magic—her own magic—had forcibly dragged her to the necropolis, an underground palace of the dead. She glimpsed barren halls. Gauzy purple-brown sheets of something organic grew on cracked walls and dripped from columns. The whole place stank of fungus.

Magnolia rested on a heap of sticky-looking treasure—tarnished coins, ornaments of jade and bronze. She had reverted to being a bodiless head. At the moment she resembled nothing so much as a cephalopod, with long thick roots streaming from the base of her neck. One root curled in a proprietary fashion around Rinlin, who was balled up on the stone floor with her arms covering her face, making sounds like a teakettle.

Another one of Magnolia's roots held the broken halves of a black feather. Crow's confusion spooled out over the course of a blistering instant during which no one moved or spoke.

A second monster dwelt in this space, too. One much larger than Magnolia or Crow.

Magnolia didn't seem tremendously concerned. She waved Crow's feather. "So that's how it works," she said. "Helpful. Here you go."

She tossed the feather up. It should have been too light to travel far, but the two halves flew towards Crow like arrows loosed from a bow. She caught one in each hand.

"I don't have full control over this creature." A slight shake had permeated Magnolia's voice. Or was that an illusion wrought by echoes? "I argued her to a standstill, but it won't last much longer. I'm tired, Carrie. All that work to maintain the element of surprise, and it ended up being barely enough to save my own skin.

"I always struggle with this type. When you get down to it, the fact is that we're simply much too alike. I hate it when other monsters remind me of myself. Why can't they all be more like you?"

Crow turned to face the other monster in the room.

Slime trails coated the floor, viscous and gleaming. At first she thought she was looking at an eel-like beast with a humanoid upper body. A well-known monster; the human bits were just a lure. It would pop up out of marshes and rivers. It would pretend to be drowning, and then it would eat its would-be rescuers, cores and all.

But this creature was not really any sort of lamia or naga. It had cobbled itself together as if to imitate the serpentine aerials depicted in countryside shrines.

The human part was not convincing. Half the torso belonged to a child, with a much shorter arm, and chunks missing where it failed to match up with the larger ribcage on the other side. The head, which consisted mostly of lank hair, slanted like that of a corpse killed by hanging. The longer adult arm dragged around a second spare head.

"A mimid," Magnolia said. "You guessed right. She's trying to look like the aerial they used to hold sacred here. What's your take—would you call this an accurate depiction?"

The snaking body and tail had the brawny grace of form you might expect from a sky dragon, but any resemblance ended there. Naked human arms and legs—splotched with strange colors and slathered in slime—sprouted at broken angles like the myriad limbs of a millipede.

Mimids were hoarders. They craved cores above all else, like any immortal. But they wouldn't let the dead flesh of old victims go to waste, either.

Fish-pale plants grew from fissures in the walls and in the wreckage of broken sarcophagi, content without sunlight, extending white air roots like questing whiskers. At first glance, Crow had assumed those roots belonged to Magnolia.

The mimid flipped its broken neck around to point its primary head at Crow. That muscular body coiled in an infinite spiral beneath it, human hands and feet smacking the slime-coated floor in a ragged wave of surreal applause.

"She didn't fear me." Magnolia managed to sound equal parts strained and indignant. "But she fears you—rightly so. I'm going to let her go any moment now. Girl, stop making that infernal noise! Thank you."

This last part was directed at Rinlin, who went silent with a suddenness that made Crow fear for her life.

The next time Magnolia spoke, it was in a very soft voice that Crow felt right in her marrow.

"Crow," she said, abandoning nicknames, "destroy that monster and bring me her core."

Now it was just a matter of executing orders. The inside of Crow's head had been washed with clear water. The crashing simplicity of it was one of the greatest pleasures she'd ever experienced. Her joints felt light and oiled, her body supple. Her magic swelled like the earth-shaking roar of a mortal army charging forth on the last desperate day of their short desperate lives.

In her hands, the broken halves of her old feather grew into perfectly weighted twin blades.

She noted that Magnolia had deliberately placed Rinlin between herself and the mimid—like a hostage, or bait, or a final fleshy shield. She considered it plausible that Magnolia had kidnapped Rinlin before the mimid seized them both. These observations swam past her as idly as decorative fish—gleaming with interest, but no fundamental threat to her serenity.

Either way, Rinlin would hear her swords filleting this monster like a sturgeon. That much was unavoidable.

Magnolia gave up on holding back the squirming mimid. It immediately surged at Rinlin. That was the only logical maneuver: to seize the most readily taken core, and then to flee. The sheer weight and physicality of the mimid made the room quake, but it was a creature meant for hiding safe in deep lairs.

Crow leapt on its human-shaped back. She didn't even really pay attention to what she was doing. Would an experienced rower think through each motion of their oar in the water?

Her swords cut down through borrowed human flesh, and then into the thrashing bulk of the serpent. As it flailed its tail behind her, stolen human limbs squelched against stone walls and columns, elbows cracking backwards, femurs protruding from thighs. It began to undulate away down the vast hall, welded-on arms and legs dragging limply as it went. It had more than one mouth, but it never said a word. The only sound it made was the thunder of its body crashing into rock.

Naturally, Crow was faster. She ported into the air above the mimid and plummeted, blades out, severing the lowest third of its tail, then the next third, then the next, until all that remained was the patchwork torso trying to crawl away across the slippery floor on borrowed arms. A bilious gunk—difficult to describe as blood—gushed out of the butchered serpent body, surging like a tide. Limbs attached to the severed segments still spasmed broken fingers or clenched discolored toes, trembling sporadically, glossy with a syrup of clear excretions.

Crow looked at the crawling torso. She put her foot on its back. It stopped moving. She pressed her blades together, merging them into one long spear.

Before she could plunge her spear down, the monster's core slipped out like a yolk from an egg. It floated towards her, glowing. The spear in her grip reverted to a broken feather and drifted down to blend with the muck underfoot, forgotten.

Her tongue had gone dry. A muscle pulsed at the back of her throat. But she didn't claim the core. She beckoned for it to follow her. She led it down the trampled burial hall and back to Magnolia, who was still posed like an octopus with her roots draping away in all directions.

"Astonishing," Magnolia said.

Crow had nothing to say in answer.

"I thought your body might struggle more with the prospect of surrendering a fairly won core. It's nice to see that I can make you bring me dinner. But you'd better take this one for yourself. You're leaking blood down your back."

The disparate parts of the carved-up mimid had begun to collapse inward with a distinct stench of rot. Rinlin remained frozen in place, an insensate ball, Magnolia's root draped across her like a threat.

Crow felt herself coming to her senses even as she drank the mimid's core down, magic flaring within her. Dirty water rose once more to fill her head. She had forgotten herself when Magnolia ordered her to kill, and she'd liked it. If anything, it had been over too quickly. She could tell from the ache in her face that she'd been smiling.

Magnolia reached out with another fresh-grown viney appendage and made Crow turn in a circle. Grabby roots yanked up the back of her tunic.

"They're the size of chicken wings now." She seemed amused. "Not suitable for flight, but perhaps you'll be able to squeeze out longer feathers if you try. Better shrink them down if you want to keep them trapped under your clothes. Or maybe you ought to cut slits in your shirt again. Anyway, it's about time for me to claim my own reward."

"What?" Crow managed. This sounded foreboding.

Magnolia gave her a puzzled look. "Surely you didn't think you'd be the only one who gets to devour a core? I let you eat this mimid *and* the cocoon monster in the mountains. Why would I feed you if it meant going hungry myself? Now, if you'll excuse me for a moment—I know you're tenderhearted. You might want to close your eyes for this."

Those last words were a mere suggestion.

Crow stomped on the root that snaked across the floor toward Rinlin. She put enough magic in her heel that the wood flattened like wet mud underfoot. She'd caught several—though not all—of Magnolia's other branches in her hands, too. They creaked and splintered in her grip.

A new root veered out from beneath the nape of Magnolia's neck. It came to curve around Crow's waist. Fibrous tributary roots branched off like hairs, each individual filament pressing at Crow through her clothing, little grasping needles. Focus her magic, and she could set it all on fire. She could burn herself; she'd done it before.

Magnolia's voice broke her concentration. "You saw this child for the first time yesterday. Leave town, and you'll never see her again. What difference could it make whether she dies now or after fifty more years of subsistence farming? Although I wouldn't expect her to live nearly that long now that the mimid is gone. Other monsters will wander through sometime in the next few years. Even if they don't, it'll be infinitely harder to scrape out a living."

Maybe it would be better if Crow didn't burst into flame right in front of the child.

"Don't," she said with difficulty. The feeling in her was so intense that it numbed her tongue. "Don't take her core. Don't you dare even say it."

Her hate roared back stronger than ever, as if tempered to a harder and hotter edge each time it sank temporarily down into her calmest depths. She remembered the light of the egret flower that had landed on Magnolia's defenseless mouth. She remembered it with a fury that defied comprehension.

"You think your righteous anger would stay me?" Magnolia said thinly.

Her teeth were an even white. The unmarked white of a creature that never drank the beetle tea of her own village, that rarely used those teeth for tearing at physical food. Her teeth were for show—like every other part of her, like her glinting earrings and the scar through her eyebrow.

Behind Crow, Rinlin remained silent. As commanded. She hadn't moved an inch. Had Magnolia ordered her to stay put even if the mimid reared over her, shedding sheets of mucous from its hundreds of tacked-on arms and legs?

"You're more worked up about this than the hunter I made you behead," Magnolia said. "Why, pray tell? Because she's younger? A rounding error. Because she's not carrying a sword? We can find one for her. There's got to be a couple fancy weapons buried beneath me in this heap of riches.

"But that won't appease you, will it? You know what's funny? You're angrier than you would have been if the mimid had managed to eat her.

Maybe I should've offered your girl up without saying a word. The mimid did find her first."

"I cut the mimid up in ten pieces," said Crow.

"More like seven. And every stroke of your blade was impersonal. No hard feelings. Now, the way you look at me—you despise me. You loathe me. I see it rippling under your skin. If I kill this girl—a kill that would be fully deserved—your hatred of me will swallow you whole.

"If the mimid killed her, you would've been filled with regret. You would've blamed yourself for not saving her. But it would never have occurred to you to nurture a seething personal resentment for the mimid herself. Why try to hold me to a higher standard? I am but a humble monster. You could say that I belong to the same genus as the mimid. Her magic had a lot in common with mine—which made her extremely difficult to command. I'm still wiped out. And I see absolutely no reason not to refuel."

"I'm your reason." Crow had to wrench each word out one at a time. "Feed on me instead. Take my hand, or my—"

Magnolia widened her eyes in mock surprise. "That won't go very far. Perhaps I can drain some magic from your flesh, but it'd be like licking dew off morning leaves when there's a spring full of fresh water ready to drink from. Not a tempting offer. You think I don't relish the ability to make you do exactly as I wish—or to make you sit there without lifting a finger, helpless? You glare at me with such passion, and you think I don't despise you in return?"

She thought blindly that Magnolia would have to go through her to get to Rinlin. Magnolia could order her to move out of the way, but—

"Move out of the way?" Magnolia said. "Why do anything by half-measures? You're my servant. I'll make you bring me my meals."

A second passed. The stink of the dead mimid and the musky fungi shrouding the walls and Crow's fatal impotence—it all swirled together inside her, a strengthening venom. Her heart beat as if seizing up with sorrow for everything that had yet to happen.

"Ah. I know how to change your mind." Suddenly Magnolia spoke in much lighter tones. "Let's go on a quick tour of the settlement, shall we? Port us back to the plaza. Carry the girl over your shoulder."

19

Magnolia turned herself into a walking stick.

She disliked sharing Crow's back with a child. Her solution was to sprout a twisted stem—a staff fit for a mage from the golden age of human magic. She resided atop it like a truncated bust on a pedestal, wood braided in a decorative rim around the severed edge of her neck.

The base of the staff ended in four claw-like prongs. It could stand alone; as soon as Crow let go, the prongs would grip the ground or burrow in like roots seeking water.

Crow shrank down her chicken-sized wings, which were starting to cramp. She ported the three of them—one saint, one human child, and one walking stick with a face—to the square.

She'd told Magnolia to lift Rinlin's vow of silence. It didn't make much difference. Rinlin was drenched with some combination of sweat, slime, and urine, and she felt alarmingly cold. She clung to Crow and shook minutely. A far cry from the girl who had confidently carried around pampered chickens. Crow had never been good at guessing the ages of human children—malnutrition tended to confound the issue. But she had to believe that Rinlin was well under ten.

They found two residents dead near the garden-filled fountain. Both were middle-aged women. They lay with their eyes open, no visible wounds, still warm to the touch and not yet stiffening. No flies in evidence, either.

"The first of many." Magnolia rotated atop her staff and eyed Crow head-on.

"What happened?" Crow could guess, but Magnolia already seemed confident in the answer.

"All of them used to have cores, I'm sure. The mimid killed them long ago. But she needed bodies to keep the town going. Mimids settle in one place for as long as they can, so people assume they're land-bound monsters. They aren't. Their real compulsion is the need to craft an elaborate disguise. To embed themselves in a settlement—and to make their puppets play out normal lives on the surface."

Crow looked at the top of Rinlin's head. She motioned to suggest that Magnolia hold her tongue.

"No need to dance around it," Magnolia said. "She's too shocked to take in more than one in every twenty words. If she does understand— good for her. Shouldn't she be made aware of the reality she's woken up to?"

"Woken up to," Crow uttered. "Were they all in a dream?"

"The living ones, yes. The dead wouldn't dream. They were mari- onettes. I do wonder if we'll find anyone else left alive ... your Rinlin was the only one with a core."

Some residents were in their homes, doors unlocked, slumped on the floor. Some had tumbled from the bleached-white stairs that cut paths up and down the steep city. Some lay at the edge of the ruins with water nipping at their fingertips, surrounded by small translucent crabs.

They were near the lake, navigating from one half-sunken roof to another, when Rinlin clutched harder at Crow's neck. A man stood silhouetted with a fishing rod.

"What a miracle," said Magnolia. "We have another survivor."

He was at the end of a long protruding sweep of stone, an inadvertent pier. It might once have been a broad guard wall. Crow set Rinlin down. She kept a firm grip on Magnolia's staff.

Rinlin began to run to him. As she came into his shadow, she slowed and stopped, stumbling. She looked back and forth between him and Crow. He must have heard her footsteps, even past the cawing and honking of the usual gossipy birds, but he didn't set down his rod, and he didn't look over his shoulder.

Crow drew closer. Rinlin hid behind her legs.

"Your world just ended," Magnolia said to his back, "and you haven't stopped fishing."

"What else should I do?" Haida said to the lake. There was a roughness to his voice—but no more so, perhaps, than any other time Crow had heard him speak.

"I suppose you always knew you were in a dream," Magnolia murmured. "On some level, you knew there was a monster below the city, a monster pulling the threads of your thoughts. It felt real enough not to matter. Let me guess—the city was still fallen, and you never had any visitors, but everyone you loved was alive, and happy, and no one ever succumbed to illness, and no one ever got into fights, and there was always just enough food to go around. A real taste of paradise. I don't fault you for missing it."

The sky was a pale sickly orange shot through with claw-mark streaks of radiant white. Haida reeled in his line, unhurried. He hadn't caught anything. He put aside his clinking equipment. His face only stiffened for a moment when he saw that Magnolia was a disembodied head on a stick.

"Do you want thanks?" he rasped. "My wife is dead. Everyone I've ever known—they're all dead."

"They've been dead for some time," Magnolia said. "You never really had to live with it until now. This girl here is alive, though, and she keeps wanting to ask for her father. She hasn't said anything yet because she's afraid of the answer. "

"She should be."

"He's sprawled in some lonely corner of the city, no doubt, just like the rest of them. You're only her neighbor—not her grandfather, not her father. You were actually born without a core, no? How fortunate. The monster had no use for you."

A precarious beat followed. Only raucous water birds moved or spoke. Crow expected Haida to raise his clenched fist and slug Magnolia into the lake. She would do her best not to stop him.

Magnolia blithely disregarded the tension. "I'm glad we're in agreement. You think you would be better off dead. So do I! But that's your decision to make, my friend. We're strangers here, and we won't keep imposing. We'll be on our way just as soon as I take this girl off your hands."

He looked at Rinlin as if seeing her for the first time. She shrank further back behind Crow. He looked at Magnolia again.

"What?" he said.

"You have nothing to live for," Magnolia explained. "Neither does she. But there's one crucial difference. The girl has a core."

"Don't," he started.

"*Don't. Stop.*" She whirled on her stand, glowering at him and Crow. "Are you all a hive mind? Why doesn't anyone ever say anything else?" She drew in air, despite not having lungs, and blew out an exasperated breath.

"I see. Are you upset because you'll be left behind? I could put you out of your misery, too," she said hopefully.

"Leave her," he said, but his voice was uncertain, as if he had only just come to the realization that he stood with his back to the crumbling edge of the ruins, lake water and the drowned labyrinth of the city behind him. Before him awaited a creature like a skull on a pike, a terrified human girl, and Crow—who, subjugated, posed no less danger than any monster. He didn't know the details, but he knew to be afraid.

"Don't argue," Magnolia said abruptly to Crow. "You won't stop me."

That was an order.

As they walked around the city earlier, examining body after body, Crow's fury had sloughed off like a molting carapace. She'd felt weirdly exposed in the lakeside wind.

Now Magnolia's order purged her mind again—without any of the exhilaration that had propelled her as she carved a path through the mimid's colossal serpent form. Instead she found an empty clarity, a piercing knowledge of the only thing she could do when she couldn't fight back.

She knelt and picked Rinlin up. Small arms went around her neck, latching on without words. She could hold Rinlin close right up until the moment Magnolia made her stop. If Magnolia never made her stop, she could keep holding Rinlin while Magnolia reached in and took her core.

After a long silence, Magnolia said in a strangely level voice: "Put her down."

The all-consuming heat of an insatiable hate burned somewhere far away. It stayed far enough that Crow could focus on looking Rinlin in the eye as she lowered her. Crow's lips formed reassuring words, gentle lies. She thought of Rinlin murmuring to her own silky-feathered chickens, silly creatures that couldn't even fly to safety if a predator came for them. Had this girl been taught by dead people how to butcher her precious chickens for their succulent meat?

She kept hold of Rinlin's hand. Magnolia hadn't told her to let go. Haida lurched forward, then stopped as if he'd hit a wall. The prongs of Magnolia's freestanding staff had drilled deep into the cracked rock beneath them. Was she trying to send all of them sliding into the lake?

"I like having someone to talk to," Magnolia said.

Haida was still alive, rigid in the sunlight. Rinlin was still alive, short fingers damp and squirming in Crow's grip, as if she wasn't sure whether she wanted to clench harder or pull away.

"One day," Magnolia told Crow, "I'm bound to do something that ensures you never speak to me of your own volition again. I suppose today doesn't have to be that day."

The staff shrank, spiraling down until her head stopped at Rinlin's height. "Congratulations, little girl," she said. "Auntie Mag will let you live."

Crow wanted to bolt from the city that very instant.

"How capricious do you think I am?" Magnolia said bitterly. "Heavens above. No, I won't change my mind. Feel free to tell me if you finally see reason, of course. Barring that—if you're going insist on making these two unfortunates live to see another day, at least do it properly. Don't expect me to help."

She told Crow to plant her in the underground shrine on the island. "I'll commune with the land," she said. "I'll learn what I can from it. That ought to keep me busy. Don't get any funny ideas about shutting me up in there, mind. I can read you like the backs of my eyelids."

Crow left Magnolia's naked head on the altar. She thought she would enjoy the exercise of rolling boulders in front of the shrine entrance— even if Magnolia made her remove them the very next day.

But she saved her efforts for other tasks.

She didn't return to the necropolis. Messy though its corpse had been, the mimid would soon collapse into tasteless ash, and then into nothingness. It wouldn't leach away into water sources used on the lakeside half of the city.

She collected the bodies of the fallen townspeople. She asked Haida about local funerary practices (her own memories were muddled, not to mention centuries out of date). He didn't know what to tell her. In the mimid's dream, people might gently fade or vanish, but no one ever really died. No one held funerals, or visited gravestones, or prayed to ancestors.

"I forget what we do for the dead," he said. "Or I never learned it in the first place. What foods to eat, what music to play, what's forbidden … Long ago, someone told me to lie with my feet toward the lake on nights when I might fall asleep sad. Don't remember why. Our whole lives were sucked away by that beautiful dream."

Eventually they took the bodies to a part of the necropolis that intersected with the surface-level city, just one or two layers down, with light falling through broken architecture as if through a lattice of forest leaves. It was far from the underground palace where the mimid had died.

Rinlin's chickens were all lively and well. They were not magically gifted animals, and so the mimid had found no reason to secretly slaughter them. Rinlin still cared for them with fanatical devotion.

Haida was neither warm nor fatherly, but he kept an eye on her. He asked her to help with the tedious chores of hauling and gardening and fishing and gutting and cooking and laundering and cleaning that would bubble up to fill most every waking hour, especially now that the entire settlement consisted of just a child and an elderly man.

Rinlin didn't speak much. Sometimes she whispered quietly to her chickens. Once she brought Crow a broken-off sunflower—she'd guessed that Haida would refuse to take it. Crow made sure to carry it around for days.

Crow could've assisted with all manner of unskilled labor, but Haida told her not to meddle. She understood his reasoning: he wanted to grasp what they would and wouldn't be capable of once they were completely on their own. For the sake of survival, he'd have to hope that Rinlin would grow much bigger and stronger before he went senile or got irreparably injured.

Ironically, they would have better odds of avoiding predation with a population of two people—only one of whom had a core. The more core-bearing survivors joined them, the greater the risk of luring another monster like the mimid. Life would be harsh without helping hands, but they might actually last quite a while.

Crow did demand permission to repair the roof of the guest house, together with other buildings that served more practical needs. She couldn't bake new clay tiles on her own, but there were plenty of abandoned dwellings she could scavenge supplies from.

"Nothing's leaking yet," Haida said.

"One day it'll be a problem," Crow said. "By then there won't be anyone here who knows how to fix it. I'm good with roofs. This is how I keep my skills from getting rusty."

"Roof repair is your hobby?" he said skeptically.

"Yes. You would be doing me a favor." She gave him a hangdog look. "You won't even let me carry water."

Haida relented.

Weeks later, when Crow had run out of important roofs to inspect and repair, she returned to the largest island in the lake. The mimid's core had sped up her recovery; she could port short distances with ease. And without bleeding through yet another set of clothing.

When she felt the soil of the island underfoot, she thought she'd materialized in the wrong place. A distant ringing gilded her hearing. It fell just short of outright pain.

A humongous tree grew in the sterile clearing in front of the shrine. It was, on second glance, the exact sort of tree she should've known to expect. Green-black leaves, waxy and thick. Unlike the mottled magnolia that she'd uprooted in the hills, all the large cupped flowers were white. As if in tribute to the orchids that were ending their bloom over in the lonely city.

It was dark under the magnolia, but when its fragrance crept in around Crow, the ringing in her ears receded.

She walked down into the shrine and picked Magnolia off the altar.

"I didn't need to wait for you. I could have left at any time," Magnolia asserted, as if they were continuing a conversation from minutes earlier. "I could have grown roots and pulled myself up the stairs one by one."

"Like an octopus on land."

"I would have gone about it much more gracefully than whatever you're picturing. Anyway, I could have left the shrine whenever I pleased. I stayed out of interest—this land had a lot to say. And it did make me wonder. What would it be like if I couldn't leave? What would it be like if I had to imagine the movements of the stars without seeing them? Even the air down here has some loose connection to the highest reaches of the sky—so long as the entrance stays open—but it must taste very different. Not much comfort, I imagine. How long was this altar occupied, and how long has it stood empty?"

Crow, who didn't want to talk about any of this, opened her mouth and said: "My feather."

"Oh, right. They did enshrine it here. The people you bequeathed it to took very good care of it. Then the mimid moved in, and that was that. Carrie, how long are you planning on standing there?"

They left the oven-like mouth of the shrine. Crow paused beneath the spreading tree.

Magnolia poked her with a twig. "Speaking of your broken feather, did you really leave it in the muck under the city?"

"I can grow fresh ones now."

"Well, if you say so."

She raised her eyes to the flowering canopy. Somewhere above them, it was noon on a summer day with anemic skies and little wind. Down here, it felt as cool and shadowed as evening.

"The tree is just a tree," Magnolia said. "Don't get your hopes up. I'm not putting down permanent roots."

"It's growing where nothing else grows."

"Who do you think you're talking to? My trees grow anywhere I want them to. Now, this tree here, it'll ward other monsters away from the remnants of the settlement ... for a brief time. Not the entire span of your little girl's life. Maybe until around when that old man kicks the bucket. It's not omnipotent.

"Oh!" Magnolia exclaimed. "That reminds me. You should tell them it's safe to take boats out on the lake. They'll have to be chary of storms and all that. But nothing infernal will rise up to drown them. The mimid made them think that to keep them off these islands. If anyone did go on a pleasure cruise, she'd have swum out to drag them under the water herself."

"The families who lived near the shrine," Crow said. "Did the mimid—"

"Mm. She drove them off the island and gobbled up their cores. It would've been one of the first things she did after moving in. A monster like that has to be extremely good at knocking out threats. Her number one priority would have been to get them away from your feather—from any memory of your existence. Didn't want anyone to break through her spell and call for help.

"She had your feather hidden in the necropolis. She must've stolen it from the shrine early on, and kept it with her ever since. Like a trophy. After she dragged me down there, I forced her to hand it over. Took me hours to get through to her."

Her eyes were half-closed, as if she'd begun looking deep into memories that had never been hers. "The mimid was rather vindictive in her treatment of the shrine. Retrieving your feather ought to have been enough to satisfy her, but she made her puppets rip down the decorations, too. They hurled it all in the lake, armfuls of beautiful artifacts. The shrine wasn't simply scoured bare by animals and natural decay. But that would've been its fate eventually, mimid or no mimid."

Crow wondered why Magnolia had spent weeks coaxing a magical tree to grow in front of the shrine. She'd been dead set against making any personal contribution to Haida and Rinlin's long-term survival. Was she lying about the tree's effects? Might it act as a beacon to draw in monsters, instead of a ward to dispel them?

No—if so, Crow would have sensed some hint of that when she breathed in its scent. Maybe this was Magnolia's way of marking where she'd been.

"Like a dog lifting its leg?" Magnolia said. "What an uncharitable interpretation. You really are determined to think the worst of me."

"Have you given me any reason not to?" Crow didn't wait for her to answer. "Why didn't you plant a new tree like this in your village?"

"No need. We'll go back there soon enough. Now, if I'd been planning to leave them for entire generations—then, yes, I would have grown a tree for them."

Before they left the island, Magnolia said offhand, "Does it bother you less now?"

"What?"

"Approaching the shrine."

Crow had never mentioned her discomfort. "Yes. It's much … is it because of your tree?"

"Doubt it." Magnolia sounded as though she had already lost interest. "What else has changed? You finished integrating the mimid's core. Now you can tolerate what you couldn't stand before."

And yet Crow had eaten the mimid before bearing Magnolia down to the altar weeks ago, back when the days were still longer. If she'd already grown resistant to the shrine's effects on her, that walk up to the underground altar wouldn't have felt like wading through boiling water.

Today was different. With the magnolia tree towering in front of the entrance, looking as if it had been there forever, those shadowed stones suddenly felt like the stones of any other defunct shrine. Nothing to do with who she was now.

20

AT MAGNOLIA'S BEHEST, Crow took her on a final stroll around town. They visited the necropolis: first the deeper palace where the mimid had lain in pieces, then the higher level where Crow had interred each dead resident in a recycled stone coffin. Down below, the mimid had been reduced to a series of incoherent dark smears.

Magnolia was a staff again. Crow plopped the quadruple prongs of the staff's base in a shrinking puddle of old slime and watched them squirm like curling toes.

"Why didn't the mimid take Rinlin earlier?" Magnolia asked, as if testing her.

"Visitors from beyond the lake are rare," Crow said.

"And?"

"Rinlin was the only human left in reach with a core. The mimid was trying to save her for later."

"Rationing, yes." The staff quaked as if Magnolia had nodded. "The mimid was too successful here. Creatures like her—they don't know when to move on. They usually don't make the decision themselves. They get discovered by neighboring settlements. They get slaughtered, or chased out. But this mimid burrowed under the old city only three decades after your last visit. The settlement has been hers for over a hundred and seventy years. Would you stop stirring that slime with me?"

Crow had been dragging the prongs of the staff around as she listened, drawing spirals in the mucky ashen leftovers of the dead mimid.

Magnolia continued. "Earlier generations would've gotten by without detailed supervision. They remembered the routines of their daily lives, the skills needed to keep the settlement going. Things went awry once entire generations began to live from birth to death within her dream. That's not a good environment for passing down knowledge, especially not knowledge that the mimid herself would fail to appreciate. You think she has any idea how to repair a roof?

"All this time, the mimid was operating on instinct. She reared these humans like an ant farm. She expected them to naturally keep reproducing all on their own, given sufficient food and water and an appropriate environment.

"Once the population started falling off, she manipulated the dream to make them reproduce more. But even if that worked, would anyone still harbor a practical understanding of how to aid childbirth? Her dead puppets would've been worse than useless. I didn't see a single woman of childbearing age around town—did you? She let a lot of them die in efforts to birth more children with cores. Their corpses were too damaged to prop up as citizens of her dream.

"With only Rinlin left to eat, she realized it was time to bail out. Mimids aren't suited for long-distance travel, and neither she nor any of the residents would've known where to find the next nearest settlement.

She meant to hold off on taking Rinlin's core until another group of traders arrived. In her memories of older times, traders came by fairly often. I wonder how long ago they stopped visiting? Trade routes die out all the time, and this place is far out of the way. Were the dreamers here capable of bartering?

"I bet the last merchants to grace their doorstep got thoroughly creeped out—if the mimid didn't go ahead and eat them all. She should've left some alive and assimilated them as new citizens. Fresh blood and fresh brains would sustain the dream longer."

Crow used the end of the staff like a stick of charcoal, dipping it in the mimid's ash. She wrote lost runic alphabets on the drier parts of the floor.

"Quit that," Magnolia said. "You'll confuse future archaeologists."

"Archaeologists are a dying breed."

"Our world itself is a dying specimen, but we don't have to write its obituary just yet."

"The mimid snatched you and Rinlin at the same time," Crow said, trying to hasten the conclusion of Magnolia's speech. "It was wary of me, but it thought you were human—or an immortal weak enough to subdue. You gave it a reason to stop rationing. It saw your arrival as its one final chance to gobble down multiple cores."

"Before migrating in search of new prey." Atop her staff, Magnolia swiveled back and forth to shake her head. "That compulsion to put on a whole masquerade, to parade around dead dreamers—it kept her well-fed and protected. And isolated. It became a trap of her own making. She slowly strip-mined the entire population of anything valuable, leaving only a pile of bones. She didn't have anyone like you to free her. When the masquerade could no longer sustain new life, she knew of nowhere else to go."

They made the ascent to the villagers' burial site. This part of the necropolis had been partly filled in to begin with. Crow had carted over more soil to pack around the borrowed stone coffins; it would tamp down the worst of the smell. The bodies decayed at a normal rate now that the mimid was no longer around to preserve them. The necropolis, luckily, had no end of sarcophagi to choose from.

"Why didn't you have the same problem as the mimid?" she asked as they hiked to the surface.

"Hm? What problem?"

"Diminishing returns over time."

"Meaning?"

"Read my mind," Crow grumbled. "After you stopped taking local sacrifices, everyone who came to you were slayers. Slayers rarely have cores."

"Ah, right. They did try to starve me out. Although nowadays, so many people are born with cores—there'd be no hunters left if only the coreless could hack it. But I do see your point. I took countermeasures. The fully coreless parties that came after me—I destroyed them before they ever stepped within sight of my tree. I encouraged them to turn on each other, or I sent other monsters in pursuit. Only parties with at least one core-bearing member would be given any hope of getting close enough to slay me. I made that very clear. Every survivor I sent out said the same thing."

"You trained them to bring you food," Crow said.

"What else was I supposed to do? I was stuck there."

They said farewell to Haida and Rinlin outside the chicken coop, which had an attached yard filled with fruit trees. Despite the intense smell of its occupants, it was overall more generously appointed than the empty shanties near the shore.

"I can make pasta," Haida said plaintively.

"Good for you," Magnolia told him.

"But I can't shape it into ears. My wife did so much. I don't know how to—"

"She was a reanimated corpse, and yet she made beautiful ears. You'll figure it out."

Haida bent and said something to Rinlin, who bobbed her head. She held a slender fallen branch like a pretend sword as she came up to Crow. Two plush black chickens tottered behind her.

She glanced at her branch, dropped it, then put both hands on her stomach. Not right over the light of her core, but close enough. Nearby, more velvety chickens pecked at the muddy base of Magnolia's staff.

It was a hot and blustery afternoon. Far below them, the wind over the lake kneaded the water's surface into small foaming waves.

Rinlin raised her head. Past her tangle of black curls, Crow recognized the look on her face. Young or old, it didn't matter—she knew what it meant when people gave her that look. Her shrunken wings buzzed as if the blood inside them had fermented to the point of erupting.

"Saint of the Carrion Crow." It sounded as though Rinlin had forgotten to breathe. She looked hastily back at Haida. He must have told her what to say. The important part was that she meant it. Crow could sense that as unerringly as a compass seeking north. It was her most vital instinct as a saint.

"I have a core." Rinlin's fingers dug into the front of her smock. Wind buffeted her dirty sleeves and her curls and her already-tearing eyes, and her puffy escort of well-loved chickens. "I—"

"Stop that nonsense," said a murderously low voice.

As Magnolia spoke, the staff beneath her dissolved into brambles. The spindly thicket wound around Crow, sewing Magnolia's head to her side. Rinlin's mouth clamped shut.

"I never promised not to kill you," Magnolia said to Haida. "I never *promised* not to kill anyone. I suppose you put the child up to this because you want to be rid of her? A more humane choice than drowning her in the lake, and yet—if you waited till we left, you could've gotten away with anything. Why do mortals have to be so hopelessly impatient?"

He had a hand on the tree beside him, as if it were all that held him up. In a matter of weeks, his beard had grown much more unkempt, his eyes increasingly yellowed and bleary.

Incredibly, he ignored Magnolia. He looked Crow in the eye and said: "She wants to go with you. No one else ever held her like a mother. No one remembered how."

"So you coached her to make an offer that Crow couldn't refuse," Magnolia said coldly. "You've dwelt in a dream cobbled together by a monster ever since you were a fetus, my man. You've only just come to your senses. I'm surprised you know that saints can't turn down a willingly offered core. Guess you'd have died young if you didn't inherit some basic knowledge of how to survive in this world."

"The dream was the same as real life," Haida said. "Only happier."

"And you'll keep missing it till the day you die. Which I expect would have been any day now, if only you'd managed to foist this girl off on us. Well, it won't work. Whatever it was she had to say, I'll never let her finish saying it."

Rinlin scooped up one of her docile chickens and buried her face in it. Her shoulders were very thin.

"You can speak again," Magnolia told her, as magnanimous as a king sparing the life of a traitor. "Just don't speak to my Crow."

This could have been Crow's escape route. Magnolia had said it herself: *It would've been different if you came to me with a promised companion.* She would never let Crow exchange a vow with a core-bearing mortal.

It's unfair to you, too, said Magnolia's voice in her head. *Humans just have to be sincere in the moment, and you're bound to accept. You can't help but say yes—that promise becomes a leash around your neck.. But they're free to change their minds after stringing you along for decades.*

Unfair or not, Crow thought, *that isn't why you stopped her. You want to be the one holding my leash.*

Of course. Never claimed otherwise. Anyway, did you want to settle down here? Did you want to watch that little girl grow older, and work her fields, and fall in love or not, and bleed in childbirth or not, and eventually wither and complain to you of achy joints, and one day fulfill her promise with a smile? Or—far more likely—change her mind and pretend she never owed you anything at all? Aren't you tired of going through the same charade over and over?

Such a promise was never empty—not at first. When petitioning a saint, humans needed to be wholly committed. Committed enough to accept death in that very moment, even if it could in truth be a long time coming. Many people had failed when offering Crow their cores.

Those who succeeded might indeed experience a change of heart, years later. Yet at the time of their initial proposal, they couldn't deceive Crow, and they couldn't deceive themselves. Signing over your core—and meaning it—was every bit as difficult as the physical act of flinging yourself into a sacrificial volcano.

Because of this, there was a decent chance that Rinlin's offer wouldn't have taken hold. Even without Magnolia's intervention, and even if Rinlin thought she spoke from the heart. Then again, Crow knew for a fact that sometimes children could surprise you.

Now Rinlin peeked out from behind her chicken-shield as if fearing a scolding. Magnolia hopped down onto Crow's arm like a strange bird and began making ridiculous faces at her.

Crow spoke in an effort to salvage the situation. "Let me give Haida my feather."

At least on her end, that was the main reason they'd stopped for formal goodbyes. It had taken her half a day to grow a feather worthy of handing over, but it would work just as well as the one that Magnolia had unceremoniously snapped in two.

The scarf of nettles eased up around her shoulders. She finished disentangling herself from Magnolia—who, rather than becoming a staff again, chose to merge with a crooked fence post.

"Make it quick," Magnolia said. Her icy anger had dissolved in an instant.

Crow made Haida hold the black feather and began explaining how to use it.

From the corner of her eye, she saw Rinlin solemnly introducing each member of her flock to the severed head on the fence post. She probably didn't understand how close Magnolia had come to murdering her. Granted, children were capable of getting used to all sorts of horrors, so long as the adults around them acted matter-of-fact. Arion had slain his first monster at the age of nine.

Crow bent closer to Haida, who was shorter than her, and said in a voice too quiet for anyone but him to hear it: "Six months from today, break the feather. I'll give you a new one to replace it."

Over the next six months, she would lead Magnolia as far away from here as possible. When Haida snapped her feather, she would be ported back to the lake town alone—stranding Magnolia in unfathomably distant lands. Hopefully it would be a great enough distance to shatter Magnolia's hold over her. If not, it might buy her enough time and space to learn a better way to fight back.

Haida spun the shaft of the feather between his forefinger and thumb. "Why should I?" He didn't sound bitter, just blandly inquisitive. "You ruined the only life I've ever known."

"Six months from now," Crow whispered, "if you break the feather and call me here, and if she still wishes to offer me her core in exchange for a lifetime of service"—she pointedly did not glance at Rinlin—"this time, I'll be able to accept."

His fingers stilled. The feather quivered; the wind tried to snatch it away from him.

"You just have to survive the next six months together," Crow said. "Just six months."

He raised watery eyes to her face. His expression froze as if he were watching a tsunami come in.

"Good thinking," said Magnolia, "but let me save you some grief. It won't work. Even if your feather yanks you back here out of the blue, I'll cling to your magic like a barnacle. I'll come right along with you."

Crow turned.

Rinlin—so close that Crow almost stepped on her—held Magnolia like a prize pumpkin. Crow wrestled with a shuddering urge to grab that accursed head and ram it deep in the chicken-scratched ground.

"Never mind," she told Haida. "Don't do it. Unless ... you can break it any time, if you need help badly enough to risk her showing up, too."

He wordlessly attempted to return the feather.

"No, no, you'd better keep that," Magnolia said brightly. "What if you take a tumble down those twisty stone stairs and break your back? It's a nasty way to get injured, let me tell you. Don't hesitate to use her feather if you need it. It's not like you have anyone else to rely on."

Crow stooped to liberate Rinlin of her burden. She plunked Magnolia down on her own shoulder. Wiry roots immediately descended to grip her.

She told Haida and Rinlin that she hoped they would have good weather and better health. She didn't mention that if they were indeed so blessed—if they never had cause to break her feather—then they would probably never see her again. Mortals tended to be far more optimistic about the chances of meeting once more during a relatively narrow window of time. To them, that window represented an immeasurable expanse of possibilities; entire lives fit inside it.

"Carrie," Magnolia said from her shoulder, "at least tell them the name of their own town. The mimid didn't care enough to make them retain it. We're basically walking away and leaving them with less than nothing, as is our right—but that's something you can toss them as an easy parting gift. To go along with your feather, and my tree."

"Which name?" Crow asked.

"Your pick."

She considered a few historical options, then settled on the one that had stuck around the longest.

"Fellshore," she said.

"Fellshore," Rinlin repeated, head tilted. She looked as if she were sampling an unfamiliar new vegetable.

"Fellshore was the name of the settlement." Crow swept an arm towards the water. "The lake was called Lake Fallen."

No one said anything.

She'd thought Haida would want them gone as quickly as possible. Rinlin was harder to read. She spoke very little, and sometimes she shook like a leaf, but she appeared to be developing a weird fascination with Magnolia, or at least with the fact that she was a talking severed head.

"Do you want..."

Crow waited for Magnolia to intervene, but no one replied except for the vigorous wind blowing off the lake. She would have to complete this thought on her own.

"Do you want to know where these names came from?" she asked.

They did. And so she and Magnolia stuck around long enough to finish telling them.

PART THREE

Artificial Immortals

21

"THAT WAS CUTE," Magnolia said after they left the two-person town of Fellshore.

Rinlin had hoisted a chicken overhead while yelling one last goodbye to Auntie Mag and Auntie Carrie. Haida, grim-faced, held his hand in the air like a flag of surrender. He would never forgive them, Crow thought, but he would keep caring for this child until his body gave out.

Magnolia had given orders for Dung to meet them on the opposite side of Lake Fallen. It was not a small lake: skirting half its length on foot would take a week, maybe two weeks, even without any need to rest or forage.

Crow didn't offer to port. The longer she could keep Magnolia from encountering more mortal prey, the better. Fortunately, Magnolia seemed content to take her time admiring this desolate shore where no one lived.

After assuming the form of a staff, she would wind a cage of woody tendrils around Crow's gripping fist. She was doing that—it pinched—when she said: "You dispatched that mimid with incredible ease. It was a dreadful sight."

"You told me to do it."

"I meant that as a compliment, Your Saintliness. I wish I could show other monsters. Some might dissolve into dust from sheer terror."

"Feel free to dissolve into dust yourself."

Magnolia laughed. "Now you're fishing for praise. Yes, you were very frightening. You can see why, can't you? You're at your strongest when you're being commanded. You have a reputation for fanatical obedience to your human companions—far more so than other saints. If a companion asked you for something within your power, did you ever tell them no? Did you even feel capable of refusing?"

"Does it matter?" Crow said flatly. "I can't refuse you." Personal questions felt like being probed for hidden weak spots.

"It's been fascinating to follow tales of you from afar." Magnolia was impossible to discourage. "There's more than one reason that the word Carrion became stuck as a permanent part of your name. Not all saints would go to war or maim poor criminals just because some human told them to do it.

"A smart saint would wander away—a smart saint would find a less troublesome companion. Saints can occasionally break promises, too, if the demands placed on them outweigh the value of a single core. It's not only humans who are allowed to change their minds. It's a promise, not a binding magical contract—but you've always treated it like something that can't be broken, at least not on your side. You aren't a typical saint at all."

"Is there any such thing as a typical saint?" Crow said. "Or a typical monster?"

It had been raining on and off, brief squalls of sideways-slanting drops, though much of the sky remained light gold and uncovered. The clouds that gathered in patches over the lake kept changing color like a slow-to-heal bruise.

Behind them, only the highest parts of the old city remained in sight, a pale mirage. Haida and Rinlin could keep living there like fleas on a sleeping animal, scrounging resources as their ancestors had done for generations. It would be harder with just the two of them, but they had an entire dead settlement's worth of inherited supplies to start off with.

Crow's devotion to her promised companions had been neither blind nor forced. Those years of willing service, even to companions who denied her—it all contributed to the weight of the gift that came when she finally harvested her next promised core. That seeming self-sacrifice was just a self-serving investment. It would pay out in the end, and the rewards would stay hers long after every companion who turned their back on her had been dead and forgotten for millennia.

She didn't resent them. They had their fate, and she had hers. Humans had the right to panic at the end of things. They had the right to take their core to the grave. They had the right to claw out a few extra minutes or days or months of writhing life.

Of course not everyone would be able to look her in the eye and tell her: *Now, Carrie, now is the time.* And of course not everyone who told her that would be able to stop themselves from shrinking away, from crying out before she could touch them. This faithful, humble servant who had remained loyally by their side for such a very long stretch of their life, perhaps longer than any other relative or friend—all along she had been the stalking shadow of their eventual death.

"Indeed," Magnolia agreed. She was rain-soaked atop her staff, her hair in dark dripping hanks. She'd made Crow tuck it behind her ears.

"You've played the role of self-abnegating servant much more effectively than most so-called saints. That's got to be the reason you've gathered more power. Quality over quantity ought to be the motto of all saints, but you've taken it to an extreme. You've made an art of it. And it's served you well. As well as you've served your companions.

"But—entirely separate from your natural imperative to collect cores—you do enjoy the act of surrender. You sublimate yourself to the fiery longings of these short-lived animals, and you find immense relief in it. You were never simply waiting for your companions to get old and die. You liked chasing their improbable dreams—even a dream of living quietly and well, unknown and unmolested. You cherished your time with them for its own sake."

"Not all of them," Crow said.

Was Magnolia still trying to position herself as the equivalent of a promised companion? If this journey ever had a conclusion, if Magnolia ever tired of her company, surely their roles would reverse. Magnolia would end it by consuming Crow's core. Magnolia's words would sedate her, like a snake overpowering its prey with venom.

One evening, Magnolia asked her to make a stop right at the edge of the lake. The crest of the city looked like a ghost smeared against the fading sky. The only visible aerials seemed impossibly distant.

"Your friend has been following us all day," Magnolia said.

"My friend?"

"In the water."

Crow eyed the lake. The creature was not difficult to make out: it trailed ambient magic like fluorescent dust. She'd noted that gliding light earlier, but had not thought much of it one way or another. It wasn't a threat.

The shoreline here was composed of smooth colorful pebbles like a million glass marbles. At Magnolia's prompting, Crow hauled an old driftwood log to the waterline. She sat down, placed Magnolia's head on the log beside her, and rolled her right shoulder, savoring the sensation of lightness.

"It's a lake whale," she said.

The whale swam closer to the shallows, though not close enough to reach out and touch. The top of its head briefly parted the water, then submerged again. It was svelter and more elongated than most oceanic whales, with vestigial back legs and a sprinkling of white spots like a fawn. Long catfish barbels crackled with magic below the surface.

"They live a long time, don't they?" said Magnolia. "A past acquaintance, perhaps?"

Lake whales were known to last centuries, but Crow honestly couldn't remember if she'd seen this particular one on her prior trip to Fellshore. When multiple whales lurked in Lake Fallen, the locals had always been better at telling them apart. Not that she didn't try.

Magnolia kept pressing. "You mentioned fables about lake whales being the earthly form of some sort of aerial. Every few hundred years, they return to the sky. Like a caterpillar becoming a moth."

That was one of many origin stories for Lake Fallen. People said a world-ending crater had carved out the lake (although it wasn't especially crater-like in shape, and the world hadn't quite come to an end yet). They said that the sky used to rain with dead aerials of all sizes, although there were varying explanations as to why. They said if you were very lucky, you might witness the moment when a living aerial descended and became a lake whale.

They said that once, long ago, an elder aerial had plummeted down to end its life on the shore of the lake, and no one would ever forget. They said that at other times, ancient machines of war had fallen to rest here, too. Plus showers of stars, wild mystical beasts, tempting demons in human guise, et cetera.

All in all, the area used to be a magnet for deadly shrapnel from the sky. Maybe that was why anyone with the means to live elsewhere had left these shores in eons past.

Crow waved at the lake whale, lighting her hand with magic. It rose and sank, sending water spattering in all directions.

"Young and playful," she concluded. "It doesn't know me."

"Come back in fifty years, and we'll see."

"Aerials are mortal beasts," Crow said. "They won't remember a random immortal passing through. They're not gods—they're more like primevals. Or those birds over there."

"Your crows and your gulls," Magnolia muttered. "Look, they're fighting again. Seems rather unjust that the crows get to use three legs. That's a whole extra weapon."

Then, apropos of nothing, and in tones of deep mourning: "I developed quite a taste for that ear pasta. Should've gotten the recipe."

Crow inadvertently glanced at her ears.

"What?" said Magnolia. "Do I look tasty?"

"Do those earrings mean anything?"

"Remnants of another time." She sounded almost sing-song. "Remnants of another me."

The lake whale kept coming back to greet them as they trekked along the ever-bending shore, though sometimes they had to detour through forested areas or walk high up across striated cliffs. They lost sight of the old city, but they kept noticing the whale's mottled back, day after day and night after night. Magnolia tried to make it a competition of who could spot the whale faster. Crow infuriated her by pretending not to care.

As they hiked through morning fog, Magnolia—now riding her back—said: "You're torn over where to take me next."

"You like to put words in my mouth."

Today Magnolia dangled a tangled moon-white shawl of capillary roots. She'd done it to maximize her chances of tickling Crow while they walked. Well—while Crow did all the walking for both of them.

"I've been thinking, too," Magnolia said, which was never a good sign. "About the issue of motivation. I've seen many hunters stuck working for terrible bosses. I've seen the struggle of mid-level supervisors trying to get a handle on jaded slayers. Yes—employee motivation is extremely important. Your problem, Crow, is that you have nothing to strive for except a vague hope of slaughtering me, and you're not tactical-minded enough to lay the groundwork for it. Except by seizing some elusive future chance that may or may not ever visit. That's no way to live."

"I'm not your employee." This was how Magnolia tricked her into reacting: by getting basic facts wrong, and forcing her to issue a much-needed correction.

"But I already paid you," Magnolia said, all innocence. "I paid you most handsomely."

For lack of anything else to do, Crow took the bait. "How?"

"By not killing Rinlin. Or Haida, for that matter, although it seems shockingly cruel to make him live out the rest of his days deprived of every beloved face and voice, knowing everyone he deeply cared for was an undead corpse manipulated by a monster. You think it's the height of virtue to nobly suffer for the sake of a child. Like I said, I could have put both of them out of their misery all at once. But I spared them. I paid deference to your saintly qualms. What currency could I have paid you with that you value more highly?"

"Will you run the same scam every time we pass a human settlement?" Crow asked wearily.

"Scam?" Magnolia sounded outraged. "What scam?"

"Will you threaten to slaughter them, and then back down at the last moment, and tell me that's my salary? Will you tell me to be grateful?

Will you tell me to rejoice?"

"No, actually. You should be grateful and rejoice entirely of your own accord, not as the result of inexorable orders. But never mind that. See, this is exactly what I'm talking about." Magnolia's mane of white roots flared for emphasis, whipping Crow wetly across the face. "You're awfully fixated on the small stuff. You can barely see two steps ahead. You need something to aim for. You need an aspiration."

"Your death."

"It needs to be something realistic. Something attainable."

"Like the promise of a promotion? A new job title? A better salary?"

Magnolia was impervious to sarcasm. "I know a better way to motivate you. I said before that we could travel together forever, but that won't do. An eternity of this will rot you from the inside out. So here's an alternative."

Here it comes, Crow thought. Magnolia had her own secret goal, and now she was ready to say it. Had the events at Fellshore proven something crucial to her? She'd tested her ability to retain mastery over Crow in a variety of life-threatening situations.

"Take me to the end of the world, and I'll let you go," Magnolia said. "Take as long as you want to get there."

"The end of the world?"

"The end of the world."

"What's in it for you?"

A laugh. "I'm surprised you care. Why not? Most humans will never see it. Anyway, you should take this bargain before I change my mind. I'm offering you a chance to be free."

"That would be motivating," Crow said, "if I had any reason to trust you."

Trust me, Magnolia uttered, deep in the least-touched recesses of her head.

Trust me.

It reverberated through discarded memories of old betrayals by long-dead and long-forgiven companions. It reverberated in the marrow of Crow's magic, and for a screaming second of silence, she glimpsed the bottomless terror of knowing that this monster's voice could at any moment choose to rewrite her entire self, everything she had ever believed in, everything she had ever cared for or rejected with abject contempt. This was only the smallest taste of that, a flick of the very tip of her tongue.

She trusted Magnolia, against all reason and evidence. She trusted that Magnolia would keep her word. Her thoughts realigned around that trust, as if bowing under the implacable pressure of a growing tumor.

"Consider the fact that you still hate me," Magnolia said calmly. "I left you that. All I did was remove one single insurmountable hurdle to a more productive working relationship. Although I won't do you the insult of telling you not to worry."

"I do hate you," Crow said dully, finding it true.

"You're welcome. Now, what was I saying? Ah—the end of the world."

"You want to destroy the world? It'll get there with or without your help."

"Hah. Are you even listening? We're on the topic of our travels. I mean the physical end of the world, not its temporal end. Parts of it have already been destroyed. That's what I want to see. The edge of existence. Take me to the very end of the corporeal world."

This was not absolute nonsense. Crow knew vaguely what she spoke of. The physical end of the world was not a popular destination for human beings. Which, promises aside, did make it an ideal place to bring Magnolia.

"See?" Magnolia said, triumphant. "You're looking forward to it.

You're already more motivated. You'll continue to be pleasant company. Couldn't wish for better."

Crow had to dissent. "I'm not pleasant company."

"With all due respect, that's for me to decide, not you."

"I've tried to kill you multiple times, and I'll do it again."

"Mm. Your problem is that your thought process isn't nearly villainous enough. What are a couple half-hearted murder attempts between friends?"

"My murder attempts have never been half—"

"Your argument would be more compelling if I were dead. Oh, look, we're already here."

Dung, shaggy with moss, awaited them warily at the far end of the lake. Magnolia made her fine white roots stand on end like hair buoyed up by static electricity, forming an unwieldy halo behind her and Crow. They must've looked like a two-headed monster surrounded by a blazing corona. Dung didn't run, but he didn't start approaching, either—not until Magnolia called out energetically, without a care for who or what might hear her.

22

Magnolia cooed at Dung, asking if he'd had great adventures. She looked more like an octopus than ever as she patted him with bulbous wooden limbs.

Crow resisted the urge to shush her. They had observed no other recent settlements along the perimeter of the lake. If any slow-moving monsters lurked here, despite the dearth of human prey, they knew better than to invite unwanted scrutiny.

She'd glimpsed scraped bark and scat and muddy tracks—cloven hooves, padded paws—but those sorts of animals would also lie low. Unless Magnolia called them over to put on a show. She only did it once, orchestrating a symphony of warbling songbirds while terrified deer tapped their hooves on rock.

"Is that all it takes to amuse you?" Crow asked.

"It's actually quite depressing," Magnolia said. "They aren't even angry." She sent the deer and the birds away unharmed.

The lake had a temperate climate, along with a near-boundless supply of fresh water and edible fish. In the golden ages of humanity, its shores would have been heavily settled. Maybe the lake hadn't been around back then, at least not in its current shape. The world had been a lot more turbulent near the beginning of its end. Perhaps there was some truth to the stories about destruction raining down from on high to carve out the lake bed.

Magnolia was still busy cuddling Dung.

With a mental apology to the whale who had followed them all this way, Crow attempted to subtly chart a path away from the end of the lake.

A vine whipped out; a tongue of green wreathed her wrist. Dung had halted, too.

"Look across," Crow said, resigned.

A narrow inlet cut deep into the shore like an inverted peninsula. Shaggy shapes loomed on the opposite bank, half-submerged, darkening the water. Initially they appeared to be a series of incongruous rock formations, dripping with greenery, like misshapen minor mountains.

"Ah." Magnolia's vine released Crow. "Ye olde machina. I've never seen any in person. There were none in the hills."

The silence after she stopped speaking had a dangerous, quivering quality to it. No three-legged crows popped out of the forest to voice harsh opinions. No gulls or swallows wheeled around the shoulders of the archaic machina—which, if you stared for a long time, were shaped like titanic bodies. Not wholly human bodies, but bodies nonetheless. They'd grown a coat of furry moss and spiky bromeliads. Reeds thronged madly around the parts sunk underwater.

"I'll never tell you to get in one of those," Magnolia said. "Too many unknowns."

Even in their current state, untouched for some untold stretch of time, the machina were still magical in a way that made Crow feel faintly drunk.

Magnolia's voice steadied her. "The magic is tempting, I'll admit. But they aren't alive. I don't like things I can't command. Give them a wide berth, Crow."

"That's what I was trying to do before you stopped me." She'd feared Magnolia's incorrigible curiosity.

"Good. You really are the perfect partner."

Crow didn't dignify this with a response. She raised her hand one last time to answer the faraway glow of the lake whale, then led Magnolia and Dung into the thickening night. The air filled with wing-whispers and soft chirps from bats on the hunt. Pretty-faced monkeys chittered listlessly in the treetops; most were already settling down to sleep.

Dung submitted to Magnolia's caresses, but he seemed gratifyingly unimpressed. She changed this by feeding him more silver dew from the bottom of her neck.

"What?" she said to Crow, who had once again been obliged to hold her in position while she dripped. "You want some?"

"No," Crow said sharply. Hours passed before the lingering honeysuckle scent of that dew began to dissipate.

She'd been unaccountably stung by how Magnolia disparaged her lack of tactics. She became aware of this gradually, overnight. Her mind wandered back to revisit it as if staring down into a dark fishing hole cut in ice.

She did like having a mortal companion around to tell her what to do. She liked being useful. Even in a dying world, there were still so many minuscule quests to embark on, so many possible ways to live.

If Crow could do anything, why not let someone else decide her direction—someone with far fewer choices before them? Her only deep, undeniable need was the need to collect cores. As for what to do with herself while waiting for harvest time—she'd rather leave that up to her companion of the moment.

One of her past companions had been a scholar of aerials. Incredibly accomplished and underappreciated, and now fallen into permanent obscurity. One of her past companions had been a midwife in a land where no one used family names. Since Crow never slept, she was always alert and ready to assist with poorly timed births.

She'd served royalty and knights, woodworkers and petty smugglers and a traveling handyman who used to be a pirate. Her role was to take their core at the end of it all, if they were still willing to let her reap it.

She had never set out to make a name for herself. Only by accident did she become renowned in certain times and places, sometimes loved and sometimes dreaded. She had no need for complex schemes. She granted the wishes of her mortal companions, to the extent that she could. That was a perfectly acceptable use of her life.

But it was not an approach that would get her any closer to escaping Magnolia. And she couldn't settle for merely escaping—she had to prevent her own recapture. Then she had to keep her vow to Arion and his mother before him. Magnolia was the last of the Four Great Adversaries, and Crow would bring her down.

They walked along in starlight. They had finally come far enough to stop seeing the hulking silhouettes of those machina against the sky. The ambient smell of the lake had faded, too.

The forest was treacherous, crisscrossed by huge deep scars: bizarrely shaped canyons with a silvery glint to them. Loose pebbles fell and water plinked in an offbeat pitter-patter of broken music.

Like many immortals, Crow could unerringly navigate to any place she'd been before, no matter how much it had changed in the interim. She could zigzag back and forth across the continent without once consulting a compass or map.

Yet she had never gone right up to the physical end of the world. It was notoriously difficult to locate. Magnolia would doubtless be pleased if the journey proved long and arduous, a search lasting decades. For Crow, it would be a desperate hunt. For Magnolia, it would be a joyride.

The border marking the end of the world was both steadily encroaching and constantly in flux. Mortal adventurers who sailed off in search of it found themselves going in circles, or never returned. Intellectuals theorized that an overwhelmingly powerful death wish emanated from that boundary. Obey its call, and you too would join the vanished. (Immortals had immunity, being fundamentally incapable of wishing for death.)

Dung seemed dissatisfied with their pace; he could always go faster. Magnolia had cemented herself to his back like an oyster on a rock.

Crow put a hand on one of his plate-sized scales. It was smooth and dry, not unlike the clay roof tiles used for the guest house in Fellshore.

"The end of the world," she said. To Magnolia, not to Dung.

"Can't tell you how to get there. You're more worldly than I am."

"I need more information to plan out our path."

"Then go get it. Although personally, I would be content with a century or two of aimless wandering first. No need to rush."

That decided their next stop. Now that they had Dung, it would only be a week or so away. In the meantime, Crow tried to keep Magnolia occupied with a constant stream of conversation. This proved devastatingly successful.

"Like most of us immortals, I don't have a maternal bone in my head," Magnolia declared, "but I was rather touched when I saw you holding that child."

Crow had no memory of how they'd gotten onto this topic. "Rinlin?"

"Who else?"

"You were about to kill her for her core."

"And? Humans can find livestock charming, too. Remember her frilly chickens? We all ate them. But in my case, it was you who charmed me, not the child. I perceive no contradiction."

"You look down on me," Crow said.

"Do I?"

"You despise me."

"I find saints profoundly irritating," Magnolia said mildly. "The feeling is mutual, isn't it? A burning-hot vein of unwarranted resentment is just the thing to keep you on your toes. A little bit of spice. You wouldn't want me to be *too* easy to get along with. That would be awfully damaging to your worldview. Anyway, it's quite possible to be simultaneously despicable and infuriating and lovable, and even cute."

"...I need an example."

"Look at Dung. What a pampered prince. He isn't classically cuddly, and there's nothing he would enjoy more than gnawing on a nice fat femur. Open your head up, and if not for my magic, he would happily suck out your brains. No gratitude.

"Then think of how he rolls around in dust, how he dangles that silly long tongue of his like a ribbon. Cute! Just not in a conventional sense. You know, I don't buy into the notion of conflicting emotions. When you get to be our age, you can hold three or four or five feelings about the same thing at once. They don't contradict one another—they blend together."

"Like mud," said Crow.

"Or black ink, or bright light. All useful in varying contexts. Don't denigrate mud, either. You can build houses with it."

They had made their way to a landscape of golden-green tussocks. Turquoise streams flowed into turquoise pools. Large reptiles with an excessive quantity of squinty eyes lay motionless amid tufts of flowering grass. They remained undetectable so long as they refrained from blinking. Dung, who was larger still, ignored those watching eyes as if they were beneath his notice. Every so often, Magnolia paused her lecture to flawlessly imitate the cry of a hawk.

Crow had prompted her to expound on her theories about the beginning of the end of the world. Its temporal end—not the corporeal boundary they would ultimately aim to reach by travel.

"Previously I compared us to maggots," Magnolia said.

"And to undertakers."

"You remembered? How endearing. In short, we immortals aren't what wounded the world so badly that it could never recover. We sprang up as the natural result of its inevitable doom—we weren't the root cause. So what was?"

"Human magic. You already told me."

The gleam in Magnolia's eye made Crow wish she'd feigned a lack of interest.

"Our world used to be peppered with vorpal holes."

"Vorpal holes?" Crow could pronounce the words, but their meaning eluded her.

"Little rifts in reality. They popped up here and there like pimples. They'd annihilate anything that fell inside them. Soldiers, criminals, children, puppies—you name it. Some states found them useful for conducting inexpensive executions. Some cultures found them convenient for human sacrifice.

"People lived in tandem with vorpal holes for a very long time. They just had to accept a certain degree of random tragedy. Like getting struck by lightning. A vorpal hole might swallow up a church, a school, your father, your neighbor—but what can you do? Life goes on.

"Then—after a devastating act of human magic, new holes appeared in multitudes. They killed many, many mortal creatures—more than even immortal minds can quantify. The thing is, those holes acted as a kind of release valve. They were the unavoidable outcome of the world's throes. Now, I can understand the temptation to stitch reality back together, like repairing a garment coming apart at the seams. But—if only they knew the eventual consequences—humans would say she shouldn't have done it."

"She?" Crow echoed.

"The devil who destroyed the world. The metaphorical devil, I mean. She's quite human."

Crow felt like a parrot. "The Devil is human?"

"Our devil is. Can't speak for any other worlds out there. The Devil is the same mage who originally made vorpal holes start breeding like barnacles. She came back to fix her mistake. She closed every last rift. She made sure no new rifts would ever appear again. No more devoured houses, no more vanishing children. She tidied up her own mess, and then she left forever. But she was like that mimid down in Fellshore— cursed by success.

"Now our world is all sealed up. No release valves. No arcane beasts wandering over from other realms. Maybe that's why we immortals emerged—as a sort of replacement? Now, at any rate, our world is like a closed terrarium. Under ideal conditions, an abandoned terrarium can last a very long time. But a very long time is not the same as forever."

Being rooted in the hills had clearly given Magnolia many years to mull this over.

"We must have an important role to play in this sealed box of ours, even if we don't understand it. Does a dung beetle understand its role in the greater ecosystem? No, but it doesn't need to. We're all saints, in the sense that we were all blessed from birth with some sort of sacred purpose, every bit as sacred as the inexorable gnawing of a maggot. We're all carrion beasts feasting on the corpse of a collapsing world. We collect and absorb and absolve magic. Maybe we're the reason the death of the world has been so long and serene. Maybe we're what keeps this little terrarium going."

"You said the exact opposite before. You said we were midwives of the end times."

"I see it both ways," Magnolia answered. "For a long time, I had no one to debate except myself. It doesn't really matter which is right. The truth might be something else entirely. I don't expect we'll ever know."

"Then why dwell on it?"

"Because I like talking at you," Magnolia said.

She should've known.

Off near the horizon, where grasslands swept up over the lower slopes of mountains, a dire fox with many tails had stopped to watch them from afar. Dung gave a warning lash of his tongue, which made a sound in the air like a whip. They were almost at the place where they could learn how to reach the border of the living world.

23

THE TUSSOCK GRASSLANDS slipped by swiftly when they rode Dung together. The sky was a dizzying kaleidoscope of color. The furthest mountains still had snow on their peaks, but the ones they threaded a path between were more modest, covered in a dense mix of dark green and golden scrub. At times the dire fox dogged their steps, but it never came close enough to attack.

They pulled up short on a ridge overgrown with gorse. Crow dismounted and told Magnolia to put on her body.

In addition to her body, Magnolia also put on clothing—an outfit taken from Fellshore. It hung off her shapelessly, with pant legs so wide that they had the appearance of a skirt. The fabric was covered in neat proud stitches that wandered like a lost ant, marking an endless series of careful repairs.

She tied back her sleeves and gave Crow a winning smile. She could have been a healthy young human of any gender, sveltely ambiguous.

"Wear these," Crow said, taking off her usual sunglasses.

They suited Magnolia's face annoyingly well, as if they'd been made for her all along. "Don't think this will fool anyone," she said.

"Wear them anyway."

"I've had my fill of magic abstention. I won't exercise the same kind of restraint I showed in Fellshore."

"They'll know you're an immortal," said Crow. "But don't mention being a Great Adversary. Try to seem uninteresting."

"Well, that might prove very difficult. What about you?"

"They've already met me."

Magnolia lowered her sunglasses to gaze down at the plain that stretched out before them. It was roughly circular, rimmed by mountains, mottled like the hide of an animal, and distressingly empty. Dung stuck his long face deep in a bush, probing for insects.

"The archivists," Magnolia said quietly. "The—what else are they called? The automagi?"

"You know of them?"

"Only a little."

Your average human hunter and your average wandering monster—Magnolia's primary source of intelligence about civilizations outside her hills—would never have heard of the automagi. Especially now that said automagi dwelt in seclusion. They stoutly refused to interfere with worldly affairs, whether mortal or immortal in nature. But that didn't mean they never accepted petitioners.

"To get what we want, we'll have to bargain," Crow explained.

"You make it sound like you've done it before."

"I have."

"Really? Bet you gave them all the clothes off your back."

"They have no use for material rewards."

"You'd better not sell them Dung."

"Why does that thought distress you more than killing a human child?"

Magnolia looked at her blankly.

"Never mind," Crow said under her breath.

Magnolia touched her wings, which poked out sheepishly through newly hemmed slits in her tunic (another Fellshore hand-me-down). Crow had extensive experience with being petted by curious mortals, especially children. This felt different—because her newly grown wings were still so raw? An involuntary shiver—painful as a hunger pang—branched through the deepest muscles of her back.

"I'm not sorry I made you tear them off," Magnolia said. "I didn't need to do it. But you would have been a real handful if you'd kept your full power all along. And it was a grisly, glorious sight. A saint desecrating her own flesh."

She'd pushed her sunglasses back up, and her face was unreadable. But there was a throaty note of remembered euphoria in her voice. Her hand clenched down harder on Crow's left wing. Then, all at once, she let go.

"They'll grow back," Crow said.

"Indeed they will."

The most frightening part of it was that sometimes Crow forgot who had been responsible for the loss of her wings. Sometimes she almost tricked herself into thinking they'd been mutilated in an unfortunate accident. She had never been adept at working up a sustained rage on her own behalf.

"Bargaining," she said, trying to get back on track.

"Ah, yes. What will we offer them?"

"Tell them your thesis about the beginning of the end of the world. The human devil who set it on the path to destruction. The terrarium theorem. They're usually more interested in hearing about first-hand experiences. But I think you'll intrigue them."

"And here I thought you were genuinely fascinated by my ideas." Magnolia pretended to be wounded. "You were just fishing for nuggets of wisdom to feed the archivists."

"You'll be the one feeding them. They'll be a better audience than me—much more knowledgeable. You might actually have to defend your thinking."

Magnolia drew herself up. "Well, I'm not one to back down from an intellectual challenge."

Crow knew this. She also knew, by now, that Magnolia was not constantly reading her thoughts. She would glance at Crow's mind as if glancing at a wall-mounted clock to check the time. The best way to keep her from picking up on incriminating thoughts was not to cling to them or desperately cover them. It was to let them flow past as if she had nothing to hide, soon to be replaced by other minor distractions—a sudden field of summer wildflowers, the sparkle of Magnolia's earrings in sunlight.

She had more than one reason to visit the automagi. They could tell her much more than the route to the end of the world, if only she found an opportunity to ask. But she didn't dwell on it, and so—at least on the surface—Magnolia seemed to notice nothing amiss.

They lingered on the ridge until the golden hours of the afternoon. The sky above the plain was an unusually blank, cryptic blue. Shreds of premature sunset colors churned around the edge of the blue void, foam swirling around an ocean whirlpool.

Then the entire surface of the plain blinked—once, twice, like a reptile's third eye—and retreated.

"*Oh*," Magnolia said.

Crow led the way down.

The automagi occupied a valley with the largest stepwells in the known world. More of a sacred location than a practical place to draw water, although perhaps it had changed over time.

The mountainous landscape gave way to an expansive rocky basin. Symmetrical flights of steps—thousands or tens of thousands of them—marched up and down the walls of the crater, angling back and forth with dazzling precision. None of the stairs had any sort of guardrail.

Dung didn't seem to mind the precariousness of their descent. Once in a while, his tongue flicked out to impossible lengths and snatched glittering beetles off the stone.

It was shadowed at the bottom, as cool as the entrance to a deep cave. From far below, the step-carved walls became a quilt-like tableau of geometrical markings, precise diamonds and triangles formed by neverending back-to-back staircases. But much of it was blocked from view now. A forest of prehistoric proportions grew in the basin, hollow trees of living stone.

"All right." Magnolia slapped Dung's flank. "Once you've eaten your fill, climb back out and go hang around the mountains. No need for all of us to be trapped in a city-sized cistern."

He trundled away, claws clacking.

"When were you last here?" she asked Crow.

"Within the past century."

"What'd you need from them?"

"Information on the other Great Adversaries."

"What'd they know about me?"

"Almost nothing."

"Hah. Guess it's mutual."

"That's one of the reasons we saved you for last."

So far there were no living residents in sight, and no birds or aerials in the eerie blue sky above. The first animal they saw (other than beetles) was the same dire fox that had observed their progress through the grasslands. Its tails flickered out of sight around a corner.

At first glance the valley felt as barren as a quarry. On closer inspection, nondescript plants grew in every available crevice, squeezing a frond or two through hairline cracks in rock. It wasn't exactly lush, but it wasn't a wasteland, either.

Deeper steps spiraled down to wells filled with milky green water, still and opaque, as though coated in a gelatinous skin. There were also places where the roots of stone trees pulverized existing architecture, and vivid geothermal pools welled up in broken sinkholes. They skirted around clouds of steam, following glimpses of the fox up ahead.

"Saint Crow!" said a husky voice.

The dire fox shook itself, as if wearying of formalities, and darted away—utterly silent despite its size.

From behind it emerged a woman in an apron. Magnolia stared. Crow put an arm out in front of her.

The woman carried a bright core in her lower torso. Brighter than Rinlin's, yet severely unstable: it twisted and changed shape like a flame in angry wind.

A metal mask covered half her face. Enough remained visible to see that she was on the older side, weather-worn, short-cropped hair faded with age. Her eyes were the same intense, unshielded blue as the glowering sky. A wooden pendant hung from her neck.

"You're the Saint of the Carrion Crow," she said.

"Yes," Crow said after a moment. "I'm Crow. This is ... Mag. I don't think I know your name."

"Tamar."

"Have we met?"

The woman didn't seem insulted. "I was away on business the last time you came by. And before that—I was practically an infant. I toddled around by your ankles. I remember you carrying me, warming me with your wings."

"How old are you, exactly?" asked Magnolia.

"Do you count your own years?"

"Not with precision."

"Likewise. I'd have to consult the archivists' tablets to answer correctly."

Tamar could have been a pickle-making granny in any number of lost villages. She looked rather pickled herself. She put her hands together briskly—she was missing a finger—and said: "Let me take you in to wait for the archivists."

She led them to one of the most imposing stone trees. Large segments of the outer trunk were missing, forming a shape like the lacy lattice left by a leaf eaten down to its veins. The tree did not, therefore, enclose them with sturdy cylindrical walls. It was more akin to stepping into a wide-barred cage. Those filaments of stone ought to have collapsed to dust under their own weight: the upper trunk and branches looked far more solid.

Tamar asked if they wanted refreshments. Crow thanked her and declined. This was not the sort of place where going through the motions of human rituals would gain you any advantage.

"Are you..." Tamar had gotten up, ready to excuse herself. She looked back and forth between them. Her glance stopped on Crow. "If I may ask—is she your promised companion?"

Magnolia lifted her borrowed sunglasses away from her eyes. She grinned at Tamar, who showed no surprise. A ward of the automagi could not be so easily fooled into mistaking Magnolia for human.

"I'm a saint, too," Magnolia said. "A very new one. She's my mentor—a wonderful teacher. I worship the ground she walks on."

Crow fought to keep a blank face.

After Tamar left, they were alone in the chamber at the base of the hollow tree. Given the state of the walls, it didn't feel much different from settling down in an open-air pavilion. Except for their constant awareness of the mass of the tree above them.

They sat at a low table spread with clay tablets. Tamar had provided them with faded floor cushions; there was no other seating. A scattering of earthenware vases, each several feet high, surrounded the table instead. They looked like the sort of crock that would normally be used for outdoor pickling, dense and heavy-walled, glazed with reddish-black marks. Matching lids lay in a jumble off to one side.

Magnolia frowned at the clay tablets before her. Crow didn't even try to read them. The language of the automagi had no spoken equivalent, and past attempts at parsing it had given her a headache lasting months.

"That woman." Magnolia sounded as if she had a bad taste in her mouth.

"Tamar?"

"She's not human."

"She's half-immortal." After saying this, Crow quickly corrected herself. "Not exactly half. Her clan—they all have mixed blood, to some extent. They all call themselves halves."

"She has blue eyes. Not red."

"Some halves seem fully human on the outside."

Magnolia had probably only ever heard of half-immortals with pink-red eyes. In truth not all of them looked the same. Blue eyes might have made it easier for Tamar to pass among humans, but it wasn't enough to guarantee her safety. People were creative. They invented ways to identify halves (correctly or otherwise), even if they weren't obvious at first glance.

"Don't try to eat her," Crow added.

"Whyever not?" Magnolia inquired in a tone that could have been either sarcastic or deathly serious.

"Her clan lives under the protection of the automagi. You don't want to pick a fight with them."

"If we picked a fight, wouldn't you win?"

"Not with shriveled wings," Crow said.

"Don't be modest."

"The automagi are skilled preservationists. They've got storehouses full of deadly artifacts. They have functional machina."

"Machina..."

"War machines. Like the ones at the lake."

"I know what they are," Magnolia snapped. She started biting her nails with a vengeance.

Crow tried to say something, then wondered why she would bother. In any case, the room had gotten cooler. The air shivered visibly, rippling like windblown water.

A small, aged man protruded from one of the voluminous pickling crocks. His atrophied arms rested comfortably on the rim of the pot. He looked like a swimmer holding himself up at the edge of a pool.

First he spoke to Magnolia. "It's very comfortable. Would you like to try one?"

She eyed the nearest empty pot. "My lower half wouldn't fit."

"You could make it fit."

Without waiting for a response, the automagus turned to Crow. He was not quite transparent, but he blurred and smeared around the edges if you focused on anything else. Automagi liked to describe themselves as creatures of the mind. They didn't often go to the trouble of taking any sort of physical form.

"You're starting to become a frequent visitor," he said with amusement. "No, don't apologize. We like repeat customers. What do you seek?"

"A path to the end of the world." Plus a quicker way to defeat Magnolia. But she couldn't ask that with Magnolia listening.

The representative automagus nodded to himself. "Very well."

Crow didn't recognize his voice, which was gratingly pleasant. It felt like the average of dozens of different masculine voices, most much younger and haler than this skeletal, toothless creature crammed in a pot. Haida would look downright sprightly in comparison.

"And how," asked the automagus, "will you pay us?"

Magnolia kept furiously chewing her nails. Crow delivered her prepared answer about Magnolia's theories regarding the true role of immortals as carrion beasts, and their world being the equivalent of an abandoned terrarium, and so on and so forth.

"She can explain it better than I can," Crow hedged. "She has a unique ability to tap into the earth, to learn from the memory of the land itself."

"That isn't quite as unique as you seem to think," the automagus said with equanimity. "Rare, yes. But in other senses, she is even rarer. She can pay us in the same way that you paid us before."

Magnolia put her hands on the table, slow and deliberate, as if to pacify an agitated mount. "How did you pay them before?" she asked.

Crow's mind whirled. "An interview. I told them about my beginnings."

Magnolia half-smiled. "Your life story?"

"Yes. But—"

"It's a fair price, Carrion Crow," said the automagus. "We wanted your story because you're a returner. We want her story because she's a returner, too."

The table shook. Magnolia had smacked it as if killing a cockroach. She stared at her flattened hand with disgust.

The word *returner* had a very specific meaning, and it had nothing to do with being a repeat customer of these self-styled archivists.

"What makes you think I'm a returner?" Magnolia said tonelessly.

"Your earrings," he replied.

She scoffed. "These? These prove nothing. Any half-baked jeweler could cobble together a perfect imitation. The design isn't anything special. Clear dangling teardrops? Yeah, never seen those before. You can't tell me that with a straight face."

"Some call us automagi," he said. "Some call us artificial immortals. Some call us archivists. And some call us appraisers. We specialize particularly in appraising inanimate objects. It's the inverse of your own specialization, is it not? You appraise and invade the minds of things with life. We, for our part, are better at understanding things that were never alive at all.

"Like your earrings. Even with that design you belittle as generic, we can tell that they date back to the beginning of the end of the world. Alas, those were more turbulent times. Every single pair was lost or destroyed, one way or another, well before the dawn of immortals. But yours aren't a copy. They're the genuine article. They returned as part of you when you—"

Magnolia stood up.

She swayed.

Crow, moving without thought, rose and caught her.

Magnolia's throat kept working beneath her skin. It was the way you would swallow over and over to keep from vomiting.

"We'd like to have a night to talk it over," Crow said.

"Of course," said the automagus, unruffled. "Please be our guest. The half-immortals will host you."

He vanished without fanfare, collapsing down into his pickling crock. The mouth of the jar breathed a cold dusty mist, but there was no evidence of anyone living there when Crow looked inside it.

Though there was hardly any daylight left, Magnolia's earrings glinted perversely bright. The scars on her eyebrow and forehead glowed, too, as if there were a fire on the other side of her skin.

"You never said anything about being a returner," Crow told her.

"Neither did you!"

"But you must have guessed," Crow said. "That's why you were excited to see Fellshore."

"Partly, yes."

Crow hadn't gone out of her way to hide being a returner herself. She hadn't gone out of her way to speak of it, either. Magnolia might have plucked the truth from her thoughts regardless, although it wasn't often at the top of Crow's mind. Her past as a returner was ancient history, in every sense of the word.

She steered Magnolia out of the hollow tree and toward an obscure lower stepwell, one shaped like an inverted pyramid. It terminated in a square pool of creamy jade-colored water. From this vantage point, the tops of the stone trees looked black. The pure blue whirlpool above them stretched to fill every visible inch of sky.

She made Magnolia sit on a stone step. Crow sat on the opposite flight of stairs, facing her. A dislodged fragment of rock plopped into the water, never to be seen again.

She'd had another life before she was born as an immortal. She hadn't made any kind of conscious choice to return, or to take the form she had now. It just happened. Had it been the same for Magnolia?

"What were you before?" Magnolia asked woodenly, as if she hadn't already figured it out.

"An elder aerial."

"The one that fell near the lake."

"Long, long ago," Crow clarified.

"The one they worshiped in that underground shrine." Magnolia laughed under her breath. "What a hometown. As an aerial, you fell down and died there. Then later you reincarnated as an immortal in human-shaped skin. Although I don't know if reincarnation is really the right term for it. What a life."

She touched the scar on her forehead as if trying to measure its temperature. She was still wearing Crow's sunglasses. She looked across at Crow and said, almost lightly, "Your automagus was right. I'm a returner, too. I, however, used to be a very different type of animal. Nothing so magnificent as an elder aerial. No wonder you were reborn as a saint."

"Before you became an immortal…"

"What? Have out with it."

"Were you human?" Crow asked.

Magnolia removed her sunglasses and studied them critically. She wore a thin smile. "Why, yes," she said. "But I hate that you're right."

24

Not all immortals were returners. Most, in fact, were not. Regular immortals came into being without any knowledge of past lives.

Some of Crow's companions had been awed to learn that she was once an elder aerial. But this had little bearing on practical issues like where they would go for dinner, or how to soothe a colicky baby (Arion had screamed nonstop for months), or how to slay the Great Adversary that took the form of a hive, its mind spread out across hundreds of bodies.

Magnolia still seemed shaken. Peeved. Maybe even embarrassed. But not afraid. Her past as a mortal human was not something that Crow could use to get the best of her.

This was true the other way around, too. Being a returner was not an exploitable weakness. It wasn't comparable to the inborn compulsions that plagued monsters until they were freed—like Magnolia, no longer bound to her hills. Or until they were killed—like the Fellshore mimid, who had fought to the end to maintain the masquerade of a peaceful settlement.

Tamar found the two of them brooding by the well water. She invited them on a casual tour of the settled parts of the haven. She showed them garden beds, netted for protection from birds and rodents. She showed them clusters of bushes and fruit-laden dwarf trees. And also a number of simmering open-air baths. No one mentioned the automagi.

"I can see why your people think of this place as paradise," Magnolia said. "You don't keep any livestock?"

"Not down here. We used to have ambrosia hares."

Magnolia nodded sagely. "They smell heavenly when you burn them. They're often raised for sacrificial purposes, no?"

That was the extent of Crow's knowledge, too.

Tamar said: "When I was a teenager, I set them all free. Steppehaven really was like heaven to grow up in. Especially compared to what the rest of the clan experienced before we came here. But I was very convinced of my righteousness. I told everyone that we halves were no different from those ambrosia hares. That we had no right to breed them for slaughter."

She spoke lightly of how her rabbit liberation phase had eventually become an inside joke. Many of the older halves had begun calling her Rabbit. She raised her necklace so Crow and Magnolia could get a better look at it: the large wooden pendant was a plump whittled hare.

"I used to spot descendants of our hares in the mountains, but I think they mostly got eaten. There are a lot of hawks up there."

Afterward, the dire fox padded gracefully in and out of sight while the three of them had supper. Magnolia only took a few sips of soup. Crow made herself eat extra so Tamar wouldn't be forced to sit there and chew for an audience. She was relieved when Tamar mentioned the other half-immortals living here. Most of them would also need to eat at some point. Hopefully no one had labored over a stove just to cook for a pair of immortals who could get by perfectly fine without food.

"Where are they?" Magnolia asked.

Tamar, who had been sipping from a lacquer bowl, gave her a questioning look.

"Your brethren," Magnolia said, pointing at her with a spoon.

Tamar's mask still covered the left half of her face. At first glance it looked crude, almost broken—just dull hammered metal. Still, it fit her exceedingly well. And it hummed with magic. Not a type of magic that Crow understood, but magic nonetheless.

All she could discern was that the magic in the mask didn't originate from Tamar herself. It had nothing to do with the core in her belly. The mask seemed to intensify a signal beamed in from elsewhere, a signal that passed harmlessly through Crow and Magnolia and the hollow trees and the array of small dishes before them.

"My brethren." There was a slight smile in Tamar's voice, if not on her lips. "Most were ill-treated in the outside world. That's why the Saint helped us escape here."

She nodded at Crow. "Most of us have sworn off contact with anyone except our fellow halves. But the automagi can't quite meet all our needs on their own. They have no permanent bodies, after all, so it's easy for them to forget about things like hydration and clothes and latrines. I represent my clan when we host guests, and I'm the one who goes out to trade for supplies."

"You're a diplomat, then," said Magnolia, still toying with random utensils.

"That's why I missed your last visit," Tamar added to Crow. "When was it—eighty years ago? I must've gone out on one of my longer supply runs."

"You always go alone?" Crow asked. "There aren't any other halves who could help?"

"We each have our own specialty. Dealing with the secular world is mine. The archivists appreciate it, too—they do like to hear of current events. Besides, I'm the youngest of my clan. I don't have nearly as many bad memories of human society."

She reminisced with Crow about the journey to Steppehaven, as they called it. She spoke of how she'd grown up among the automagi after Crow left. They'd let her climb in their jars; they'd let her draw all over the floor with chalk.

"I was everyone's kid," she said. "The older halves raised me, and so did the archivists. They would play hide and seek with me for hours. It's hard to track intangible voices. I loved having an excuse to explore every little cranny."

"You always call them archivists," Magnolia observed.

"When I was little, I couldn't pronounce *automagus* or *automagi*. No deeper reason."

"Is it lonely here?"

"This whole valley is filled with my family. I've never been lonely."

"How do the automagi treat you all?" Magnolia asked innocently. "They have quite alien sensibilities."

"You're one to talk," Crow said.

Tamar stifled a chuckle. "We've got some surprising luxuries down here. Remember those baths I pointed out?"

When the meal was mostly over, she took them out to stretch their legs. Her stone tree was a good distance from the automagi, clustered in a grove of other silent trunks. They had enough room to house many, many halves.

She climbed down into a cellar, then emerged with a bottle of snake wine. She poured three cups.

"The archivists keep a small selection of grape wine," she said, "but I can't recommend it."

"How old is it?" Crow asked.

"A century or two. Or three. This snake wine I can vouch for. We made it ourselves."

Magnolia took a sip. "Tastes venomous," she said blithely.

They kept drinking while Tamar lit candles to place outside the nearest hollowed-out trees. The candles hung upside-down—and actually burned that way, the flame trickling downwards like water.

"The wax drips into long stalactites. Like the points of an upside-down crown," Tamar said. "We light candles for anyone who might be coming home late."

"Why invert them?" Magnolia asked.

"To confuse evil."

"What makes them burn that way?"

Tamar touched two candles together to pass a flame from one to the next. "The springs have special properties. We dip our candles in the pink spring, and they learn to burn downward. Drops of water from other wells can preserve cooked food for months."

For much of the meal and their subsequent stroll, Crow's mind had been on other things. She'd worried that, following their discussion with the withered old automagus, Magnolia would decide there was no longer any point in walking around in a human body.

While they sampled pickled ferns and perilla leaves, Crow had mustered arguments about how the appraisal skills of the automagi would not extend to Magnolia's living flesh. There would still be some merit to putting in the effort to look deceptively ordinary. Crow herself, in all her years, had never encountered any other immortal in the shape of a severed head.

If the automagi started thinking that Magnolia was really something singular, they might decide to preserve her as one of their specimens. Which, from Crow's perspective, would be one of the best possible outcomes. But she could hedge her bets—she could warn Magnolia about it, and thus convince her to stay in her human body. To sleep. For just one night. She'd have to pray that Magnolia would be too vexed with the automagi to make a deeper study of her mind.

In the end, Crow didn't have to say a word. After their walk, Tamar served a dessert made of sweet agar jelly. Crow ate her helping, and then she ate Magnolia's, which remained untouched. Immediately afterward, Magnolia left to sleep in her human body, though the night was still shallow. Tamar showed her to a bed in another stone tree, whose walls were more intact than the tree where they'd met the potted automagus. Magnolia pulled the covers up over her head.

Crow watched over her until she felt absolutely certain it wasn't a ruse. She left soundlessly, making her way back to the center of the grove.

Tamar hadn't warned them not to wander. She'd simply mentioned a couple stony hollows on the far side of the haven where bats liked to roost—thousands of them, perhaps tens of thousands. She'd suggested avoiding those caverns unless they wanted to go wading in guano.

The dark of night closed in around Crow like a river. The wind rustled as if in a living forest, though none of the stone trees had leaves. Short, spiny trees (the wooden type) grew between and among them like flat-crowned mushrooms. At one point in the evening, Tamar had listed off about fifteen different uses for their resin, needles, and roots.

Crow navigated more with her magic perception than with her physical vision. A smog of drifting magic showed her the way from tree to tree. The scattered stepwells and untamed pools shone as if each harbored a fishing net full of stars.

She slipped back inside the cage-like tree and knelt before the low table. Tamar had diligently taken away every last cushion, and the bare floor felt like cold rock.

As she waited, automagi materialized in open crocks. They whispered together in voices like fingernails scratching a cliff.

Only one spoke to Crow. It was the same one who'd appeared earlier in the day, with naked eyes sunk deep in huge sockets.

"You come to bargain alone," he said.

"I want to kill the monster I came with."

"Go on, then," he told her generously. "We won't stop you."

"She's bespelled me. I'd like advice on how to escape her control."

The whispering of the automagi died away.

"Bespelled you," said their representative. "*You?* The slayer of Calamity Bridge? The slayer of the Singular Horde, and the Beautiful Scourge? She must be a formidable foe."

It was the first time Crow had ever heard an automagus speak with emotion.

"It's not that she's strong," Crow argued, though it wasn't in her best interest to stop them from developing a deeper fascination with Magnolia. "I'm weak to her. We're a bad combination."

After some thought, the automagus said: "You could take a new promised companion while she sleeps."

"Like Tamar?"

Tamar had a core. Unlike full immortals, she might prove capable of swearing to give it up. But Crow couldn't offer her much that she didn't already have here with the automagi. Additional safety? An escorted tour of the outside world, like Magnolia had demanded?

"We can't allow that," the automagus said coolly. "Another option would be to borrow our machina. We're not sure you have any stories worthy of such an enormous loan."

"If I try to pilot a machina—"

"The machine will establish a profound connection with you. It will sever or weaken the roots she's put in you." The automagus paused. "That's a simplified explanation. The answer, however, is yes. It should work as you hope. Let us think on it. In the meantime, we advise you not to take shortcuts."

"She might never sleep in front of me again."

"It can be arranged," he said. "So long as you linger in our domain."

The automagi snuffed themselves out, diving back inside their pots. Crow was dismissed. She walked out and found the dire fox swishing its tails, luminous amid the fragments of moonlight that spilled down through interlacing branches many stories above.

"Are you a half-immortal, too?" she asked.

The fox deemed her unworthy of an answer. It slipped away into a space that looked too small for it, then slithered out of sight.

She didn't know where the automagi had concealed their machina. Common sense would suggest that it was too large to keep hidden for long. But searching the entirety of this crater would be like searching the old city of Fellshore. The subterranean portions extended at least as deep below her feet as the full height of the stone trees above.

If she were lucky enough to stumble across their machina, she'd climb right in—with or without permission. For now, it would be smarter not to antagonize them. If only she hadn't already told them everything there was to know about her past life as an aerial. She'd severely overpaid them last time. If only she had more to offer—

An owl hooted. She ignored it until she began to get the distinct sense that it was hooting at her in particular. She peeked inside the hollow base of the tree where Magnolia was supposed to be sleeping, and found it empty. The owl hooted again, sounding piqued. Crow gave up on searching for secret machina. She couldn't do it stealthily with that fox monitoring her, anyway.

She climbed the smooth stone tree, using magic to make her bare hands and feet stick like the toes of a gecko. She discovered Magnolia lounging in a crook near the top, one leg dangling, scowling balefully at the half-swollen moon. She'd hooked Crow's sunglasses on the V-shaped front of her slumpy button-up shirt.

"How long did you sleep?" Crow asked.

"Long enough. What sort of mischief did you get up to while I conked out?"

"None," Crow said. "We're guests. Can't do anything disrespectful. How'd you climb up here?"

Magnolia's eyes slid away from the moon to study her. Then she smirked. "Hoping I'll fall?"

She followed this up by hooting like an owl again. She did it so convincingly that any owls in the area must have been deeply confused. Woody vines came shooting out from behind her.

To Crow, who stood on a branch lower down, it was like getting attacked by a pack of gliding snakes. One vine curled around her neck, tightening vindictively. Others seized her upper arms.

"That's how I pulled myself up," Magnolia said haughtily.

Crow pictured her swinging like a corpse from a gibbet. Her human body would've flopped around uselessly while her tentacles did all the hard work of summiting the stone tree.

The vines wrung at Crow harder, making her muscles creak and her throat squeak pitifully.

"You have a ridiculous imagination. I didn't look nearly that silly." Magnolia released Crow, her vines withering. "Don't just hunch there like a dolt. This branch is large enough for both of us."

As soon as Crow joined her, she flopped on her back and plopped her head in Crow's lap. The branch in question was indeed wide enough to treat it like a bench.

Crow looked down, down, down—past Magnolia's now-relaxed face, past her own feet dangling in empty air. She debated the merits of falling together. It would be a much trickier landing than when she'd shoved Magnolia off the plaza in Fellshore. The main difference now was that Magnolia had stopped restricting her magic. Even if they only spent a couple seconds in the air, she could force Crow to magically soften their fall—or to land beneath her and become a cushioning carpet of meat.

"Do you ever stop thinking gory thoughts?" Magnolia asked. "Save some brainpower for other matters."

"I think gory thoughts because of you," Crow said.

"Please. Are you trying to flatter me?" Magnolia exhaled hugely, as if savoring the physical reality of her lungs. She took of one Crow's hands, securing it in her fingers, and held it firmly to her breastbone.

From the outside, this might have looked affectionate. But it seemed clearly intended to ensure that if Crow pushed her off, she wouldn't plummet from the tree alone.

"You don't like it here," Crow said. In the space of a single afternoon, Magnolia had bitten all the nails on her right hand raw. They healed sluggishly, as if perplexed by their predicament.

"Of course not. I've never been so uncomfortable in my life."

"No one forced you to lie in my lap."

"Aren't you funny." Her scowl returned. "I can't command the automagi. Wasn't sure of it until I faced them. If I'd known, I'd have forbidden you to come here. But this curiosity of mine, it's like a disease. Now, I'm not saying that I could never learn to command them—I haven't completely ruled it out. They aren't alive in the same way as us, but they aren't dead, either ... or are they?"

Her eyes glittered. "Automagi. Automatic mages. Automated mages. Artificial mages. Artificial immortals. Who made them, Carrie?"

"Human mages," Crow said.

"A mind-blowing accomplishment. Guess they were mostly building on the work of their predecessors. Did they even understand what they'd created? If they hoped for their automagi to save the world, they must have been severely disappointed. Well, it could definitely have turned out worse."

That sharp smile slipped on and off, quick as a blink. "Why did you become a saint? Were you just that saintly in your past life, too? I put down deep, deep roots when I perched on the altar in your shrine. I know what they did to you. Humans found you and raised you after your rebirth—but why didn't you kill them all? Why couldn't you have been a monster?"

She stopped and then said: "I suppose there's still time for that. Monsters never rise. But saints fall. Saints do fall."

"Saints do," Crow said. "I won't."

"You know I'll take that as a challenge."

Crow changed the subject. "You must have theories about the nature of returners." This might tempt the automagi more than anything she could offer.

"I don't want to talk about it."

"You ranted about my past life. But you won't speak of yours?"

"No," Magnolia said flatly. "What's the point? You won't sympathize. You won't caress me and vow to commit mass murder to make it right. There's no one left to kill, anyway. Not even direct descendants. What's there to get excited about?" Her voice grew more distant. "Do you ever miss the sky?"

"I have wings. I *had* wings, until you—"

"Having wings isn't the same as being an aerial. Or else we'd call all birds aerials, and everything in the ocean would be a fish. Do you miss it?"

"I've been in this form for far longer than I ever lived as an aerial," Crow said.

"But elder aerials live a long time, don't they? Longer than tortoises and sharks. I wonder if we were ever alive at the same time, back then. When we were mortal. When you were an aerial, and I was human. I wonder if I ever saw you coasting around up there, not a care in the world. I'd like to think I did, somehow." She snorted. "Of course, there's no way you ever looked down far enough to spot any one individual human."

True enough, Crow thought.

"You might not know why you were reborn as a human-shaped woman with wings. But I know exactly why I became a living head." Magnolia sounded drowsy—as if she were talking to the wind combing through a million invisible leaves, not to Crow. "That man in a pot was right. My earrings are part of me. It's too aggravating for words. They were just regular earrings in my previous life. Now they have a sense of touch."

Crow squeezed one of the clear dangling teardrops. It was as hard as polished crystal, but warm, as if someone had already nursed it between their palms.

She dug at the gem with her thumbnail. Magnolia let out a tiny pained noise, but made no attempt to squirm away. She couldn't risk toppling off the branch.

"You wanted me to do that," Crow said.

"I never—"

"You just bragged about how sensitive they are."

She pinched the earring with supernatural strength. She must've come close to crushing it into glassy dust.

"You could order me to stop," she said.

Magnolia gasped. Her eyes were closed. The sound of her gasping hung suspended between them like a powdery winged creature, a moth that Crow could catch and crush in her fist.

A tide flooded Crow. Heady elation—almost powerful enough, in its primitive way, to knock her off the branch herself. Then came coupled fear and self-loathing. Then a wordless want as total and simplistic as the feeling of parting her lips to drink down the core of a defeated monster.

No—it was closest to the feeling of stooping over a human who had loved and trusted her for years, who still loved and trusted her more than anyone mortal. The gutting exhilaration of rummaging about in their flesh, dragging out their brilliant core as if wrenching fruit from a tree, ending their one short life by mutual agreement, surrendering to the all-encompassing hunger that slept dormant at the murky bottom of her being. There was often a split second of terror and regret reflected deep in the eyes of her dying companion. By then it was much too late to change their mind, and much too late for her to stop.

No one ever talked about the ugliness of the corpses left by saints. Whether you ripped out a human's magic core right away—as monsters did—or claimed it decades later, the culmination of a faithful promise … the end result looked the same. A mangled body, sometimes with a gaping tunnel bored all the way through from belly to spine.

The relatives and friends of Crow's dead companions would always look at her differently afterward. They might have treated her as one of their own all their lives, but everything would change once they smelled blood and organs. Once they saw Crow without a scratch on her, shedding no tears. Wouldn't it be rude to cry in front of mortal mourners? She hadn't lost anything; she had gained something infinitely precious. She had reached out and taken it.

The impulse that made her do this was the most inexorable aspect of her immortal existence. It was the only urge remotely like the selfish desire that clawed its way up to the back of her mouth—now, out of nowhere, when Magnolia winced in her lap.

25

The light changed, as if a cloud had moved in front of the moon. Crow's disgust with her bestial self, that senseless longing—it all washed away in an instant, leaving her as hollow as the tree beneath them. She let go of Magnolia's earring.

Magnolia sat up shakily and scooted back towards the crook of the tree. She kept a wary eye on Crow.

"You loved that," she accused. "You *loved* that! I thought you were a masochist!"

"What about you?"

"Huh?"

"What do you want?" Crow asked plainly.

One of Magnolia's hands darted up to her left earring, as if feeling around the outlines of a bruise, then retreated. "I want..." She brightened and said, totally shameless: "I want to hear about someone else's suffering."

"Maybe you should go to bed," Crow said.

"Tell me about your terrible past."

"You already know it."

"All I did was glean clues from the land around your shrine. It would be much more delicious coming from you."

"No." She regretted squandering her chance to fling Magnolia off this branch. She started to pick at the bark of the tree, then recalled that it was stone.

Magnolia tipped her head back and drank in the night air as if using some secret hidden sense of hers to sniff out the torments of others. "The half-immortals. What's their story?"

"You know what a half-immortal is."

"I know of them in theory, but not in practice."

"Now you've met one. Ask her."

Magnolia pretended not to hear this. "Half-immortals fled human society. They erased themselves from history. And the survivors ended up in Steppehaven?"

"It's happened more than once," Crow said. "Wherever they live—even without bothering anyone—they get persecuted. I brought Tamar's enclave here a couple centuries ago."

Magnolia gave her a look that was disconcertingly empty of mockery. "You saved them all, then. You rescued them."

"Just in passing. I had other business with the automagi."

Half-immortals were longer-lived than typical humans. But they were also more vulnerable to sickness and injury. (Their susceptibility to plagues gave them another reason to seek refuge far from the rest of humanity. They were the first to succumb to disease, and they were unfairly blamed for spreading it.)

They could live with debilitating wounds, but their flesh refused to regenerate. It was as if their bodies expected to heal like immortal bodies, only to flounder helplessly when no such healing took place. They weren't immune from the need to eat or sleep, either, although they could get by on small meals and short naps.

"They aren't born with a compulsion," said Magnolia. "Unlike immortals."

"Unlike monsters."

"Are you still stuck on that? Goodness. My point is that from the start of their lives, half-immortals can go anywhere they like, and do anything they wish. If only they have the means."

"Having the means is the hard part."

Immortals never had children with each other. It was probably impossible, for one thing, and most would find the mere thought of it profoundly disturbing. Immortals were inherently disinterested in making offspring. But humans could carry their children. Intercourse wasn't a prerequisite: a human of any gender could spawn a half-immortal child. It would be the result of magic, not biology.

Some humans were very interested in copulating with immortals. Some wanted to infuse their family line with longevity. Some thought that eating half-immortal flesh would grant them true immortality.

"Can't imagine any monsters cooperating with this nonsense." Magnolia pulled a face as if to say that she, at least, would never be involved in such foolishness. "Anyone ever ask you for children?"

"Before my time," Crow said, "there was a saint whose companion wanted to breed a half-immortal army. Back when people had ambitions of conquering the world."

"What happened?"

"The saint made all the men of his existing army pregnant. So they had to stop fighting."

"Lovely," Magnolia said.

"Half-immortal soldiers aren't any more likely to survive than a throng of regular humans. They're just as killable. In fact, they're more delicate. Leave them be, treat them well, and they'll live longer ... that's the only material difference."

"No one made similar demands of you?" Magnolia pressed. "Tragic old stories were enough to dissuade them?"

"I met that saint," Crow said. "They'd turned into a monster. They told me: be careful who you allow to become your companion. Be careful who you tell you're a saint."

She wondered—in a sudden dream-like leap of logic—if Magnolia had been one of her past companions. Magnolia used to be human. But the timing didn't add up. Magnolia had been an immortal for longer than Crow herself.

Garbled stories of the Woman in the Hills had washed up in Fellshore for centuries before the world regurgitated Crow. Before she awoke as an immortal in a field of furious three-legged birds. She had been naked, fully adult in size, slick with blood as vivid as the many-colored sky above. Her wings had been enormous and deformed, a confused mix of skin and oversized feathers. They had no idea what shape they were supposed to take.

A man with a burned face came up to her. He spoke incomprehensible words. The cawing crows made more sense. She uttered something in response, but afterward, she had no idea what she'd said.

Her magic perception seized on the core buried in his torso. It shone through the wrapping of his body, unmarred and beautifully radiant, quite unlike the rest of him. It looked as though it were the only thing in the world that could slake her thirst. How she craved it.

But from the start, something in her had balked at the notion of doing the straightforward and easy thing, of growing claws on her hand and liberating his perfect core from its wet slimy cage of warm flesh. She didn't know what a saint was, and yet—in the way of a migratory bird following magnetic fields, below the fumbling level of conscious thought—she always knew her path.

At the time, she hadn't understood that the man with the burned face was pointing a weapon. Perhaps something would have been different if she'd been alarmed enough to defend herself. But he beckoned to her. He walked away, and she followed him out of the furrowed field like a duckling while crows jeered all around them. He had been a father to her, and a grandfather, although immortals weren't supposed to have either. He had been the first of her promised companions.

High up in the stone tree, Magnolia caught at her shoulder. "Look," she said.

"What?"

"A falling star."

"It's very slow," Crow said dubiously.

"Maybe not a regular meteor, then. According to the old lore—"

"Which old lore?"

"Of the north," said Magnolia. "If this does count as a falling star, then seeing it means we've been cursed. Better to be cursed together than to be cursed alone."

"Is that why you made me look at it?"

"Of course. I'm glad our star took its time."

Magnolia slept a few more hours in her human body, though she was up again before dawn. The white dire fox peeped in on them while they drank bitter bark tea with Tamar, who informed them that the automagi were diurnal. They wouldn't be ready to interview Magnolia until more sunlight poured down past the step-carved walls of the valley.

"Guess old habits die hard," Magnolia muttered. "Does your fox have a name?"

"We call her Pothos," said Tamar.

"We've been traveling with a primeval called Dung."

"How evocative."

Magnolia pointed at Crow. "She named him. All the blame goes to her."

Upon further questioning, Tamar explained that she'd rescued Pothos from a trap during one of her trips outside Steppehaven. Pothos later showed up to save her from bandits, and subsequently followed her home to the archivists' haven without being asked.

"That was several decades ago," Tamar said. "She must have part-immortal heritage, too."

Magnolia swirled her cup of tea. "Dire foxes live many times longer than the single-tailed type. Over half a century, if no one hunts them. But perhaps you're right."

Tamar told her to join the automagi after the morning light reached a certain angle. Until then, Magnolia wanted to wander. Crow followed her away from the central grove of stone trees. A firehawk's shrill cry echoed in the distant blue sky.

Magnolia grumbled extensively about having to face a panel of ethereal beings hunkered down in jars like humanoid hermit crabs.

"They're going to make me get in a jar, too," she said. "I just know it. The worst part is that I'll probably like it. You'll have to carry me around in a giant pickling crock for the rest of our journey."

While Crow envisioned this, Magnolia added: "The automagi already interviewed you."

"A while ago. No one told me to get in a jar."

"Their loss. All you had to do was talk? What'd they do, make half-immortal scribes take down a transcription?"

"Only the automagi listened."

"Maybe I'll ask them to show me."

"What?"

"Their records of you," Magnolia said impatiently.

Demands for more information would require additional compensation, Crow thought, but she didn't say anything. Let Magnolia pay the price.

"If the automagi try anything funny, I expect you to come to my rescue," Magnolia informed her.

"Your expectations don't much matter. You'll make me do it either way."

"Just remember, we're bound by a star now." Her shoulder twitched. She touched her earring as if she felt a sudden pang in it.

Crow looked away. Was it because she used to be human that Magnolia seemed so at home in this human-shaped body? She kept putting it on and discarding it and then putting it back on like a well-worn robe.

Tamar resurfaced moments after Magnolia reluctantly went over to be interrogated. Perhaps the fox named Pothos had made her aware that Crow was alone now. Pothos followed from a distance as they strolled together, a diffident silver-white shadow in the periphery of Crow's vision.

Crow asked if there was anything she could help with—menial labor, moving rocks around, basic repairs.

"Are you looking for something?" Tamar said.

Had she been that obvious?

"A machina," Crow said, abandoning subterfuge.

Tamar's mouth quirked. The rest of her expression was hard to read. Sunlight glinted dully off the plain metal of her mask. She appeared as aged and ageless as the countless steps carved around the valley.

Upon reflection, however, Tamar was by far the youngest creature here. Or the youngest bipedal creature, rather. Fox tails kept lashing at the corner of Crow's eye.

"There are places I can't take you," Tamar said carefully. "But I can show you our pickling fields."

The fields were made of stone—sweeping sunlit courtyards where royalty might have entertained courtiers, or bedraggled pilgrims might have appealed to the priests of long-lost faiths.

Now the courtyards were filled with rows of waist-high lidded pickling crocks, some dark brown and some a color closer to rust, painted in thick layers of rough glaze. They lined up all the way into the distance like soldiers standing on display.

"Thought it was better to bury these," Crow said, "or to keep them in shade."

"When was the last time you did any pickling?"

"A long time ago," Crow confessed. "We made larger batches in winter than in summer."

Tamar put a hand on the lid of the nearest jar. "Some of these are empty."

"Are you sure you don't want help?"

"They don't need maintenance."

She began walking between rows of anonymous jars. Crow followed. This field would look like a perfect dotted grid from above, the tall jars acting as sundials throughout the day. At least until the quarry-like walls on the horizon folded in enough shadow to cast an early gloam over the lands below.

"The other half-immortals—" Crow began.

"They're shy."

"I saw some last time. While you were away."

"Did you?" Tamar said politely. "That's nice."

She wore a dark green apron again. A stained handkerchief covered her hair. Each row and column of pickling jars was oriented with such precision that no matter how many steps they took, the scenery never seemed to alter.

The only reason Crow could tell they were making progress was because of Pothos the fox, who refused to set foot on the field arrayed with jars, and who instead watched from far behind them—a fluffy white shape receding into the distance as they moved. It was like being glared at by a displeased cloud.

"You know how the automagi were created," Tamar said.

"I wasn't there."

"But you've heard stories."

"The ancients volunteered for it," Crow dutifully recited. "Each volunteer got split into a heavenly self and an earthly self. They left their human bodies behind."

Tamar had stopped to listen, her face turned so that only a slice of the metal mask remained visible.

"Later generations debated over whether the abandoned bodies had any real purpose," Crow continued. "The bodies kept living for centuries, in a minimally functional sense. They became natural mummies. Cults stole them and kept them as relics. They grated dried fingers as if grating ginger. They sprinkled the dust in sacred wine and drank it for health and longevity."

"Even those who drank the mummies have been dead for an age and a half." Tamar thumped at her lower back to soothe an ache. "I'm no scholar, but I think those bodies served as a kind of anchor."

"The bodies of the automagi are long gone now."

"But their spirit selves keep shifting. Aging. They didn't always rely on empty pots to hold them."

She turned toward Crow, her back to the sun. "When you brought us here, Saint Crow, did you think it was all your own idea?"

"What?"

"To take us halves to this secret refuge."

"Of course not. It's been done before. Plenty of tales—"

"Yes. All the happy tales of our kind end with us escaping to hallowed land, a place ruled by benevolent spirits. But when you brought us down into the basin, there weren't any other halves waiting to welcome us. It was empty except for the automagi. I was too young to remember much, but I remember that. It was very quiet. Didn't you wonder why?"

"Tamar," Crow said, "what's in these jars?"

They could have been standing in the middle of this dizzying grid for a very long time now. The rock underfoot seemed so much paler than elsewhere. Combined with the black dots of infinite jars, it became blinding. The furthest jars appeared to shift as if caught in a heat mirage, tiny pinpricks crawling about Crow's vision like flies.

"The jars are for pickling," Tamar replied.

There was something written on the jars, every one of them. Large blobs of lighter or darker or rustier brown. It could have been random smears of glaze. Or it could have been an obscurely painted rune. Yes, a rune—the word for some sort of animal. Crow's head was too sun-addled to remember which.

"Tamar," she said, "what's under your mask?"

Tamar drew one finger down the edge of the metal. The finger next to it was just a stump. "Perhaps I had acid thrown at me the last time I went out. Perhaps I haven't actually left Steppehaven in many years now. We don't need much from outside anymore. We don't need much of anything."

Both her eyes seemed bluer than ever, even the one under the mask. By human standards, she could have been a woman of forty who'd aged prematurely, or a woman of eighty in remarkable shape.

"You'll pity me," she said, "and you won't ever ask me to take it off."

Crow remembered half-immortals with wounds that never closed. Raw holes that showed unprotected bone until the day they died.

"Do you want to take it off?" Crow asked.

Tamar backed up a few steps, her expression unchanging. She backed up some more, and then she ran. She ran like a young girl.

26

CROW TRAILED HER at a distance, nonplussed. She knew the thrill of the chase. She knew what it was like to be feared. Tamar ran as if her life depended on it. But she didn't seem afraid.

Afraid or not, she kept running, and Crow kept chasing her. She couldn't scan Tamar's mind like Magnolia, reading reflections off the surface of a lake.

Had Magnolia stealthily read Tamar's mind while they dined on pickles, or while they sat around sipping bark tea? What had she seen, and what was she hiding?

Tamar raced past silent ceramic crocks, row after row of them, a somber and critical crowd. As she neared the edge of the courtyard, a fleet blur of pale fur came flying around a corner. The dire fox stopped momentarily to snarl at Crow, then bolted away in Tamar's wake.

To avoid overtaking them, Crow stuck to more of a restrained jog than a flat-out sprint. Tamar kept wheezing. Pothos huffed noisily, too.

They drew closer to the shadow of a colossal step-hewn wall. Steam gushed from jagged cracks at the bottom of a sudden ravine to the right.

Crow glanced behind her. From this standpoint, the largest grove of stone trees felt startlingly remote. The pickling fields could have been mistaken for an elegiac memorial from a prehistoric war. The steep valley wall looked like a mosaic, with its perpetual pattern of stairs. In the shade of the wall, the blue window of sky above became unbearably intense.

Tamar waited with her back to the lowest tier of steps. Pothos crouched between her and Crow, bristling, puffy tails fanning out like a peacock.

"I wasn't chasing you," Crow said. "You were leading me."

Further and further away from the automagi. Further and further away from Magnolia.

"Your woman," Tamar said.

"My what?"

"The immortal you came with. They want to keep her."

Close up, Pothos was about the size of a small pony. She looked from Tamar to Crow, and gradually her growling died down to nothing. Her tails twitched. As if realizing something, she padded away, then turned and leapt lightly up onto the stairs behind Tamar.

"If they want her," Crow said, "they can have her."

Tamar blinked behind her half-mask.

Some crucial balance of power had begun to shift, a fault line grinding underground before a quake. Long experience whispered to Crow that a chance was coming her way, a chance that she could snatch or miss, a chance that might never come again.

She started to say something.

You traitor, Magnolia pronounced in a disembodied voice so distinct that all the stones seemed to echo with it. Tamar went rigid. Pothos dropped flat and unleashed a brain-piercing scream.

Crow, I'll deal with you later. Tamar, take off your—

Tamar shifted into fluid motion. All at once, she ripped her metal mask off; she stood on tiptoe; she slapped the mask against Crow's face and pressed it in place like a branding iron.

—mask, Magnolia finished.

Crow barely noticed. It should have hurt to get smacked with a piece of crude metal, but she didn't feel that, either. She sensed the world—and Magnolia in particular—as if from behind a rushing waterfall.

"Hold it there," Tamar said hoarsely. "Follow me. Hurry!"

Crow clapped a hand over the mask. It skewed at an angle, blocking her eye. She stumbled down half-hidden steps hacked into the nearby ravine. A path fit for a mountain goat. Clouds of steam alternated nonsensically with patches of frigid mist. The mask pulsed from hot to cold in answer.

Back among the hollow trees, Magnolia was raging. Her fury came through in a rumble like the seething of a volcano, but it had no power to really touch Crow. It grazed her skin as would a rain of already-cooled ash, flaking and falling away.

Tamar pulled her through a dark entrance, an open gash in the side of the canyon. Crow blindly kept pace with her. The magic in the mask held Magnolia at bay. In exchange, other presences—slippery and unfamiliar—scrabbled at her mind. But they couldn't get a grip. This mask was not designed to control her.

Light—or something resembling light—oozed from a larger cavity up ahead. It trickled along their path in the way of a thin stream of leaking water.

Tamar whipped around, one hand to her chest, as if to hold her heart while it spasmed. Her mask hadn't sheltered a mass of rotten flesh. It hadn't done anything, seemingly, except give the automagi a way to relay orders.

"My core," Tamar said.

That was all it took.

No special words of ritual had ever been needed. Sometimes no words were needed, period. Crow had started to back away, but she moved for naught. Dread pooled like liquid mercury in her lungs, cold ballast weighing her down. For forty years, she'd avoided taking another companion. All that effort to resist, and now—

Their eyes met. Tamar's were dark in the low light, her sagging skin textured as if she were a creature born from the rough tunnel of rock around them. She faced Crow with her utter willingness to give up everything, to hand over her burning core and perish on the spot.

Crow lowered the mask. She was calm to the point of dullness. She no longer needed a shield. Magnolia's consciousness beat at her like fists pounding on a locked door in another town. No amount of intricate magical trickery could get between a saint and their promised companion.

"Break it," Tamar told her.

Crow snapped the mask in half as if breaking a crispbread. Its magic hissed and fizzled like hot coals in winter water. She let the dead pieces drop from her fingers.

"You brought us here," Tamar said. "All of us halves—my whole clan. Find us and save us. End us. Even if it makes you a monster."

"The automagi—"

Tamar pointed at the gelatinous light. Together they moved toward the next cavern. Tamar's footing was less certain now, as if she'd expended years' worth of pent-up energy in a few short bursts of movement. When Crow caught her arm, she felt shaky and old, flesh hanging off her bones like an empty bag.

But her voice remained strong. "Use that," she said, "and they'll be helpless."

They had to stop at the cavern entrance. It was little more than a window onto a mass of mottled green. It could've been the world's largest deposit of precious jade. Crow traced the outlines of foreign magic beneath the earth. This magic sang a tune so deep that it had completely escaped her notice.

"Those stone trees grow sprinkled all over the valley for a reason," Tamar said. "Their roots are much stronger and deeper than their branches. Their roots hold down this machina."

"This is—a leg?" Crow asked. "An ankle? I'll need to find the cockpit."

"You're a saint," said Tamar. "Do you need a door to enter? Let yourself in. Take me with you."

Crow hesitated. "Rousing the machina could prove very destructive."

Tamar regarded her coldly in the jade-inflected light.

"Your dire fox," Crow clarified. "If she's waiting nearby—"

"Pothos will know to get out of the way. Board the machina."

Tamar's order reverberated in the roots of her still-shrunken wings. Magnolia might as well have been a writhing nightmare from another life. Magnolia's voice and Magnolia's magic clawed at boarded-up windows in a place where no one lived, failing to reach her, and yet still trying over and over. It was all rather pathetic.

Keeping one hand on Tamar, Crow touched the mammoth jade leg of the buried machina. Her mind felt as superbly hollow as a bell waiting to be rung. She took hold of the intangible magic that dangled like a rope to welcome her. She tugged, and it reeled both of them in.

27

SHE'D NEVER been inside a working machina. She'd seen them piled like bizarre monoliths on the coast, some eviscerated, some caught in a mutual rictus of violence. Different civilizations gave them different names: sky pillars, behemoths, colossi, meteor soldiers, and so on. Most had been defunct for eons, like the ones overgrown with shrubbery at Lake Fallen.

Tamar inhaled sharply when they got ported into the cockpit. It was like being trapped in a geode with no windows and no air holes. Just jagged crystalline walls imbued with the same gooey, pliable light that the machina's leg had shed in the cave outside. Gravity bent together with the light: Crow's gut insisted that the smoother floor was in fact a vertical wall, and yet they stood there without falling.

At the back of the cockpit was a structure like a set of enormous animal ribs pried wide open. At the front was a place to sit, but no reins or any other sort of steering mechanism.

"I don't know what to do with this," Crow admitted.

"Sit," Tamar said. "Put your feet in the bath. I'll go to the back."

"Bath?" Then—"Have you been here before?"

"I've looked inside." Tamar motioned for her to hurry up and get seated. "I have an idea of what needs to be done."

The bath turned out to be a dried-up depression in the floor in front of the pilot's seat. Thankfully, the lining appeared smooth; no nail-shaped crystals waited to spike Crow's soles. She had no shoes to take off—she rarely wore them away from human society, as her feet were mostly impervious to discomfort.

A creaking came from behind her, like an old door opening. She started to turn.

"Face forward," Tamar ordered. She was adapting quickly to having a saint on her side.

As was her wont, Crow obeyed. She put her feet in the empty bath. The air here tasted as though it had been filtered to nothingness, as though there wasn't enough substance left in it to satiate human lungs. She suppressed the urge to glance at Tamar behind her.

A lukewarm substance crept between her toes.

The shallow bath began to fill, viscous liquid welling up like groundwater. It rose to her ankles. It stank like fatty pork broth boiling away in a cauldron for days on end. Together with that smell, a cloudy magic infiltrated the crystalline cockpit.

Crow said: "Before I do as you wish, please tell me to kill the woman I came with."

"Do you need an order for that?"

"It would help."

"Go on, then." Tamar's voice was strained. The onslaught of odor couldn't have made it any easier for her to breathe. "Kill the woman you came with."

The fluid in the bath thickened like gelatin. It seized up, gripping the bones of Crow's feet, and then the magic in it surged to coat her entire awareness.

Like Tamar's now-broken mask, it wasn't a good fit. This machine had been calibrated for a human pilot. Or, at minimum, for someone or something utterly different from Crow. Her skin felt tight enough to burst. Every sense doubled up. Her eyes saw the cockpit full of crystals pointed like knives—and her eyes saw out through the translucent jade shell of the machina's body.

There wasn't much to see yet. The machina lay interred below the valley basin. The roots of stone trees wound around its limbs like implacable ropes—stretching miles away from their aboveground trunks. Crow's muscles trembled at their grinding pressure.

But she could move the machina as if it were an extension of her own body. She was simultaneously the size of a giant and the size of an insect. She kept suffocating on the stench of bubbling bones. The air in the cockpit had clouded until it too resembled long-cooked pork broth, milky white and thickly emulsified with collagen and marrow.

Kill the woman you came with.

Crow and her machina burst out of their stony grave. She found herself distantly aware of rock cracking, the earth shaking, hoary walls crumbling, steam billowing, hot springs flooding their banks.

The machina was somewhat humanoid, but it had a tail that she wasn't sure what to do with. Wings would've been easier for her to maneuver. The tail dragged noisily as she trudged forward, well over a hundred feet tall.

She looked down at herself as the machina, all in hues of cloudy jade. Uneven protrusions traced a ragged ladder along its thorax and lower limbs, like hand holds for a rock climber.

Her magic perception had ballooned together with every other sense.

Tamar's core burned like a pile of coals in the cockpit behind her. The automagi cowered, cobwebs in corners. Magnolia was still hidden in the furthest grove of hollow trees, which had tilted precipitously as a result of the violence done to their far-reaching roots.

Crow thundered forward. She could spring into the air on mighty legs and reach the trees in a single leap. But if she fumbled the landing, she would cause more reckless damage to the already-fragmented haven.

She wondered why Magnolia wasn't scrambling to escape.

She stopped wondering once she'd trampled a path up to the hollow trees. A tight band of tension ran round her head, an unwanted crown. Piloting this machina might leave her with the equivalent of a hangover. But Magnolia was there inside the tree before her, an ant-sized blot of magical essence.

The tree didn't look quite so titanic from the perspective of a machina. Crow clamped overlong jade arms around it, ripped off the solid-walled upper half, and tossed it aside with a bone-jarring crash. She leaned her bulk forward and peered down into the remainder of the tree as if examining the interior of a dollhouse.

Tablets of clay and stone were strewn about like leaves after a storm. Most of the crocks appeared empty. Several had tipped over or cracked in half. The low table lay in pieces, as if someone had snapped it like Crow breaking Tamar's mask.

Only one pickling crock had an occupant, and that crock held Magnolia's head. Frenzied roots grew to fill the gap between her neck and the rim of the pot, spilling down past the fragmented table, gripping random tablets as if ready to hurl them at the machina. She glared up with what might have been hatred or indignation or terror. It felt like locking eyes with a housefly.

"I came to you," Crow said, though the machina had no voice, and only Tamar in the cockpit could hear her.

"I came to you with a promised companion."

There was no room for thought. She raised the many-fingered right hand of the machina, a hand large enough to crush a cottage. She leveled the lacy-walled stump of the tree in a single blow. A shudder went through the earth.

Her aim had been true. Magnolia should have been reduced to a bloody smear on stone.

When Crow made the machina lift its hand from the wreckage, the ground beneath was broken and sunken. Magnolia's roots had whirled up around her to form a protective ball of yarn. Distressed automagi gyrated like ghostly eels between the machina's ankles, then eddied away to hide.

A substance that could have been either blood or crude oil leaked from the tight hairball of Magnolia's roots. Her pickling crock had burst like an eggshell. Crow waited for her naked core to slip out and present itself for consumption. She waited for a frisson of triumph, of satisfaction. All that intensified within her was the reek of overcooked bones.

She would have apologized for forcing Tamar to witness this, but Tamar couldn't see anything outside the sealed cockpit.

No core emerged for eating.

The machina shed its unseelie light on Magnolia's roots. Crow flexed its excessive fingers with a resounding crack of joints. Magnolia must still be alive in there, albeit barely. She could pound this mass of roots with her mechanical fist—causing more earthquakes—or use claws to surgically slice it open.

She opted to use her claws.

A millisecond before she cut into the bleeding roots, they unraveled. Magnolia and her roots rocketed away, bouncy as a jumping cricket, brackish blood spattering.

She flung herself into the nearest teetering treetops.

Crow and the machina remained stock-still. Another missed opportunity to slaughter the Woman in the Hills. Another maddening chase. Yet the instant those roots unfurled to reveal her head, a matching knot inside Crow had come hopelessly undone.

She sent the machina crashing after Magnolia, then staggered to a halt. With each massive stride, rock dust huffed out of the pummeled ground. Hunting in this form would be like attacking a spider with a sledgehammer.

"Tamar—"

"Don't forget your promise." Tamar seemed to be fighting not to breathe through her nose. The air in the cockpit had gone increasingly chalky, almost opaque.

"I won't," Crow said. "I'll be back."

While synced with the machina, she could open the hidden lid of the cockpit as if winking an eye. A segment of the crystal-encrusted wall flipped out of sight, and daylight charged in. Tamar shifted audibly, as though the sudden brightness had stunned her. She was still mostly hidden by the lingering fog from the foot bath.

Crow had opened the door (instead of porting out) so Tamar wouldn't be stranded alone with the reek of pork broth. The long strides of the machina had already brought her close to catching up with Magnolia's frantic darting.

Magnolia had never hinted at being capable of porting herself. If there were ever a time for her to use hidden skills, it would've been now. But she didn't: she scrambled about on her roots, shedding splats of steaming blood. Crow overtook her by bounding from one broken stone tree to another.

Tamar called out from behind, high and desperate, begging Crow not to leave her all over again. Crow ignored her. That was Magnolia, who could bend her voice around corners, who could imitate anything from a nighttime owl to a dead boy she'd never met.

Crow reached her at the edge of a modest stepwell, one untouched by the machina's trail of destruction. She pounced on the flailing mass of roots—it felt like embracing a rabid squid—and began ripping them off the base of Magnolia's neck. She tore them out as emphatically as she'd torn out her own wings. They grew anew, pale and larval, and she pulled up the fresh roots like fistfuls of weeds.

At last nothing remained but Magnolia's head in her hands. She could do anything. She could pulverize Magnolia on the edge of the uppermost step. She could use magic to reinforce her fingers; she could dig them into the crevices of this defenseless skull and crack it open like a walnut.

She'd thought Magnolia would fight harder.

"You'd be dazed, too, if you almost got crushed to death by a giant hand," Magnolia said through bloodied lips.

Something was wrong. She wasn't ranting or screaming. She wasn't bargaining. She wasn't pleading coyly for her life.

"I won," Crow said.

"Didn't peg you for the type to rub it in. Me, now, I'll rub it in every chance I get. But you're not me. You're a saint."

"I came to you with a companion," Crow said.

"No, you didn't," retorted the head in her grip. "Not this time."

"She's right over—"

Magnolia giggled wetly. Crow almost dropped her down the staggered stepwell.

"Better get started," Magnolia said. "Dash me on the rocks."

Crow lifted her higher, above eye level. Crow's arms would not tire. She could hold this rigid pose without ever reaching a point at which she'd be forced to make a choice, to lower her burden gently or smash it like pottery. Why did both seem untenable?

"There's nothing I detest more than a willing martyr," Magnolia said wearily. "Did you know that? Now you do. If you hate something, destroy it. If you love something, destroy it. That's what saints do, right? Don't make this difficult."

If Magnolia would just stop talking, she'd already be dead.

"I'm not so sure about that," Magnolia said. "Let's put it to the test."

With perfect aim, she spat at Crow's cheek.

A repugnant gluey wetness tracked an agonizing path down toward Crow's jaw. She didn't move a muscle.

Magnolia abruptly stopped leering. "I'm not sure what I'm trying to prove," she said emptily. "It's a moot point. Whatever happens, I'd save my own life in the end. There was a sliver of time in which you had a genuine chance to murder me, and it was gone before you grabbed me. You may be under the illusion that you could kill me or spare me, but you have no reason to spare me, and the illusion will shatter as soon as you work yourself up to the point of actually killing me. Put me down, Carrie."

Crow remained frozen.

"Put. Me. Down."

The order hit her like a cannonball. By the time she could make sense of what had happened, she'd let go. Magnolia's head lugged itself out of reach on truncated wooden knobs like the legs of an inbred dog.

"Yes, yes, bask in your shock," Magnolia rattled off. "You're mine again. You missed your one shot."

Crow reached up and, as if in a trance, wiped Magnolia's saliva from her face. She glanced at her palm. It was blood-laced spittle, ugly and raw.

28

THE WORDS *put me down* were still lodged in Crow's marrow. "But I had a companion this time," she said.

"You *had* a companion," Magnolia sniped. "Let's go see what's become of her, shall we? Where is she—languishing up in that horrid machine of yours?"

"When she cried out to me..."

"What? Finish your thought."

"Was that you?"

Magnolia eyed her without answering. Her head—which had been considerably lumpier and more dented than usual, hair matted with all kinds of leakage—was beginning to magically shudder back into a healthier shape.

"I'm tempted to let you believe what you like," Magnolia said. After a long pause, she parted swollen lips. Battered though she looked, she would be healed before any real bruising had time to develop.

Tamar's voice emanated from somewhere over Crow's shoulder, husky and cracking. "Take me with you," she pleaded. "My god, please don't leave me."

In her normal voice, Magnolia said, "Excuse me while I sprout a body."

Moments later, she sat buck naked at the edge of the stepwell, shooting sidelong looks as if it were Crow's fault that she had no clothing. She smacked the tops of her bare thighs in much the same way that she sometimes smacked Dung to encourage him to pick up his pace.

She rose—and lurched in the wrong direction. Crow caught her before she pitched headfirst into the glossy pink water.

"Maybe you should stay as a head," Crow said.

"Believe it or not, sometimes I don't want to be carried about like a suckling pig on a platter," Magnolia sniffed. "Take me to your machina."

"Naked?"

"I know where to find clothes."

For all her insistence on not being carried, Magnolia draped herself over Crow like limp laundry. Crow gave up on walking all the way back. She grabbed Magnolia around the waist and ported over with a wrenching heave of magic.

When they materialized in the cockpit, she reacted like a bodyguard. Before her brain could process anything, she'd thrust herself out in front of Magnolia.

"I was thinking of taking her clothes," Magnolia said, muffled. "Never mind that. You win this one, Carrie. I'll go back to being a humble head."

The sleek body that had been pressed up against Crow evaporated. Magnolia's head clung to her shirt with familiar hooks, climbing a stabby path to her shoulder. They gazed together at the back of the cockpit.

At last Magnolia said: "Didn't think it'd be so messy."

Clothing hung in shreds from the ribcage structure bracketed on the back wall. Nothing recognizable remained of Tamar's living self. Just ravaged physical matter—an unnaturally symmetrical pile of mincemeat.

The foot bath in the floor looked larger, somehow, as if it had expanded to meet growing demand. Not a trace remained of the transparent jelly that had welled up around Crow's feet. Something different filled the sunken basin: darker, looser fluids. All this liquid had come running from the back of the cockpit, flooding grooves in the floor that fed the bath like thick veins. Unspeakable odors mingled with the lingering stench of bubbling pork broth.

"The machine separated liquids from solids," Magnolia said. "Like separating an egg for baking."

Crow found her voice somewhere in the depths of her stomach. "You knew this would happen."

"I was stuck with the automagi when you started attacking. Had time to ask a couple short questions." She repositioned herself, twisting to bury her nose in Crow's hair. Mutated thorns budded from the base of her neck; they cut Crow's shoulder like the talons of a raptor. "It gets fouler in here every second. Let's retreat."

"The automagi," Crow said, still primed for combat—though she had no idea who she would be fighting, or why.

"They're extremely put out, and they do have other toys, but they won't be a threat. Now hurry up and climb down. You seem shaky. You'd better not port."

They descended. The jade machina remained standing on its own, lifeless and impossibly heavy. Its surface felt as hot as sun-baked rock, though light-muffling clouds surrounded the blue hole in the sky above the valley.

"Did she die because I left her alone?" Crow asked.

"How should I know?" Magnolia said bitingly. But she kept going. "Tamar cheated you. She died before you could retrieve her core. Oh, I'm sure she understood what would become of her. Did you even need the machina to shake off my influence? Or would it have been sufficient just to take a new companion behind my back? Her mask tided you over well enough, it seems."

"Why'd you tell her take it off?"

"I was being charitable! That's the last time I ever do anything nice. The automagi were our common enemy. I was going to propose an alliance."

Crow removed her hand from the smooth jade skin of the machina. To stand below it and look straight up felt like gawking at a skyscraper in a classical city, the sort of monument that had all but vanished from mortal memory.

"You underestimated Tamar," she said tightly.

"...You're angry," Magnolia said in tones of dawning disbelief.

"I couldn't kill you. I'm seething."

"Don't try to talk your way around a mind reader." Her eyes narrowed. "You're angry—because I let her go cantering off to her death? No. You're angry because I slipped up and let her become your companion. However briefly. You're angry because she broke your forty-year streak of abstinent mourning. Well, no need to include her in your official list of past companions. Her tenure was too short to count."

"They all count!"

Crow felt herself shout, but she scarcely heard it. It was as though she had fists stuffed in her ears, as though her voice spurted out into a soulless vacuum. There was no God of the End—there were no gods at all, no impartial witnesses. Arion was just as gone now as he had been forty years ago; just as gone as every single prior companion. She would meet random strangers with his hair or his ears, with the same squeaky sneeze, but there would never be another Arion, and the same was true of every human Magnolia had ever eaten.

"Everyone counts," she said through the broken glass wedged in her throat.

"Even if they don't last an hour?" Magnolia asked.

"Tamar was my twenty-fourth companion."

"Then make your peace with it. No point in getting irate over things you can't change," Magnolia said reasonably. "What'd she do after she slapped her mask on you? She was a quick thinker, I'll give her that."

Crow's heart beat double-time, as if it had split itself in two. She reeled herself in. She focused furiously on the facts. "I'd said I was looking for a hidden machina. She took me there as soon as you freed her."

Magnolia snorted. Her breath ruffled Crow's hair. "The automagi kept me well informed of your interest in their machina. They're experts at playing multiple sides."

"Tamar might have known it would kill her. But we boarded that cockpit because I—"

"Nonsense," Magnolia barked. "You haven't the faintest notion what she thought, or why she did anything. You two destroyed a huge swathe of this venerable haven. Was that her real goal, or yours? Not at all. But she didn't make you pilot it for your sake."

"Then—"

"Start with the result and work backwards. The automagi are powerless. Have they come zooming out to scratch your eyeballs? Have they raised an army of skeletons? Nothing of the sort. In fact, your vicious rampage remains completely uncontested.

"That machina served as the engine for much of their power. Now that it's clawed its way out of the ground, now that you've interfaced with it—they can't use it anymore, not in its current state. Their other tricks and tools pale in comparison. That's why Tamar made it her top priority to get you in the pilot seat, to make the machina rip free of its stony cocoon like a reviving immortal.

"You wanted to neutralize me. She wanted to neutralize her masters. I doubt she gave a fig for *your* desires, but stealing that machina was the only way to quickly achieve the latter. Mask or no mask, she couldn't have done it alone. If she tried, the machina would've kept sleeping while she turned to half-human soup at the back of the cockpit."

Getting chased by a legendary war machine hadn't cowed Magnolia for long. She sounded as imperious as ever. She commanded Crow to hustle over to the wreck of the proudest hollow tree: the place where Crow had found her and tried to smack her like a fly.

More was left of it than Crow had expected. She set Magnolia on a half-buried stack of tablets. Then, as requested, she sifted through a jumble of bark-textured rocks and broken crockery in search of Magnolia's clothes. Everything was coated in a layer of flour-fine colorless grime.

"They talked me into getting in one of their stupid pots." Magnolia's voice had gone thick with rage. "I went along with it just to be diplomatic. Shed my body so I would fit. Lost everything I'd been wearing. The pot trapped me there—that's why I was a sitting duck when you came to kill me."

Crow tossed undergarments at her. She sat back to watch while Magnolia burst out coughing in the ensuing clouds of dust.

After the dust settled, Magnolia's expression cleared, too. It was like she'd never stopped talking. "Although I suppose that may have worked in my favor. How'd you like the sight of me anchored helplessly to a pickling pot? Did I tug at your heartstrings?"

"Not at all," Crow said with emphasis.

"You're like a loving family hound, you know, one that every so often gets possessed by some ancestral killer instinct. Once your jaws close, you won't let go. But you waste too much time dithering before your reflexes kick in. Has thinking things over ever done you any good? Certainly hasn't helped you wriggle out of my clutches."

"You told me to think more tactically," Crow said.

Magnolia gave her a wolfish grin. "Surely by now you've realized that I say a lot of things I don't mean."

Crow found her sunglasses buried under a heap of potsherds. They had been mutilated beyond any hope of repair. She held them up in the light.

Magnolia let out a series of curses that had drifted out of common use a thousand years ago. "You ought to be much more upset," she tacked on at the end. "Can anyone still manufacture new sunglasses of this style and quality? Highly doubtful. You'll have to settle for something rather less sophisticated. It's your own fault, anyway. They wouldn't be in such an awful state if you hadn't been trying to kill me."

Crow placed her broken glasses on the broken table. "I'll donate these to the archivists' collection."

In past eras, many saints had worn similar sunglasses. It had been a way to signal polite deference to human society. But very few still wore them to this day. At best, it had made Crow look old-fashioned.

She'd spent another handful of decades living among people who considered it taboo to look a saint in the eye. To make it easier on them, she'd go around with a blindfold, using her magic perception and echolocation to navigate.

"How very like you to blind yourself for the convenience of mortals," Magnolia said. She donned human form again. Then she donned her dusty clothes (with no end of complaining).

"What's the body for?" Crow asked.

"For paying my respects," she said obscurely. "Consider it my version of formal wear."

She raised both hands, frowning, and groped her head as if feeling about for missing chunks and oozing brains. Parts of her hair were audibly crusty with blood. "Your mind is an open book—not that I always put the work in to read it—and yet you confuse me. I thought you would be beating yourself up over your failure to permanently smash my head in. You're dwelling much more on Tamar."

"I'll have other opportunities to crush you. Tamar won't live again."

"Unless she becomes a returner."

"What are the odds of that?"

"Infinitesimally small," Magnolia conceded. "I've never heard of another returner who used to be human. That's the main reason the automagi wanted me for their zoo. So much for my historical credentials as a Great Adversary of humanity."

"She was only half-human," said Crow.

"Makes it even less likely, huh?" Magnolia shook out her arms as though testing to make sure they were fully connected. Gray vines sprouted from the nape of her neck, looping around the front of each shoulder to bind up the excess fabric of her hanging sleeves.

"You mentioned pickling fields," she said afterward.

"No, I didn't."

"Not out loud. Show me the way."

"Tamar's remains are still—"

"This is relevant. Trust me."

The landscape had changed considerably from earlier in the day, when Crow followed Tamar to the pickling fields. Now Magnolia followed Crow along shattered and rubble-filled paths. No matter how far they went, the motionless machina never fully left their sight.

"I have to keep my promise," Crow said, trying and failing to come up with a more persuasive way to phrase it.

"To Tamar? Even though she cheated you?"

"She was truly ready to give up her core."

"She was truly ready to give up her life. Which might be effectively the same type of readiness, as far as saints are concerned—but then she went ahead and did just that, and she kept hoarding her own core to the end. She must have guessed that the machina would gobble her up before you ever got around to it. By extension, she must have trusted that you would carry out her wishes even in her absence, and even without any promised reward." Magnolia's mouth twisted. "You sure you want to prove her right? I heard you brooding over it. She asked you to kill all her kin. Not the type of request you would usually leap to fulfill."

"First I have to find them," Crow said. "I left the half-immortals here. I left them, and I never wondered what became of them."

She'd led them on a long and arduous march toward freedom and safety. Toward the valley of the automagi, which some half-immortals called Steppehaven. This was supposed to have been the one place they could escape persecution.

She remembered vivid, disconnected snatches of Tamar as a clumsy toddler. Long-forgotten scenes had resurfaced, bobbing up like flotsam, after reminiscing with her the night before.

Tamar was the only child among all those half-immortals. She'd eaten too much and then vomited on Crow's knees. She'd cried in that strange way of hers with blue eyes wide open, no sound passing her lips. She used to laugh the same way, too—a silent, fearful shaking.

She'd spit up in Crow's lap after tasting bitter bark tea for the first time. She'd thought she was looking at a horrible stranger whenever Crow removed her sunglasses. All of a sudden, she'd been too shy to come say goodbye when Crow left.

Whatever Crow felt in the pith of her body was not grief. She spoke numerous mortal languages, but she knew of no words to describe the staccato sensation of meeting a child and then an old woman without encountering any of what lay between. Or, as happened more often, returning to a town to find the graves of everyone she'd previously met. When she turned her back on a place, the mortals there were essentially dead to her. One day she might come back, but it would be a miracle to encounter the same stranger twice. If she did, it was typically after years of irrevocable change.

"You delivered up your motley band of half-immortals," said Magnolia. "You trusted the automagi not to mistreat them. I dislike the automagi on principle—I have a severe aversion to anything I can't order around—but I can understand how it turned out this way. They never lied to your face. They never swore not to put senile old halves to practical use."

"You know what they did?" Crow said.

Magnolia didn't answer directly. "They're archivists, after all, and they contain most of their own records. They preserve and extend themselves. They honor the purpose instilled in them by dead creators. They have to. It's all they can do. It's all that makes sense.

"Elderly or sickly half-immortals might decline past any hope of recovery—anyone could see that. They'd just keep deteriorating. They'd stop contributing to the community. Why not assign such individuals a grander purpose? It's even possible that most of their brethren knew about it, and never objected. Safety has a cost."

She stopped, tugging at the long tails of Crow's shirt. "Looking for Tamar's kin, are you? Here's a start."

29

THEY WERE AT the border of the pickling fields. It smelled like the retch-inducing aftermath of a combat zone in summer.

"I've seen headstones arrayed less lovingly," Magnolia remarked. "A shame that the machina's stomping knocked them over." She pointed at the nearest spilled pot. "Solids and liquid. Neatly separated. Look familiar? I wonder what kind of smell-erasing magic the automagi used to seal in all that soup."

The crock lay on its side, lid askew: a compressed mass clogged its open mouth. A fermented dark fluid spilled out onto the off-white slabs of courtyard stone.

Suddenly Crow recognized the rune painted in random-looking strokes on each jar.

"Rabbit," she said.

"What?"

"The word on the crocks." Her voice was not whole.

"Ah," Magnolia said dryly. "Symbolic."

She put her hands on her hips. She had the air of a farmer surveying an uncooperative field. "A bit of a mess, and it'll only get worse over time. I'm not so heartless as to force you to—"

"Are these all the half-immortals?"

"Just the dead ones. Minus Tamar."

"I'll clean this up," Crow said. "That's part of my promise."

"What, right now? I don't think she meant—oh, stars! You're actually touching that?"

"You don't have to help."

"Wasn't planning on it. But that leaves me with nothing to do here."

"Do what you're best at."

"Lounge around and look intelligent?"

"Talk," Crow said through her teeth, righting another jar. There was a subtle sealing magic tattooed inside the lid. She could reinforce it with a bit of her own power, as if sprinkling blood from a cut finger. But she would have to come back and scour the wet rock underfoot with magical fire, or water, or both.

Magnolia trailed after her, careful to tread only on clean swathes of pavement. "I'm more talkative in moments of triumph. But I suppose I can try. I made a dire tactical error—it almost got me squelched to death by your magical fist. Where'd I go wrong?"

She didn't give Crow time to guess. "I judged Tamar based on what she was like with her mask. Extremely controllable. The second she removed it, I thought I could slide into place and become her new puppeteer. Easy-peasy.

"In my defense—I could absolutely have controlled her. It just wasn't as simple as I'd assumed. I needed more time and less distance. She was a whole different beast without the mask. You know how it went—you were there. She made all the right moves.

"Want to hear about my other big mistake?" Magnolia asked. "Needless to say, I was furious with the automagi for trying to trap me in one of their jars. But I was cognizant of the risks, and I went along with it anyway. Wanted to see what they had in mind for me. Long story short—I was counting on being able to call on *you*. No back-up plan. What a blunder! Having access to you has made me careless," she added accusingly.

"I'm sorry," Crow deadpanned. "How terrible."

She straightened her back. The stench seemed duller now, but she wondered if she would lose her ability to smell or taste anything else. There was only one of her, and the vast courtyard contained an overwhelming number of pots.

"Yes," said Magnolia, catching the tail end of her thoughts. "Too many, isn't it? More half-immortals than you've ever met in your life. Some would've hailed from Tamar's group—a couple dozen, I guess? The rest predate them.

"Were they always spread out in the sun? Maybe their jars used to be stuffed down in some cave. Were the remains kept out of reverence, by fellow halves—or did the automagi hoard them? They might've been driven by a scientific reluctance to dispose of evidence. It's a treasure trove of spent fuel."

Crow could have released her magic like a tidal wave to right every fallen crock at once. But that would inevitably result in toppling others. So she went one by one. She checked each jar for cracks. She fused the cracks with magic. On to the next, and the next, and the next. She fought the urge to wipe her itching face with filthy hands.

"You could send the whole place up in flame," Magnolia suggested. "You'd be done much faster. Tamar might have liked that."

"You read her mind," Crow said without looking back.

"What, did you expect me not to?"

"When did she start wearing a mask?"

"I didn't absorb her entire life story. She noticed older halves disappearing, and she became dissatisfied with whatever explanation they gave her. She must have kicked up a fuss. Eventually the automagi forced that mask on her. Might've been her own brethren who held her down and made her wear it.

"She was a fortunate child. All her formative memories came during and after her journey here. The other halves would've given up anything to stay on good terms with the automagi. To avoid going back. Living in peace demands its own price, you see. She ended up being the only one of them who ever went out for supplies. Because she was the only one without red eyes? Or because none of the rest could bear to leave their haven."

Crow listened, but she didn't say much else until she was halfway through fixing the courtyard.

The next crock was a splintered morass of broken ceramic and gooey innards, like a great beetle ground beneath the heel of a giant. She reached for her chicken-size wings and began yanking out handfuls of feathers. Soon she would have few left to spare.

Teeth-rattling magic flared, and flared again, as she anointed shattered jars with her feathers. Glazed potsherds glued themselves back together.

"You knew what was going on here," she said. "Since last night, or since the moment we arrived."

"Yes?" Magnolia sounded puzzled.

"You knew what the mask was doing to Tamar. You knew there was a reason we didn't see other halves. All your chatter, all day and all night, and you didn't breathe a word about what really matters. What would have happened if the automagi didn't scheme to keep you?"

"Tamar would be alive," Magnolia said immediately, "and still wearing her mask, and we would've waved a friendly goodbye when we left.

What other answer is there? This isn't like Fellshore, with a mimid hiding underfoot. Well—there might be a tasty meal or two lurking here, too, but I wouldn't go out of my way to antagonize the automagi if they didn't antagonize me first. You came to negotiate in good faith, didn't you? You've gotten along with them in the past. Whatever you think of me, I'm not an agent of thoughtless chaos. I wouldn't have messed that up for you—not without good reason."

Crow had not paid attention to anything she said after *This isn't like Fellshore*. "What do you mean?" she demanded. "It's just like Fellshore. It's the same pattern. You gazed into the secrets of a settlement, and you chose not to mention it. Knowing about the mimid or Tamar's mask might not have changed your behavior one whit. But it would have changed mine, if only you'd—"

She couldn't finish. Why waste her breath? Why would Magnolia ever choose to tell a servant anything? Out of the goodness of her monstrous heart?

She strode towards a part of the courtyard where no dry pavement remained. Magnolia flitted on the unsoiled outskirts, shading her forehead with her hands.

Crow had to raise her voice to be heard again. "Don't leave me oblivious," she said. "If I seem unaware, tell me. Let me decide if I care."

She patched a crock that had inky fluid leaking from a hairline crack in its painted rune. Magical strain darted through her flesh like a cloud of razor-sharp minnows, too quick to catch, not truly located in any one muscle or joint. Magnolia would not be motivated to cooperate. Magnolia liked to watch her stew; she watched as avidly as a child tormenting ants.

"Sure," Magnolia said.

"...What?"

"I value your goodwill more than you think."

Crow checked the next few jars in a rush of rage-induced efficiency. "You could've made our travels miserable." Magnolia was quite skilled at pretending to be oblivious herself. "You could've poured all your effort into torturing both of us. I do realize that your mind simply doesn't work along those lines. I appreciate your goodness, even if you just can't help it. And look—time passes so quickly when we're having a productive dialogue. You're almost done."

This was an exaggeration. Crow had fixed all the broken and open crocks. She had set them back in place. But she would still need to purge the mingling liquid that she hadn't separated and siphoned into individual jars. Perhaps someone skilled in other types of magic could have determined which molecule belonged to each jarred half-immortal, but that was beyond Crow's abilities.

She sent an ankle-deep tide of liquid fire washing gently down the pavement. She scourged away every last bit of clinging organic material, which looked so much like sticky spillage from a tar pit.

"More a show of sheer force than a show of finesse," Magnolia said, as if she were a critic sent to review Crow's magic. "Still, a job well done. Any lingering stench ought to clear in a matter of days, I expect. The sun is low now. You'd better take a bath."

Crow wanted nothing more than a bath. She'd washed her hands in fire, and she still felt polluted. "Tamar first," she said.

"If you must. She had a jar picked out for herself—it kept crossing her thoughts. I'm not sure where she stashed it."

They searched Tamar's tree, located in a separate grove that had mostly stayed out of the machina's path. They searched storerooms and cellars, greenhouses and garden beds. They waded their way among an immense collection of carvings depicting the God of the End. At last they found what they sought near a cave kiln shaped like a hole left by a tunneling serpent.

There were plenty of similar crocks, some small enough to hold in one hand and others large enough for Magnolia to climb in without discarding her legs. Some were already in use: holding water, assorted seeds and grains, liquor, pickled radishes, fermented sauce.

"Where'd they get the material for all these pots?" Crow said.

"Must've brought it down from the mountains. Or perhaps they've got a secret well that serves as a neverending font of clay."

A few old jars were painted with spica leaves. But out of all the crocks they examined, empty or otherwise, only one had the rune for *rabbit* dashed on it with accidental-looking black glaze.

"Don't try to transfer her in with a ladle," Magnolia warned. "You'd better use magic."

Crow gritted her teeth. "Would you like to contribute?"

"She'll be in good hands with you," Magnolia said. "Teleportation, levitation, telekinesis, gravity manipulation—all outside my realm of expertise."

"You mean you can't do any of those."

"I bend minds, not the laws of physics."

In the machina's cockpit, Crow plucked her last feather. She jumped when Magnolia rubbed curiously at her exposed wing-stumps. They stuck out from her back like fleshy antennae, naked and crooked and skeletal. They retracted hurriedly to flee Magnolia's touch.

Crow's feather fell into the sunken pool of drained blood and interstitial fluid at the front of the cockpit. It dissolved. Over the next few minutes, Tamar's remains—streams of liquid, floating solids—arced soundlessly through the air, coming together inside the hefty open pickling crock that Crow had ported up to receive her.

Tamar's pendant drifted past, coated in goo, half-hidden amid a bobbing parade of teeth and knuckles. It poured itself into the pot along with the rest of her. Crow made no attempt to extract it.

After she sealed the pickling crock, nothing remained at the back of the cockpit except sullied clothing and a pair of sandals.

"Leave it," Magnolia said. "A sordid reminder. If the automagi want her rags cleaned up, they'll have to cut a deal with some other visitor."

She placed a firm hand on Crow's back. "Now, are you finally ready for your bath?"

30

Magnolia dismissed her body, saying: "I can create a cleaner one next time." She used her lack of limbs as an excuse to make Crow first wash her hair, then massage cleansing seed oil all over her face and neck, from the gleaming scar on her forehead to the curves of her ears. It gave off the same nutty scent as Tamar's cooking oil.

"I do smell edible, don't I?" Magnolia said.

"I'll dice you like a mango."

"Go back—you missed a spot. There. Below my jaw. Haven't you ever bathed anyone before?"

"Just children and the elderly."

"I've got to be the oldest of them all."

Her head lay across Crow's bare knees. Crow thought wistfully about spreading two oily fingers and poking her eyes out.

In lieu of violent eye-gouging, she reached for a leaky wooden bucket and rinsed off all the residue. Once her ministrations were deemed complete, Magnolia sank down to soak the lower half of her neck in the bath. Any onlooker might have mistaken her for a human bather submerged past her shoulders. The water sloshed when Crow climbed in, revealing stilt-like roots supporting Magnolia's head as if she were a tree in a swamp.

Crow eyed those roots sourly. "Everything you made me do, you could have done yourself."

"Fingers feel better. I have delicate skin."

"Use your own fingers next time."

"But I like being catered to."

Crow had already attacked herself with a dried-up sponge gourd outside the bath. She closed her eyes and imagined grabbing another sponge to attack Magnolia, too. Her skin would be a lot more sensitive once Crow scoured it like a burnt pan.

Immortals could get by without bathing. Crow could have rolled naked among the leaking jars in the courtyard—and, given time, the foul stench and filth would leave her even if she never washed herself with anything heavier than summer rain. If wounded, the body of an immortal would consume magic to repair itself. If soiled, the body of an immortal would consume magic for a similar purpose—to revert to a default state of cleanness.

Lose a crucial limb—like Crow's wings—and eventually it would grow back. (Magnolia had been an isolated head from the start, but she'd regrow her eyes if Crow ever found a way to mash them like potatoes.) Bathe in the blood and bitter hatred of your enemies, and eventually you'd come out looking and smelling as if you'd bathed with filtered water and high-quality soap.

But it took time to get clean. Just like how it took time to regrow a limb. Washing up like a human could offer a quicker path to relief.

On that note: a day ago, Tamar had shown them the round stone cistern where she did laundry. Before bathing, Crow went over to drop in some clothing. It immediately transformed into a turquoise whirlpool, foaming with magic.

"We're being very leisurely," Crow said in the bath. Not that she had any inclination to get out.

Magnolia flicked water at her with a sprout as green as the jade machina. "You spent all day neatening up jars full of dead-people pulp. We'll approach the automagi when we're ready to parley, and not a moment sooner."

"What are they doing now?"

"Watching us use their facilities like homesteaders watching a wild bear in their garden. They're just hoping not to get attacked."

Crow took her word for it.

They still needed to decide where to install Tamar's pot. But they wouldn't seek advice from the automagi. It didn't seem fair to let them dictate her final rites—they'd already dictated everything else in her life.

The peach-tinted pool simmered with geothermal heat. This hollowed-out grotto could have fit dozens of other bathers. Crow stretched her legs out as far as they would go. Beside her, Magnolia looked disturbingly peaceful.

The pearly stones that lined the bath radiated low-level magic like a feeble massage. Falling droplets tickled the air with tiny ripples of sound. Her feet kept bumping Magnolia's swamp-tree roots, warm as blood in the water.

It was midnight by the time Crow reluctantly left the bath. Their soak had lasted for hours. She salvaged more borrowed clothing; their laundry would need another day to hang-dry.

Magnolia hopped onto her shoulder. Crow squished her wings down to hummingbird size and shifted them forward into the groove of her collarbone, like an ingrown necklace. They'd regenerated a decent selection of feathers over the course of her bath.

Find us and save us. End us. Even if it makes you a monster.

"Tamar wasn't the only living member of her clan," she said.

If they were all part of the pickling fields, Tamar wouldn't have told Crow to go find them. If they were all dead, there was nothing Crow could do to them that would result in her becoming a monster.

She plucked Magnolia off her shoulder. "Where are they?" she asked.

"I did promise to tell you more, didn't I? You'll have to excuse me for being a little slow on the uptake. There are things it simply doesn't occur to me to share."

"And there are things you withhold out of malicious caprice."

"That, too, yes. How'd you know?" The base of her neck grew thick vines that twined like a harness around Crow's wrists.

"Just say it."

She tilted her head back in Crow's hands, looking theatrically at the sky. The viney reins attached to Crow's forearms pulled tight.

"All those stars," she said, "and none of the others feel like falling. Did I ever share my thoughts on how this valley was formed?"

"Do you need to?"

"A giant vorpal hole spawned and took a bite out of the earth. I bet Lake Fallen got carved out by one, too. A vorpal hole could be any shape—as round as a hole in a sock, or splattered like ink. There could even be chunks missing inside it."

"A hole filled with reality ... inside a hole in reality?"

The vines squeezed Crow's wrists. A nod by proxy. "Like a bagel," said Magnolia. "If my theory is right, the vorpal hole at the lake had gaps in it. Hence the islands. Anyway, back to Steppehaven. Some time after the beginning of the end of the world, all vorpal holes vanished. People descended into the basin. They carved it up. They covered every available surface in stairs. They prospered—until they destroyed themselves—and eventually the automagi moved in.”

Crow was losing patience. “What does this have to do with finding the rest of Tamar’s kin?”

“I’m getting there. This place was born from a random rift between worlds, and physical labor, and old-school human magic. These days, much of its borrowed magic stems back to that one machina. You can see the results. The laundry cistern and the bath we soaked in and the other stepwells and chemical springs all draw on unnaturally disparate sources.”

“You think I should dredge the springs?” That would be the work of days, if not weeks. She’d have to pray that Magnolia wouldn’t lose interest.

“Let’s be strategic about it. Put me back on your shoulder, would you? That’s my girl.”

Crow almost knocked her off on reflex.

Magnolia clung on, undeterred. Choking vines looped around Crow’s throat and chest and upper arms. “Look for the pools that stink more of magic than of sulfur. Look for opaque water. If you can see down to the bottom, skip it. If there are fish or turtles or other critters, skip it.”

With some concentration, Crow conjured downy feathers from the lines on her palm. They germinated like moss growing between bricks, then floated up in the air, as buoyant as milkweed fluff. They hovered around her in little flame-bright puffs, descending to illuminate the bottom of each spring and well and cistern that Magnolia told her to check.

“Not sure what we’re looking for,” Crow said, although Magnolia seemed confident whenever she declared it was time to move on to the next.

“Did Tamar talk to you about anchors?”

"For ships?"

"For the automagi, you dunce. A guillotine of the soul was used to create them. It took all those poor saps who volunteered for the experiment, and it cleaved them in two. Body and spirit. The abandoned body would eventually wither and die. But that doesn't mean they didn't need it. So the automagi used some half-immortals as fuel for their machina. Others had the honor of becoming substitute anchors. I can say from experience that it's definitely better to have a body on hand—even if you opt not to wear it."

Crow heaved herself up out of a well with machina-size steps, monumental in scale. "How does that affect our search?"

"Tamar had flickering thoughts of watery graves. Graves for the living. We'll find the anchors preserved in ... embalming fluid goes on the inside, doesn't it? So this is like reverse embalming fluid. They'll be hidden and immersed in it. Let's take a closer look at that green pool over yonder."

Crow made repeated treks up and down many stories' worth of stairs. There were wells with lower steps blanketed in slippery moss, and wells where mineral-dyed walls hinted at a higher water level in the time of the ancients. There were pools that spit scalding mud at her, and pools surrounded by graffitied rocks proclaiming undying love in obsolete alphabets.

Dawn came before she descended the shallow steps of a well that seemed cruder than the rest. It was a curving corridor hacked out of solid rock. Like walking into a mollusk shell the size of a mansion.

The stairs had expanded over time. On the left, they were an unreliable series of bony ridges. On the right, they were newer and somewhat sharper, though still beaten down by the feet of lost civilizations.

The burgeoning morning sun didn't venture far past the entrance. An incoherent whispering teemed near Crow's hips, like a memory of disembodied voices in the mountains. The automagi must be displeased—but, as Magnolia had asserted, they were too cowed or cautious to intervene.

Crow's bobbing feathers shone their light on the spiraling steps, and then on a pool of murky orange liquid that smelled intensely of frankincense. Muddled etching on the walls spoke in flowery language of how this well would bring longevity and prosperity to the worthy.

When Crow crouched at the edge of the water, Magnolia dangled down a skinny white root. She let her root sit in the pool as if idly sipping from an straw. Then she abruptly yanked it out.

"This is the one," she said. "Start dredging."

Hours later, Crow had gone nose-blind to the fragrance of frankincense. She was soaked from head to toe. Even her vision had acquired an orange tint.

She'd found eight bodies underwater. She'd counted rather more than eight automagi swirling around the valley: like the Fellshore mimid, they'd been forced to ration supplies.

A passing rain had swept through while she dredged the well. Now a broken sort of sunlight leaked down onto the bodies. When had they last lain out beneath the sky? Her mind tabulated the years. If they'd come to Steppehaven together with Tamar—if they'd known Crow by name—

"They spent less time submerged than you spent on that altar," Magnolia said softly.

They weren't breathing in any noticeable way. Out of eight people, Crow detected only one heartbeat. Their skin had a texture like seaweed. They were hairless, for the most part, and had the bloated look of raisins soaked in wine.

Yet they were undeniably alive. All eight cores still brimmed with magic, undimmed by decades outside the cycle of day and night, drowned out of sight, forgotten by everyone in the world except Tamar. And the automagi. Magic tethered them to the automagi—it kept them nominally in the realm of the living.

End us. Even if it makes you a monster.

They would die slowly if Crow left them to shrivel in the sun. They would die faster if she savaged the bodies herself, or if she severed the magic tying them to their ethereal masters.

She'd killed core-carrying humans without becoming a monster. But only under the direction of a promised companion. The sole exception was the hunter she'd beheaded in Magnolia's hills. She'd been straining against Magnolia's orders. It had all unfolded too fast for her eyes to go to his core.

Would she be able to suppress the core-reaping reflex with willpower alone? Outside combat? Without the protection of an existing promise? It might happen regardless of her intent—like swallowing something forced to the very back of her throat.

She wouldn't know unless she tried. If she tried and failed, she would be remade as a monster. These bodies were not capable of exchanging a conscious promise with anyone. But Tamar hadn't liquefied herself so Crow could toss the last living halves out to be picked apart by animal scavengers.

The eight bodies were clad in a matrix of impoverished threads. Nothing that could reasonably be called solid cloth. That orange fluid might have preserved their flesh, but it ate away at everything else. Like their hair, their fingernails and toenails had all but dissolved.

"Right," Magnolia said briskly. "I'll do it."

Crow grabbed her by the hair. She pried Magnolia off her back as if pulling a starfish off a rock. She realized belatedly that she was holding Magnolia like a trophy from an enemy army—and, remarkably, that Magnolia had yet to start complaining.

"Tamar told me to end them," Crow said. "She told me to do it myself."

"Did she use those exact words? Didn't think so. Put me up there," Magnolia ordered.

Crow dropped her on a mountain of ritual clay bowls by the stepwell entrance. "She said to end them, even if it makes me a monster."

"She's dead, and she didn't even give you her core. She just up and died at the back of that machina. You don't owe her anything. This would be a very foolish reason to fall from sainthood."

"You wanted me to become a monster."

Magnolia flapped her roots in exasperation. The pile of bowls rattled beneath her. "Not out of obligation to a woman who currently exists as human soup in a pot for pickles! She gave up her right to have input. Anyway, I don't need to convince you of anything. I give the orders here. Stop trying to steal these cores out from under my nose."

Those words of command sewed Crow's frankincense-anointed feet to the ground. Her breath petered out as if she were trying to blend in with the orange-stained half-immortals. The sun warmed them. Could they feel it?

She watched a monster harvest living cores from eight unresisting victims, and she did nothing to stop it.

31

THE EIGHT CORPSES would have been difficult to squeeze into storage pots. Frail and elderly though they seemed, every single one was substantially taller than Crow. As if they'd been loosened and expanded by their time in the water.

No, they wouldn't fit in any available crocks—not without judicious dismembering. Crow had been thinking of building a pyre.

But there was nothing left to burn.

Enthroned atop her heap of bowls, Magnolia sent a forest of roots racing toward the salvaged bodies. Loose bowls tumbled to rest at Crow's feet. The roots were prolific and dense and powerful, so ancient-looking that in comparison Magnolia's head appeared unimportant, a strange vestigial burl. Anyone would have thought that her real self was a ravenous tree.

Eight brilliant cores went shooting along those roots as if suctioned up pneumatic tubes. Each core disappeared in the maw under Magnolia's neck. Crow's consciousness tracked their movement like a circling hawk.

Yet she failed to see what happened to the bodies. They were there, drowned by plundering roots, and then they were gone, leaving only a lingering scented dampness on the ground. A shadow fell across her mind, a shadow like a throng of aerials covering up the sky.

When Crow's head cleared, all the roots were gone, too. Magnolia rested at a slight angle atop the now-sagging pile of bowls, which had begun to cave in like a collapsing volcano. Her eyes were no lighter than before, but the sun seemed to shine right through them, rays reaching to the bottom of a crimson well.

"Would you rather stop being a saint?" she asked bluntly. "Can't blame you for being tempted."

Crow shook herself as if she were trying to get water out of her ears.

"Life would be easier if you fell from grace. If that's what you want—for yourself, not for Tamar—you should say so. I can read your mind, but it's incredibly difficult to decipher your actual desires. Too much noise."

"I want..." Crow began.

"Yes?"

"I want to get what we originally came for. A route to the end of the world."

"Very well," Magnolia said grandly. "Leave the bargaining to me."

She made Crow lay out a few strategic clay bowls, as if an alluring empty vessel could snag the disembodied automagi like flies on flypaper. (Their favored jars were all in smithereens.)

The automagi did come when she called. They came, and they lurked like sullen globs of mist in the waiting bowls. Occasionally the illusion of faces appeared in the haze. They bore more of a resemblance to gloomy catfish than to anything human.

Magnolia said: "Give us our path to the physical end of the world.

Tell us how to get there, and we'll put your machina right back where it belongs. After that—once we're ready to go, we'll leave you in peace. What more could you ask?"

Crow didn't hear their answer. The rest of the conversation was mind-to-mind. Apparently they knew they had little room to negotiate.

"They recommend heading north," Magnolia told her. The automagi had ungraciously dispersed. "Rather far north. At least it isn't all cold. We might stumble across a tropical oasis or two, if we're lucky."

"That's all you talked about?"

"I also learned that they call their machina Flytrap."

"A small name for a big machine," Crow said.

"Oh, and they claimed they only took the most decrepit half-immortals. Whether for fuel or for anchors. They took those who were practically already dead. They compared it to harvesting cores at the end of your companions' lives."

Crow scrutinized her orange-dyed nails. The automagi would not say things just for the sake of being provocative. That was the truth of how they saw it.

Magnolia wasn't done yet. "The half-immortals were tired. They'd left behind the outside world and its horrors, but they could never forget it. The automagi considered them willing participants—at least as willing as your companions. Tamar disagreed."

"That's one way to put it," Crow muttered.

"The automagi plucked away everyone she loved, one by one. Not time, not sickness, not grief. It was all the automagi, the gods of this place. They reaped the other half-immortals until no one remained. The real question for Tamar was if those sleeping anchors were even sleeping at all. Did they dream, like the people of Fellshore? Were they lonely? Did they suffer? They wouldn't have been capable of crying for help.

"The automagi were just doing their job as they always have, perpetuating themselves and their immeasurable knowledge. They never violated their own code. Tamar, for her part, was well within her rights to fight back. But I'll never forgive her for stealing you."

During Magnolia's discussion with the automagi, Crow had stood off to one side like a guard on duty at a ballroom. She ran her fingers through her hair. It had dried stiffly after repeated dives to the bottom of the hidden well.

Magnolia had faced them as a bodiless head. She and Crow had the upper hand: no need for humble disguises. She'd made Crow drag over a tall slab of rock for her, so she could look down her nose at the automagi cupped in their unglazed bowls. She remained on her makeshift dais well after they departed, holding forth like a political speaker in a public square.

Crow inserted herself deftly into the split-second divide between one sentence and the next. "How do we keep our end of the bargain?"

"Bargain? You mean the part about putting their machina back? They already gave us what we wanted. Let's skip town."

"They gave us what we wanted," Crow repeated. "We should do as we said."

"Tamar wouldn't mind, would she? She'd tell us to punish them."

Debate had never been Crow's strength. She couldn't cobble together arguments about rightness and wrongness. She knew how she felt: no more, no less. She could think of reasons to explain it, but the reasons came after the gut reaction, and they always seemed somewhat contrived.

She rubbed her forehead. "You gave them our word," she said ineffectually.

She'd lied and gone back on oaths plenty of times in her life, usually at the prompting of a sworn companion. Nothing about being a saint required unswerving honesty.

Maybe, if they kept their promise, the haven would start to recover. Maybe it could return to some semblance of how it had been before the machina chewed up Tamar, and Magnolia guzzled down eight comatose half-immortals.

"It wasn't exactly heaven on earth," Magnolia said. "Tamar's mask made her a collaborator. When the machina juiced her brethren, she scraped their remains into jars. She got down on her hands and knees to scrub the cockpit. She carted each sealed urn over to that field in the sun.

"How would you feel if the automagi trapped a monster to feed to the machina? They did try that once or twice. I asked. They sealed a monster in their Flytrap and let it die and regenerate and die and regenerate over the course of many years, until the larva that crawled out of the cocoon was weaker than a human infant. Then they discarded it. Not quite a perpetual motion machine—but it helped tide them over in eras when no new half-immortal clans came seeking refuge. Would you like them to do that again with a different monster, or perhaps a saint? Or me? You'd love to see me installed in that cage of bone, wouldn't you."

Crow collected the clay bowls where the automagi had puddled themselves like supplicants to a tyrant. "Let's just put the machina underground," she said. "One day we'll—one day I'll come back here. If I meet another Tamar—"

"Then you'll destroy the automagi?"

"Yes."

"She wasn't the first of her kind. But all right. Your stomach turns at the thought of annihilating their millennia of remembered history, does it? Go back over to Flytrap, then."

Crow walked, opting to conserve her magic for the task ahead. Her wings—still in hummingbird form—beat nervously against the front of her neck. Magnolia strapped herself on like a misshapen backpack, suspended from a network of painfully knobby roots, facing outward so as not to smother her nose in Crow's spine.

Flytrap glistened with scattered remnants of morning rain. That wetness made it look less mechanical; it could have been a sky-high mutated succulent.

"Not all machina work the same way. But for this model, at least, someone's got to get stabbed at the back of the cockpit." Since she was pointing away from Crow, Magnolia had to raise her voice to be heard. "I'm not volunteering."

"We could switch roles," Crow suggested.

It struck her that Magnolia might actually be a genius pilot. She could flexibly manipulate numerous tentacles. She was accustomed to wearing her body like an accessory. She was gifted at controlling others—mortal, immortal, and everything in between. Flytrap was not a living being that she could push around with words, but she might find it laughably easy to merge her mind with a machine.

Magnolia swung around to the front, griping as she collided with Crow's chest along the way. "I'm not volunteering you to get stabbed, either. Use magic to move it. Like bending the legs of a child's doll."

"A very large doll," Crow said. Her tiny wings fluttered inadequately.

"This would've been a breeze if you'd swallowed those cores."

"You forbade it."

"All I'm saying is that in another world, if you'd taken them, you'd be throbbing with power right about now. You'll just have to make do with your magic in its current state. Half-recovered—at best. Too bad."

Magnolia would grow bored of needling her if she ignored it. Crow went to speak with the automagi instead: she wanted to know if they could lend her a mirror.

The only ones they could offer were made of obsidian or polished bronze. Heirlooms that vastly predated even the beginning of the end of the world. The bronze mirrors were hopelessly tarnished. The obsidian mirrors had retained more reflectivity, but showed an image too dim to be useful.

Magnolia cheerfully informed the automagi that Crow might lose her temper. "She wants to move Flytrap for *your* sake. Fail to offer the bare minimum of good-natured assistance, and what do you think will happen? She'll throw her hands up, climb back in the machina, and finish the job she started yesterday. I, for one, wouldn't mind seeing this entire valley in shambles.

"Don't doubt me, now—she may look outwardly placid, like a water buffalo content to graze in her own little pasture, but she's quite wild at heart. She's not the same as you and me. We all were born or reborn from human beings, whether naturally or artificially. Come to think of it, you're almost like fake returners ... it's just that your original bodies kept lingering on as meaty anchors.

"One way or another, I was human in my past life, and you lot were human in yours. On some level, we understand each other. What about Saint Crow? She looks human enough, but she used to be an aerial. You don't understand her nearly as much as you think. Who's to say what might drive an aerial to true raging destruction? If I were you, I'd be as cooperative as possible. If I were you, I'd play it safe."

Much as Magnolia relished giving this speech, it had probably been unnecessary. The automagi were quick to tell Crow which of their bronze mirrors she could attempt to buff. They supplied recipes for compounds to rub off the tarnish, too. A rough paste of flour, salt, and vinegar; a finer mix of powdered stone and precious clove oil.

Though large for a handheld mirror, it would still be inconveniently small for Crow's purposes. At least the limited surface area meant that it wouldn't take long to polish.

It was mid-afternoon when she passed the mirror to Magnolia and asked her hold it.

Then, some distance from Flytrap, Crow did a handstand.

"I was too fascinated by your new career as an antiques restorer to question any of this," Magnolia said. "What are you doing?"

"Looking in the mirror at the machina."

"I can see that. Why are you doing it upside down?"

"My magic—" Something about being inverted made it difficult to speak coherently. "I'm better at moving myself around. Porting and flying and such. Than moving other things. Helps to view it from a different angle."

"You had no problem levitating your feather-sword when you first fought me." Magnolia sounded baffled.

"That's different. That's part of me. Like how you have no trouble moving your vines."

Said vines dutifully tilted the bronze mirror at just the right angle to show the looming machina. Magnolia kept this up for about half an hour before she set the mirror down with a gentle clink.

"You've consistently made the machina move in the wrong direction," she said. "It's almost impressive. Are you telling me things would be worse if you went right-side up?"

"Maybe not," Crow allowed. "Let's—"

"Let's try something else. Get down from that handstand. Good. Now hold me up—yes, higher—and open your mouth. I'll give you the gift I gave Dung. Might function as a sort of stimulant. See the dew beading up along the rim of my neck? Catch it all—don't you dare let it spill."

Crow caught three drops on her tongue. The fourth hit her chin. She lowered Magnolia (who frowned darkly) and swiped the last drip off with her knuckles. The dew tasted like sweet watery sap. There was magic in it, but it wouldn't do much for anyone who was already immortal.

"Your wings are still growing back," Magnolia said, "but I can't see why you're so reluctant to flaunt your power. It's not like you have any hope of concealing your abilities from me, of all beings. Here's a tip: hop on that machina's back. Like me going for a ride on your shoulder. Face the way its head faces, and move that body as if it's part of you. Pretend you're walking on stilts." Her voice deepened. "Go get it done, and make it look easy."

Crow's stomach muscles rippled as if liquefied by an electric shock. That jolt went all the way out to the tips of her fingers and toes, and kept going. The valley and the sky and the whole world felt extraordinarily large. Magnolia's dictates left no room for choice. Yet some essential part of her responded like witless leaves reaching for sunlight, like a dumb animal following the smell of food.

If Magnolia had ever fed her a stimulant, it was this, the phantom shiver when a true order kicked in. In its own way, it was as good as eating a core. Good enough to make her despair. Each mindless taste of magical ecstasy would dull future attempts to escape. Even after taking Tamar as her companion—when she tried to flatten Magnolia beneath the machina's implacable hand, had she really been fighting with all her strength?

Her blood vibrated. She ported to the machina's shoulder. She coaxed it back into its underground grave without trampling any undamaged parts of the haven. She restored the machina's roof of stone, hiding it from the bottomless blue sky above, and she made it look easy.

32

Magnolia wanted to pack up before they left.

"Pack what?" Crow said.

"You'll see."

"Tamar comes first."

"Who gives the orders around here?" Magnolia asked, but she went along with it.

After putting the machina back, Crow tended to the most precariously fallen stone trees, and other unstable-looking rubble. This would not be her first time leaving irreparable scars on a site of historical value, but she hoped it might be the last. At least for a while.

They brought Tamar's pot to what appeared to be the newest end of the pickling field. (They determined this after much argument, and a scrupulous examination of the other crocks.) The breeze was still hot, with no hints of fall. Crow held Magnolia up one-handed, like a tea shop server with a tray.

She kept inhaling illusory whiffs of frankincense—or something more sinister that ably mimicked its scent. The courtyard was devoid of the fouler smells that had stained it earlier, before she washed it with fire.

"We can hang an inverted candle for her tonight," Magnolia said. "What else do people do at a funeral?"

Crow repeated the question back at her. "You lived an entire human life. I've lived with humans and halves, but I've never been one."

"*An entire life* would be a generous way to describe it," Magnolia said under her breath. "Trust me—following the ways of my people would not result in giving her a dignified send-off."

"Some funerals are held in silence," said Crow.

"Easy for you, difficult for me. Fine. Let's give it a try."

Magnolia grew roots into the shape of a sturdy staff, as she had at Fellshore, so Crow could lower her hands. Side by side, they gazed at Tamar's pickling crock, and at the regularly spaced rows of other crocks filling the palatial courtyard. *Rabbit. Rabbit. Rabbit.*

Each sniff of frankincense was like the taste of an old meal creeping back up Crow's throat. She pictured the cavernous well filled with a liquid like carrot soup. The worn curving stairs untouched by wind and light and rain.

This courtyard was one of the least sheltered parts of the basin. No hollow trees or shady arched corridors or eroded monuments on plinths or old stone walls built atop a foundation of even older buildings. Maybe Tamar had kept all these pots out beneath the open sky because she knew other halves wallowed—not yet dead—at the bottom of a lightless well.

"Did Tamar know your story?" Magnolia had succeeded at holding her tongue for a grand total of ten minutes.

"My what?" said Crow. She had not been primed to listen.

"About what happened after you fell to earth as an aerial. About being a returner."

"Not unless the automagi deemed it worth sharing."

The middle portion of Magnolia's wooden staff twisted, creaking dramatically, like a neck being wrung. She switched her focus from the graveyard of crocks to Crow.

"You haven't told me, either," she said.

"You already learned everything from the land back in Fellshore."

"You are you, and the land is the land. Different perspectives."

"Will you force me to tell you?" Crow asked. The words did not come easily. The breeze had quieted, as if fearful of interrupting, and the blasted blue sky was horribly devoid of aerials.

Magnolia met her eyes. "If I did, you would relate your story as fluently as a bard, and you'd be flushed with pleasure the whole time. You know it. You would love it, until you finished, and then you'd be disgusted, and you'd train yourself not to look at me for the next couple months.

"No, I won't force you to tell me. Not about your aerial life, and not about your Arion. I'm familiar with the basics of that one, too. You made an entire countryside town evacuate before the two of you fought the Singular Horde. They weren't eager to go. You terrorized them out of their homes. As a result—during that last awakening, the Horde claimed fewer victims than at any other time in written history."

"It wasn't the Horde's last awakening," Crow said with difficulty, although she would have been better off not speaking at all.

"Oh?"

"A fragment escaped."

These were words she had never uttered to any human.

She would have pursued the fragmented Horde, but Arion was dead. She'd been right there, and still the Horde had breached her protection.

The Horde had taken his core.

If she'd chased the last surviving element of the Singular Horde, if she'd massacred it and swallowed its collective core—she might have returned to find Arion's body already half-eaten by wild animals. The Horde was very desperate, and the Horde was very fast, and the Horde was supremely good at survival.

Arion's body was just a body. She had seen and touched and created many similar carcasses, mortal and immortal, human and animal. If he could speak, he would have told her to forget him. He would have ordered her to go after the fleeing Horde.

Would his mother before him have told Crow the same thing? His mother, too, had once been Crow's promised companion. If she'd been the one lying there, she would've ordered Crow to leave her. But would she have ordered Crow to abandon her son?

It was just a body, twenty-two years old, and one day it would decay to nothingness no matter what Crow did. It was also everything Arion had ever been or ever would be. Crow could fight the Singular Horde a thousand more times before permanently putting it down, if she wished. But she couldn't ever take Arion's fallen body in her arms again.

His real mother was gone. He had no family left to hold him precious above all else, above justice and glory and doing the right thing and slaying monsters. He had traveled too much to make true lasting friends—though, in every settlement they stopped at, people loved him and remembered his face. She'd watched with pride and wonder at how effortlessly he moved among strangers. He had never grown old enough to fear them.

Here in this scorched and evacuated land, he had only Crow. It had to be her. She needed to stay with his body before the world took it and chewed it up. She needed to stay, no matter the cost.

She couldn't leave him—not him—to the mouths of carrion beasts.

Magnolia murmured something, a statement or question that slid between Crow's ribs like a knife. Jarred back to the present, she clapped a hand to her head as if she could physically stop memories from dribbling out to betray her. In a different corner of her mind, she perceived herself from the viewpoint of a passing bird, clutching her own skull, and she knew just how foolish she looked, and how futile it all was.

"He was renowned," Magnolia said, "for a time. You two became known as the heroes who exterminated the Singular Horde—the periodic scourge of humanity. Starting about forty years ago, all the hunters who came to me knew Arion's name."

"That won't last."

"Not forever, no. And none of them realized that a portion of the Horde slipped away from you." The staff creaked again, though it didn't look like she'd moved. "I do understand why you never mentioned it. You don't want to sully Arion's name. You won't taint the memory of the feat he died for. Besides, the Horde has shown no sign of coming back yet. It used to reemerge every thirty years or so. After the near-fatal damage you dealt out, it'd take twice that long to get in shape to swarm again.

"A severely wounded Horde would pose no threat to humans. It would devote all its scant resources to burrowing underground, licking its wounds, rebuilding its forces, undetectable to those on the surface. You must've been hoping to track down any remnants before its next emergence."

"The trail died out," Crow said. Confessions were always like an avalanche, the weight of one all too easily bringing down the next. "I never found the last of the Horde."

Magnolia rotated slowly atop her staff, as if swiveling on a barstool. "At your most optimistic, you'd have to assume that another immortal came across the Horde in its weakened state and destroyed it. An opportunistic passing monster, or a vigilant saint. The alternative would be to think that a human slayer gave it an impermanent death, not knowing what they fought. Or that it tunneled so deep and hid so effectively as to eliminate all hope of discovering it before its resurgence.

"You ran out of places to search. You gave up on hunting down the elusive last scrap of the Singular Horde. You turned your sights on me instead. And I'm glad of it."

She seemed about to continue, but they'd both heard growling. She spun at the top of her staff like an owl looking backwards.

Crow swiftly turned, too, and stepped in front of her just before a furious dire fox sprang at them. Any human would have been bowled over. It was like getting rammed by a full-grown bull. Crow held her ground, but the fox's jaw closed on her forearm.

"Tell me to—subdue it—without hurting it," she squeezed out. Bones crunched. Her shoulder guttered in its socket. "Tell me to—"

"Quiet!" Magnolia snapped. A second later, her voice crawled up from the ground like a thicket of invasive vines. "Pothos, you stupid animal, release my Crow before she vaporizes you."

The jaws came open. Crow shuddered. The fox backed off jerkily, unwillingly, its mouth discolored with inky blood.

"You don't have to like us," Magnolia continued, "but you will respect the fact that Tamar knew what she was doing. If you're going to wage war on anyone, go fight the archivists."

Pothos let out a piercing whine that threatened to tip over into a full-blown scream. With her uninjured arm, Crow seized Magnolia's staff and stepped hastily out of the way, striving not to drip blood on nearby jars.

"If you don't hurt us, then we won't hurt you," Magnolia said. "She's all yours."

Little by little, side-eying them all the while, Pothos crept up to the crock that held Tamar's remains. Her white tails and paws were dingier than before, and she gave off a much gamier scent. Crow hadn't noticed any animal prints while fixing cracked jars and cleaning the courtyard— but then, she hadn't been looking.

Pothos paced several circles around Tamar's pot with vulpine delicacy. She touched her black nose to the bold glazed rune. After her examination was complete, she folded herself up on the flagstones, tails fanned out like a warning, snout resting on her front paws, eyes fixed on Crow and Magnolia.

"Stay or leave, as you please," Magnolia told her. "We'll be going soon enough. You don't have a core—the automagi won't interfere with you. Unless they get really desperate. Which I suppose is entirely possible. I'll warn them not to use you as anything, not even as fuel for their machine. Keep an eye out, just in case, and maybe spend a little more time outside the basin."

Pothos growled again.

"Up to you," Magnolia said. "Tamar won't be going anywhere. She's all used up—the automagi won't touch her. Unlike some of us, they won't be cruel for cruelty's sake. So, barring any natural disasters, her grave will be safe. Go sleep in her tree if you want to feel her presence. We left it unchanged."

Pothos lay there without moving while Crow—living staff in hand—walked slowly out of sight.

33

Several nights in a row, they lit hanging candles around Tamar's grove. They gave Pothos space; no more biting ensued.

Crow's injury healed quickly enough, but they weren't yet ready to leave. Magnolia insisted on packing a cart full of plundered supplies.

"Get a harness, too," she said. "So we can hook it up to Dung."

Crow was still stuck on the notion of needing supplies. "Supplies for what?"

"What do humans need in the wilderness?"

"That depends on the wilderness, and the season. And the human."

Magnolia cast her eyes at the upper edge of the basin. "It'll be hereabouts. The season: now. The human—we'll get to that later."

"Are you planning to kidnap someone?"

"Other than you? No."

"Are you planning to start a human farm on the side of a mountain?"

"No," Magnolia said, "so don't make any dramatic declarations about how you'll wrap your arms around me and walk into the deepest trenches of the farthest sea before you let yourself be used as a tool for the systematic cultivation of human livestock." She paused. "I was hoping to surprise you."

"We very recently talked about not concealing vital information."

Magnolia laughed. "Oh, Carrie. You're starting to sound like me. That's the final fate of any two beings who spend too much time together. Voices meld."

"The mimid," Crow ground out. "Tamar's mask. If it's something like that—"

"Not quite."

They'd entered a hollow tree near where Tamar used to live. For Pothos's sake, they left Tamar's room untouched—and, for the time being, still soaked through with her scent.

This other tree must have been unoccupied for years. There were musty chests packed with blankets, and knee-high jars of brown liquor with round fruit steeping at the bottom. No, not just fruit—coiled snakes and lizards, too. Furry grey dust grew everywhere, as soft and thick as moss. Magnolia kept coughing, but she pulled out a few articles of clothing that she deemed appealing enough to merit a wash.

While Magnolia (having assumed human form) tried on various outfits, Crow cut and stitched shirts to make slits for her wings.

"You really are quite domestic," Magnolia said.

"Don't get distracted."

At the moment, Magnolia had on a simple wrap over loose trousers—a style that could almost be called timeless, given its recurrence in multiple eras. She undid the sash and shrugged the top off her shoulders.

"I have a hunch that we might meet someone in the woods."

Crow pushed her needle through fabric. "Someone who needs food. And fluids. And shelter."

"Most likely."

"You don't know who?"

"I have certain suspicions," Magnolia replied, "but it would be extremely embarrassing if I'm wrong." She made a bundle of clothes and swung it as if wielding a slingshot. Dust puffed out like fine-ground flour. "If I'm right, it's someone who has nothing to do with Steppehaven, or Fellshore, or my hills, or your past companions. Remember that falling star? Remember how slowly it descended?"

"That wasn't an aerial," Crow said. "I know how aerials fall."

"No. Although it would have been very poetic if we discovered a fallen aerial and nursed it back to health. Or killed it, I suppose, to end its suffering. That star we watched together—I think it was human. It didn't fall far from here, either. As we set off north, we can take a few extra days to track them down. A saint wouldn't leave a mortal to die of starvation in the wild reaches between settlements. Right?"

Crow couldn't argue otherwise. But this didn't make the cart-packing project seem any less like some manner of devious trap.

"How many days of rations should we bring?" she asked. "How much drinking water?"

"Are you any good with magic for collapsing big things into small spaces? Other than your wings, I mean. If not, then pack however much fits. We'll make do. Of course, whatever we don't take will just sit here and rot, and Dung is stronger than you think. So no need to hold back—pile it on."

Crow's wings twinged as if she'd pulled a muscle. She'd overworked herself while rehabilitating the smashed-up haven.

It was a relief to take on tasks that involved no use of magic. She hauled barrels and jars and sacks over to Tamar's cart with her arms alone. Even unloaded, the cart was too heavy to imagine a half-human woman pulling it around by herself.

She wondered vaguely where Tamar pastured her pack animals.

"They might live out by the foot of the mountains," suggested Magnolia, who had put herself in charge of spectating Crow's labor. "They're probably half-feral, or at least self-sufficient. Or maybe Pothos loved her enough to play at being a draft horse. Or the automagi lent her magic oil to grease the wheels. Her cart could've flown along like the wind, pulling itself."

"She needed a way to get it past all those stairs." Crow indicated the towering wall of the basin. The diamond shapes formed by rising and falling steps resembled a jagged pattern of scales.

"Ah—there's an elevator."

"...Really?"

"Let me know once you're done packing," Magnolia said smugly.

As she worked, Crow speculated about what kind of person would fall from the sky. Human mages and airships were both long extinct—as much the stuff of legend as the machina that littered the land, feared and untouched. In the absence of mages, she couldn't conceive of any human figuring out a way to ride aerials, either.

The elevator turned out to be a round porting platform covered in scuffed runes. The cart fit on it like a prop on a revolving stage.

"It was powered by animal sacrifice," said Magnolia. "See all those rusty cages? The automagi used to have quite a menagerie. Like the ambrosia hares that Tamar released."

She joked darkly about sacrificing the animal nearest at hand: Pothos. Crow, pretending not to hear her, fed a little magic to the device. Then a little blood, for good measure. It wrenched sideways as if gearing up to rotate. They and the cart found themselves instantly transported to a similar platform out above the rim of the basin.

The matching platform was sunken in soft ground, almost completely hidden by silky grass. There were hardly any roads or trails out here. A thorough archaeological inspection of the landscape would reveal old traces, of course, but they had long ago lapsed into disrepair.

The automagi, increasingly eager to see them off, had bestowed them with magical cart wheels capable of churning across uneven ground and through thick untamed brush. Just stay away from bogs, they warned. Magnolia had thanked them sweetly. She'd also made Crow anoint the wheels with her dew. She saw it as a kind of magical panacea, or at least a good luck charm.

The last time they visited the pickling fields, Pothos was still there in the same spot, haunting Tamar's crock. She snarled at them under her breath.

Day after day, they'd placed food and water near her as if leaving offerings at a shrine to the God of the End. She wouldn't touch any of it while they watched, but each time, they returned to find empty bowls. At first she took only a little and overturned the rest—then, later on, she ate all of it.

At the lip of the valley, surrounded by mountains, Magnolia planted her head on one of the wooden crates strapped to the cart. A few grayish roots snaked out from under her neck.

Crow, meanwhile, focused on shrinking her wings and hiding them in gill-like flaps of skin beneath her clothes. Magnolia was still acting coy about the human star. Whatever came next, it might behoove Crow to conceal her distinguishing features, like Magnolia putting on a body to meet the automagi.

"You never recognized that fox's name?" Magnolia said.

"Pothos?"

"Tamar named her after another half-immortal. One who helped raise her. One who came with you on the desperate march to reach Steppe-haven. Tamar was testing to see if you remembered."

Crow didn't. Not with any specificity.

She'd recalled Tamar in more detail (after a couple conversations jogged her memory) because Tamar had been a child, and children needed to be watched. Who better to keep an eye out than Crow? She was faster and stronger than the rest, and above all, she could function without sleep. The other half-immortals cut into their own rations so Tamar would never go hungry.

She'd been extremely quiet, so quiet that she'd disappear without warning if you glanced away for half a second. With all the food and love the other halves showered on her, she had more than enough energy to toddle off and hide inside rotting logs, to shove bugs in her mouth and in the communal pot of soup, to stumble down toward deep rocky streams as if she were making a concerted effort to bash her head in and drown.

Already half-filled with shadow, the Steppehaven basin looked like an intricate diorama. Magnolia hummed as they waited for Dung to heed her call.

They spoke briefly of the automagi. "They'll survive this," said Magnolia. "After all, they're experts in preservation. They've gone long stretches without physical anchors in the past—although it'll make them fade faster. You're more worried about Pothos, aren't you?"

Crow nodded.

"Then you'll be glad to know that in the wild, dire foxes spend most of their lives in noble solitude. She was made for this."

Was Pothos still a wild creature, though? Had she ever been a wild creature like any other, or did her rumored immortal heritage set her apart? Crow herself had once been a mortal animal, patrolling a vast territory in the sky. But it was extraordinarily difficult to remember what that had really been like, or to imagine going back to it.

"If the Singular Horde has another awakening, would you let me go fight it?" she asked.

"It's only been forty years since you and your Arion culled nearly the entire Horde, no? We'll reach the end of the world first. I guarantee it."

"If the Singular Horde shows up tomorrow—"

"I'll tell you to terminate it." Magnolia's roots swished along the bottom of the cart. "But you'll have to give me its core."

The cart creaked, though Dung hadn't come yet, and they hadn't lurched forward. Crow's compressed wings beat involuntarily beneath her skin. The Horde had swallowed Arion's core. Part of Arion—the last remaining part of Arion, sublimated beyond recognition—now belonged to a monster's store of magic. She pictured Magnolia's lips opening to take in the conquered core of the Singular Horde, her tongue as red as her eyes, raw with desire—

Crow might mind. Crow might mind terribly. Such indignity, for Arion's essence to be passed from Adversary to Adversary, from one apex monster to another. But Arion himself wouldn't have cared one whit. He would have wanted Crow to finish killing the Horde forty years ago.

"Fine," she said harshly.

Wind touched the ends of Magnolia's hair. "Such agony over a hypothetical question." She spoke with a tinge of bemusement. "Why do you torment yourself like this? That's my job. Believe me, Carrie, you won't need to worry about the Singular Horde for a long time to come."

After that, Crow occupied herself by contemplating the ponderous journey north. Originally they'd traveled southwest to reach Fellshore, and they'd come a long way. Steppehaven lay even farther from the village of beetle tea and radishes.

From here they'd have to loop around, northward and eastward, going up past Magnolia's hills again. And much further, onward to places that a human party would take years to traverse, stopping and starting, stalled during apocalyptic seasons of torrential wildfire or endless snow. Not to mention the deadly migratory volcanoes, which had reawakened en masse over the past millennium—as if in celebration of the world's otherwise slow and quiet death.

They would reach the northern end of the world, and then Magnolia would let her go. Or she would go back on her promise; she'd ask Crow to first complete other impossible tasks. She'd chuckle wryly at her own audacity. She'd rattle off some convoluted line of reasoning to justify her latest act of betrayal.

If it came to that, Crow would find a way to fling both of them off the edge of the world and into oblivion. She would take Magnolia with her, either to permanent exile or death beyond any hope of return.

She didn't care if anyone heard these thoughts. Magnolia was not infallible. She made mistakes—most often due to arrogance. She would do it again, sooner or later, and Crow would be ready. Refusing to release Crow would prove to be the worst mistake of her life.

Part Four

A Saint and a Devil

34

Dung balked at the sight of the cart. He seemed to blame its presence on Crow. Magnolia circled him with budding green tentacles, murmuring soothing nonsense, until he let Crow fit the harness around his chest and back. She struggled: the straps were configured for an animal with different anatomy.

Luckily, they didn't need to use reins. Dung would heed Magnolia's commands.

Despite the magic-greased wheels beneath them, the lack of well-kept trails made for a rocky ride. Wherever she went, Tamar would probably have gotten out and walked most of the way alongside her beast. Dung, however, was capable of chugging along faster than anyone would consider safe for a vehicle of this nature, even with both Crow and Magnolia adding their weight to the supplies piled out back.

Sometimes Magnolia made it even worse by donning her body, despite the limited space available, and the fact that the cart was not at all conducive to humanoid comfort. She would wear a loosely tied shirt (if even that) and stretch her legs out at just the right angle to jab Crow in the diaphragm. Once Crow moved to flick away a pitch-black ladybug, and instead found herself picking at a mole on Magnolia's thigh.

Sitting in the cart left her with a lot of time to fill. More so than when she jogged beside it, or when they'd ridden Dung together without a saddle. If Magnolia stopped talking for long enough, scattered thoughts would leave Crow's lips as though sucked out by the vacuum of unaccustomed silence.

That was how she found herself discussing the inborn compulsions of monsters. Land-bound monsters, like Magnolia before Crow freed her. Time-bound monsters, like the Singular Horde with its alternating intervals of dormancy and ravenous reemergence. Magnolia criticized its lack of precision; most time-bound monsters adhered to an exacting schedule. But the Horde had never taken more than half a century to go on the attack again.

Other odd compulsions resisted easy categorization—like the mimid's need to maintain the outward appearance of a functioning settlement. Magnolia had acquired many curious stories by plundering the minds of unfortunate hunters. There were monsters who would only attack people wearing blue, and monsters who became active only during specific hours of the night.

"It's like a tooth that can be pulled," Magnolia said. "It's like a shackle that can be broken. Only we immortals can free each other from our native compulsions. Similarly—only we immortals can sentence each other to an everlasting death. But we can't free ourselves on our own, and we can't kill ourselves on our own. Those are services we can only perform for our peers."

She leaned forward. Her lazily closed top fluttered in gusts of sun-heated wind, threatening to come undone. "If you think about it, compulsions are the only factor that might motivate immortals to cooperate. We don't reproduce—at least not under ordinary circumstances, and certainly not with each other. We don't have families or any other sort of kinship group. In every other way, we're mutual competition from birth to death. And the ability to lift one another's compulsions clearly hasn't been enough to make us form a civil society. Most of us live with our compulsions, sometimes without ever comprehending their true parameters. Only a lucky few ever get freed."

"Such as yourself."

"Such as myself," Magnolia agreed cheerily. "And yet you still claim you don't have a compulsion."

"Not that I know of."

"Wouldn't you feel it? Wouldn't you chafe against it? No ... perhaps you wouldn't. Perhaps the Singular Horde never thought of its periodic dormancy as a type of restriction. Maybe, each time its compulsion kicked in, it just started getting sleepy—and behaved accordingly."

Crow shrugged. The jolting cart made her insides feel like a tankard getting sloshed around a tavern. "Maybe mine was removed long ago. But I don't think saints are saddled with the same sort of compulsions as monsters. Ever heard of a land-bound saint?"

"Or saints are just too stuck-up to talk about it. Or they tend to be so immersed in human civilization that they know little of their own nature as immortals."

The cart rattled past a scattering of trees with bark the pale powdery green of aged copper. The sky resembled marbled paper, a vertiginous fractal of bruised red and gray and violet and gold. Crow thought she smelled wildflowers, then realized it was just Magnolia.

Early the following day, Magnolia made them stop at a wild pawpaw patch. She picked a few off the ground while Crow floated up to gather an armful of yellow-green fruit from higher branches. She asked if these were for the human—the falling star—who Magnolia expected to find on the far side of the mountains.

"Oh, no. I've never had pawpaw before," Magnolia said. "It's for me."

Crow reluctantly dug a knife out of their luggage, sliced a pawpaw in half, and warned her to discard the large lumpy seeds. Magnolia considered the pale yellow flesh; Crow hadn't offered her any utensils. A broad root extended from the back of her neck, draping down like a hank of long hair. The end of the root shed its bark and reshaped itself into a facsimile of a wooden spoon. Victorious, she scraped at her pawpaw halves until there was nothing left but skin.

This would have been impossible to pull off while the cart bounced around behind Dung. Crow cut open a pawpaw for him, too. She knocked the seeds away, then held it out so he could scour the pulp with his whip-like tongue.

The low, easy mountain pass bore old scars of human passage—a thread-thin trail that kept vanishing and resurfacing like the shaky stitches of a child's first sewing project. When they got back on that road, such as it was, Magnolia cast away her body and nested in a tangle of curly vines.

"Tell me about mages," she said.

"I only really knew one."

"But she was the last human mage, wasn't she? Sounds important."

"She only knew how to use one type of magic."

Magnolia looked at her expectantly.

"Basic first aid," Crow said. "She worked at a family woodshop."

"A noble profession."

And then Crow found herself saying more, because to leave it at that would leave an incomplete impression of a woman long dead, who had no one else to speak for her.

She may have been the last living mage, but she didn't understand much more about mages than anyone else around her. She learned first aid magic from an elder in the settlement who died immediately after teaching her. As soon as she was old enough, she went looking for students of her own. She didn't want to let human magic die with her.

She spent over half her life away from home. She found countless people with cores, but none of them actually had the capacity to use magic. Even if they wanted to, they couldn't be taught. Eventually she decided that she wouldn't waste her entire life looking in vain.

She returned to the family business. She returned, and she found that the quality of their work had plunged. They'd switched to using sunset wood—cheaper and weaker, and a garish orange color. The varnish they painted on it was shinier and stickier than it used to be, too. Crow had been obligated to mediate a number of cross-generational blowouts. The last mage had been young when she left, and now she was old, but she hadn't been present for any of their subsequent struggles.

"Why work so hard to max out profits at the end of the world?" Magnolia asked.

"They weren't making much profit. By the time she came back, sunset wood was the only type they could reliably obtain."

"And is the family business still going?"

"It died out three generations after the last mage," said Crow.

"Not bad, really."

"No. Not bad at all."

Once the last mage gave up on finding a student—once she knew the storied history of human magic would only live as long as she did—she'd lost interest in everything magical. She gave her neighbors first aid whenever they needed it, but she preferred deferring to the wisdom of doctors and herbalists. She never bragged to her grand-nieces or nephews about knowing magic.

As an old woman, she became much more devoted to the woodshop.

Even if it wasn't as good as it used to be, the furniture they built would outlast her, and it would outlast the final days of human magic use.

In mortal years, both then and now, the end of all things seemed to come on very slowly. The God of the End was the sort of guest who would always arrive late to a party. People lived their small lives in the only way they could: as if the world would last forever.

"An intriguing family saga, but I don't feel like I've learned much about mages."

"My mage had the same complaint," Crow said dryly.

Dung pulled them past the shaggy hulk of an old ghost city, long since overtaken by forest. Heaps of leaf litter softened the jutting bones of collapsed buildings.

Later, Magnolia lifted a root to point out the rusted remnants of a bridge that had once reached ridiculous heights over a dense river gorge. The middle of the span was gone, but vertical steel trusses still rose on either side of the ravine, supporting nothing, threatening the air like a spike trap to maim any unfortunate aerials who ventured too low.

Many mountains on the horizon looked like they'd had bites taken out of them. Magnolia attributed this, too, to her fabled vorpal holes.

Crow had never thought about there being an explanation for the current shape of the world. She imagined despair choking the continent as holes opened at random, swallowing factories and military bases and civilian settlements—only to stop one day, forever vanishing, like the end of a divine storm. Magnolia claimed that humanity had been severely depopulated at that point, both by the cataclysm of physical reality splitting open all over the place, and by each other.

After an age of ceaseless magical disaster and war, cowering survivors must have wondered if they were finally safe. Then came the advent of immortals. Saints and monsters—but mostly monsters.

They made several stops to go hunting. Magnolia wanted Crow to get her strength up before collecting the human who had allegedly fallen from the sky. (And who was probably dead by now, Crow thought, although she didn't say so.)

During one such stop, Magnolia plunged a root deep in the soil as if to measure its moisture. Crow asked if she ever talked to isopods.

"What?" Magnolia said distractedly.

"Never mind."

She withdrew her root with a frown. "There aren't many of our kind around, but it'll have to do. Might be able to catch a few migrating toward more populated areas."

In her usual fashion, she sat back and watched while Crow fought a monster in the form of a wolf with an absurdly long tail. Next they found a withered land-bound monster: a colony of enormous tree-burrowing worms with human faces. Magnolia expressed vituperative disgust in four ancient languages.

"They're not so different from you," Crow said after ingesting the colony's core.

"Exactly. I have every right to be disgusted." A few young green vines coiled from the base of her neck. She twiddled them together like coquettish fingers. "I am prettier, aren't I?"

"Than a mass of greasy worms that only wear human faces for show?"

Magnolia batted her eyelashes. Crow looked away and flexed her wings, testing how wide they could spread when she wasn't trying to limit them. Magnolia had asserted that they appeared almost the same as when Crow first came to her hills. Indeed, their healing had exponentially accelerated. Crow should have welcomed this, but some aspect of it disturbed her. It felt like a sign of her body growing overly accustomed to her new environment, her servitude, Magnolia's constant presence and knowing smiles.

"You don't feel any great urge to fly?" Magnolia asked. "I thought you'd take to the skies as soon as your wings grew back in full."

"Humans don't fly," said Crow. She felt Magnolia staring at her. "I've spent this whole life as a saint among humans."

"That doesn't mean you have to bind yourself to the ground in solidarity."

"Never got in the habit of flying for no reason."

"You don't crave it?"

"If I can fly anytime, why now? Why not later?"

"Some aerial you are," Magnolia said.

"I haven't been an aerial since—"

"Right, yes, I get it. And you don't even use your wings to fly, do you?"

"Not physically."

"Thought as much. It's more a matter of magic. Well, they may be about as decorative as a soldier's epaulets, but they do look nice."

"Only nice?" Crow asked, then immediately wished she could take it back. She really was starting to sound like Magnolia.

"When you let them all the way out, they're magnificent."

Flying didn't require any special exertion for aerials. They didn't claw against gravity as if fighting ocean currents. Rather, touching ground felt unnatural to them, as unnatural as it would be for a deep-sea fish to come all the way up and breach the surface. A fish like that might get beached in a freak accident, but it wouldn't survive to swim away with the tide. Likewise, a fallen aerial couldn't simply get up and flap away.

Of course, Magnolia immediately brought up the whale in Lake Fallen.

"That's different," Crow said. "The whale is a kind of larva. If it becomes an aerial later, that's like becoming a moth."

"Were you ever a larva?"

"I was always in the sky."

The creaky rocking of the cart seemed to hypnotize her into matching Magnolia word for word. Between hunting sessions, she spoke about more than just the life and death of the last human mage. She spoke of other companions, too, with only a minimum of prompting.

A violet haze in the sky reminded her of the blighted country where a pregnant woman had stepped away from a gaggle of gaunt children. The woman took Crow aside to ask: "If you eat my core, will you have enough magic to end the drought?"

That wasn't an answerable question. Crow had intervened with local weather in other regions, in other eras, but on a much smaller scale. Pushing back snowstorms, or blunting their teeth. Making rain sprinkle down steadily and thinly—no faster than the ground could absorb—rather than release itself in a deadly waterfall. She'd never manufactured moisture out of nothingness.

"But there's a chance," said her new companion. "Then do it."

She killed the starving woman and took her core. While that core still rested hot in her belly, she ended the drought.

Later, after seven years of bounty, the land abruptly became a desert. One large enough to dim half the continent with silver-purple dust every spring. A shameful reminder blown on the wind, making people in far-flung realms rub burning eyes and break out coughing.

"Ah, yes," said Magnolia. "I've tasted that infamous dust. So that's why you avoid using weather magic."

"If you'll let me avoid it," Crow said coolly.

"I'm a benevolent overlord, aren't I?"

Another unanswerable question.

35

IMMORTALS WERE NOT, on average, completely devoid of erotic desire. Those who experienced it considered it a fleeting glitch, like a human catching hiccups.

Any vestigial yearning Crow ever felt was a weak and shadowy thing. She became more prone to it after long stretches spent in human society, as if picking up a local accent. Move to different surroundings, and the accent would fade. She was a moon inadvertently reflecting the intensity of human passion all around her. She would feel nothing in isolation.

So there was really no need to glance across the cart at Magnolia, each time reaffirming that, no, she would not lust after a severed head. She'd lived among humans long enough to have acquired some of their squeamishness.

Her fingers itched for other reasons. If she ever fantasized, it would be about bouncing Magnolia on pavement like a bloody rubber ball. The problem was that her fantasies of murderous punishment felt increasingly disconnected from the physical drudgery of day-to-day life.

One of her companions had been a poet. He'd railed at Crow for her disinterest in his endless saga of romantic drama. There was always someone coming by to yell at him or sleep with him. Often they'd save time by doing both in short order. She didn't even try to keep track.

"*You* don't have to recruit a dozen lovers," he'd said. "You don't have to take pleasure like a conquering general. But at least leave the door open for joy to steal in. Your life is too long not to marvel at the new clouds of every new day, the yearly screeching of summer insects, the meteor showers you'll see more times than any of us mortals ... even if you never go out of your way to find them."

Magnolia turned out to be surprisingly intrigued by Crow's poet. She hadn't heard his name before. No one had—not in his own era, and not later. He was really more of a dilettante, embarrassed by his inherited wealth, living in luxury in an apartment that from the outside looked as if it were falling apart.

"Tell me what else he said," Magnolia ordered.

As the cart jostled them, Crow was startled by how much of it came back to her. She hadn't taken him seriously at the time. He'd been prone to hysterics, acting like each quarrel with each jilted lover meant the loss of all hope and goodness. The things he'd said when lecturing her went utterly at odds with the way he chose to live.

For example: "If you're lucky, life is mostly made up of quiet moments. The ones you have to work to remember. The work is worthwhile, I think, especially for you. If you don't put in the work, centuries will slip by, and nothing will stay with you except cruelty and fire. What about the satisfaction of clean clothes, the sound of rain running down gutters—what about bright white clusters of snowberries, and spiderwebs spangled with dew? Who will be there to remember any of that at the end of the world, if not you? Who else will remember young swallows learning to fly on summer evenings, or the taste of long-lost fruit, or the shape of a child's footprints in snow?"

"Did you do as he said?" Magnolia interjected.

"I've tried. From time to time. It does take work."

He was a foolish man, in life and in death. When the plague came to town, he'd ordered Crow to treat the poor before she treated him. So she did. She went to the faraway slums and spent five years working to perfect a cure—bending magic in ways that had little to do with her natural abilities. She healed several beggars and rag-pickers, but by then, that particular disease had already burned through most of the urban population.

She returned to find that her companion had taken ill and succumbed soon after he sent her off on her charity mission. He had been too proud to call her back. Even if he had, she would've lacked the skill to cure him at the time. But she would have been able to say goodbye. She would have been able to retrieve his core, and his sheafs of poetry, and maybe she would have been able to save some of his work to give to the archivists.

"Seven cores out of twenty-four people is really an awful record. I would say that you've had terrible luck with your companions—but the only common factor between all of them is you, my friend." Magnolia sounded amused. "You're congenitally predisposed to putting their wishes above your own."

The sound of late summer insects came in waves as they rode through the night. The wheels of the cart gave off a piercing magical tone akin to a leaf whistle.

Dung thumped forward through old-growth forest despite the lack of light, leading them on a convoluted but surefooted path around swampy patches and fallen logs. Primevals were known to thrive in dark places: deep cave systems, for instance, and abandoned mines.

The poet had been much better at giving advice than taking it—and he'd been hopelessly self-involved, to boot. Then again, so were most humans, and Crow thought no less of them for it. When you had such a truncated life to live, it made sense to focus primarily on yourself.

Out of all her past companions, the poet was the only one she would've liked to ask for advice about Magnolia. Not because she would expect a wise reply. Anyone sensible could come up with the same conclusion that Crow had reached on her own: that she should bide her time and kill Magnolia whenever she got another good chance. Either before or after they reached the end of the world. The poet's input might, in comparison, be utterly ridiculous. But at least it would be something different.

The first light of dawn had the same wistful quality as the hour before sunset. It found hints of red and gold in Magnolia's hair, which was normally a dark, dark brown.

Her hair hadn't grown at all in the months since they'd first met in the hills, and neither had Crow's. It stopped at the length it was meant to be, like the coat of an animal. In Magnolia's case, that was just long enough to card with your fingers—if she forced you to—but never long enough to get trapped beneath the end of her neck.

Before them, the trees began to open up. More specifically, they lay flat, as if blasted by a volcanic explosion. The few that still stood were bare sticks snapped in half. Dung's steps slowed in consternation. There would be no way to thread a clever route through this.

"How nice to have a sign that we're on the right track," said Magnolia.

Crow hopped off the cart and walked next to it, infusing the wheels with additional magic until they hovered higher than most imminent obstacles. She and Dung jumped over logs that had been flayed of all their bark. She could no longer hear a single bird or insect, and the nearest aerials were far over by the bitten-up mountains.

The cart made it across the maze of fallen trees without losing its contents—although, with each lurch, Magnolia acted as if she were about to get flung off the face of the earth. If only.

Past the silent flattened trees, the landscape yielded to a huge charcoal blot where nothing grew. It was more of a barren pancake than a crater, made from roll upon roll of corrugated rock like dried magma. Liquid puddled in crevices: glistening shallow streams with fat fish waddling between them on short anxious fore-fins.

Crow eased the buoyant wheels to the ground. The trip across this stony plain would be much smoother. But the cart inched along as if mired in mud. Dung didn't care about crushing any number of unlucky traveling fish; some other instinct made him drag his heels.

The magical whine of the wheels reached a pitch that seemed liable to burst a hole in Crow's head. The only other detectable sounds were the trickling of water and the weak splatting of land-walking fish. She eyed Magnolia, who had gone freakishly quiet. Then she found herself incapable of looking anywhere but at the center of all those frozen waves of stone.

A figure sat there, head in hands. Hair as white as bleached paper. A spindle-shaped cloud dipped down from the sky like a stationery tornado. All it did was pour rain in a single specific pool next to this human who Magnolia had known would be here.

A dark eye peered across at them through parted fingers.

Crow grabbed Dung's harness. He gladly halted. She needed another moment to translate this sensation in her, to understand it as fear. She'd suffered at the hands of mortals. But this was the first time in her thousands of years that she had ever feared a human being in the way that humans feared monsters.

The figure rose. It was a tall woman—a very tall woman—but she remained hunched, as if she were about to keel over. Her right hand pressed on her stomach. Like she had to hold her magic in to keep it from spilling like sliced-open guts.

The woman had more than a core. She had so much magic that Crow's thoughts ground to a halt. Branches sprouted from her core like veins and arteries, an infinite tangle. This was the type of magic that humans could actually *use*, if someone taught them. She carried enough to be bursting with it, as if she were composed more of magic than mortal flesh.

Crow hadn't seen a single human with a single magic branch since the death of her old companion, the last known mage in a fading world. The last human to have more magic to her than just an isolated, sterile core. Crow herself had brought the glorious history of human magic to an unceremonious end. Although the last mage had ultimately been much more invested in improving the quality of sunset wood and building sturdy tables than in the magical part of her legacy.

Now Crow had to do something she'd never done before. She had to shutter her magic perception, as if clamping her hands over aching ears. It was the only way she could keep looking at this woman and not lose her mind.

"Go," the mage said.

It reached her with terrifying clarity despite the distance between them. The same voice-carrying trick that Magnolia so often relied on. The pronunciation was unlike anything she'd heard in either of her lives, and that word—an archaic form—was one she'd only seen in written scraps.

She felt herself take a step backwards, one hand on Dung's harness.

Then Dung shifted. He folded his back legs. He bowed forward until his puny rows of forearms almost grazed the igneous ground. The cart tilted dangerously.

"What treachery!" Magnolia cried at him. If not for her roots gripping tied-down stacks of luggage, she would've tumbled off like a dropped ball. "My word. It's not even possible for you to have any sort of ancestral memory of her. Ridiculous. Crow, unstrap him."

Crow mechanically obeyed, taken aback to find that her fingers still worked. She liberated Dung and stabilized the cart. As soon as she finished, Magnolia told him to go hide deep in the woods. "Don't let me catch you lurking around and fawning at that—that—"

Dung bolted like a gazelle.

Magnolia reached for Crow's shoulders with grasping vines and swung herself up into her usual seat, leaving the cart behind. Her barked commands—and the physical motions of dealing with the harness—had chopped thick layers of paralyzing rust from Crow's brain.

When she next spoke, though, it took the entirety of Crow's attention to comprehend what she said.

"We know who you are," Magnolia called to the mage. "From the way you're sulking, I'm guessing you didn't come here on purpose. You must want to return. Perhaps we can help."

The mage stared mutely at her.

Magnolia had said it all in the variant of Continental language commonly used during the beginning of the end of the world. In the time before Crow's fall. Myriad regional languages were heavily shifted descendants of this tongue. Crow knew enough of those, older and newer, that she could follow along just so long as she didn't think too hard. It was a new experience to find her ears so shocked by a dialect. She'd taken no conscious note of how different Tamar sounded from Haida and Rinlin.

The mage gave no response.

Crow put a hand on Magnolia's head. She meant it as a rebuke. She was more than just a convenient perch. She was the last line of defense for both of them, and she had no idea what was going on.

"Step closer," Magnolia said.

As Crow moved forward, a wary current of magic went through the white-haired mage, and through all the rivulets of water coursing between ridges of volcanic rock.

"Red eyes," said the mage, still in archaic words.

Crow started to look at Magnolia, but it would have been quite a feat to make eye contact with a second head perched on her own body. Their only pair of sunglasses had been pulverized in Steppehaven.

"Oh, I see." Magnolia kept addressing the mage. She had no words to waste on Crow. "Your knowledge is many, many lifetimes out of date. Red eyes don't mean what they used to. Mortal bodies change when they age and deteriorate and get ready to die, and so do worlds. First of all—surely you can tell that we're not human."

"Who is she?" Crow asked, deeming herself unlikely to get answers by waiting.

Magnolia seemed briefly perplexed about having to explain it.

"Who?" she echoed. "A visitor from afar. As the saying goes, you really do meet all kinds of people on the road."

Crow smacked the side of her head to make her stop stalling.

"Ouch! Show some respect, Carrie. No, not to her, to me! Like I was saying—this lady hails from a very different time and place. Long ago and far away. She's the devil in human skin who dealt the dying blow to our world, and then left us. I'm awfully curious about what's brought her back at such a belated hour."

36

The mage began to speak.

Magnolia immediately cut her off. "Isn't it enough to be our Devil? Do you need any other title?"

Said Devil shook her head.

Trust Magnolia to take this sort of tone with the half-mythical mage who'd destroyed the world. That alone convinced Crow to believe her. Of course Magnolia would talk back to the Devil.

"Had a little chat with the land in Steppehaven," Magnolia said quietly from her shoulder. "Several times. It was especially easy to reach deep after you riled the ground up with Flytrap. I had a nagging feeling about that slow-falling star." A breath of laughter touched Crow's ear. "If only the automagi knew. They would've killed for a chance to interview her. Or to preserve her in a pot. What could possibly have more historical value than the person who triggered the end of the world?"

The Devil was not talkative. She regarded them with an air of caution.

Despite her white hair, she seemed relatively youthful, as far as humans went. Maybe a decade or so older than Arion, who'd died early in his twenties. Quite a bit younger than the likes of Haida or half-immortal Tamar.

As Crow approached her, more and more ashen powder had crunched underfoot. This was not ash from the faux-volcanic impact of the Devil's descent, or whatever else might have charred the ground here. This was the ash of dead immortals—likely dead monsters, though saints and monsters all looked the same when they reached a permanent end.

A permanent end?

"She's human," Crow said, for Magnolia's ears only, so soft that a second later she wasn't sure if she'd said it at all.

"She's human," Magnolia affirmed.

"But she can kill us." Crow ground immortal ash under her heel. "She can kill us for good."

"We're mere servants of the dying realm that spit us out. She predates us. She punched the world so hard that it started coughing up immortals—including regurgitated returners like us. If any human mage could figure out how to break the rules of our existence, it'd be her. But she hasn't gotten there yet."

"You don't want me to run?"

"Take a closer look at that ash," Magnolia said. "It's not precisely the same as ash left by a permanent death. One day, cocoons will form. Might take longer than usual. But all the monsters you've been treading on will revive."

If the Devil was that falling star, then she'd already been here for days. Over a week? Multiple weeks? Crow hadn't been counting. Had she survived by summoning rainwater and plump ambulatory fish, or had she avoided starvation by putting herself in magical stasis? Had she done anything except fight wave upon wave of hungry monsters?

So many immortals must have been drawn to the extraordinary light of her magic. So many must have flooded in to be slaughtered. They'd shivered with the same terror that pressed on Crow when she locked eyes with the Devil. It was a dread so large that it seemed to come from outside her, more akin to the weight of the ocean or the weight of the atmosphere than an internal emotion. Other immortals had felt that, too, and still the Devil's core had been a lodestar too potent to ignore.

"You'd be tempted, too, if you didn't have me gripping your reins," Magnolia murmured. "You'd kneel like Dung—you'd vow eternal loyalty. Don't pretend you wouldn't."

Was Magnolia any different from the other immortals who had stumbled out of the skies and woods and mountains, pulled inexorably by the gravitation of this woman's magic? Even if they hadn't known who she was, and Magnolia did—it meant only that Magnolia understood how rare a prize her core would be. Why else would Magnolia have been so determined to come find her where she fell?

"For your information, Carrie," Magnolia said in her most lordly manner, "I have a good head on my shoulders—hah!—and I know not to bite off more than I can swallow. I'm here for altruistic purposes."

While they debated, the Devil sank down to huddle on comfortless rock. The slim spout of rain next to her—a targeted waterfall—never splashed her. From the way she cradled her torso, she might have been felled by hidden pain. Or mortal disease.

If she'd come from some unimaginable other place—if she hadn't been back here since the beginning of the end—then she would be defenseless against modern plagues. But maybe she'd had minimal contact with mortal creatures. The ash on the ground spoke of ceaseless waves of avaricious immortals, culminating in the arrival of the last Great Adversary.

As this shadow play of thought unfolded in the confines of Crow's mind, Magnolia raised her voice. "We're wise, rational, and peaceable immortals," she told the Devil. "Unlike those who came to try their luck with attacking you. Want to know what an immortal is? I'll get you caught up."

The Devil appeared as though she wanted nothing more than for them to go away.

"Bring me closer," Magnolia said, undaunted—which was how Crow, reduced to chauffeuring about a severed head, discovered herself in close quarters with the human Devil.

Magnolia made her kneel so they would all be at eye level. She kept talking, always in that prehistoric form of Continental that threatened to bypass Crow's understanding.

No magical lightning descended to smite them. The Devil had her arms around her knees, head down, but sometimes she squeezed out a few truncated words. None of her questions carried any of the expected intonation. They dropped away like a final statement, rocks in water.

Magnolia spoke intensely about the fate of the world. "It's still on its deathbed. But something on the scale of a whole world has to take a long, long time to finish dying. It's difficult work. A protracted form of labor—like a mammal giving birth."

Little by little, Crow observed details that she had previously been too tense to take in.

An empty tin with a picture of a fish on it nestled in a wrinkle of rock between the Devil and her ever-raining pool. That kind of tin would have been manufactured in a full-blown industrial cannery. She hadn't seen anything like it since the earliest days of her second life as a returning immortal.

The Devil's clothing, too, incorporated techniques and materials that Crow suspected she had not laid eyes on in a very long time. Nothing she wore seemed egregiously alien in design. But it looked strikingly new: no repair stitches, no patches, no signs of having been let out or taken in.

The long coat that hung from her shoulders—better suited to late fall or winter—was a color like springtime honey, with fabric that appeared remarkably soft and buttery. The left sleeve was, mysteriously, much shorter than the right—it only came partway down her forearm. Maybe her culture valued asymmetry.

The one time the Devil asked Magnolia to repeat herself was when she explained that there were no longer any human mages. All magical knowledge and capability had been lost many generations ago; humans with cores could only use them to bargain with saints. Otherwise, a core was nothing but a liability, a beacon for monsters.

Those with cores would have been cast out of society as a fatal security risk if not for the fact that nowadays, nearly everyone had them. In the days when it was closer to half and half, Crow had interceded in bitter battles between core-bearers and the coreless. Both had thought they were fighting for their respective right to exist.

When the topic of returners came up, the Devil lurched to her feet. She strode away, her back to them, and then—almost politely—bent over to vomit.

She came back. She rinsed her mouth with water from her pool of ceaseless rain. She wiped her face. Her expression remained unnaturally blank.

Her voice, too, remained a low, flat line. "The erasure of all vorpal holes ... I did that." She waited a minute before saying: "Should I find a way to undo it?"

"Can you stay afterward?" Magnolia asked without sympathy. "Can you see it all the way through, come what may? No? If you were prepared to stay, you would never have left in the first place. You don't belong here—you haven't belonged here in a very long time now. This is a world that's reached its final shape without you. Let it die on its own time."

The Devil nodded. Earlier she'd uttered something incoherent about how she'd plunged back into this world by pure chance. As if you could trip across the impermeable border between realms of existence as readily as you might slip off a lakeside dock.

Before its extinction, human magic had been highly regimented. Immortal magic, in contrast, had much vaguer limits. Humans grew their collective body of magic through cooperation: they had to teach one another how to use it, for the most part, whereas immortals simply followed innate instincts. Humans named and delineated and measured and recorded and experimented with their magic, which they divided into discrete skills that could be passed from one mage to many students. As individuals and as a group, they knew exactly what they could and couldn't do.

Crow had never been sure how to put her own limits into words. Ask her to perform an act of magic she'd never done before—like ending a years-long local drought—and she could try. She could always try. Like how she could try to run fast, or jump high. But she could not reach the moon in a single jump, and by the same token, she doubted she could ever use magic to pull the moon down from the sky.

There were many forms of magic that just didn't come naturally to her. Like Magnolia's commands. To attempt the same would, for Crow, be like attempting to write sheet music for a song she'd never heard. She could stop rain from falling, but she couldn't begin to imagine how to read even the most frivolous thoughts from a stranger's mind.

Many years before she took the last mage as a promised companion—back when the study of magecraft had still been somewhat centralized—she'd frustrated scholars with her inability to articulate the rules of immortal magic.

"It's different for each immortal," she'd said, and: "Why are you a scholar, and not a poet? It's like that."

They never seemed satisfied. She didn't mind helping with their research, although all her contributions seemed to backfire. But she also failed to grasp why explaining any of it would matter.

She could see what they couldn't. Rather, she could see what they couldn't accept: the inevitable erosion of knowledge, slipping away from civilization like sand trickling through the neck of an hourglass. The population was thinning and dispersing, turning away from the pursuit of science. The understanding they strove for would scatter like ashes tossed off a mountain. Which didn't mean they shouldn't bother— she had never been one to dictate how people lived—but she hoped they could at least have fun with it, and she was sorry to stymie them with her ignorance.

She resumed listening to the conversation between the Devil and a severed head. At the moment, Magnolia was proudly (and not all that accurately) summarizing several millennia of human history in a few pithy sentences. The Devil had her head in her hands again.

Her left hand—

It wasn't missing—but it wasn't all there, either. It kept distorting like a limb seen through warped glass or water.

The Devil took that rebellious hand away from her face and regarded it with a blankness that bordered on loathing.

"Ah. There's something we can help you with," Magnolia said suddenly.

Without warning, she slipped into her human-shaped body. Naked from head to toe, without a single gesture at modesty.

Crow and the Devil—both still on their knees—gaped up at her with what Crow felt certain was a mutual sense of horror. The Devil must've been wondering why she had to get terrorized by an exhibitionist on foreign soil.

Magnolia put her hands on her hips, still wearing nothing except an irrepressible grin.

Crow ported to the cart. She grabbed the first garment in sight. She ported back. She threw the clothing—a long shawl-like wrap—around Magnolia's shoulders. Magnolia permitted this to happen in the way of a king getting dressed by attendants.

At last Crow drew breath to apologize on her behalf. Different cultures had different standards for appropriate dress around strangers, true. But the Devil had been fully clothed when they first turned up. It seemed best to continue returning the favor.

"Do it again," the Devil said, eyes on Magnolia.

Her empty stare of shock might instead have been a look of intense concentration.

"Just once more," Magnolia replied. "I'm not a sideshow."

Her wiry naked body vanished. She was a head again, and she was falling. Crow dove forward, catching Magnolia in one arm and her discarded wrap in the other.

The moment she had them both secure, Magnolia regenerated the rest of her body. Crow found herself clutching a bare torso. Her right hand gripped the wrap as if she were about to use it as a makeshift boxing glove. She was in a very good position to bring that fist around and punch Magnolia square in the nose.

The Devil got up, wincing minutely. She drifted off, pacing, muttering to herself. Crow flung the wrap like a shroud over Magnolia's face.

Magnolia let her body evaporate beneath her, taut heat exchanged for empty air. This time, when Crow caught her, her head was entirely swaddled. Her mouth worked against the fabric. Crow wrung the shawl tighter.

"I'll haul you like a sack of flour," she said.

"Let me out, you cretin," Magnolia retorted.

She meant it. A familiar opiate calm loosened Crow's fingers. She unwrapped Magnolia's head as if peeling an exotic fruit.

The funnel-shaped cloud—the one that had been directing a precision bombardment of rain into the Devil's pool—began to retreat. It untwisted as it went, growing wider and mistier. The rain softened, quieting, and then stopped altogether. The Devil kept walking in circles.

"Let's give her time to work it out," Magnolia said, unconcerned. "You'd better pick something to cook for dinner. She doesn't seem like the type to focus very much on nutrition. Practical matters are for peons, I suppose."

Magnolia was the one who'd made Crow pack a cart of human supplies. There might be some grain of truth to her assertion of altruistic motives. If a core-stealing fight was all she wanted, they could've found the Devil and fought her much faster if they hadn't been carrying around excess luggage.

On the other hand, a straightforward confrontation didn't seem like Magnolia's style. She might still be plotting a way to take the Devil by surprise. Or had she given up all thoughts of dirty tricks after witnessing the Devil in person? Had she felt the same breathless fear as Crow—that unknowable mass bearing down on her, a premonition of being buried alive?

37

Magnolia poked Crow with an accusatory tendril. "I'm offended. What you see as underhanded, I see as doing things the smart way. We can't all blast our problems away with balls of plasma."

Crow went back over to the loaded cart.

"Now, I may have more in common with the archivists than I would care to admit," said Magnolia, riding along in the crook of her elbow. "Call it a scholarly spirit of inquiry. I heard a great deal about the Devil from the land—from its deepest memories. Given the chance, who wouldn't want to meet the person who started it all? She's like our mother. If not for her, the world wouldn't have spawned either of us, nor any other immortal. Is it so wrong to be curious?"

"No," Crow said. Then: "If you thought I had a chance, you would already have told me to go for her throat."

In the distance, the Devil kept pacing.

"You might have more of a chance than you think," Magnolia said idly. "She's weak and overwhelmed. All that magic pains her. Astonishing though it may seem, she really is only human. Immortals aren't the strangest creature this world's ever hacked up. But I also suspect, somehow, that ambushing her at her very lowest point would be likely to backfire."

Crow hauled the cart closer to the center of the stone field, bumping noisily across the rippling ridges of a lava flow gone cold. As Magnolia's words sank in, she ground to a halt. She cast an eye over the bounty of strapped-down crates and clay jars packed in reeds.

"We brought all this to rehabilitate the Devil," she said, aghast. "Once we've nursed her back to health—that's when you'll tell me to attack."

"Only with her consent. In true saintly fashion." Magnolia hung down over Crow's breast with vines slung around the back of her neck, like a stupidly heavy necklace. "You seem to think me very devious," she added. "Even a monster can be a philanthropist."

"Pitting me against a world-destroying devil doesn't seem like the best way to prove that."

"Don't worry," Magnolia said serenely. "It'll all be aboveboard. She'll cooperate."

A few hours later, Crow had planned out a week's worth of menus utilizing various combinations of their supplies on hand. Magnolia made her carry over several boulders to serve as seats around their future campfire. It was early afternoon, but the sunlight had never become palpable enough to heat the rock beneath them.

Elaborate fuzzy dragonflies—like flying clusters of golden-brown eyelashes—coasted above confused tributaries of inch-deep water. The walking fish (which had mostly stopped walking) soaked their bellies in the largest puddles.

The dragonflies scattered when the Devil drifted closer. She sat on a boulder. She pulled her left hand off—as matter-of-factly as if she were removing a glove—and hurled it at the ground as if bashing a cockroach.

The severed end of her arm looked, briefly, like the wound under Magnolia's neck. No blood, no bone, just a starry abyss. Then it took on the appearance of a healed stump covered in skin. Meanwhile, her severed left hand scampered crabbily around the circle of boulders.

When she held her wrist out, the lost hand rocketed up and seamlessly reattached itself. The entire time, not a single twitch of any sort of expression crossed her face. She rubbed her knuckles.

"Well done," Magnolia said sourly. "You just had to put your own flamboyant twist on it." She cast a look at Crow. "The Devil reinvented the magic I use to summon my body. Might not have been the best idea"—now she turned to the Devil again—"as you're clearly in bad shape."

The Devil wasn't listening. "I should have killed him," she said in a very low voice. "I—"

Magnolia unfurled a sharp root, like Dung unslinging his whip-thin tongue. That root jabbed the Devil in the ribs. She doubled over, soundless, but with visible sweat on her forehead.

"Pay attention," Magnolia said, ruthless. "We're about to start cooking supper."

The Devil shook her head, though her stomach had been growling since the moment they met.

"Are you the pickiest of all eaters?" Magnolia demanded. "Does a rarefied mage like yourself refuse to dine on anything except rainbows and gold leaf?"

"And preserved fish," said Crow, nudging the anachronistic discarded tin with the tip of her toe. Had the Devil brought it from another world in her pocket? Was it some kind of tradition, where she came from, to carry about canned goods?

The Devil had such a dark unrelenting stare that it was difficult to hold her gaze, but Crow persevered. "I'll make stew," she said. She spoke at a careful pace, in the oldest descendant of classical Continental she knew, and hoped it would be close enough to get the point across. "You can watch each step of the way. Tell me if there's anything you can't eat."

"Why?" the Devil said at last.

"Why would we want you hanging around?" Magnolia asked. "The faster you recover, the faster you'll get out of here."

With a tinge of irony, the Devil glanced down at her core. So she had, after all, absorbed some key aspects of Magnolia's interminable ranting about immortals and terrarium theory and the way of the world.

Crow built up a fire with the Devil as her unblinking audience. The stew took hours but came out quite well, considering that she hadn't cooked since Arion's death. She made a translucent umber stock from dried fish and mushrooms. After straining it, she added beans the size of chestnuts, and hearty chunks of vegetables, and seasoning from Tamar's stores.

She served the Devil first, ladling a modest portion into a wooden bowl. The Devil took it, though there was a tremor in her hand. Crow began eating from her own bowl as a sign of solidarity. Every so often she had to stop and spoon-feed Magnolia, who liked to pretend that she wasn't perfectly capable of gripping utensils with her prehensile roots, and who kept smacking her lips in an overexaggerated show of pleasure. Crow strove not to ponder the eternal question of where food went after Magnolia swallowed it.

Some time later, the Devil risked a small taste. "It's good," she said unconvincingly.

"It's excellent," Magnolia shot back.

As a growing child with a rebellious stomach, Arion had been ornery no matter what Crow fed him. She didn't need praise; in her book, any meal that didn't end in tears was a wild success.

The Devil kept eating. Having secured a captive audience, Magnolia returned to one of her favorite topics: what, precisely, is an immortal? What separates monsters from saints?

"Long ago, closer to the beginning of the end, many people called us angels and demons," she said. "Or spirits, or fairies, or elves. My favorite old name for us is Children of the Void."

The Devil dropped her spoon.

Crow picked it up and wiped it. Stormy whitecaps rippled across the Devil's bowl of stew.

"No need to be so tense," Magnolia said pitilessly. "Think of how much time has passed. Maybe there used to be other apocalyptic threats lurking in the shadows—but you locked in this world's fate. You sentenced it to a drawn-out death. Maybe the solidification of destiny helped avert every other possible end.

"Crow here was witness to wars that consumed the entire continent. Why, over generations, did those wars just sort of peter out? I think it's because you gave our world an appointment with death by gradual deterioration. It lost its ability to go up in sudden flames."

The Devil wordlessly raised her reclaimed spoon to her lips.

Crow kept an eye on the other two—one woman and one head—as she cleaned up afterward. The sky behind intermittent gray clouds was a glorious gradation of flaming purple—redder towards one horizon, bluer towards the other. Lightning flashed among distant clouds without thunder or the scent of rain.

The Devil's eyes were dark holes where charisma went to die. But she was also very well-built, even statuesque, though she didn't show it in how she carried herself. Look more closely, and you might easily picture her strangling a grown man with one hand.

"You ruined the world by *accident?*"

Magnolia's voice rose. Crow flinched.

"You started a plague of vorpal holes, and then you came back to fix it. I thought that was a sign you'd changed your mind! You weren't even trying to destroy anything in the first place? None of it was on purpose? What kind of devil are you? I'm so disappointed."

Crow strode back and forth from the extinguished campfire to the cart. On another return trip, she heard Magnolia cry: "*That's* why you did it?"

The silent lightning in the clouds suddenly felt too close for comfort.

"That's why you couldn't bear to speak of returners." There was an unusual edge of heat in Magnolia's words. "You fear that returners are a twisted reflection of your original sin. The closed-up world reenacting its own trauma again and again. What a terrible thing to face. Terrible—and laughable, isn't it?

"I was human before I was immortal. Did I mention that? I was human in a time when some people still remembered your name, your legend. Would you like to hear my confession? Would you like to know how I died?"

The Devil kept still. She had her head bowed, white hair falling forward to hide her face. It seemed a touch longer than it had been when they first spotted her after dawn that very same day. Her fingers were laced together, but her left hand was a thing of shadow and smoke, seething and bulging, impossible to contain.

The magic within her moved the same way: fitful nauseous heaves, growing stronger with each spasmodic pulse.

"Magnolia," Crow said. Louder: "Magnolia. Mag!"

Magnolia stopped haranguing the Devil. She stopped right in the middle of a multisyllabic word.

"Why, Crow," she said. "That's the first time you've ever called me by name."

"No, it isn't," Crow countered, more from her innate urge to disagree than from any real conviction that Magnolia was wrong.

"I do like being called Mag."

"No one asked."

They both looked anew at the Devil's writhing threads of magic. Some burst out of her skin like arcs of lightning.

"She's about to lose it," Magnolia pronounced, all too calmly. "Frankly, we should have addressed her magical injuries long before feeding her, but I enjoyed watching her squirm. Nothing soothes my soul like the sight of a powerful being wracked with pain. Such a beautiful thing—one of nature's great wonders, like aerials in the sky at sunset."

This was not a good time for lengthy speeches. In fact, this felt like sitting around and doing nothing while tongues of fire crept toward a stack of explosives. Crow asked if they should give the Devil some space.

"Her self-control is to be commended," Magnolia said, still unperturbed. "I was interested in seeing how long she'd torture herself before asking for help. Before asking for the one thing she needs above all else—certainly more than she needed your stew. I guess the answer to that question is: possibly forever! Oh, well. In terms of lived time, we're several thousand years her senior. We'll have to be the adults here. Have you ever detangled human magic?"

"Um," Crow said.

Her sole mage companion had only possessed a single thread of magic. Sometimes it tried to tie itself in knots. Crow had learned to soothe that obdurate strand in the same way that she'd learned how to massage human shoulders. The Devil, in contrast, had too many tangled threads to count. Going in there would be more like performing amateur neurosurgery than soothing stiff muscles.

A skein of fine pallid roots flowed out from the decapitated edge of Magnolia's neck, as lacy as a veil. "You're better equipped to fiddle with her magic," she told Crow. "But I do have a certain rapport with complex branching threads. I'll tell you what to do. Go behind her—put a hand on the small of her back. Be sure to touch skin."

Power rippled away from the Devil like heat from an open oven. She seemed paralyzed, holding her magic in with all her might. She'd shrugged off that fine coat of hers while eating from the bowl Crow had given her. Hot stew was not an ideal summer meal—but it had stayed cool here all day, as cool as a cave untouched by sunlight.

Crow sat on an empty rock next to her. In old and simple language, she asked if she could touch the Devil's back.

The Devil's left hand was slightly more controlled now. She had it balled up in a fist pressed to her lips. Her other hand gripped the offending wrist like a tourniquet.

"You'll heal my magic," she said through her fist. A question, probably, though it lacked all inflection.

"I'll try," Crow said cautiously.

"Let her try," said Magnolia, now perched on a white filigree of hair-thin roots.

The Devil made a noise of pure despair in her throat. She looked at the deepening sky, as if she could see something on the other side of it. Then she wordlessly lifted the back of her shirt.

As apologetically as she could, Crow put her palm against the lowest portion of the Devil's spine. She felt even sicker than she looked, with clammy skin that seemed both too hot and too cold. This was as close as Crow could get to her core without actually reaching in and ripping it out.

"Get comfortable," Magnolia said. "We'll be here for a while."

38

AT FIRST, Magnolia was all business. Step by step, and with surprising patience, she instructed Crow how to tease apart the Devil's snarled magic. This was an excruciatingly slow process. Crow had to translate convoluted verbal advice into precise metaphysical nudges, one hopelessly knotted thread at a time.

The Devil's reactions were minimal. But the fact that she had hitherto shown almost zero emotion made the tiniest stutter of breath sound worse than an all-out scream.

Night fell. A handful of aerials swam beneath the stars. Crow took occasional breaks. No one had any energy left to make small talk.

Dawn came, and gradually gave way to a rich green sky stippled in a multitude of wildflower colors. Crow's pace improved with experience. Every so often, the weary Devil nodded off. She kept awakening with a half-finished gasp and a name on her lips.

Having decided that the worst was past, Magnolia became noticeably less helpful. She began to go off on tangents. As the Devil dozed, head drooping, Magnolia regarded her with narrowed eyes. "Logically speaking, she's the greatest of all great adversaries—of humanity, and of every species. You should take her out before you even think of targeting me."

"She's human," Crow said dully, too drained to muster a more considered response.

"She's human, and worst of all, she always had good intentions. Want to debate whose kill count is higher?" Magnolia asked. "Don't bother. Even the Singular Horde can't measure up. Our Devil didn't witness most of the mortal deaths we could reasonably pin on her—she skedaddled off to pleasanter planes of reality. But she seems like the honest type, doesn't she? If only we could hold her accountable.

"I should have used her real name from the start, now that I think about it. I should have convinced her that she still belongs here. Might've been a strategic misstep to let her so easily shoulder the role of our irredeemable Devil. Hmm."

The Devil was no longer sleeping—though she made no attempt to defend herself. Magnolia didn't care about being overheard. Maybe she thought it unlikely that the Devil would understand more than a fragmented word or two of modern language.

"If she's honest," Crow said, "if she has good intentions, then it's in your best interest to let her go. If she stays, if she learns what you are, she won't let you roam unscathed. You already tried to control her, didn't you? You tried, and you failed. Did she fight you off, or did she not even notice you planting roots in her?"

"Carrie..."

"Don't call me that."

"Carrie, are you jealous?"

Crow methodically unbraided a stubborn clump of the Devil's magic.

"You *are* jealous," Magnolia exclaimed. "You think I'll ditch you for a higher-powered servant. Monster, saint, or the Devil herself—you think I'll happily upgrade as soon as I get a chance. Do I really seem so disloyal?"

"That's the reason you wanted to find her," Crow said levelly, and she knew she was right.

Magnolia would gladly devour the Devil's core if she could take it by force. But more than that—far more than that—she would want to test out her power of command. If it worked, she would be far more than a Great Adversary. She would be a monster with absolute control over a destroyer of worlds. She wouldn't need Crow. No matter what Crow did from then on, no matter how many armies she called to her side, Magnolia and the Devil would be unstoppable.

"Carrie," Magnolia said gently. "Crow. I truly didn't expect to succeed—and I didn't. She's impermeable. But I did have to try. You can see that, can't you? There is very little in our immortal lives that can be described as a once-in-a-lifetime chance."

Crow redoubled her efforts to sort out the Devil's jumbled magic. Nearly a full day later, she was finally beginning to get the hang of it.

This was a form of emergency treatment. Without intervention, mages with tangled magic would eventually go berserk. At that point it would not matter how good or true or cruel or conniving they were at heart. They would erupt like one of the wandering volcanoes of the north, a random catastrophe that spared no one in sight. They would become human avatars of indiscriminate violence, worse than monsters—who, if nothing else, were predators with drive and purpose.

By now, the immediate danger had passed. Magnolia kept hinting that she could stop, but Crow continued. The more comfortable the Devil felt with the overwhelming burden of her magic, the better equipped she would be to fend off Magnolia's attempts at mental conquest. Magnolia was an eternal opportunist—one with boundless time, patience, and optimism about her chances of victory.

"You think so little of me," Magnolia sniffed.

"But I don't underestimate you," Crow said. "Not anymore."

"True! Very true." Magnolia beamed.

It was nearly night again when Crow took her hand off the Devil's back for the final time. The Devil promptly curled up next to the largest boulder and closed her eyes.

"When you get to be my age, you run out of things to pray to," Magnolia said piously to the burgeoning stars. "Who will save me from devils and saints?"

The stars didn't respond, and neither did Crow, who had gotten up to make camp for the first time in forty years. On her own, without a companion—without Arion—she'd never needed to concern herself with the rudimentary basics of shelter.

Arion had been courageous beyond measure, a true hero to the people. He had also been prone to distraction, and wasn't always the best at getting through a simple list of tasks. She'd send him off fishing to catch his own supper, and he'd end up chasing bandits or saving drowning children. Or else he'd come back with an armful of half-starved kittens.

Crow usually took care of the menial business of travel, like setting up tents. Arion would've been just as happy shivering in wet blankets under an open sky, but Crow hadn't sworn a vow to his mother only to let him wander through the wilderness without any semblance of shelter. She hadn't collected his mother's core only to turn around and let him neglect his own needs. One day, she'd be compelled to collect Arion's core, too—until then, she'd give him the best life she could. Or so she'd thought, until the Singular Horde cut him down and stole his core instead.

She picked up the sleeping Devil and laid her on a mat inside a goatskin tent. This brought another pang of memory: the smell of smoldering fire, and Arion's body.

The Devil was older than him, and taller, too. Or had he only seemed smaller when he was dead? Had he shrunken in Crow's recollection because she'd always thought of him as a child? The same child who ran tirelessly through tall grass and mud, who climbed trees like a monkey, who had a horrible predilection for falling in bogs.

She'd carried him each time she rescued him, and she'd carried him after he died to the Horde—a warrior, a grown man, but still so young that she'd felt it like glass shards in her chest. Four decades had passed since then: almost twice as long as the entire span of Arion's life. The shards cared nothing for the passage of time. They would work their way through her body at their own pace, sometimes digging deeper, sometimes rising to the surface and making themselves known with every breath.

When she emerged empty-armed from the tent where the Devil now slept, Magnolia sat in human form on the most prominent boulder. She was draped in a lazy low-hanging robe that left her shoulders bare to moonlight.

If Magnolia dared to utter a single word about Arion, Crow thought she might actually go mad.

Magnolia gave her an inscrutable look, one reminiscent of the painfully expressionless Devil. Magnolia's eyes were not the same flat black—but at night, with no fire left burning, they could have been.

By human standards, the Devil woke late. Magnolia was a decapitated head again, mindlessly drumming hardened roots like wooden mallets on the rock around them. Crow offered the Devil tea and sorghum porridge as soon as she stumbled out of her tent. This time she ate quickly, trying to get it over with.

Then she looked Crow in the eye and said: "I should repay you."

Magnolia stopped drumming. "That's a collective *you*, right? I played an integral role in the extremely grueling process of healing your magic. We worked all through the night and the following day, to boot."

Crow began to tell the Devil that she owed them nothing.

"Excuse me?" Magnolia said dangerously. "Carrie, don't interrupt the nice lady when she's trying to—"

"I'll steam your clothes," said the Devil. "All of them."

Magnolia's mouth hung half-open.

"Steam-cleaning," the Devil continued, evidently concerned that they had not understood her. "Steam. To clean. Your clothing." A pause. "With magic," she tacked on, quite unnecessarily.

Magnolia pulled herself together. "Sorry—this is how the Devil chooses to clear her debts? After all we've done for you—"

"Steam-cleaning would be wonderful," Crow said loudly. She caught Magnolia's eye. "Her clothes are spotless. If only we could say the same."

They glowered at each other. Magnolia heaved a sigh. "Well, then. Anything for my Crow. Can't say I have much interest in watching you two do laundry, magically or otherwise." She hopped off her boulder. "I've sensed lesser monsters approaching us. I'll go off and have some snacks."

She scampered away across the flowing plain of black rock in her usual squid-like fashion.

As she went, her voice cut through Crow's head, cold and sudden.

Don't ask the Devil to free you. Don't ask her to kill me, either. If she makes any such offer of her own accord, you won't accept. This is not an order dependent on legalistic wording. This is an order based in pure intent. You can't squirm your way around it, so don't even try.

While Crow collected garments for cleaning, the Devil said: "She can see your thoughts."

"Some of them."

"Are you bonded?"

It took Crow a prolonged moment to recall what that meant. An obsolete human concept—something to do with mages and their retainers. Irrelevant to a world without mages, and especially irrelevant to immortals.

"No," she said.

"But you belong to her. Do you want to be free?"

"No," Crow heard herself answer. It came out painlessly, and only afterward could she futilely grind her back teeth.

The sunlight was stronger this morning, as if it had recovered in tandem with the Devil's magic. Crow followed her to an open area without any stray fish or water-filled seams of rock.

The Devil held out her right hand. Crow handed her a pair of trousers.

The Devil took them, and—without glancing up—hurled them high in the air with all her might.

Crow stared. The Devil stared back. Was this some sort of insult?

The trousers began falling, and Crow dashed to catch them. They were dry, hot, and smelled like heaven.

"Next," said the Devil. She'd been drastically underselling her abilities when she described this magic as steam-cleaning. If there were any hiss of steam, Crow couldn't hear it—but those scant seconds in the air were enough to purge fabric of all dirt, wrinkles, and mustiness.

The Devil kept flinging garments about without any care for where they fell. Crow gladly ran around to rescue them before they had a chance to touch ground.

"She calls herself a monster," the Devil said, once Crow's arms were full of blissfully revitalized clothes. "She eats human cores."

"So do I," Crow said carefully.

"You do it differently." The Devil fixed her with that unsettling gaze. "Should I kill her?"

Crow's wings jumped. Just a little. She'd diminished them, folded them down to hide inside temporary flaps of skin that, for the moment, lay flush along her back.

"No," she said again. She had no other choice.

The Devil regarded her without scorn, without confusion, without concern.

"Don't ever offer an immortal your core," Crow told her. "Don't offer it to her—and not to me, either."

"I won't," the Devil said instantly. "I need my core to get home."

Crow relaxed. Magnolia would never be able to sweet-talk this woman into doing anything she didn't want to do already.

"How did you come here?" she asked as she carried her bundle of freshly cleaned clothes to the cart. Magnolia had already touched on this topic, but Crow hadn't been listening closely.

The Devil twisted at her left wrist, turning her hand all the way around and around as if trying to remove a lid from a screw-top jar. This should have torn a ligament or two—among other things—but she appeared unaffected.

"I was angry," she said. "Angry enough to kill some people who deserved it, and many who didn't. Instead I turned away from them. My magic drilled a path from one world to another. I came looking for something I'd lost. But it had already been eaten up by the space between. It was already gone."

This sounded like a riddle. Crow let it be: any attempt to explain the wandering paths of her own past would probably come off as equally nonsensical.

"You have no reason to linger, then," she said. "You just want to go back."

The Devil nodded with surprising vigor—and more enthusiasm than she'd shown throughout any of her long discussions with Magnolia.

Over the next couple days, they got the Devil on a semi-regular schedule of sleeping, eating, and magic detangling. Every evening, Crow would gaze with awestruck despair at the state of her magic: a jungle that seemed to grow denser each hour. She simply couldn't work fast enough to fight the natural tendency toward tangling. At best, she could try to keep the Devil from reverting to the thoroughly matted state she'd been in at the beginning of it all, her magic threads woven together into a solid tapestry of continuous knots.

At night, after the Devil disappeared inside her goatskin tent, they didn't have much left to do but bicker. Sometimes they went out past the flattened trees and picked off a few circling monsters. Crow would take one core, and Magnolia the next.

There was a visible difference in how it affected them. Having mostly recovered from the self-inflicted damage to her wings, Crow stood little to gain from monstrous cores. Human cores were her real sustenance, and the sustenance came not in how quickly she managed to nab one—instead it built up like the rings of a tree, year after year, across decades of promised waiting.

"Like how some human food needs to be cooked a long time for proper digestion," Magnolia said. "You saints are lucky to be able to swallow monster cores at all, given that they can never be surrendered with consent. We're constitutionally incapable of self-sacrifice. Well—to you it's all just a feeble appetizer. You're used to lengthy deprivation. Not even one good meal per century. Feast and famine, but without much feasting."

Magnolia said a lot of things. "I was excited to meet the Devil," she told Crow under moonlight, "but she's got the same stink as you."

Crow sniffed herself.

"Figuratively, you meathead! And no, I won't explain any further," she said mutinously. "Sometimes even I get fed up with having to elucidate myself to lesser minds." Minutes later—as Crow had anticipated—she doubled back and explained herself anyway. "It's the unbearable stink of goodness."

"Oh," Crow said. "Thanks?"

When Magnolia was in the mood for it, she'd elaborate on the Devil's classical turns of phrase, or snatches of vocabulary that Crow had been at a loss to interpret.

"You've done a decent job of parsing it, all things considered," Magnolia said. "It's not just that she's speaking a dead language. Her cadence isn't at all typical. Very suppressed."

"Are you a linguist?"

She'd spoken in jest, but Magnolia answered in earnest. "A form of classical Continental was my native language as a mortal. She understands the old dialects you use with her—but maybe not quite as much as you think. If you ever have anything important to tell her, I'll do the talking."

"Do you ever not do the talking?" Crow asked. Magnolia scoffed.

During the day, the two of them would retreat to the border of flattened trees while the Devil made various attempts to depart. This felt a bit like sitting in the audience of a summer fireworks show. The sky would go black, or blue, or yellow. The interplay of light and shadows on the ground would form sharp crescent shapes, as if near the peak of a solar eclipse. Sometimes the Devil vanished, or went all wavery, or appeared as a tiny speck in the sky, searching for a door to a hidden attic.

The pancake-shaped plain of dried lava turned to sand combed in flawless concentric circles, not a footprint in sight, and then churned until all the sand had been replaced by silken blue grass.

"None of which has anything to do with breaking away from this plane of existence," Magnolia commented. "She's leaking wild magic all over the place. Not the safest state of affairs."

After the Devil appeared to give up for the day, Crow walked back over with Magnolia attached parasitically to her shoulder. The ground had mostly reverted to black stone, but flowering moss grew all over in tight, agonized lines: the shape of a rigged labyrinth without any feasible exit.

The Devil turned down supper. She was markedly quiet—even more so than usual. Thunder crunched like knuckles cracking in the heavens, but it was too far away to be coupled with rain.

"You're mortal," Magnolia said in the tone of a doctor delivering a sad diagnosis. "By definition, your time is limited. If you have something to tell us, then you might as well say it."

The Devil's left hand spasmed into a claw-like shape, then subsided. With that deliberate air of hers, she dragged her gaze from Magnolia to Crow. Only now, days later, did Crow abruptly wonder why she had not once questioned Magnolia's existence as a living head. Was this a common sight where she came from, or was she just incredibly inept at showing surprise?

"I think," the Devil said, looking only at Crow, "you need to kill me."

This was followed by one of her signature pauses.

"Try to kill me," she amended. "Please."

39

AN UNHOLY GLEAM entered Magnolia's eye. "You say that as if Crow can't actually do it. Have you ever fought an immortal saint, my friend? I think not."

She stretched out a hefty branch to smack Crow on the back, right over her hidden wings. "Buck up, Carrie. At worst, you'll end up cocooned. I'll wait around for your revival if she wins. I'll wait like Pothos at Tamar's grave."

Crow, feeling perennially left behind, asked the Devil why she would want to be killed.

Magnolia jumped in again. "She forced her way here under immense pressure and stress, head-splitting fury, homicidal grief. It's taking too long to craft the right combination of magic to travel back. She wants a shortcut. She wants the type of power that she can only unlock in the face of a legitimate threat to her life.

"None of the monsters who came before us were a legitimate threat.

You're different. Which makes her just like me—a princess waiting for dear old Crow to come to her rescue. Isn't she lucky we tracked her down? Think of it as doing her a favor."

Magnolia had not said any of this in a language that the Devil would understand. The Devil, in turn, waited without complaint for them to finish conferring. She had a pebble balanced on the tip of her smallest finger. It spun like a globe, at dizzying speeds, until it went too fast to see.

At this stage, an all-out battle might have multiple benefits for Magnolia, too. She wouldn't be a direct participant. But unless the Devil put both her and Crow in cocoons, she would win.

If the Devil gained the ability to go home, a great peril would vanish. If Crow got the upper hand, then Magnolia might worm her way in to seize control over the Devil instead. If Crow slew the Devil, then Magnolia could force Crow to hand over her core.

Crow caught the Devil's eye. "You really want me to kill you?" She didn't use the word *try*.

"I'll defend myself," the Devil told her. "That's all."

"She's more worried about hurting you than she is about being hurt herself," Magnolia said to Crow with derision.

"You can't harm me in any way that matters," Crow promised the Devil. She hoped it was true.

On the one hand, the Devil was only human. On the other hand, no other human had ever made her blood rise as if she were about to battle a Great Adversary—a behemoth like the Singular Horde. Not a comparatively obscure figure like the Woman in the Hills, who was really just there to round out the numbers. Storytellers liked having Four Great Adversaries. No more, no less. To match the cardinal directions, maybe, or the classical temperate-zone seasons, or the pantheon of that lost religion where everything came in fours....

"Watch yourself," Magnolia said coldly. "I hear you disparaging me in your head. What does that say about you, Carrie? You felled the other Great Adversaries, and yet you crumpled to your knees before me. Doesn't that mean I win the tournament? Aren't I the greatest of them all?"

She used root-nubs to twist her neck towards the Devil. "You want to do it right now, yes? Let's get ready."

Crow and the Devil cooperated to set up a safe zone around the largest pool of old rain, which still hadn't shrunk. Magnolia floated in the middle of it like a sentient lily pad, roots hanging down in black water. Parts of the pool went as deep as a sinkhole. Little silver-blue fish clustered around her, nibbling at the edge of her neck.

"Go on," she said to Crow. "Take revenge for our broken world—for all its lost possibilities. Wait, no ... that won't get you fired up at all, will it."

The next words she spoke came out in the tone of a command. "Fight with everything you have. Fight like a monster. Like you're trying to reap her core. She's our Devil—give her hell. Stop hiding your wings, and stop hiding your self. Make me proud."

Crow's conscious self froze. She went as blank as the sinkhole where Magnolia roosted with her entourage of delicate fish. She was a cave shaped for the sole purpose of echoing those orders ad infinitum. It felt so deliciously heady, purposeful, so right that she could have wept from relief. She was never so sharp as when she became a tool of someone else's unwavering will.

Ordered to attack any other mortal, she might have tried to hold back. In this case, she surrendered without protest to the rising tide. Because the Devil herself wanted it, and because of Magnolia's orders, and because a core element of Crow's own being had registered the unassuming Devil as an existential-level threat.

The Devil waited in the summer sky, winter coat flapping, standing on air as if she belonged there.

Crow's wings emerged through the slits she'd sewn in the back of her shirt. A single dark feather wafted into her waiting hand, where it metamorphosed into an obsidian blade too long for any human to wield.

She felt Magnolia's eyes on her as she flew to meet the Devil. A twitch of her wings convinced the air to bear her up as if with thousands of admiring arms. In her head resounded the din of whole cities clamoring for her and her companions, lauding their feats. A bitter echo, now that those cities were gone. But the repeated drumbeat of Magnolia's orders soon overwrote it, and then she didn't have to think about anything at all.

True to her word, the Devil did not attack. Crow met her midair with a sword that should have sliced her from shoulder to hip. The blade ground against a translucent barrier. In the now-extinct pantheon of human magic, this was an effective but also very old-fashioned shield. A second later, it cracked like window glass in a fire.

The Devil very nearly looked startled. It was the closest thing Crow had seen to raw emotion on her closed-off face. If Crow were her own master, this would have made her pull back. Instead, as the Devil flickered out of reach—narrowly avoiding getting cut in two—Crow let her wings bear her forward. She swept her blade sideways, an arc meant to behead. Again, the Devil ported away at the last second.

The Devil could port, but so could Crow, dropping stray feathers as she went. They twisted and snapped to every corner of the sky, high and low, Crow never more than a millisecond behind. They sneakily ported pockets of air about in lieu of themselves—squares of the game board swapping places even while the pieces in play simultaneously danced together and apart.

"What is it you fear most?" said Magnolia's voice.

Magnolia was just a speck in the middle of a sky-mirroring pool. The pool looked like a weak filmy eye, an aged thing tucked amid the wrinkled bulk of the rolling dead lava flow that the Devil had created, in some way, upon her arrival. Yet Magnolia's voice canceled out the wind and the furious whip-crack of magic. Crow only saw the Devil in fleeting glimpses, white hair borne aloft, but she knew without question that the Devil could hear Magnolia, too.

"How fitting it would be if you ended up trapped here forever. Your destiny might be to die alone in the world you once abandoned."

The Devil repelled Crow with invisible wells of gravity. The more Crow whirled about the sky, the more feathers she shed, the more the atmospheric pressure dropped—a precipitous downward slide. Her feathers floated, arrested, like dragonflies hovering. Clouds of different colors slid together at alarming speeds, grappling for supremacy. It felt as though the sky and the air had roused themselves, remembering her, rallying to her side.

"It's even more fitting," Magnolia's clear voice said to the Devil, "that what brought you back to us was, essentially, a fit of pique. Uncontrolled magic, emotions beyond bearing. Other people can rage impotently against the injustices of life, but if you rage, it's never impotent. Surely you've heard that before."

Now Crow was fast enough to nick the side of the Devil's neck. She caught sight of red blood, indisputably human. The cut sealed itself in an act of self-repair as dramatic as time reversing—faster than an immortal's natural healing. The Devil certainly did perform better under duress.

This time, however, Crow had not been slashing to kill.

The feathers bobbing around them looked like detritus carried by a ghostly tide. Some were distant specks, and some were nearer.

All looked randomly placed, forgotten.

Before drawing first blood, Crow had chased the Devil to the precise center of those scattered feathers.

Raindrops careened sideways, slapping them as hard as birds hitting window glass. The Devil's honey-colored coat billowed, dyed dark with rain-splats like the hide of a spotted animal.

The Devil was no longer moving. As soon as Crow's sword met her skin, every black feather in the air had reoriented like iron filings around a magnet. The slender shafts pointed at the Devil, a volley of fletched arrows awaiting release. But none went flying. Concentrated light shot from the feathers like the sun extruded through a pinhole—dozens of taut yellow beams.

The shafts of light intersected where they met the Devil's flesh, forming a giant cat's cradle of luminous string. None of it touched Crow. She slipped away, careful of her wings, and wove through the rays as if escaping the bars of a cage.

Any magic she attempted could be strengthened through rituals of delay. The power of her woven light came from the extra seconds she'd spent porting back and forth, trying and failing to catch the Devil with her sword.

All subsequent action—lashing rain, the Devil's binding, Crow's retreat to the edge of the matrix of feathers—had taken place in less time than a spectator would've needed to gasp in surprise.

But their sole spectator didn't sound remotely startled. She didn't miss a beat.

"What, originally, made you flip over the chessboard of our world?" Magnolia asked. "What made you kick the table across the room and walk out and slam the door behind you? There was someone you couldn't bear not to save. All the rest of us, mortal and immortal, just have to live with our mistakes. You're different. You could tap into god-level magic, if driven hard enough—if the world failed to please you, you could change the world itself. What launched the beginning of the end? You gave into grief and threw a tantrum. Simple as that."

Beyond the boundary of feathers, Crow—floating effortlessly—gazed at her sword. There was meaning in waiting now, too. Although the longer she waited, the greater the risk of the Devil escaping.

Every day, humans waited for water to heat before brewing tea. Every year, they waited for fruit to ripen in orchards. Some magic would be more potent if you put it off till just the right moment. At least for Crow, who watched faithfully over each companion until they told her they were ready to die. Knowing from the start that some would never be ready at all, no matter how sincerely they'd first promised her the gift of a life spent in tandem, and a core at the end.

"You've done it again," Magnolia said. "And in a perfect accident of fate, it's sent you right back to the world you condemned so long ago. A fascinating realm, I tell you. Crumbling slowly into a quiet abyss."

The Devil's clothes had begun to scorch. Thin colorless threads of smoke rose where the shafts of light touched her.

Magnolia's voice kept going, building momentum like a preacher. "You sacrificed this world for a woman. Only to find yourself stuck here with us, your spiritual children. At this rate, you might be separated forever."

The Devil raised her head. She'd reacted more to that than to the fact that her skin was starting to smolder.

"History echoes itself in strange ways across the cosmos. People here were devastated when their one hope went missing in the middle of violent chaos. How they cried out for you, their greatest living mage. How they begged for you to save them.

"Later you dipped back in, just once, to close off all those pesky vorpal holes. By then, millions of prayers had already gone unheard. Good for you! You got away without having to listen."

The weight of Crow's sword had changed. She was ready. She tossed it up, impossibly high. It got sucked away into opaque clouds that formed a ridged tunneling shape like an open throat.

"Now it's your turn." Rather than traveling through the air, Magnolia's voice infused it. "You let emotion take over, and it sentenced you to join us, to fight monsters, to look upon what you've wrought. This time, you left your beloved behind. This time, she'll think you've forsaken her. She'll rage impotently, with nothing to show for it. Now *her* prayers will go unanswered."

At last faraway clouds regurgitated Crow's sword. Blade pointed down. Poised directly over the Devil's head. It had grown to the size of a pre-apocalyptic skyscraper, a black tower. It wouldn't just cleave the Devil—it would obliterate her. It was not a weapon sized for combat with anything less than the earth itself. It looked like a stake made to split the world in two.

Magnolia whispered to the Devil: "You have no idea what might be happening to her back in your chosen world, your better world. Your departure wasn't planned. She must be very vulnerable."

The building-sized blade began to fall.

"For all you know, she might already be—"

The sword stopped. The Devil hung in its shadow like a speck of dust under the tip of a pencil. But it fell no further. The pressurized air that had been Crow's ally now betrayed her, immobilizing her swollen blade, holding everything in place—the blood that had stopped in her veins, the magma that had stopped deep below the crust of the land.

A force struck the towering blade, a force that left cracks from tip to hilt. Crow thought her own bones would crack in answer, too.

Another blow. The blade splintered into ever-smaller pieces, black and reflective, a host of obsidian mirrors.

The Devil's magic hit it until nothing was left but ashen dust. She kept hitting it while the shafts of light binding her bent and sagged like loose ribbons. She kept hitting it when there was nothing left to strike, not even looking up to observe the impact, eyelids half-lowered, utterly intent on something beyond Crow's comprehension. Her magic struck emptiness, and it felt like a crazed soldier beating a voiceless captive.

As she kept pounding at nothing at all, there came a broken fraction of a second during which the air itself seemed to give way.

The Devil's body had not moved. Not even when the light rays that scorched her began to slip and fray and then, unraveling, released her. But the instant the air buckled, her magic stopped laying siege to it. "Oh," she said, and she appeared more taken aback by the sound of her own voice than by anything else that had transpired thus far. She wasn't paying any attention to Crow.

40

Magnolia's omnipresent voice addressed the Devil. "You wanted a fight for your life, and that's what you'll get. As for you, Crow—you never needed wings."

Now. Stop hiding your self.

The same command as before. It pierced Crow like a poison dart; it took effect before she knew what it meant. Her rational mind dropped off the edge of a cliff.

Life with humans had trained her thoughts to trickle through filters of language like water through charcoal. Her far-flung feathers—the ones she'd strewn about to trap the Devil—rushed back to her. She had no words for what came next.

Her wings twisted up and retracted inside her with frightening force. She hung suspended from the sky without their help, a marionette on unseen strings. The heretical rapture of not having control over anything—not even her own form—reached its peak.

In her old life as an aerial, she had drifted on undetectable currents. She had been a mortal creature of magic that the ground repelled like an opposing magnet. She hadn't needed to understand the forces that bore her up in the sky where she belonged. Where aerials had belonged, unchanging, since before humans first fought over the land below.

As an aerial, she had never made a conscious decision to spare a life. As an aerial, she had never held the frail bodies of shorter-lived creatures and granted them a swift passage to whatever came after. As an aerial, she had never clung to memories of the irrecoverable dead. As an aerial, she had felt nothing beyond the eternal sensations of the present moment: wind and cold, light air and heavy air, stars and clouds, all equally welcoming.

Stop hiding your self.

Her brain shed the burden of language like an infection burning out.

She didn't need wings. This was true. She felt herself turning inside out. She became what she had been in another life—what she had been all along, regardless of the flesh she wore like a capricious change of clothing.

She became an elder sky serpent.

She looked nothing like the disintegrating icons in roadside shrines. The Fellshore mimid, with its conglomeration of substitute parts, had only been able to produce a grotesque imitation—drawing on fuzzy images from the minds of humans who had never seen an aerial close up.

Long before the beginning of the end of the world, countless people—including powerful mages—had died in pursuit of elusive elder aerials. Trying to tame or capture them. Trying to harvest some vital substance from their organs.

She clamped the Devil-woman in her jaws. As she bit down, many-layered magical barriers snapped like plates of sugar. She hurtled head-first toward the ground.

The field of volcanic rock was shaped like an arena. Or, from the perspective of an aerial: a giant target. Her sheer momentum would open a rift in the earth, pulping her skull and her mouth and the woman she'd taken inside it. She plunged without fear, lightning crackling between her teeth. She had nothing to dread from even the steepest of dives. In her long life as an elder aerial, she had never fallen without meaning to.

Except at the very end.

As she crashed down, black rock faltered beneath her, yielding like a bed. She bounced and tumbled sideways, tail lashing, frenzied. The softening of the ground was not her doing. Foreign magic crawled like lice over the surface of her colossal body. She writhed furiously to scrape it off.

She spat something out. A scorching lump of human magecraft. In her wrath, she had a vague sense of fire and water scouring the stones she clawed at, unstoppable tides of elemental fury sweeping the barren field from end to end. The border of flattened trees looked like twigs, a clumsy bird's nest. She hardly knew what she was fighting—a creature too puny for the scale of her aerial senses; a biting midge. When she attacked, broken magic crunched like broken glass.

She didn't stop until she noticed that the entire sky had gone blue.

It was very plain. But it ached like the sight of something lost. Had she ever known such a sky herself, in either of her lives? She wondered how far this blueness really stretched. She wondered if anyone in far-off settlements would see it. The people of the radish village, perhaps—or the automagi and Pothos the fox, or Haida and Rinlin and her chickens.

No one was fighting anymore. Crow realized that well after the fact. She had shed her aerial form. She had arms and legs, and a pounding head, and dove-sized wings that had migrated to the nape of her neck. They flapped loudly, right by her ears, as if to beat her awake.

She sat up. The plain of melted black rock appeared unnervingly intact. The fallen trees beyond it had become burnt skeletal things, as mangled as a shipwreck. If any other immortals had been lurking in the wings, lured by the Devil, they must have been smart enough to beat a hasty retreat.

Had all the winding streams gone up in steam? She saw no waddling fish, no furry dragonflies.

Magnolia had been down here, too. The protections around that placid pool could not have been nearly enough to save her.

Incoherent emotions swept through Crow one after another, passing too swiftly to catch or name them. If she were dead, Crow would sense her defeat. She'd reach out and close her fist around Magnolia's waiting core even if her cranium and her roots and her face and her bitter smile had been reduced to specks of dust too small to see.

Unless the Devil had killed Magnolia instead. Unless the Devil had gotten to her while Crow lashed out blindly, no better than a maddened animal.

A wiry green vine coiled around her forearm.

"I knew what was coming," Magnolia said pointedly. "I'm good at getting out of the way."

She pulled herself closer, scooting across dry rock with feeble runners. Crow bent to pick her up. There was dirt on her face and in her hair, as if she'd buried herself like a digging mole, but she appeared otherwise unscathed.

A corkscrew-shaped tendril pointed accusingly past Crow's shoulder.

For some reason, the campfire boulders were now stacked six high. The Devil sat at the top. She didn't seem wounded, although Crow distinctly remembered clamping down hard enough to bite her in two.

She pored over her coat like a finicky seamstress, magically erasing holes and scorch marks.

"She had her epiphany," Magnolia said dourly. "She knows how to go back. Doesn't want to show up looking like she nearly got murdered in another world." She squinted at the wide blue sky. "My word, that's depressing. If the Devil were more devious, I'd accuse her of trying to rub it in."

"More devious," Crow repeated. "More like you?"

Magnolia jabbed stiff vine-stalks skyward, as if to spear the heavens with a pitchfork. "What do you make of this, Saint Crow?"

"It's like the blue pocket over Steppehaven."

"You're always so literal. Well, enjoy it while you can. Once she's gone, you'll never see a big blue sky like that again."

Up on her stack of boulders, the Devil kept tending to her clothes.

Magnolia was still grumbling. "The really annoying part of it," she said, "is this. Despite our excellent—and effective!—performance, I doubt we'll merit so much as a single line when bards pen the Devil's love song. We're in the wrong world for it, after all. We dwell in a shadow, a cast-off, a leftover shell."

You sacrificed this world for a woman.

"What kind of..." Crow trailed off, uncertain of what she was trying to say.

"What kind of person would the Devil go to such lengths for? As far as I can tell," Magnolia said glumly, "it's someone that neither of us would give a second glance. Someone quite powerless. Someone without a core, if you can believe it. Who can ever hope to understand the vagaries of mortal affection?"

"You were human before you were immortal."

"I died too young for true love," Magnolia retorted. "I was a starving peasant. No one important. I couldn't use magic. And yet no one doomed the rest of the world to save me. No, Crow, I don't understand it."

She picked up the thread of that thought again after a protracted silence. "But if I did destroy the world for the love of a woman, I would damn well make sure to do it on purpose. I would only do it for myself, in fact—not for love, not for anyone else. I'd do it with glee and panache, and I wouldn't regret it for an instant."

"It's a good thing you aren't the Devil," Crow said.

"I know. You love to hate me just the way I am. I'll do you a favor, Crow. I won't ever change."

Crow would have objected on principle—but the Devil had at last paused to look down at them. Crow stacked Magnolia atop her own head, as if carrying a jug of water, and together they approached the column of boulders.

"I'm in your debt." The Devil said it with her usual flat affect.

"The pleasure was all ours," Magnolia replied, tart-voiced. "Tell us more about your breakthrough. Then we can consider the debt repaid."

She and the Devil spoke of eldritch voids and wormholes and other esoteric vorpal and corporeal affairs. The Devil's boulders probably understood the conversation better than Crow did. At any rate, Crow and the boulders were equally vocal participants.

After descending from her tower, the Devil magically dismantled it. Hands in her pockets, she wafted the boulders down into a misshapen ring. Any traces of past campfires had been thoroughly obliterated when Crow thrashed about with her aerial body.

The Devil excused herself, despite the fact that Magnolia wasn't done talking. She promptly set about weaving the beginning of a work of magic that made Crow want to flee across the wasteland and go find Dung and never come back.

"She'll leave as soon as she can," Magnolia muttered. She sounded decidedly put out. "Of course—who would expect goodbyes or gratitude from the Devil? Not I."

The Devil showed no inclination to stop and rest, but eventually she collapsed like a fallen leaf. Crow put her to bed again, this time without a tent.

There was little to be salvaged from the wreckage of their cart. Only a few lucky jars had survived—along with, curiously, all the garments the Devil had steamed. They'd refused to burn; they remained persistently clean. But humans couldn't derive much nutrition from chewing clothes. If the Devil lingered much longer, someone (presumably Crow) would have to forage for extra provisions to tide her over.

The Devil slept deeply. She failed to stir even when Crow knelt beside her and sorted through her matted skeins of magic. The knots were so dense that she couldn't see down to the Devil's core. Like hair so tangled that you couldn't glimpse any of the scalp beneath. Crow couldn't do much to fix this—she'd need years to make a dent in it—but she tried. Magnolia grudgingly offered guidance.

When the Devil finally woke again, she didn't waste time looking around and blinking. She took the long coat that had been pillowed under her head and shook it out with a snap. She put it on despite the fact that a muggy heat had descended while she slept. She opened and closed the fingers of her left hand until they stopped trying to turn transparent.

It was an hour or two before dusk. The cloudless blue sky had been watered down, steadily losing depth. Only a few timid insects croaked in the shadows. Crow and Magnolia had gone back to sorting through the remnants of their battered cart. The magical wheels had all melted away, carving distinct shapes in the rock beneath, like a mold awaiting molten metal. Crow collected scraps to craft a sack. They could carry around extra outfits for when Magnolia used her body.

The Devil walked up to them. Magnolia rested on the remains of the cart as if upon a throne of garbage. Crow, busy rummaging around, didn't glance up fast enough to understand the look on her face.

"I owe you a debt," the Devil said.

Her eyes were on Crow.

Magnolia's drapery of vines fell away from the base of her neck as if someone had chopped them with a machete. They flailed, worm-like, spraying droplets of clear sap. By then Magnolia had floated off her pile of trash, whisked away by the Devil's magic.

There was a venomous look in Magnolia's eyes. But she didn't screech in protest. She didn't say anything at all.

Crow could not read minds, but she could read this.

Magnolia was afraid.

She hovered unsupported, a buoyant head without a body. The Devil gazed past her.

"She eats people," the Devil stated, as if it were as simple as that. Maybe it was. No—of course it was. There was nothing simpler in all the world.

Crow began making promises. She promised to stop Magnolia. From doing what? From doing anything that would give the Devil a reason to pass judgment on her. To dispose of her.

She halted in the middle of a sentence, aghast. She couldn't explain any of what she was saying, or why she'd said it. The Devil and Magnolia watched her without blinking.

"Can you do that?" the Devil asked. "Can you stop her from behaving as a monster?"

Magnolia's mouth stayed clamped shut. Crow felt her there all the same, a growing pressure building up in her eyes, her skull—even in her core, as if it too were a fluid-filled orb.

She wasn't mortal. Nothing in her—no organ, no matter how tender—could be irreparably damaged. Just so long as she never suffered defeat at the hands of a fellow immortal. But it felt as if Magnolia had done something irreversible. Even in the absence of orders, it felt as if Magnolia would never leave her head.

41

"You can't ask me to free you," the Devil said. "You can't ask me to kill her. You'll never seek help. But I don't need permission."

She was utterly matter-of-fact. As matter-of-fact as Magnolia would have been when suggesting that they murder the nearest human. If not for Crow, she would have devoured Rinlin without hesitation. If not for Crow—

"She's mine to punish," Crow blurted.

Only afterward did she remember that whatever the Devil did to Magnolia, it couldn't result in permanent death. Unless that had been another of her revelations—one of the puzzles she'd solved while Crow pursued her across the sky. New magic for killing as immortals did. Could the Devil lay claim to Magnolia's core?

"Don't take away my chance to punish her," Crow said. It pained her to speak. It would have pained her more to keep silent.

"What chance?" the Devil inquired.

And then: "Is she making you say that?"

Magnolia opened her mouth. Before she could breathe a word, the Devil reached over and twisted at the top of her head as if screwing it tighter. There on a bed of air, Magnolia's eyelids fluttered shut. Her chin dipped forward. Until now, Crow had only ever seen her sleep while wearing the costume of her human body. In her true form, she had no reason to leave herself exposed—head tilting, lips loose.

It took the Devil no effort to keep her aloft. She kept floating, forgotten, while the Devil studied Crow.

There was a warning thump in Crow's chest. She seemed on the verge of becoming an aerial again, right then and there. Even though she knew no one left in this old world—mortal or immortal, human-shaped or aerial-shaped—would be a real match for the Devil herself.

That didn't matter. She was like Pothos growling by Tamar's grave. If anyone was going to erase the unholy light from Magnolia's eyes, if anyone was going to extract whatever blood could be wrung from a body that only consisted of a head and a neck, it'd be Crow. No one else would get past her.

"You don't want this monster dead." The Devil made it sound like a question without a question mark.

"That's not—" Crow stopped to regroup. "At my hands," she said, illogically. "It's different if she dies at my hands."

A very subtle shift took place in the Devil's face. Crow didn't know her well enough to hazard a guess at what it meant.

"Another option," the Devil said. "I can break her hold. Without killing her. But I can't give you future immunity. You'll have to flee, and you'll have to stay far away from her. For as long as you live."

For as long as it took to acquire another heroic companion, one who would understand the danger of letting the last Great Adversary roam unchecked. She would find Magnolia again as soon as she could.

Soon enough to stop her from cutting a swathe through the nearest settlements?

Crow stared at the ruts that the vaporized cart wheels had inscribed on solid rock. The stifling afternoon heat had thinned as the once-blue sky turned the color of a fading bruise. The Devil, clad comfortably in her ankle-length coat, seemed to have simply opted out of summer.

Magnolia's head rotated in the air, as if she dangled from a long and subtle string. As if she were on display at a fine museum, the sort that would have been looted to its bones in ages past.

"Can you perceive what she's done to me?" Crow asked the Devil. "Can you tell how her magic affects me?"

"It affects you more than you know," the Devil said, "and less than you think."

"Has she softened herself in my sight? Has she made it harder to think of hurting her?"

"Not in the way you fear. Her commands are absolute, but they come from outside you."

"You're sure of that?"

The Devil's magic stirred within her. It was a wall of tangled branches. "She could do it. You might never know. She could order you to worship her, and she could order you to forget it'd been forced on you."

"She wouldn't be interested in any worship that comes so easily," Crow answered, and was startled to find that she fully believed this.

It would be child's play for Magnolia to reap adoration, to found a lasting cult, to spread the good word of the Woman in the Hills. But she would quickly grow bored. She would revel more in the mastery required to bend—or break—someone resistant to her will. She would have more fun toying with an enemy who hated her guts than a fanatic who fawned over her every syllable. She was a villain who would rather be surrounded by heroes than sycophants.

The Devil turned abruptly and hissed something under her breath. "What?" Crow said.

The Devil didn't hear her. "Clem would..." She crumpled her unruly left hand, which was attempting to escape her wrist again. It settled down after repeated flexing, like a young animal desperate for exercise. "If Clem were here..."

She pivoted to face Crow, the smashed cart, and Magnolia. With an unexpectedly vindictive air, she flicked the side of Magnolia's hovering head. Magnolia—though still dozing peacefully—began spinning much faster.

"I eliminated vorpal holes," the Devil said. "I removed a basic principle of the world, as if erasing the existence of gravity. I thought I was making things right. Now, instead of vorpal holes, you have red-eyed monsters. Which do much the same thing, with respect to human lives. Except the monsters have mobility, and magic, and intelligence, and hunger. I should have known. I should have guessed."

Water welled to fill dried-up rivulets in the plain of hardened lava. It had an inexplicable brackish smell, though they were many miles from the nearest coast.

"You might never get away from her," the Devil warned.

Crow was under no illusion that she could make Magnolia into anything other than the monster she was. Yet she balked, irrationally, at letting the Devil play executioner. She balked at leaving Magnolia, too—which would mean leaving her to eat as she pleased.

Crow told herself she had an obligation to stay. To see it through. She had to escort Magnolia to the end of the world, a place devoid of people who might become collateral damage.

She wanted to yank Magnolia away from the Devil—to rescue her from hanging like a melon in a net. She wanted to leave a mark on Magnolia to show that no one else was allowed to hurt her. She wanted to hurl Magnolia into the brokenness at the edge of the living world, and she wanted to be alone when she did it. The urgency of it pulsed in her like blood in an artery, a force outside her conscious control or understanding.

She could only scrape together threadbare logic to clothe her thoughts. The Devil would see right through her.

"One way or another," Crow said, "I'll take care of her."

Stars pricked the dusk sky like needle holes. The Devil contemplated Crow as one might contemplate an open casket.

Magnolia's head stopped spinning. She drifted over to the burnt-out wreck of the cart. The Devil's magic deposited her there, the crowning touch to a mountain of refuse.

She opened her eyes. She looked immediately at Crow. "I had a dream," she said, indignant. "I was riding some sort of dreadful carousel. I almost got sick! What would you have done if I vomited in my sleep? What on earth would I even vomit—I'm a head without a stomach!"

"What do you exhale when you sigh?" Crow asked.

Magnolia glared.

The Devil's face had gone quite blank. She turned to the cart. Magnolia dug probing roots into the heap beneath her—looking once more like a mollusk stapled to a pier, bracing for the sea.

Neither of them said another word. But Magnolia's eyes flickered. They were conversing mind-to-mind. Crow's downsized wings itched with frustration.

At last the Devil walked away.

Crow, watching her go, said to Magnolia: "If you went to Fellshore or Steppehaven without me..."

"I could never have made it so far on my own."

"Pretend you did. If you were alone with Rinlin, if you were alone with Tamar—what would you have done?"

Magnolia's voice lacked its usual tinge of amusement. "You already know. I'm not sure why you want me to say it."

Crow didn't answer. She jogged to catch up with the Devil. Magnolia made no attempt to tag along.

She found the Devil near her former campsite. The tent had been atomized during their battle. The Devil tilted her head back as if she were noticing stars for the first time in her life. She gazed at them in the same way she had gazed at Magnolia: like there was something profoundly wrong, something she couldn't translate into words.

Suddenly Crow wished she'd told the Devil more about their world.

There were far fewer people than before—but as time went by, they fought amongst themselves far less. Maybe it was just that no one had the energy or imagination to wage war on a grander scale. Maybe there was less to fight over. Maybe the human species had lost some essential inner fire. Crow, who had seen empires fall and cities eat themselves alive, much preferred the sort of age in which humanity's last mage could live out her days in happy obscurity, surrounded by bickering woodworkers.

She wished she could talk like Magnolia. She'd tell the Devil that it wasn't all bad. The world as it was now could not have come to be in any other way. The earliest years of apocalypse, the decimation of humanity—that predated Crow, and every other immortal. It was not a crime she had any standing to prosecute.

Fairly or unfairly, enough time had passed to turn atrocities into facts, and facts into stories, and stories into myths. Even with diminished land and resources and culture, life in these late-stage end times was—on the whole—good enough that people entreated the God of the End to keep waiting another couple generations.

Please, not in this lifetime, they would pray. *Please, spare our children and grandchildren. And their children, if you can.* Crow did not believe in any deity, much less the lazy God of the End. But so far, it appeared as though all their prayers had been answered.

The Devil said: "You're a returner." She pronounced the word with exaggerated care. It was borrowed vocabulary, unfamiliar to her mouth.

"Yes?" Crow said gingerly.

"Do you consider yourself the same being as you were before? Are you the same soul in a different shell? Or are you a child to your past self—an offshoot?"

Crow pointed a thumb over her shoulder. "Did you already ask her?"

The Devil kept waiting.

Crow said she thought she was the same. Her memories of being an aerial were sketchy, but so were her memories of long stretches of immortal life. Unchanging days, repeated seasons, faces that appeared imbued with the ghosts of previous generations.

She might have become something unrecognizable to her previous self, but the change had taken place so gradually that she saw no natural stopping point to mark the end of one soul and the beginning of another. Not even the moment of her mortal death.

Maybe that blurring of lines was something unique to her, and what had happened after her fall. But even humans were capable of growing into the opposite of their younger selves—in the span of a single life, and with far less time to spare.

The word for *aerial* had changed surprisingly little over the course of eons. The Devil understood it more readily than anything else she'd said.

Crow left the Devil to her magecraft. She brought Magnolia over to the boulders that poked up out of the otherwise flat land like a half-hearted monument. This gave them an ominous view of the Devil at work. She'd resumed lacing together magic that set Crow's teeth on edge with its strength.

"We're dead to her," Magnolia said flatly. "She won't think of anything except getting out of here. Now that she's worked out the necessary mechanics, it's only a matter of time."

Crow sat on a boulder with Magnolia on her knees. Restless vines unfurled from the darkness below Magnolia's neck. They twined about her ankles, locking her in place.

"When you went chasing after her, I thought you'd changed your mind," Magnolia said. "About letting her kill me."

"You didn't stop me."

A harsh laugh. "If I made you do an about-face—that'd have gotten her attention faster than anything. She was very ready to have a go at ending me. I'd give her fifty-fifty odds of devising a way to make it permanent."

"She spoke to you in your head," Crow said. "Before she walked away. What'd she say?"

"None of your business."

How childish, Crow thought.

"Think what you like. The only good thing about today—aside from the Devil's impending departure—is that I got to see you as an aerial."

"I didn't know I could do that."

"You probably couldn't, before. I bring out the best in you," Magnolia said with easy confidence. "You were beautiful. Spectacular. Graft me to your back, and we would make a truly fearsome creature."

"No free rides," Crow told her.

Without warning, there came a sound like air getting sucked from lungs. Then there was no sound at all, just a hideous internal pressure with no way to relieve it. Vines bit Crow's ankles, bristling with thorns. She covered Magnolia to shield her from a blast that never came.

The Devil's left hand glowed like a glove filled with fire. She stood silhouetted in front of a vertical crack without anything whatsoever on the other side of it. Its mere existence—or the lack thereof—stabbed Crow's senses. She doubled over, Magnolia warm and hard against her. She couldn't look up.

The first noise she heard was a smothered squawking. She straightened, no longer crushing Magnolia's head in her lap. Her back felt as though it had been hunched for years. The bleeding skin of her legs kept trying to heal around Magnolia's thorns.

The crack had vanished, taking with it the Devil and her left hand and her windblown winter coat. She hadn't left anything behind.

"That was a vorpal hole," Magnolia said tightly, "or something very like it. See what I mean? She makes rules, and then she breaks them."

Crow felt obscurely compelled to defend the Devil, who was no longer here to defend herself. "She spared you."

"And is that a sign of good decision-making?" Magnolia demanded. "Is it?"

Crow couldn't say yes.

"There you go," Magnolia declared. "That's what makes her our Devil. Our creator, even, if you carefully trace the chains of cause and effect. I'm sorry if you miss her, but she won't be coming back. You know, I shouldn't be surprised that you prefer the strong, silent, responsible type. Like calls to like. I suppose she has a certain mystique that I lack."

"What are you talking about?" Crow finally managed, bewildered.

"How glad I am to be getting out of this wasteland. Almost as glad as the Devil was to turn her back on us, I'd say. No, leave these boulders here. Don't try to salvage anything else from the cart. Dung will be delighted to see it destroyed."

42

Was Dung delighted? He didn't pay any attention to the debris of the broken cart. Instead he spent half an hour sniffing his way around all the places where the now-absent Devil had walked.

"Not you, too," Magnolia said irritably. "Stop moping!" For once, her orders had little effect.

Crow still thrummed with the aftershocks of her aerial transformation. She felt as though she could expand her wings and port the three of them straight to the radish village. She didn't mention it—and if Magnolia picked up on her thoughts, she either deemed them delusions or chose not to mention it, either. Crow was grateful. She would keep Magnolia away from mortal settlements for as long as she could.

The next day, the once-blue sky turned a subtly different color. More like periwinkle, shading towards lavender. The day after that, it was covered from horizon to horizon in a pattern as pronounced as a peacock's tail. No sign remained that the Devil had come to visit.

Magnolia led them on a roundabout path toward her hills. First she urged Dung east, all the way to the coast. "The dregs of the Devil's water gave me a hankering to smell real salt," she said.

"Ever smelled it before?" The hills were thoroughly landlocked.

"I've perused the minds of seafarers, but I've never seen the ocean."

Dung carried them through a land of dolmens: rough megalithic tombs that seemed to predate the apocalypse. He was less impressed by these than he had been by the Devil. He showed a similar lack of reaction when they stumbled across a ghost forest. Gray trunks speared the sky, still standing despite having been dead many hundreds of years.

"Name the killer," Magnolia said.

"Salt water?"

"A tsunami, presumably."

They had a ways to go before they reached the shore. No picturesque beaches here. Just abandoned settlements and an accumulation of shipwrecks that must have piled up over the course of a thousand-plus years. There were few seafarers left anywhere on the continent nowadays—and none foolish enough to lose sight of land. It looked as if the tide had swept every last far-off tragedy into this one crowded corner.

The limb of a machina protruded crookedly from beneath the fused wooden hulls of ships. Nothing here had been seaworthy in generations, but the whole mess served as a kind of inadvertent breakwater.

To Dung, it was a many-tiered display of hidden delicacies. After they dismounted, he tromped on ahead, tongue flicking. All those sea roaches scurrying in the shade would leave him too full to move another inch.

"Don't get buried," Magnolia yelled at him.

She had been in a mercurial mood—sometimes gloating over the Devil's absence, sometimes scowling at collapsed dolmens. Crow took her up to a rocky bluff, so she could see the ocean past the mass of shipwrecks. She appeared prepared for disappointment when she sniffed the breeze blowing off the water, but then her face shifted.

Wooden hooks emerged from the shorn-off rim of her neck, fastening her to a stone growth that tilted out toward the sea like a broken tree trunk.

"Comb my hair," she sad.

"I don't have a comb."

"You have hands."

Magnolia's hair wasn't long enough to get drastically tangled, which made this much pleasanter than tending to the Devil's many-branching magic. But the instant Crow lifted her hand away, the wind erased her work. She let those heartwood-colored locks slip between her fingers again and again. She had unlimited time.

There were fewer water birds crying out than at Lake Fallen. Maybe they had an animalistic taboo against nesting in the graveyard of ground-up ships.

"I owe you my life," Magnolia bit out, "and I strongly dislike it."

"Because I asked the Devil to let me kill you instead?"

"She held back on your behalf. But I did it first," Magnolia said. "I restrained my natural impulses for you alone. Why should the Devil get all the credit? Then again—she was absolutely ready to scrub me out of the world like a nasty spot. She really did only stop because of you. She felt sorry for you. Or she thought she'd better let you make one single choice, in that one single moment, seeing how as I've denied you every other true moment of choice.

"Even if you suddenly found the strength to break my magic and grab me and dash me on the rocks right now, you did save me from the Devil. I hate it. I hate even the hint of a shadow of a vague sensation of owing repayment. You'll drive me crazy one day, Crow. You ought to be very happy with yourself."

Crow continued carding her hair. "How did you die?"

"What, in my first life?"

She was about to utter something flippant. Crow could see it on her lips. But then her throat made a phantom motion of swallowing. She pressed her mouth shut and leaned her weight, just a little, against Crow's hand in her hair. Her thorny claws scraped the pitted rock.

"There's a theory of returners that I strongly disagree with," she said, detached, as if they were discussing the principles of post-apocalyptic economics. "Some think our power comes from suffering and sacrifice in our previous lives. I don't know if that has anything to do with why we became returners, but I doubt it. In any case, it definitely has nothing to do with our magic as immortals.

"We're all born weak, grasping for cores—whether taken from humans, or cannibalized from each other. It's just a question of how fast and how far our magic scales with each acquisition. That does vary—it's not predictable, and it's not fair. I don't think returners have any sort of leg up, except perhaps in knowledge of the world, and sometimes of human society. Equally powerful immortals have been born from nothingness."

"How did you die?" Crow asked again.

"I've tasted ambrosia hares. They aren't very good."

There was a trance under Crow's skin, as if the breeze had infiltrated her empty spaces. She had a strange buzzing sense that she could no longer stop or turn away. Not even if the dangerously angled spur of rock shattered and flung her down in disgust. She remained settled there, as though in the crook of a jutting tree limb, and ran her fingers over and over through Magnolia's hair.

"Did I ever mention being an illiterate peasant?" Magnolia said.

"Once or twice."

"When I was human, I lived far, far north of the hills. Way past the modern-day end of the world. So we won't be seeing my homeland. At least—I hope not. It must be uninhabited, if any sliver of it still exists. Empty of people, and empty of immortals. Why live in a place with no prey?"

A shadow scuttled over them. Too fast to be an ordinary cloud. "Aerials," Magnolia breathed, like an epithet. She twisted so that Crow's hand momentarily came to rest on her cheek.

"My birth village was surrounded by vorpal holes. Not always, obviously—but they grew and they grew. *Holes* isn't a very good word for them. They're ruptures, an unraveling in the earth and air. Anyway, you wouldn't have been around back then. Aerials were almost extinct before our Devil sealed up all those cracks in the world. And that came much later.

"The important part is that no one came to save us. We lacked the funds or daring or coldblooded decisiveness needed to get the hell out of there in time to survive. Who knows if going south would've been any better? Half the world was eaten by vorpal holes, and the other half was at war over whatever remained. Even way up north, we saw foreign machina flying and fighting and crashing.

"Plus, there were undeniable merits to having a wall—or a moat—of vorpal holes between us and other settlements. No one bothered trying to pillage us. They'd have to file through the gaps one at a time, orderly as you please. We wouldn't need to be soldiers to hold out our pitchforks and gut them.

"People said it was bad luck to look directly at vorpal spaces. But by the time I grew up, our village was completely ringed by holes. No room left to get out. Imagine the bars of a cage swelling and growing and merging together into a solid wall. We couldn't fly high enough or dig deep enough to escape. All we had inside the ring were some fields, some wells and ponds—lucky, that—and some livestock that had to be herded away from the rift at all costs. We were a microcosm of the world as it is today, with a slow-encroaching boundary of death. Or you could say we were like a terrarium forgotten on a shelf of an empty house, environmental balance deteriorating, no one to fix it."

Crow asked if the circle of holes had already closed before her birth.

Magnolia cast her eyes up to think and then said, as if surprised: "When I was littler than Rinlin, there was enough of a break in the ring for a thin adult to slip out. Some of them lost bits of clothing—or bits of flesh, or more than a bit—in the process. One day it became so narrow that not even a child could get through unscathed. My father got caught on the other side. He had to settle down in another village. He would toss fruit to us, and pass letters on a stick. Nothing too big. I saw a falling star around that time, but I knew better than to tell anyone.

"Another night, the ring completed itself. I thought it was because of me, my star—my ill fortune. I still didn't say it. We couldn't see my father anymore, not even the tips of his feet. He would come every day and shout to us, for a while, but eventually he stopped. We never knew why."

"You still don't know," Crow said.

"A generous heart would hope, in retrospect, that he just got tired of shouting. Wherever he went to seek shelter—he may have been known as a traveler, a distant neighbor, but he wasn't one of them. It wasn't an era famed for kindness to strangers. A couple times, people shot flaming arrows over the top of the vorpal wall. As if they could purge their own troubles by burning us in our beds. As if our fire might distract the gods that cursed them."

"What was the curse?"

"The usual thing," Magnolia said. "The same problem inside our wall and outside it, I'm sure. Too many people and not enough food. One morning, yet another vorpal hole formed out of nowhere—yes, even inside the outer ring. The new hole swallowed up our granaries. What do you do during a famine, Crow?

"In our case—and this did have some basis in local tradition—they started offering up sacrifices. The human sort. Which had the added benefit of reducing the local head count. Our livestock were much too precious to throw away for a prayer."

"Sacrifices to who?"

She laughed. "To anyone or anything that would listen, no? I'm sure they had some appropriate demon or deity in mind—could've been the Devil herself—but I didn't find the religious element of it important enough to remember across multiple lifetimes. The automagi would've been so disappointed. Never did get around to telling them that part. So where do you think we tossed our sacrifices?"

"In the moat," Crow said. "In your vorpal abyss."

"They threw out the elderly. They threw out useless little children. They threw out young girls. I helped, no doubt. Everyone helped. Eventually it was my turn. Not first, not last, but right in the middle."

A cruel inversion of glee entered her voice, hard and bright. "By then, you know, they'd stopped shoving entire bodies into the abyss. Too wasteful. They performed the bare minimum of traditional gestures: they put these earrings on me to take to the land of the dead. Some sort of bargaining chip—I think that's how the story goes. I did get the very last pair of earrings, so someone cared enough to give me that. No more pretty dresses to spare, though. I was probably wearing a sack, or nothing whatsoever.

"I knew what they'd do. They'd dunk my face in nothingness, as if holding me underwater to drown me. They'd pull me out, and my head would be gone without a trace—severed at the shoulders, so cleanly that it might almost seem cauterized. Much less blood than you'd think, or possibly none at all. I knew what would happen because I'd seen them do it before. I'd participated. They'd stick my head in to go through the motions of a proper sacrifice. They'd keep my body. For a while after that, the starving village would feast.

"By then my mother was gone, too. And my sisters. Hm, did I have sisters? Brothers? I'm assuming I did, but who knows. If they were still alive, maybe I would've been glad to get eaten. But I wasn't. I didn't go with dignity. I caterwauled. I bit and scratched and kicked like a wildcat. I fought them with strength I didn't have. I gave them a pretty hard time, honestly. By then, even grown men were getting weak. It's funny, when you think about it. Life was hellish inside our fortress of vorpal holes. I still didn't go in peace."

Wooden thorns gripped the rock like spiny crab legs. She shifted minutely, and her earrings shook and gleamed against what remained of her neck. "Well, you understand how it goes in the end. They put the sacrificial earrings on me. They forced my head in."

Her claws turned her a few more degrees. The sea and all its detritus lay behind her. She looked straight up at Crow. "What bothers me most about being a returner is the randomness of it. Why me? I say this with zero humility: there was nothing special about me. No reason that I should have come back when others didn't—others better or worse than me, more or less innocent. I ate from the sacrifices we murdered before me, just like everyone else, and I suppose I ended up feeding those who outlasted me, even though I fought it to my very last breath.

"If this life is a reward, I did nothing to deserve it. If it's a punishment, I did nothing to deserve that, either. I wasn't the only one who went unwillingly to my death. When you think about it—our village getting walled in by vorpal holes was total happenstance, too. Why us? Why anyone? There was another town, bigger and richer, that got devoured by a fresh-blooming vorpal hole in the space of a breath. No time to fear, no time to mourn, not even any pain. Just gone.

"We merely had the bad fortune to get plopped down in the middle of a deadly donut. The vorpal holes had no malice—and no more rhyme or reason to them than bubbles in water. But when all was said and done, I'm sure everyone would have much preferred instant annihilation. When life is a possibility, it's very hard not to fight for it, to fight long and hard and dirty. To trample whoever you can, and weep as you suck badly cooked meat off their bones."

She gave Crow a short cutting smile, showing teeth. "Eventually I went from thinking *Why me?* to thinking *Why not me?* One's as unanswerable as the other, and I like the sound of it better."

Down below, Dung nosed his way around the corpses of decaying boats. "My body was not my own in life or in death," Magnolia said. "Was I lucky to be next in line to be sacrificed—before our little society completely broke down? No one tried to lay hands on me, although virginity was hardly a requirement for sacrifice. After a certain point, they couldn't afford to be picky.

"So later—quite a bit later—the world had a minor convulsion, a fit of hiccups, and it hacked me up again. There I was, reborn in a different time, in hills I'd never seen before, and I was still trapped in one single place. Even after I became an immortal creature, a returner, my territory hadn't gotten all that much larger compared to when I was an emaciated villager girdled by vorpal holes. I was inextricably bound to the land. I was a prisoner in both lives. Hilarious, isn't it?

"For a long time my monster self kept taking sacrifices, kids just like me. I never felt bad about it. Didn't even need to demand victims, really. People dragged them to me, as they'd dragged me to stick my head in a vorpal hole. They cried lots of tears over it. But they must've thought it was a fair trade, or they wouldn't have done it. This way, they could choose who the monster took. Instead of shivering in their beds, always wondering who would go next."

Crow touched one of her hanging earrings. It was like a drop of colorless amber, a frozen thing, but as warm as her tingling fingertips remembered from Steppehaven: moonlight, a head in her lap, a pained hiss of breath.

Words didn't fail Crow. She hadn't expected them to do much for her in the first place. She was not a poet or an orator. In one of her lives, she'd had no words at all. Maybe she'd been happier for it, existing as a creature too vast and free to countenance the smallness of abstract philosophical concepts, the sort you'd only brood over if you were rooted to the ground.

But she was not an aerial anymore, not at heart, and she couldn't revert to being one even if she wanted it more than anything. Like how a fallen saint would—as far as anyone knew—stay a monster forever. Some changes could not be undone.

There wasn't anything in particular she wanted to say. She focused instead on Magnolia's wary look, and the earring in her fingers. She felt the tender curve of Magnolia's neck beneath it.

Magnolia had gone very still, in the way that a mortal might freeze if you pricked them in the back with a knife.

"I'm a severed head," she enunciated, as if Crow were hard of hearing.

"I used to be a serpent long enough to tie the whole sky up like a package with string."

"You're exaggerating," Magnolia said severely. "And that's not what you are anymore."

"I can take the shape of an elder aerial again. Do you like me better that way?"

Magnolia gave her a helpless glare. "None of this has anything to do with me being a *severed head*."

"We have enough in common," Crow said. "We're immortals. We're returners."

"Crow," Magnolia pronounced, so deliberately emotionless that she began to sound like the Devil. "Are you flirting?"

Crow, jarred, stopped caressing her earring.

She had not been thinking about anything beyond this precise moment. The smell of stale salt. The way that Magnolia's moles liked to secretly move around but always put themselves back in just the right place. The smooth jewel that was part of Magnolia between her fingers. The sweet life-giving scent that bloomed and heightened, a heady floral, as she rubbed it.

She hadn't known what she was saying. She hadn't known what she meant.

"Did I make you do that?"

Magnolia's voice was sharp with horror.

They stared at each other. Something creaked—way back in the marsh of dead trees, or below in the bones of ships that the wind played like a macabre instrument.

"No?" Crow said. But it was only a guess.

PART FIVE
Carrion City

43

Magnolia seemed eager to get away from the coast. It was a peculiar transition: Dung had waded through mud flats during their initial approach, but everything grew rockier on the way out. Hollowed-out caves, crashing waves, sea arches worn so thin that they might collapse overnight.

Then, as Dung left eldritch footprints below tree-crowned cliffs, they began to see barnacle-crusted stumps, some submerged by the lapping tide. More ghosts preserved in salt water. Perhaps for much longer than the gray trunks in the marshes.

Crow pointed out dotted marks where small birds had run about in dark brown sand. She'd always excelled at helping her companions track animals—as would any immortal that put their mind to it. Most saw no need. The only prey they tracked were humans.

Magnolia made Dung stop by a stump large enough to bathe in. Its center had hollowed out, leaving a shallow tidal pool. Fish smaller than a fingernail darted around; they were the same color as the wet sand. She dipped in a tentative white root, only to wince at the taste of salt.

"What'd you expect?" Crow said.

Magnolia wiped her salty root on Crow's clothes.

After they'd left the seaside far behind, she said: "Time lost all its friction once I became a living severed head. It wasn't nearly as bad as you'd think."

Why are you telling me this? Crow thought.

"To make it clear to you that I don't require sympathy. In fact, I forbid it." This came out in Magnolia's conversational voice, not her commanding voice. She would be relieved to know that Crow had no excess compassion to spare.

"Your scars," Crows said.

"My what?"

"Why don't they heal?"

"You mean my neck?"

Crow tapped her eyebrow, then her forehead. "Your scars."

Magnolia remained skeptical until Crow made her look at her face in a puddle.

"In my defense," Magnolia said, "the hills weren't exactly littered with mirrors. Forgot I had these. They aren't an artifact of my first life, if that's what you're asking. Jaunty, aren't they? Debonair, even."

"Did you make them yourself?"

"To enhance my beauty? No. There were a few semi-successful attempts to kill me, early in my career as a ghastly monster. They stabbed me everywhere. Lost an eye, I think. The problem with being a bodiless head is that even the noblest enemies have no choice except to go for your face. The total damage was much worse than these measly scars. But I never suffered a temporary death, and I was never again wounded so grievously by human hands. Oh, I made sure of that."

"You kept the marks as a reminder?"

"Now, why would I do a thing like that? A poor reminder—I'm not the one who sits around admiring them." She nudged Crow's questing hands away with an impatient root. "There were lingering traces of humanity in my mentality. Like a hangover from my first life. Like an infection. Something in me was convinced that I'd been hurt too badly to heal without scarring.

"Time passed, and I learned the art of being a monster. Slayers ambushed me again and again, but I never kept any other scars from them. Although I must say ... you'd look good with a scar or two yourself."

"Mine fade," Crow said. "They always fade."

"I know. That stab mark by your shoulder—long gone. I'd better enjoy them while I can."

It was late at night when Crow asked her again about her final conversation with the Devil.

"We've been over this."

"You dodged the question."

For a time, there was no reply except the warbling of frogs and the mournful ululating of unseen wolves.

"I told her," Magnolia said stiffly, "that I doubted I'd commit any future atrocities so egregious as to justify her executing me in the name of all humanity. I told her you could stop me."

"She believed you?"

"Either her magic showed me to be honest, or my simplicity proved persuasive. Whatever the reason, it worked. Who knew the Devil would be so gullible? Surprises all around. Are you satisfied, Carrie? I'd rather not speak of her now that she's gone. Gives me a real shudder. Legends are much more delightful with distance."

In the languid weeks that followed, they rode Dung beneath clouds as heavy and textured as mountains of clay. They passed a bizarrely warm pocket of land, one that resisted any encroaching hints of fall. Temperatures stayed subtropical all night long.

It had attracted a substantial colony of peacock pheasants, which normally would not have been able to survive a single mild winter around these parts. Magnolia, fascinated, said she was tempted to linger. She wanted to figure out how they'd avoided predation.

No people dwelt with the pheasants. "We can stay," Crow said.

Magnolia demurred. "It would be a nice diversion, but no. I crave socialization. Our time with the Devil rather whetted my appetite."

"Socialization," Crow repeated.

"Yes. Time in human society. Real society, not some hamlet with a single-digit stock of survivors."

Time in human society would mean something very different to a monster than a saint.

"Fear not," Magnolia said. "I'll be subtle."

"That's not what I fear."

"I know what you fear. I was showing tact by not giving voice to it."

"You can show tact by not killing anyone," Crow said.

"That's asking a lot of a monster. I wonder how long ago people lived nearby? Not recently enough for the pheasants to fear us."

Crow wished she were better at stalling. "Dung likes it here."

This was true: he'd found a pit of bones of ambiguous provenance and was happily slobbering away at them, even though they had no juices left to slurp.

The underside of Magnolia's neck sprouted growths like green caterpillar legs, or nubby orchid roots. She used them to skitter down from Crow's shoulder to her hand. Crow held her like a serial killer conversing with a human skull.

"*You* like it here," Magnolia said, narrow-eyed. "You know why it's so much hotter than the surrounding climate. Tell me."

Crow understood, then, how she could delay their departure. She settled at the edge of the bone pit in order to keep an eye on Dung.

"If only we could all be as joyful as a primeval in a mass grave," Magnolia said wryly.

"An elder aerial fell here," Crow told her.

Magnolia raised her eyebrows. She flicked a look at the sumptuous pit. "Those aren't from an aerial. Do aerials even have, er, bony-looking bones?"

"Those are human bones."

"Mostly," Magnolia corrected. "It's a bit of a motley mix."

"Aerials don't leave bones on the ground," Crow said. "This warm pocket—all the tropical plants—that's what the aerial left instead of a skeleton. Altered air. Altered seasons. Altered weather."

"You didn't leave a rainforest at Lake Fallen."

"Not all aerials have the same effect when they fall. I didn't. The rumored oases in the north, melted holes in the middle of winter—that's from a different sort of elder aerial."

"I'm surprised there aren't more places like this," Magnolia said after a moment. "The apocalypse has been good to aerials. The population really exploded. All over the continent, and probably all over the world, or what remains of it. Humanity shrinks, and aerials multiply. If only we immortals were meant to feed on aerials instead."

"It isn't normal to fall when you die," Crow said. "It's like a whale getting beached. Many more sink to the ocean floor."

Aerials—especially elder aerials—were supposed to dissolve in the air. To get eaten by thousands of tinier flying beasts. Falling far enough to touch ground would make you an outlier.

She didn't remember why she'd fallen. Perhaps she'd been hunted. Perhaps she'd become senile in her prodigious old age, flown too far into empty skies. She might have ventured too high or too fast for the swarming companion parasites who would have been diligently waiting to scavenge her corpse. Perhaps she'd encountered a storm cell she could neither escape nor control.

At any rate, she fell.

She fell, and she didn't die.

Three-legged crows flocked to her bloated aerial body on the ground, as distorted as a deep-sea creature forced up out of the water. The crows were vigorous—the biggest flock any locals had witnessed in generations— but they couldn't begin to make a dent in her.

Even then—pecked by crows, insensate with shock, reduced to a massive ruin of flesh like a ship run ashore on rocks—even then, she was not entirely dead. She had been a truly singular type of elder aerial, a species with no agreed-upon name, a body with a voracious ability to cling to some semblance of life even when no good could possibly come of it.

How much of this story had the automagi sucked out of her? As she spoke to Magnolia, her own skin seemed to constrict her, warning her not to continue. It felt as though she had never put anything that mattered into words.

People exclaimed over the miracle of her still-living body. They assumed that the liquids flowing from her were an elixir, that her solid parts might hold the secret to human longevity.

In her half-dead state, she looked more like a horrifically enormous worm than a respectable serpent, or a proper dragon. But she was not the type of worm that could survive as two new worms after you cut it in half. When they carved away chunks of her tail, she fled into the rest of her body. The carved-off parts were the first to perish.

Those who dined on her flesh died the very next day. Even infants—who'd only had a tiny sliver placed on their tongues, a transparent slice as thin as gauze, shaved off with the finest of ceremonial knives. She had no awareness of this: she only came to know it much later. At the time, she knew nothing except her own neverending pain.

She unconsciously called down cold rain to quench the feeling of burning, the wounds that refused to heal. It rained and rained and rained, flooding streets and fields, and eventually filling up the whole bed of a half-dry lake.

It rained so much that the people who came to dispose of her had to wear waders. Their hands kept slipping. Several of them accidentally chopped into each other, instead of her. Many such tragedies occurred as they sawed off thick rings to give to intrepid mages and scholars, like cross-sections from an ancient tree.

They cut off her head, and she let it die. She escaped into what remained of her body; she always sought refuge in the largest piece of her that was still (however improbably) alive. The rain fell more lightly, and finally it stopped. There was much rejoicing.

"I bet there was," Magnolia said. Occasionally she would call out to Dung, telling him he'd missed an especially scrumptious bone. For the most part, though, she listened quietly.

Crow described how—through some tortured logic that she still failed to fully comprehend—they had settled on worshiping her. Perhaps the intent was to appease her. Someone had perceived a face in the pattern of her ... well, she didn't have true scales, but she could see why people claimed she did. A smudged patch near the underside of her long throat had, to human eyes, looked like the somber face of a mourning woman. An utter coincidence.

Because that was the last part of her left after they sawed up all the rest, it was also the last part to stay alive without rotting. Her final refuge. A piece of a serpent's neck, with only a whisper of magic to hold it together. A piece small enough that a band of farmers with knives could have put her out of her misery. The flocks of three-legged crows could have eaten her until nothing remained.

But people saw that splotchy face-like shadow on her skin as a sign. They wrapped up the last living hunk of her in rich cloth, like something beloved, and they built a temple to her on an island in the middle of the nearby lake. They hauled over the poisonous dead flesh they'd cleaved from her—everything they could salvage, that hadn't been bought by foreigners—and they buried it in the patch of land in front of her shrine. Nothing would grow there afterward, but it made for a clear path to the entrance.

They placed her on an altar. They posted guards and procured defensive spells to ensure that no scavengers would wander down to gnaw on her. The dead land out front seemed to be its own kind of deterrent, too.

She was ostensibly a mortal creature. Without intervention, she would have perished. It would have taken an extraordinary alliance of crows and vultures and maggots and isopods and low-flying aerials, ones inconspicuous enough to be mistaken for insects—but eventually she would have been eaten by creatures that wouldn't keel over after a tiny taste of her. She would have vanished bite by bite, as was her right.

The locals treasured that one final dismembered fragment of her. Over time she became dessicated. She looked like a ragged piece of brown rock, not like the remnants of something that had spent its entire life in the sky. There were no coincidental patterns left to perceive in her— certainly not any that resembled a human face.

And yet, even then, she lived. She lived on that altar. On and on and on. She lived long enough for human language to seep into her awareness like rain after a drought—at first rolling off soil too parched to take it. Hundreds and hundreds of years passed before it really began to soak in and penetrate.

She couldn't move. She couldn't fly. She couldn't force wind down through the oven-shaped mouth of the shrine. She was just a splinter of self buried like shrapnel in a dried-up relic that only lived because it hadn't been given permission to die.

She came to understand their prayers. Not that she could do anything about it. She could neither crush dreams nor grant wishes. She had all the power and magic of a sentient piece of beef jerky.

"That's a lovely way to put it," Magnolia said. "So how did you die, in the end?"

"You tell me."

"I did converse with the ground by your shrine. But the land isn't always concerned with the finer details of a narrative. It's just land, after all. It's not a bard."

"The city thrived," Crow said, "and they thought it was my doing. Then it stopped thriving, and they thought that was my doing, too. They brought me fruit from faraway countries, and lit nice-smelling candles. They collected funds to lavish attention on the shrine."

"No human sacrifices?"

"Goats, yes. Humans, no."

"How enlightened of them. Did they become angry when you failed to listen? Did they grind you to dust in a giant mortar and pestle? Or did they toss you out like fish food in the lake? Did they flee for more fertile lands?"

There had been a girl in the family who cared for the shrine. A mage—the extraordinarily rare sort who could teach herself to use magic without a mentor. But no one saw what she did as magic, anyway. When livestock seemed wounded or sick, she could immediately pinpoint what pained them. It wasn't anything so astonishing as outright talking to animals.

From a young age, she knew that the lump of flesh in the shrine was suffering. She knew it had no hope of controlling floods or famine or drought. She knew it had been kept waiting a very long time against its will. She knew that the only thing it wanted was to die.

"She dragged me out in secret, in the night," Crow said. "She soaked me in lake water, and left me exposed. She knew I had to be consumed, and that it would kill her if she did it herself. Three-legged crows came, and gulls, and crabs the size of cockroaches, and beach hogs, and salt ants. An incredible torrent of life, as if she'd called them. They all arrived before dawn. For centuries I had dreamed of nothing but being eaten by carrion crows. It happened quickly, once the water softened me."

"And you never knew what happened to the girl who saved you," Magnolia murmured. "Brave, noble, and heroic, just like all your favorite companions. How beautiful it would be if that were me, if that was my story, and now you could pay me back. Too bad—no poetic justice governs who gets to become a returner. It's as random as a lightning strike, and it's got nothing to do with good deeds."

By the time Crow emerged as an unwitting returner, anyone who had ever known that girl was long dead. No one recorded her life on tablets for the archivists who lived in jars. If anyone had made note of her fate, the notes were lost to history, and so was her grave.

"I assume they killed her," Crow said. "Once they found out what she'd done. I was the living god of that land. The people were desperate."

"Indeed. Desperate enough to swear devotion to a scrap of dried meat." Magnolia, who had taken a seat (of sorts) on Crow's knee, suddenly pivoted. "You see why I feel a certain kinship with you, Crow. You know what it's like to be helplessly bound in one place. You know what it's like to exist as a single living piece of a body."

Exhausted from speaking, Crow gave her left earring a warning flick. Magnolia yelped, then started sulking.

The sulking was just for show. She'd lapped up Crow's story like a mosquito guzzling blood. It left her in excellent spirits all through the deepening night. Her mood had improved enough to announce that they would stay there longer, after all, and observe how the peacock pheasants spent their days.

44

A WEEK LATER, Magnolia decided it was time to leave the pheasants. If they went northwest, they would reach a city, which she knew of from past visitors to her hills. Crow resigned herself to the inevitability of Magnolia being around people.

"You were so determined not to mention the city," Magnolia said fondly. "Have you been there before?"

"Not recently."

"What will you do once there are no humans left to make promises with or protect?"

"Go somewhere else."

"Once there are no humans left anywhere, I mean," Magnolia said. "Once humanity goes extinct. Like—what was that drink called? Like spica. I had a taste of it once, in my first life. It was rare where I came from. Used up the last dry leaves in an old canister, and then we could never get any more. Spica was still grown in fields back then, in other parts of the continent. We were just unusually hard to trade with."

She refocused on Crow. "So what's your plan for after the end of humanity? It'll come eventually."

With no human cores left to seek, saints and monsters would tear one another apart. Perhaps all immortals would lose their minds and fade away, deprived of the sustenance that came just as much from the act of hunting and waiting as it did from actually swallowing human cores. They might all end up living as wraiths like the automagi.

Crow said: "You've shown me that I can take aerial form."

"My pleasure."

"After humans die out, I'll go live among aerials."

"I could speed up that process," Magnolia said helpfully.

"By wiping humanity out ahead of schedule? You're technically a Great Adversary—"

"Technically?"

"—But you wouldn't be able to decimate them like the Singular Horde. Or the Beautiful Scourge."

They had been walking for some time now. Dung had grown fussy after long days and nights of nonstop riding, and he'd stomped off to take a mud bath. Crow hoped he would sleep, too, while he could. She didn't like how Magnolia tucked a sly dripping root in a crevice of his mouth, force-feeding him dew as he ran.

Early that morning, Magnolia had attached herself to Crow's hip like the hilt of an outlandish sword. Her roots hugged Crow's waist in the shape of a belt.

"You don't want to hurry up and go live as an aerial again?" she said. "Fine. Less work for me."

"Your name doesn't fit with the rest," Crow commented.

"The rest of what?"

"The Four Great Adversaries." She listed them off. "Calamity Bridge.

The Beautiful Scourge. The Singular Horde. The Woman in the Hills. You sound much less fearsome than the others."

"Ah." Magnolia's confusion cleared. "Humans came up with most of those. I was the only Adversary to name myself—I planted it in the heads of everyone who entered my territory. I encouraged it to stick."

"Wouldn't you prefer something more..."

"Grandiloquent? No, this is better. Say Woman—not even Lady—and most people can't help but picture someone with two arms and two legs. A witch living alone in a hillside hut, perhaps. Some look shocked even if they've been told in advance that I'm only a head.

"And if they do have it all settled in their minds that I'm a gruesome decapitated head, dripping red blood like I carry around an endless supply of it—then I show up in a body instead. Really throws them for a loop. When you're stuck in the hills, you have to find your fun where you can."

They spoke of many things on the road. On the whole, this seemed less dangerous than letting Magnolia's mind go idle to seek out other forms of entertainment.

She told Magnolia about a past companion who had set animals on fire as a child. He had been quite in earnest when he offered Crow his core, though he wasn't yet grown. He had been equally earnest when he stabbed one sister and nearly blinded another. Crow accepted his offer, and she took him out of that house. She babysat him for the rest of his life.

He gave Crow a lot of orders, but she usually found a way to turn them inside out. Of course, he denied her his core at the end, as she'd known he would. He'd promised it to her in a spasm of violent sincerity, or sincere violence, and that was enough for her to accept. She could see even then that it would pass, like any of his other fits. She could also see what would happen if no one guarded him. So she did, and it was a tumultuous forty-something years. She'd had time enough to spare.

"Do I remind you of him?" Magnolia sniffed. "I'm not sadistic towards mortals. There's nothing pleasing about picking on the weak. I give them a quick, decisive death. Like you would. You know, this is what galls me about saints. We both kill people—why should you get all the credit just for doing it by appointment instead of by surprise? Anyway, what's the difference between dying at sixty and dying at thirty? Humanity as a whole already has one foot out the door."

Crow trotted out the usual arguments. She had lost none of her conviction. But all the while she heard a cold strange voice at the back of her head. A detached part of her that rarely spoke up. She wondered if Magnolia could hear it, too.

Magnolia valued Crow's power. She'd needed Crow to break the compulsion that tied her to the hills. But it didn't really need to be Crow's legs that strode with her along the sketchy traces of disused roads. She could recruit any number of other immortals—individually less powerful, maybe, but since when had she exploited even a fraction of Crow's full magic? Instead she'd gone out of her way to diminish it, making Crow break her own wings.

If Magnolia had less firepower on her side, she'd simply have to avoid sticky situations. Fellshore, Steppehaven, the black field and the fallen Devil—none of those meant much to her; she would have been just as content with other sights. The entire world was new and wondrous. She'd only ever felt it secondhand. That was why she preferred touring slowly to porting.

She could go slower still. She could burrow into any human settlement of her choosing, and she could do it more successfully than the buried mimid. She could use her voice to make herself a queen with an endless parade of willing victims.

The power Crow brought her was replaceable, and not all that vital to the nature of her journey. She could achieve a similar level of protection by collecting multiple monstrous bodyguards. So what else did she value in Crow? What quality was so uniquely precious that Magnolia couldn't recreate it with some other combination of useful immortals? Surely not her obedience. Surely not her unwillingness.

It was something beyond that. The contempt that would never burn out. The fury that would never break itself like a wave crashing on rocks. It was still bottomless. It was still there, if Crow reached for it. But she had to reach hard, and deep. She had to remember beheading the slayer in the hills.

That was more effective than the memory of ripping out her wings, which seemed duller and less inspiring in retrospect. She'd met women who, right after giving birth, would swear that the world could end before they ever had another child ... then somehow proceeded to forget the worst parts of labor within a year. Crow might forget the pain of losing her wings. But she wouldn't forget murdering a young slayer who could have been just as heroic as Arion.

This loathing would abrade her like a joint losing cushioning, nothing left but the agony of hard bones. But she needed it in order to react with sufficient force and precision when Magnolia inadvertently bared her own throat. She needed it so Magnolia wouldn't try to replace her.

Magnolia didn't have a single self-flagellating bone in her (she didn't have all that many bones to begin with). She bragged about never changing. Maybe, perversely, she luxuriated in the fact that Crow would never change at heart, either. No matter what she was forced to do. No matter how little choice she had left.

"I like having you around, Crow." She sounded amused, and faintly alarmed. "It's not that deep. You might need socialization more than I do."

"I loathe everything you stand for."

"Everything?" Magnolia said. "Really, everything? I don't think so. I gave you the entire sob story of my first life."

"You didn't want sympathy."

"Not at all. You ought to be wringing your hands, stiff with discomfort, mind all twisted up in knots like the Devil's magic, trying oh so hard to figure me out—struggling to reconcile the victim with the killer, the human sacrifice with the devourer.

"It's working rather too well, actually. I'll make it easier for you, my friend. All that stuff was long, long ago, and I've been a devourer for much longer than I've ever lived as anything else. Don't let your flame go out, Crow. I was very proud to have been the one to light it. Oh, look! A road."

It was, indeed, a proper road. There was something surreal about seeing one in actual use—not just a historical artifact running below the land's surface like the puckering of an old scar.

They retreated into a hazel coppice, and Magnolia donned her body. Normally she would have ordered Crow to dress her like a handmaiden, but this time she turned her nose up and dressed herself. Crow slimmed her wings down and shifted them to her head. They blended with the shag of her hair like feathered ornaments.

"Charming," said Magnolia. "You could be a hero wearing laurel. Like it or not, you're my hero now. Tell me, will the people of this city stay calm if they see a wild primeval?"

Crow thought it unlikely.

Magnolia blinked into the distance. "I'll warn Dung to stay away, then."

They descended to the road. Without Magnolia's weight on her back or her hip, it felt as though she'd forgotten something important—the legendary sword that would defeat a demon king, for instance, or a hard-won wheel of really excellent cheese. But the modern-day equivalent of a potential demon king was walking right at Crow's side, and as far as Crow could tell, she didn't care much for dairy.

She linked arms with Magnolia the instant they spotted human figures. Most parties traveled with a substantial distance between them. Nearly all were on foot, though some walked alongside large wagons.

Magnolia promptly broke the social contract by yelling and waving and announcing herself as a saint. She went up to bristling groups, some flanked by coreless hunters, and had them eating out of her palm in a matter of seconds. Crow's jaw clenched at the sounds of mirth and laughter.

A gigantic old man with a halberd ruffled Magnolia's hair and called her a cheeky young lad. "That's right," she said, pointing at her eyes. "I'm the cheekiest saint you'll ever meet!"

If Crow kept grinding her teeth like this, she'd lose her molars faster than she could hope to regrow them. She doggedly trailed Magnolia from one isolated party to the next. Men generally took the two of them for a pair of men, but with women, it seemed to go any number of ways. Crow couldn't begin to guess which set of assumptions was more likely to elicit giggles and blushing.

There was no reason for these travelers to believe they were saints. Crow had some claim to fame in the region, and could probably have reassured them by announcing her title and spreading her wings. But the need never arose. Everyone took their hands off their weapons. They didn't request proof.

"Is it a strain?" Crow asked between groups.

"To stop myself from gobbling all their cores right on the spot? It certainly is, Carrie. Thanks for thinking of me—didn't know you had it in you."

"Is it a strain," Crow said tautly, "to make them swallow your every word?"

"Oh, that? It's just a bit of passing suggestion. Takes no more work than a gentle tap on the shoulder." She tapped Crow to demonstrate.

Crow couldn't leave her on her own, not even for a moment. Not that Magnolia didn't try. "Turn around," she said hopefully. "I see another peacock sky in the distance. Why don't you scratch your nose and look at the horizon for a bit? You don't have to spend every single second of every hour so utterly focused on your beloved lady. I'm flattered, of course, but it must be exhausting."

Crow held her arm tighter. "No."

"Come on. Let go of me, look the other way, and you won't have to see it." A dangerously persuasive note crept into her voice, like a hand slipping under clothes. It grazed the edge of becoming an outright order. "You wouldn't have to know. Maybe I'll just slip away to stretch my legs. Maybe I won't take a single core."

"No," Crow said, and the only reason she could still utter this was because Magnolia just barely allowed it. What twisted pleasure did she get from the farce of asking permission from someone she could easily force to say yes?

Magnolia sighed and leaned toward her and playfully bumped their heads together. "You just can't stand to be separated? Very well, then."

The city walls were not complete. Still, the road came to an obvious entrance point where cautious groups converged into an orderly line.

Magnolia lined up with all the rest of them. She savored the grinding slowness of it like a tourist attraction. Every so often there would be whispers with the word *saint*, but the whispers died out before reaching them, and no one stared. She made the two of them all but invisible, and she watched the progress of the line contentedly, without further chatting.

A giant lizard sunned itself near the checkpoint, oblivious to all the noise. Magnolia perked up—"An immortal?" she said—but on closer inspection, it was just a placid lizard the size of a trebuchet.

The guards had been fairly diligent in their questioning of every prior party. When Magnolia and Crow came up, all they would speak of were their husbands and wives and children and elderly parents, their opinions on tax law, their problems with bedbugs. Magnolia made sympathetic noises. She and Crow strolled past without voicing a single word of importance.

"Bedbugs are no joking matter," Magnolia said reverently.

The city they'd entered had a variety of names. Crow just thought of it as the New City, since it was only a few decades old. It had grown from the burnt shell of a town with nothing left.

The streets that permitted vehicular passage were crammed with oxen, rabbit-eared horses, and sad stringy beasts that bore only a passing resemblance to a proud wild primeval like Dung. There were many piles of his namesake awaiting collection. As they ventured deeper, arm in arm, Crow was gratified to feel Magnolia recoiling from the stink that infiltrated every orifice like an invisible fog.

Crow had been prepared for this. It stank in the way of many young cities—a natural reek, like unwashed human adolescence. Some cities lasted long enough to grow out of it. Most didn't. She asked if Magnolia would like to retreat back to the wilderness, where Dung awaited them, and Magnolia let out a short bark of a laugh.

45

PEOPLE, PEOPLE, so many people clopping about in wood-soled shoes and sandals. And just about all of them had cores. Magnolia swayed on her feet as if she were drunk. This might be far more people than she had ever seen in one place, in either of her lives.

But Crow didn't know that for a fact. In the past, entire armies might have come after her, or unknowingly battled each other across her territory. The village of white radishes might once have been a provincial powerhouse of commerce. Crow knew the radish village as it was now, and she knew about Magnolia's other village, too, the one that had become an island encircled by a moat of all-devouring nothingness. She knew hardly anything about the vast stretches of time that lay between them.

As they made their way about, they saw shrines to the God of the End tucked in small cubbyholes. Nothing too impressive. One out of every four or five people wore little gauzy scent sachets; they were tied upside down to hang like jellyfish. Others wore tasseled charms shaped like bundles of round leaves.

At an outdoor market, Magnolia made a beeline for a stall of plain wooden dolls—smooth limbless things with minimalist features.

"We had similar dolls in my old village," she said. "The donut village. These aren't exactly the same, but they're close. How remarkable! I suppose simple crafts are more likely to get passed down through times of upheaval."

"They aren't as simple as they look," said Crow, who had retained some knowledge of woodworking from her time with the world's last mage. She moved closer to Magnolia's ear. "We don't have any money."

"I can barter."

"With what?"

"My dashing good looks," Magnolia said, "and my winning smile."

She bartered, if you could call it that, for a small wooden doll. At a different stall, she bartered for a present for Dung. In a dark corner hidden by confusingly layered sheets of canvas, she bartered for two pairs of glasses with green lenses. They were cruder than the mangled sunglasses that Crow had left in Steppehaven, but this would be a marked improvement over not having any at all.

Magnolia took whatever she wanted without giving anything in return, and no one breathed a word of complaint.

As they turned to leave the covered booth full of primitive colored eyeglasses, the seller plucked at Crow's shirt. "You can't wear those."

Crow, who had already donned her green glasses, looked back in puzzlement. The wrinkled seller mimed taking them off.

Ah, so here was someone immune to Magnolia's extortionary tactics. She tried to hand the glasses back.

The seller waved her away, impatient. "Take 'em, but don't wear 'em. It's against regulations. No eye shades, no patches, no blindfolds, no goggles. If you're saints, you gotta get registered."

"*If* we're saints?" Magnolia said delicately.

"I don't know nothing, and I don't remember nothing. Maybe you've got pinkeye. Maybe you're aspiring saints—trying to move up in the world, eh? Maybe you'll hold it in your mind that I didn't give you no trouble. Keep an eye on the sky, would you?"

Magnolia laughed silently as they wound their way out of the market, ears ringing from all the touts shouting and banging gongs and clapping blocks. "Aspiring saints," she repeated. "Well, Crow, shall we go get registered?"

"I don't—"

"Trust me, you'll feel much better if we do things properly. Let's be good citizens."

"You can start by using less magic," Crow said.

"Do you want people to see us and panic? What's wrong with making ourselves a reassuring presence?"

"No more thieving."

"I paid them richly for everything we received." Magnolia lowered her voice. "I paid them by not ripping their cores out. Why, what better gift could there possibly be? Come, now, do you really think I've been too conspicuous? In a crowd like this?"

After turning two or three corners, there wasn't much of a crowd left. The smell of human and animal urine and other excretions had subsided to a more bearable level. Someone was playing a hurdy-gurdy; someone was shouting at either a dog or a child.

Magnolia leaned on a plaster wall painted with slender branching shadows from a young tree. She looked like a lanky stranger, her mouth curved in a secretive smile.

"All in all," she said, "it's rather lightly defended. The outer fortifications might as well be lines drawn by chalk. I see a few immortals—true saints,

I'm assuming—but it doesn't seem like nearly enough. Does the city have a standing army?"

"Don't ask pointed questions," Crow said.

"If anyone has the wherewithal to get seriously suspicious of me, I'll applaud them."

Magnolia was right to wonder about the city's defenses. Truth be told, Crow had been wondering the same thing. Most monsters lacked Magnolia's ability to sweet-talk border officials, and many would struggle to physically blend in, too. In all likelihood, the crowd was not sprinkled with malicious shapeshifters.

Still: the bigger the settlement, the worse the monsters it pulled in. Smaller human settlements had a better average rate of survival, although some of this came down to plain old luck. Many places where Crow lived had been very idyllic. It took her generations to realize that peaceful security was not the default state of human society, but rather the direct result of her presence.

Larger settlements needed at least one patron saint to avoid becoming quick fodder for monsters. Tiny rural hamlets would attract lesser predators, and might succeed in fending them off with human weapons alone.

In a small town, it was also easier to recognize strangers and enemies. Not even immortals could accurately categorize each other with a glance. It was a bit like one human trying to guess the occupation of another. Uniforms and vocabulary and quirks of behavior might give you away. But saints had no shared uniform—no shared culture to call their own—and neither did monsters.

A clever monster might bribe an unscrupulous mortal to pose as their promised companion. A saint might, after centuries of sainthood, grow tired of waiting and decide to collect cores the quick way. Nothing would change about their appearance in the process. Outside of instinct and guesswork, there was only one reliable way to identify a monster: to catch them in the act of mauling a screaming human from behind.

In a settlement like this, successful monsters would find some way to pass for a human or a saint. Regular human murderers might get falsely called monsters. Anyone born albino would be better off never coming to the city at all.

Crow had last come here thirty-something years ago. There had been no city then. An age had passed since she'd last seen one spring up so fast.

Most of the buildings were made of timber, wattle, and plaster. They were virtually all one story tall, though some had high roofs. Little would remain if the city succumbed to another disaster—traces of a thriving past wouldn't linger like the necropolis under Fellshore. But then, stone walls would be of no help to anyone after the population fled or died. As an immortal, Crow felt entitled to assert that there was no inherent virtue in the simple act of lasting longer. She supposed the automagi would disagree.

Magnolia did not appear eager to plunge back into the fray. She turned her wooden doll in her hands. Sometimes she pressed it to her temple, or to the mouth-like scar on her forehead. When she tipped the back of her skull against the dappled wall and closed her eyes, she could've been a local battling a hangover.

"You've never tried to be a saint?" said Crow.

She detested saints, but Crow could envision her giving it a try just for kicks.

Magnolia made a skeptical noise. "I can make people feel like they want to give me their cores, but I don't think that counts. At least not for the purpose of ascending to sainthood. To a monster, a willingly given core is just about useless. You saints brew power by waiting for it, by drawing the anticipation out as long as possible. You gain power from patience. We monsters gain power by taking it."

The interplay of light and shadow on the pale wall dimmed, staunched by a cloud. Magnolia opened one eye and shot Crow a nasty smirk. "You'll get a crick in your neck if you keep this up," she said. "You look awfully stiff. You've been trying so, so hard not to glance at the beautiful sky."

She made a show of looking up. Crow begrudgingly followed her gaze. The sky was a limpid hue of greenish teal with a few cottony cumulus clouds, and a daytime glimpse of moon. One might think that it held nothing else.

An aerial hung there, high over the city, spread wide and translucent like the gossamer bell of a jellyfish. It looked as though it would cover the entire city if it fell, although that was surely a trick of perspective. Still, it was a behemoth, a floating coliseum. Transparent sunlight sketched out intricate shadows inside its veil.

"Any city this prosperous would be bound to have a formidable patron saint," Magnolia said. "You can't think I'm surprised. Well? You should chat it up. Go talk to your aerial friend."

Crow shook her head. "It's only shaped like an aerial."

"Don't nitpick."

"Are we human because we've taken on human shape? That guardian is no different."

It wouldn't be anything like communicating with a real aerial. Besides, she couldn't let Magnolia risk catching the attention of—or picking a fight with—a saint of that caliber.

"What, isn't that half the reason you brought me here? In hopes that Saint Jellyfish would notice, and immediately smite me?"

"I didn't bring you," Crow said. "You demanded to see the city."

"Liar. You wanted me to come. If I had to descend on another settlement, you figured it might as well be this one." She tapped the side of her nose. "Nicely done, I'd say. You have a real talent for acting all reluctant and cheerless. Even inside your own head, you let dismay blot out all other thoughts. I'll give you this: you were sincerely worried about my ability to mingle peaceably with mortals. Helped cover up your darker schemes. Are you disappointed that I haven't keeled over yet?"

"If it's given you a headache, then it's been worth the trip."

Magnolia ground her bland-faced doll into her forehead again. It was like a pestle for crushing seeds: a good shape for pushing at a throbbing skull.

"Congratulate yourself on your success," she said icily. "Tell me, Crow, what's this smell that's been plaguing me?"

"The city doesn't smell like jasmine and myrtle to me, either."

"Oh, please. You sound as wooden as the Devil."

"It's ashwort," Crow said.

"Ah. In those little potpourri bundles people wear?" Magnolia lowered her hand and looked balefully at the side of Crow's face. "Guess they cut it with other herbs, hm? Just so you know, I've smelled this before. Sometimes the better-funded sort of hunter would show up with a sprig tucked in their clothes. I usually thought they were gassy. Not my favorite scent, but it won't make me swoon. Sorry to disappoint."

To most mortal creatures, ashwort seemed scentless. Saints found it mildly unpleasant: to Crow, it blended with the rank summery stench of the streets. To lower-tier monsters, it would be debilitating. But stronger monsters could push through their discomfort.

She'd never seriously hoped that a whiff of ashwort would do much to a Great Adversary. Still, better to guide Magnolia here—where she would suffer with every breath—than to a settlement where she might revel, unrestrained, in the bounty all around her.

Magnolia couldn't spend months or years or decades in the city, a self-styled anthropologist, observing the rise and fall of leaders and cultures while furtively picking off victims in hidden alleyways. Even if the ever-present aroma of ashwort wasn't enough to deter her, the saint in the sky wouldn't let her get away with it for long.

"Ashwort..." Magnolia made a face. "Isn't it supposed to be extremely rare and precious? It grows in the path of migratory volcanoes, popping up out of ruined land. And it grows—ugh, I can't remember. It grows—"

"In places of devastation caused by monsters. But most stories of ashwort are rumors. It didn't even sprout after Calamity Bridge. The only monster that—"

"The Singular Horde!" Magnolia exclaimed. "Of course."

She'd momentarily forgotten her malaise. She tossed her bangs about with careless fingers and smiled darkly up at Crow. "You think I don't know my geography? Yes, I see. There was a town here, a town that got ground to dust by the Singular Horde. A saint chased away the inhabitants. She saved their lives. She fought the Singular Horde across the ruins of the town. Everyone thought she killed it.

"And—as if to prove what a great deed she'd done—ashwort began growing in that unlivable town. Ashwort often grows after the Singular Horde comes through. But this was more ashwort than anyone had ever seen in one place. It kept growing and growing. I suppose that's why a new city sprang up in a matter of decades. A classic gold rush.

"The Singular Horde," she said again, more pensively. "Mortals all think you and your Arion slew the beast. Until the day it reemerges, they won't have any reason to believe otherwise."

"Do you still want to get registered as a saint?"

"As opposed to what?" Magnolia asked.

"We could leave."

"It's here, isn't it—the place where your Arion died. Don't you want to visit?"

"Not with you."

"No need to act stoic," Magnolia said. "We'll go see him. But first you'll have to locate whatever government outpost we need to show our faces at." She waved her hands, gesturing for Crow to get a move on.

In a coldly practical sense, ashwort was arguably not that useful. A packet of dried leaves would only drive away monsters that—even with magic—posed about as much threat as a mammoth wild hog or a southern bear.

To residents of a settlement without a patron saint, though, this made ashwort more valuable than any number of coins minted by withering civilizations. Why battle off the equivalent of a bear when you could avoid fighting altogether?

A more dangerous monster might still come through, regardless of how much ashwort you festooned on your walls. A more dangerous monster would leave no survivors. But a more dangerous monster might overlook a modest cluster of homesteads; it might seek out juicier settlements.

So it was with good reason that rural folk feared everyday monsters more than the legendary sort that got memorialized in tales of broken empires. And it was with good reason that they coveted ashwort.

For all its value, ashwort was impossible to domesticate. It grew only where and when it wished to, which was hardly anywhere at all. Harvested leaves would lose their protective effect within a couple of years. You couldn't pass them on to the next generation, although people certainly tried.

As they went looking for the Bureau of Saints, Magnolia clung feebly to Crow's arm. She dragged her feet. She asked for Crow to stop and rub her back, to fan her, to towel off her neck. All in all, she showed herself to be spectacularly good at mining even the narrowest vein of physical distress for drama. In her telling, you'd think the single drop of sweat on her throat was a pouring waterfall of pain.

Crow didn't waste time humoring her. "I'll leave you in the gutter," she warned as Magnolia flopped about, feigning incapacitation. All of a sudden, Magnolia recovered just enough to cling to her arm even tighter.

They cut through a smoky-smelling area that Crow at first took to be a craft district filled with potters, charcoal burners, wheelwrights, metallurgists, and so on. But there were plenty of residential structures, too. Whenever she spied bare-legged children playing with tops or whistles or sticks, she wondered if they should have brought Rinlin here.

"She might make it out of Fellshore eventually," said Magnolia, forgetting to sound decrepit. "Life is long."

"No, it isn't."

Magnolia chuckled. "Humans don't think their lives are short until they get to the end. Every day seems drawn out when you've been here less than a century. Don't worry—Rinlin's got time. You're imagining her all grown up and alone now, aren't you? It's only been a couple months."

Somehow it felt as though they had been traveling together for ages. As if this were not their first summer or autumn, nor their first time heading north. Perhaps every day was also bound to seem longer when you spent it in the company of a monster.

46

The Bureau of Saints was supported by a host of smooth pillars. It felt like an indoor forest.

"Don't give anyone orders," Crow had said quietly before they entered.

The wood of the pillars appeared mostly untreated. No obvious varnish. Here and there, someone had painted the motif of a curling leaf, as if marking a secret path home through dense trees.

They stood before a caftan-clad clerk equipped with an inkwell, a brush, long black hair—neatly parted—and an efficient mustache. He looked at their eyes and delivered a rote speech welcoming them to the city.

Crow hadn't encountered a human bureaucracy this organized since her earliest travels with Arion's mother. When the clerk asked their names, she put a cautionary hand on Magnolia's head and started to say: "She's a very young sai—"

"Millet," Magnolia said.

The clerk's brush paused. "You're ... the Saint of Millet?"

"Not a glamorous grain, but very useful. Earthy and wholesome."

He noted down her title without further comment. "And you?" he said to Crow.

She could have lied—and if she avoided using flashy magic, she could have gotten away with it. Being known for who she was would be both a benefit and a burden. Especially here, of all places. But if Magnolia did anything untoward, she'd need to call in old favors.

"Carrion Crow," she said. She heard the clerk's breath catch. She turned around and grew her wings to full size—briefly and quietly— then put them away and turned back.

He looked every bit as starstruck as she'd feared. Magnolia wore an enormous grin.

"We should," he stammered, "we should announce—"

"I'd like to spend my time in peace," Crow said. "Unnoticed."

"At least a welcoming ceremony. Or a festival—"

"I would rather not," Crow said gently.

"Ah," Magnolia murmured, "there's that famous humility."

The clerk's hand remained frozen on his elegant brush. "The Dame will need to be informed."

"In confidence, please," said Crow.

A minute of silence passed.

"I remember you." It burst out too loudly. He flushed like a boy of eighteen. "I do. I was—I was three years old when the evacuation happened. My family always told me I couldn't have seen you, and even if I did, I would've been too young to remember. Perhaps it's a false memory, after all, but I could swear ... and your wings..."

Crow inclined her head in acknowledgment.

He was in his early forties, then. He'd been born in the town that used to exist on this same soil, the one that fell to the Singular Horde.

Now an upstart city had risen in its place.

After that, he had no questions about their cover story. He asked shyly if they were looking for promised companions, implying that the city might help find a match. "We provide a screening service for potential—"

Crow hastily jumped in, before Magnolia could come up with any dastardly plans, and told him that their companions were doing business in another town.

The clerk wrote a quick note. With elaborate apologies, he requested that they each perform a rote demonstration of magic. Crow pulled out a feather, transformed it into a black sword, then made it vanish. Magnolia plucked the brush from his fingers with dexterous pale roots that slithered out from the opening of her sleeve.

"Millet roots?" he inquired.

"Why, of course."

He passed them each a small booklet to serve as proof of registration. It also listed various benefits that the city conferred on visiting saints, such as free meals and lodging. That would have been a compelling incentive if they'd come together with human companions. Immortals had no real need for food or shelter ... but from the gleeful way Magnolia capered about, she intended to take full advantage of both. (To be fair, her body below the neck would demand rest if she never took it off.)

"Perhaps," the clerk said, sounding anxious, "before you choose a place to stay—perhaps you'll have an audience with the Dame?"

Crow attempted to demur. The clerk smoothed his hair, seeming troubled. Magnolia rolled her eyes, nudged Crow aside, and began chatting cheerfully with the clerk about various options for accommodation. "The silkworm nuns," she said at the end of it, decisively. "That's who we'll stay with. And Crow will dictate a formal greeting to pass to your Dame."

The message ended up being relatively short. With frequent corrections from Magnolia, it took half an hour to finalize the wording.

Crow praised the state of the city, expressed admiration for the Dame's decades of leadership, alluded warmly to their brief past acquaintance, and expressed her strong desire to go unheralded. She would only stay for a few days, she said, and she'd come purely on personal business. She wished to pay a private visit to the statue of Arion that the Dame had planned and funded, all those years ago—after Crow, in her grief, had departed the lands scarred by the Singular Horde.

The clerk looked tremendously relieved once this missive was complete. He assured them that it would be delivered to the Dame posthaste, and that the silkworm nuns would know to expect them in the evening.

Outside the Bureau, alone again, they walked past a gracious courtyard of decorative trees, songbirds, and colorful spotted fish.

"I never told you about the Dame," Crow said.

Magnolia scoffed. "I can read between the lines. She's the city leader—whether by codified law or unwritten understanding. She's held power all this time, yes? She's promised to our friend looming in the sky."

The mass evacuation before the coming of the Singular Horde had been a historic success. Far more blood was shed in subsequent years. After Crow lost track of the final survivor from the Horde. After she let everyone think that the Horde had been slain—that Arion hadn't died for nothing.

At first the old town's plundered earth refused to grow anything. Some families gave up on resettling. Then ashwort began to sprout, all on its own. Thus followed bloody struggles for land rights and political dominance and control over commerce. Crow, bereft of her companion, had departed before anyone could make her a serious offer. She'd stayed just long enough to glimpse the saint shaped like an aerial—and to meet the ambitious Dame, who had dubious claims to some sort of heritage in the region.

The Dame had been in her thirties then; she'd be her seventies now, veering toward eighty. Once she seized power, she'd held it with a minimum of conflict. Her saint shielded her from sabotage and assassination.

"You and Arion are a key part of this city's founding myth," said Magnolia. "Its fabled saviors, who paved the way for prosperity. Stay more than a day or two, and soon enough, people in the streets will start to whisper about how Saint Crow has come back. No one can keep a secret like that for long. Our pal in the Bureau looked at you like a golden idol come to life."

She laughed merrily. "Don't give me those furrowed eyebrows. You just might get away from here without anyone throwing you a massive parade. It would've been best if you agreed to an audience with the Dame, but I know why you didn't. You don't want me coming under closer scrutiny from her saint. Fair enough!

"So no audience—fine—in which case you should at least have pretended to accept her hospitality. She would have been the first to offer accommodations. But you didn't want that, either. Well, you can't snub her by staying with any of the other gentry."

That must have been why Magnolia had pounced on the silkworm nuns instead.

"You weren't listening to our clerk's advice," Magnolia said without rancor. "The nuns aren't in a position to compete with the Dame. Politically speaking, they're aligned with her, but they belong to a different sphere of society. You can take a room from them without blatantly slighting her."

"Mm," Crow said. Her companions had never expected much from her in the way of diplomatic nuance.

The silkworm nuns worshiped a deity of commerce. They kept their god alive in the thin lines of trade woven back and forth between settlements. *It's a fragile flame, and we devote ourselves to tending it.* Or so they'd told Crow, at some point long in the past. No one in the world made finer silk.

"Not that it matters to us if the Dame feels slighted," Magnolia added later, "but people find the strangest reasons to undermine one another. Who knows? Your innocent decision to comport yourself as an ascetic—to refuse all celebration—could be interpreted as a silent condemnation of the city as it stands today.

"Perhaps the seesaw of power will tilt away from the Dame in her old age. Perhaps the next generation will openly jockey to succeed her. Perhaps they can't wait for her to surrender her core to her aerial saint. At any rate, you don't want to be responsible for stirring the pot."

This much was true. Crow didn't thank Magnolia, but she let her take the lead for the rest of the day.

Magnolia soon tired of acting sickly. She dragged Crow into a bookstore. "Look!" she cried. "They have printing presses. They have culture!"

It was a low-traffic shop of suspect profitability. "Can you read?" Crow asked dubiously.

"Don't be hateful. I read very slowly, I'll give you that, but I graduated from being an illiterate bumpkin not long after I graduated from being dead. Language acquisition is much easier as an immortal."

Crow could read, too, but she mostly contented herself with watching dust motes waft about in sunlight.

She found an entire shelf devoted to the Dame's memoirs. If forced to choose, she would have flipped through just about anything else—almanacs, religious texts, how-to manuals, flimsy songbooks. She picked out a collection of prayers to the God of the End, most of which wished the deity a long, peaceful, and uninterrupted sleep.

Magnolia elbowed her until she glanced over at a pamphlet of poetry. The author was listed as *Snowberry*.

"It's your poet," Magnolia said. "The one who died of plague."

"That's not his name."

"It's what people know him as now. His most popular poem talks about snowberries."

His estate had scattered on the wind long before Crow learned of his death. Yet as soon as she skimmed a few lines, the memories came back. She didn't feel qualified to assess whether this was good poetry or bad poetry, but the bulk of it was undeniably his. Maybe with some parts changed, words missing or substituted—but still his at heart.

Scanning further, she encountered verses that had been inserted by other authors. As well as entire poems that, despite being composed in his style, referenced events after his death. Perhaps the poet Snowberry was more of a concept—or a genre unto himself—than a historical figure limited by mortal time and space.

"Remember the tea shop in my hillside village?" Magnolia leaned over her shoulder. "The owner has a little chapbook. *The Best of Snowberry*. When you told me about your poet, I thought something sounded familiar. The silhouettes of swallows flying, the taste of long-lost fruit— it's all in here, too. Want to ask for a copy? We're honored saints. We can probably get one for free."

This bookstore would be better served by paying customers. "No," Crow said. "No—his work should stay out in the world, with people, for as long as it can. I thought it was already lost."

She turned the pamphlet over in her hands. It was thinner than her registration booklet from the Bureau of Saints.

The poet would have liked being called Snowberry. No one who'd known him could have imagined that his poems would still be referenced centuries after his death. So little material from his time had survived: he'd outlasted most competition. The language had evolved so greatly that perhaps now his turns of phrase seemed fresh and striking.

Poets in general were mostly a thing of the past, in the same way as machina and skyscrapers and mages and large-scale wars of territorial conquest. That alone made him special—at least from the perspective of today's connoisseurs. Perhaps some of his poetry had made it down to the Steppehaven archives after all. Perhaps Tamar had sourced a copy.

Crow put the pamphlet back. Beside her, brilliant sunlight pierced one of Magnolia's dangling earrings. It was the sort of moment that the poet would have insisted on twisting into a love story. In his telling, the light from that earring would have pierced right through to Crow's core. Magnolia's lingering fingers on the spines of books would have been an unsubtle proxy for the way those same fingers might touch a naked hip, an ankle, a—

They left the shop. Magnolia glanced up at the saint above the city. "Do aerials have a soul?" she asked. "Do aerials have a heart?"

Crow explained—not for the first time—that no language could describe the experience of being an aerial without tinting it with human perspective. Her own mind, shaped by borrowed language for over a millennium, had settled into ruts and grooves that would have been unfathomably alien to the creature she'd been in her previous life.

"Huh," Magnolia said. "You imitated human lifestyles long enough to grow a human heart. Meanwhile, I gobbled down enough sacrifices to thoroughly distance myself from having ever been on the side of the sacrificed."

She inhaled, cringed, then cocked her head. "They have the makings of a decent sewer system," she said. "Impressive planning, given how fast the city shot up out of nothing. This stench comes more from fields of ashwort than human effluent."

"It's both," Crow said.

"You would know, I suppose?"

"From long experience."

It seemed as though they might make it through the rest of the day without further incident. Around sunset, Magnolia tugged her towards a rickety noodle shop with a line outside running ten people deep. After glimpsing their eyes, a plump woman motioned them to the front of the queue.

Crow shook her head, even as Magnolia stepped forward. A man built like a barrel knocked into them and said a word so rude that it took Crow's brain a full second to parse.

She felt the bleat of danger in her blood. The man kept shoving her, failing to understand that he couldn't make her budge. She ignored him. Magnolia was the one she grabbed and pulled close.

She gripped Magnolia's wrist hard enough to leave marks, hard enough that it felt as though her fingers would sink through flesh and bone like clay. What did it matter if she bruised a body that Magnolia would eventually toss away like a tree shedding dead leaves? What mattered was blocking her. If Crow had moved any slower, if she'd clenched Magnolia any less fiercely, then the red-faced man would already be dead.

He was still, incredibly, spitting nonsense. The plump woman and several others in line started yelling. A harried-looking person in an apron stuck their head out through the sliding door of the shop. Crow shot the man a look over her shoulder, and he abruptly lost his voice.

He carried no ashwort, but his sweat and breath were redolent with liquor. He was starting to retreat.

He had stumbled to the other side of the street by the time someone said: "You're hurting the little lady."

Another man. One waiting patiently for noodles behind them. He had large fleshy ears and a well-meaning frown. His frown was aimed at Crow.

The little lady? Crow thought.

Magnolia was very good at using her body. So good that you'd think she wore it all the time. With only a slight shift in posture, she'd utterly changed. Before, she'd looked like an insouciant pretty-faced man. She'd had a swagger even when she didn't move. Now she was a whip-thin woman who appeared too cowed to talk back.

Fury and embarrassment twined somewhere at the fringes of Crow's awareness, as distant as a birdcall heard from the other side of the city. She pried her hand off Magnolia's arm even as every instinct told her it would never be safe to let go. She apologized to the rest of the line, and to the cook who stood wringing their hands by the door. She said they would come back another day. The drunkard had gone far out of sight.

47

ONCE THEY'D TURNED several corners, Magnolia checked her step. "I don't know why I bother asking—but what do you care?"

Crow didn't reply.

"A man like that will rot in a ditch," Magnolia said, "or get careless and fall off a ladder. Or he'll drink till his organs wither. Or he'll start a fight behind a pub and get punched in the head and die. Or he'll live to a hundred, taking out his frustrations on everyone around him all the while. What? Don't look at me like that. You know the type. What would have been lost if I took his core a few years early? Nothing whatsoever. I'd be doing the city a service."

"Those are just words," Crow said. "You care nothing about doing the city a service."

Magnolia smiled without humor. "Everything is just words, Carrie."

It was possible that Crow only felt protective toward humans in the way that a farmer might feel protective towards livestock. Not everyone who had a core would be ready to make her an offer. Nonetheless: as a saint, a thriving human population would ultimately be to her benefit. With a larger pool to search in, she'd be more likely to find her next companion. And the next. And the next.

It was possible that her internal conviction about everything that was right and good all flowed from the same buried spring of self-interest. Wherever it came from, her conviction was her conviction, her beliefs were her beliefs, and she still didn't think she was wrong. Even if she questioned herself later, her body would move according to her deepest reflexive instincts.

Forget that man who'd accused them of cutting in line. The lives Magnolia had already taken, and the lives she would take if Crow escaped her, and the grief of their children and neighbors—those were not theoretical, not merely a matter of philosophical differences.

Few humans would care about Crow's reasons for saving them, but they would care very much if she failed. So what if she acted out of a half-understood urge baked into her by the world that made her? Maybe she was no more inherently moral than a herding dog following the imperative of its breed, striving to corral everything living in sight. Be that as it may, she wouldn't do anything differently. She wasn't interested in trying to change.

"That's right," Magnolia said, almost tenderly. "No matter what I do, you should stay as you are. You're a being thousands of years in the making. You've already been changed by mages and poets, rulers and heroes, midwives and scholars and farmers and homicidal maniacs. I have nothing to add to that."

It had grown dark quickly after sundown. The moon on the other side of the saint in the sky looked ever so slightly distorted, as if viewed through a pane of water. Mosquito coils smoldered outside storefronts and houses.

Crow remained on edge. There was something clinical in how Magnolia eyed everyone who strode or wheeled past them, from yammering peddlers to women whose heads balanced towering stacks of baskets. She contemplated them like they were all nothing more than walking cores. A glazed look came down over her face.

"You don't need it," Crow said, when she could no longer stand it. She pitched her voice lower. "You don't need it now. You can survive ages without reaping. You can survive almost forever."

Magnolia leaned very close to her and whispered against her ear. "I could survive almost forever without eating cores. But I can't survive without pursuing them. An earnest pursuit gives us sustenance, too. Didn't you know? You should learn more about monsters."

"You don't need it *now*," Crow said again, refusing to feel the touch of breath on her skin, refusing to feel anything.

"Give me something else to need instead."

They were on a loud and busy street. The moment slipped away like a bird taking wing. Magnolia stepped back and smiled crookedly. She gave Crow an exaggerated wink. They walked on, no longer touching, except when a pair of children almost barreled into Crow's knees. She jerked toward Magnolia to spare the children a painful collision, and watched with bemusement as they scampered off down the dusty brick paving.

"You'd have been pickpocketed if you had anything worth stealing," Magnolia said. "I suppose few thieves are heretical enough to take the papers we got from the Bureau. It must happen every so often, though. A humanoid monster could work wonders with these." She took out her Bureau of Saints booklet and waved it like a fan.

Crow checked that her own booklet was still there, too. She resolved to get Magnolia out of the city the very next day. Even that felt too late—but they'd already agreed to accept the hospitality of the silkworm nuns. Best not cause a diplomatic incident by vanishing without a word.

By the time they reached the convent, the moon was as bright as a brand new coin.

"We only require one room," Magnolia told the nuns smoothly.

The windows of their chamber were fitted with wooden screens caved with intricate swirls. No glass. The air that filtered through the tight-packed lattice seemed cleaner than in busier parts of the city.

As soon as they were alone, Magnolia explored the room. There were no perforated vases filled with ashwort. Perhaps it would have been considered insulting to act like saints needed special protection. Instead, she found a little soapstone box with empty silkworm cocoons tucked inside. They looked like soft hollowed-out eggshells.

"For good luck." She held one up to her eye. "These symbolize the triumph of man. When humans defeat monsters, they go in cocoons."

"Which means they'll eventually come back," said Crow.

"Maybe they're praying that cocooned monsters stay wrapped up as long as possible."

She threw herself down on the bed, bounced, and instantly reverted to being a disembodied head. Empty clothing lay like a heap of snakeskin beneath her.

She eyed Crow. "What, were you expecting something else?"

"No," Crow said truthfully.

Stay in her body long enough, and Magnolia would need to sleep. She would never be so unguarded around Crow again, if she could help it.

Nor would she go rolling out into the city streets in the form of a head. But a private transformation on property owned by nuns was unlikely to catch the attention of the saint up above, which had a much larger population of subjects to monitor. Magnolia wasn't the only stranger in town. She certainly wasn't the only nonhuman.

Magnolia kept looking at her as if displeased with the only answer she could have reasonably given. The sound of nighttime insects seemed tinnier, somehow, than out in the wild. The hand-carved window lattices admitted a miserly helping of moonlight.

"Come scratch my head," Magnolia said. "Did you feel these sheets? There's silk in them."

That was the voice she used when she was about to play a trick. Crow went over anyway, while she still had a choice in the matter. She sat down. Just as her nails found Magnolia's scalp, the weight on the bed shifted, and Magnolia was in her body again, blinking sleepily, not wearing a thread. Her breasts smoothed out to almost nothing when she lay on her back like that, arms above her head, heedless of the shed clothing crushed into the sheets.

If Crow had better control over her faculties, it would have been an excellent moment to rip Magnolia's heart out bare-handed.

"Such passionate thoughts," Magnolia sneered, and suddenly Crow was the one on her back, pinned down by vines.

Magnolia sat on top of her, as if waiting for her to tap out of a fight. The vines grew from Magnolia's spine, curving around her shoulders and sides, pressing Crow into the bed.

"You wanted me to scratch something," Crow said, not without difficulty.

Magnolia's face went colder and colder. Then she went back to a head again, landing on Crow's stomach with a vine-cushioned thump and a gust of breath. Her eyes were on the latticed windows.

"Even if I told you that you could say no, you wouldn't believe me. Understandably so." She sounded resigned. "What's the point? Perhaps you'll believe me by the time we reach the end of the world."

If pressed, Crow would have confessed that in the moment, she hadn't been capable of believing in anything except the vines that tied her. She sat up gingerly and shifted Magnolia to the bed beside her. The vines lashed back up inside Magnolia's neck, going wherever they went when she no longer needed them. Crow rubbed her arms, which felt too light. They felt bereft.

"It's for the best," Magnolia said. "Magnificent immortal creatures though we may be, the world didn't build us for romance."

The same could be said of their first lives, too. Elder aerials knew nothing of hatred or love, of betrayal or friendship. Magnolia had once been human, but she'd been too busy starving to spare any thoughts for canoodling. Then she'd been beheaded.

"Some immortals have love affairs in stories," Crow said.

"Hah. It's always initiated by some randy mortal. Humans sing those songs, not us. They can't resist the idea of love blooming in the most unlikely places. Our sheer indifference drives them mad with desire. Some of them, anyway."

Was desire the word for the fever that made her want to grab Magnolia and shake her until she went back in her body? Next—if she could—she would seize Magnolia from behind and yank her head back with enough force to snap her neck. That particular maneuver would only be feasible when she had the rest of her body attached.

"I should have expected no less," Magnolia said through suppressed laughter. "It's only natural for you to crave the sound of my neck breaking. Well, it's a good thing I didn't plan on getting any sleep tonight. How else will you entertain me, Carrie?"

Crow got up and padded over to the latticed windows. She felt like a spy peeping out through holes in a folding screen. This part of the nunnery must have been lightly occupied: no glow of lamps or candles spilled from the rooms on the other side of the garden, connected by covered outdoor corridors. All clinking of tools and dishes had ceased.

Thwarted violent impulses seemed to rise off her skin and dissipate into the night like steam, like something Magnolia could weigh with her eyes.

"I'm not a bard," Crow said. "I won't entertain you."

But the more she spoke, the longer Magnolia would stay out of trouble.

She began by relating semi-humorous stories of farm life from centuries past. Cows loved being scratched. They especially loved when Crow did it, because she never got tired. When she wasn't available, they'd go abrade themselves on trees instead, rubbing and rubbing until the living wood had been polished to a mirror-like shine.

The farm had been prosperous enough to keep a large family fed. Crow's companion grew into an elderly matriarch. For all her competence, she had difficulty perceiving her offspring as anything but grubby mischievous kids. Even after they were past seventy, and she in turn had reached her nineties.

When she became bedridden after a fall, her children and grandchildren and great-grandchildren barred the doors. They called on hunters and exorcists and priests of at least four different religions, all in the name of stopping Crow from coming to claim their matriarch's core. As if Crow were a monster who would take cores by force. They didn't care about a promise made before they'd been born. They cared about losing their mother, their grandmother, their great-grandmother.

Crow, for her part, had to commend them for caring. It was not an ideal outcome, but she preferred this to being shoved in a sickroom by inheritance-hungry descendants.

"Thank goodness you're not a debt collector," Magnolia said. "Your recovery rate would have been far below the industry average."

"Actually—"

"You've worked for moneylenders, too, have you? Fine. Shower me with all your insider knowledge."

Later in the night, as Crow caught her breath, Magnolia said without warning: "You never talk about Arion."

Crow was on the bed. It creaked beneath her, though she hadn't moved.

Magnolia had placed herself atop a chest of drawers like a prideful bust sculpted by a forgotten artist. "Do you want to hear his voice again?" she asked.

"Not from you," Crow said. "Never from you."

"*Never from you,*" Magnolia echoed in an eerily perfect copy of Crow's intonation. "Never mind Arion, then. Now tell me where you were when you and your mage saw the Cat Comet..."

After that, Crow did the talking. At least she thought she did. She wasn't aware of stopping. Magnolia only commented once more, saying—seemingly unprompted—"Your poet wrote some folderol about mourning the lives of candle flames, and mourning the lives of bees. Can't say I've ever mourned the lives of candles or bees, and I doubt he did either. Not truly. Only in a poetic sense." Their eyes met. "I know people aren't candles or bees to you. I do know that."

More words were said after that. Mostly by Crow.

Gradually, as though rousing from a trance, she became consumed by a creeping sense that no one was listening.

There was something different about the sky outside the window-screens. It was still dark—darker, in fact. The moon had moved far out of sight.

She felt a strange dropping sensation, as if a trapdoor had opened under her. In reality, she was still on the bed. She had been on the bed the whole time. There was nothing on the chest of drawers except a closed soapstone box. She had been talking to an empty room, as if talking in her sleep.

48

THE INSTANT she grasped that Magnolia was no longer in the room with her—in that very instant, Crow ported. Those sheepdog instincts kicking in again. It was like assuming the form of an aerial: she didn't know how she found Magnolia so unerringly.

One moment, she was on silken bedding, taking in the silence of the convent. Then, with a rush of adrenaline, she landed in a narrow alley in the dark.

It wasn't wide enough to qualify as a street. Just a dead-end space between buildings—restaurants or shops, long since closed for the night.

A brick wall blocked the end of the passage. Magnolia crouched there with a core turning like a globe of flame above her fingers. She was clothed again. Of course. Her garments had vanished from the bed.

She glanced at Crow, surprise showing only in a microscopic flicker of her eyelids. The captured core limned her with fiery light.

"Before you explode," she said, "look more closely."

There were two people folded up against the black-smeared brick wall. One was mortal. A gentleman. Finely clothed, and thoroughly dead. His abdomen had been torn open as if he were a toy with jewels smuggled in his stuffing. Only an immortal would leave a wound like that.

A sachet of ashwort had been attached to the sash at his waist. It was bloody now, sodden with the mess spilling from his torso. White graffiti scratched into the bricks over his shoulder seemed to leap out and press at Crow's eyeballs. Irrelevant names, professions of love and crude intentions, wordplay, insults, scraps of lyrics....

The other body belonged to an immortal. Child-sized, with a doll-like rosy-lipped face, but wrapped from chin to toe in an overlong cloak. The bent shapes under the fabric looked like a bunch of broken sticks, the skinny folded legs of a mantis. Blood as silver as mercury flowed out from beneath the closed cloak, hissing where it touched the gentleman's shoes.

"Watch this." Magnolia snapped her fingers in front of the child's unblinking face. All the while, the luminous core pulsed in her other hand.

The child's eyes were an odd muddy hue, as if milky with cataracts. They cleared briefly, then clouded again. An extra eyelid had shuttered into place over her cornea, translucent like the third eyelid of a snake. It was remarkably effective at hiding the tell-tale hints of red.

"Pardon me," Magnolia said.

She ate the monster's extracted core.

"You tricked me," Crow said as she swallowed. "You left."

She waited for a response, any response, but Magnolia just looked sideways at her with a curious half-smile. *Yes. And?* It didn't even need to be put into words.

The corrosive silver blood of the child-sized monster kept spreading, fizzing resentfully. Magnolia stepped back as it slowly turned to ash, black spots appearing like oxidation marring a mirror.

Crow went on. "You want me to think she killed him. But it was you. You took his core."

"Is there blood on me?"

There was, in fact, an almost unnatural lack of blood on her. No acid-eaten holes marked her trousers, and no human-colored blood dyed her hands or arms or had splattered anywhere on her front, either.

Crow touched the back of her neck. Magnolia remained quite still. And yet Crow had the impression that, on some other level, ripples went through her when that hand found her nape. Like a stone thrown in quiet water.

Magnolia's collar was very simple. Just a hemmed strip of light-colored fabric. Light enough to show a few scant drops of human blood.

She would have kept her distance. She would have stood casually at the entrance to the alley, her head tilted back as though stargazing. She might not have said anything. She might not even have looked at them.

A root would have come poking out from between the subtle ridges of vertebrae on the back of her neck. It wouldn't shoot straight through the air like an arrow aiming at the other end of the alley. It would have run silently along the length of the nearest wall like a growth of naked ivy.

Or perhaps it would have veered down to meet the stones of the street. It would have crept forward unseen, its movement seemingly having nothing to do with the woman relaxing at the alley entrance. It would lie there uncoiled like a long wick attached to deadly explosives. It would fork as it found its targets—simultaneously incapacitating the monster and striking for the gentleman's core.

Only after they finished thrashing or collapsing would Magnolia have turned, as if noticing them for the first time, her roots wiping themselves off on stones and brick, retreating gracefully to meet her. The roots would zip back inside her like they always did, but maybe they went a little too fast, or maybe they hadn't been scraped as clean as she'd thought. A smidgeon of blood had grazed the back of her collar.

Magnolia reached up to feel it for herself. She patted at her collar, then laid her fingers in the grooves between Crow's knuckles, which still rested on the back of her neck, tickled by her hair. It was a gentle touch, and not at all hurried.

"I'm used to murder, but not to cover-ups," she said ruefully. "Live and learn."

Nothing remained of the defeated monster now except a crumpled cloak and a smear of ash.

"I swiped her prey out from under her nose," Magnolia said. "He was nanoseconds away from death. She'd gotten him alone. She'd covered everything but her face with that cloak, and she'd covered the red of her eyes. Wish I could grow a third eyelid, too. In any event, why do you think he followed her down to an obvious dead end? What did he mean to do with a child—what he thought was a child—wandering at this time of night, anyway?"

"That creature might have reeled him in with a power like yours."

"Maybe she did," Magnolia agreed. "Maybe she didn't."

Even in the dead of night, even with that small mask-like face framed by a hood, the illusion of being human would not have lasted long. How had the monster moved, limbs clicking, beneath the disguise of its cloak? Now all was ash.

Crow's hand tightened on Magnolia's neck. Magnolia, unconcerned, led her out onto the wider street as if they'd stopped in the alley for an emergency bathroom break. Or to avoid paying for a room to do other things.

No one saw them.

"We have to leave," Crow said.

"We just did."

"We have to leave the city."

"I get the impression that"—Magnolia pointed up—"the eyes of the city's patron aren't quite so all-seeing as you fear. A saint tasked with guarding an entire population isn't going to pick up on every last domestic incident. That aerial probably focuses on monster assaults coming from outside the city borders. And on protecting the Dame's life, above all else.

"Someone will find his body sooner or later. When they do, they'll see obvious ashen traces of the monster that killed him. Strange, yes, for the monster to have been slain, and for the human corpse to have gone unreported. But there's really no reason for them to link it to me. There are plenty of others like us lurking in the city."

"We have to leave," Crow said, "before you do it again."

"That hurts," Magnolia said mildly, twisting her neck. "Are you trying to squeeze my head off?" She prised Crow's fingers off her nape, one by one, and twined her own fingers through them. "There. Keep my hand. Pretend you're arresting me, if that's what gets your blood going."

"We can't just go around killing people."

"That's been rather standard in some historical cities, no? I told you, he would have—"

"He's dead," Crow said, "and it's your sins I'm concerned with, not his. Say anything you like to try and make this more palatable. Nothing will ever prove it true."

"Likewise, nothing will ever prove it false. Why would I make things more difficult for myself, Crow? It's easier if you don't automatically think everything I say is a lie."

Crow remembered the eight swollen bodies she'd dredged in

Steppehaven. It came to her with a suddenness as violent as being struck in the head from behind. Magnolia had made those comatose bodies disappear. She'd devoured them with her roots, right after she devoured their cores.

"You didn't need to leave anything in that alley," she said, too confounded to know what she felt. "You could have erased him."

They were still, ridiculously, holding hands. They might have looked like lovers in search of the moon—too self-absorbed to fear monsters dressed up as mortals. A observant spectator would come away thinking that Crow was overbearing, unpleasant, maybe too possessive in the way she jerked Magnolia around.

"Did you want me to eat all the evidence?" Magnolia murmured. "I left his body as a kindness. I do have a feel for how much I can test you before you snap." Her tone turned incredulous. "I didn't pounce on the first convenient victim. I had dozens of other options. Do you have any idea how long I left you alone in that room?

"I thought of you as I searched for just the right situation to feed. I'm always thinking of you, even though I would much rather act freely. It's laughable—between the two of us, who gives the orders, and who's being dragged along unwillingly? Who is the vassal, and who is the lord? Can't you see that I would do much, much worse without you on my mind? One dead monster, and one dead human, in one evening? Why, that's nothing. Age and blood clots have slain more men in this city tonight."

Her eyes dropped to her hand in Crow's grip. It was likely going numb. "If we must, we can leave today," she said coolly. "Dawn will come soon enough. Don't you need to pay your respects to Arion?"

They needed to pay their respects to the silkworm nuns, too, who had hosted them on short notice. Crow ported the two of them back to the convent before sunrise. She participated jerkily when Magnolia greeted the nuns. The early-rising birds of the city sang shrilly.

A sense of treachery ran through her like poison. But she couldn't cling to it, couldn't justify it, and the dregs of her anger turned as ashen as the damp dust left by the monster that Magnolia had killed in the street. She felt that Magnolia had sworn not to deceive her, not to take prey in secret, not to turn her own mind against her. Which was ludicrous. When and why would Magnolia ever have made such a promise?

This insidious fog of betrayal was worse than reflexive revulsion. Worse than the hatred that Crow had carefully carried with her all the way from the hills, the one precious belonging that was exclusively hers, the one thing she couldn't afford to lose even if she gave away every last scrap of clothing and other mortal possessions, all of which she had understood would be transient.

The betrayal she felt now was worse because it meant she had expected something better. It was like scrutinizing a carved woodblock for making prints: the art pressed on paper would come out in reverse. You could guess at the final flipped image even if you would never have wanted to see it, even if you would never have wanted to know.

49

THEY VISITED the noodle shop again, at Magnolia's bidding. They sat at a counter of sunset wood. Magnolia made small talk with the bemused staff, asking them if they had ever heard of noodles shaped like human ears. (They had not.)

Once she pronounced herself satisfied, they left for the old town district.

The city had started as a thin ring around the dead territory where returning settlers discovered sprouts of ashwort. In each subsequent year, the ring dramatically thickened, spreading outward. At the middle of this expansive settlement lay not a palace or a monument but instead a giant hole of uninhabited land.

Even beyond its official outer boundary, the city extended a generous radius of protection to agricultural workers and favored traders. Magnolia commented cynically about how this scheme might come tumbling down once the Dame died. The aerial saint might prefer other skies. It might flit off to some quieter place, rather than select its next companion from among all the citizens, high-born and low-born, who would scramble to offer up their souls in exchange for continued safety ... or for a chance to seize more power than even the Dame had ever taken.

The old town district appeared to be more heavily defended than the city border. The walls were much higher, and had been topped with spikes draped in threads from shrieking spiders. Guards stood at regular intervals.

Neither the guards nor the wall nor the spider-threads could stop an immortal from flying, or porting, or simply vaulting much higher than a mortal creature could ever jump. But it would keep out human bandits. A thief couldn't scale the wall without brushing those near-invisible strands of silk, which would trigger deafening screams. The larger the living animal that touched them, the louder the spiderwebs got; unlucky ants would only produce a tiny peep.

"If I were human," Magnolia said, "I'd sedate a mule and throw it up there."

"It isn't easy for humans to throw around mules."

"You know what I mean. You could use an animal to make a nice big distraction. Then you could tunnel under the wall. Guess you'd have to go unfeasibly deep. They must have traps buried underground, too."

"I'm sure it's happened before," Crow said.

They showed the guards their saintly booklets. The clerk at the Bureau had stamped a symbol that meant they could pass freely in the most sensitive parts of the city.

Once they were past the walls and out of earshot, Magnolia made an extraordinary face. She turned and spat, dryly, as if trying to get a bad taste off her tongue.

"Cover yourself." Crow motioned toward her nose and mouth.

"It isn't really something that comes in through your nostrils," Magnolia said gloomily. "It's only pretending to have a scent. Not all monsters have noses, anyway. It's more of a presence than a smell."

Magnolia had no reason—other than morbid voyeurism—to view the site of Arion's death. Crow started to say that she didn't need to tag along. But the words faded as they crossed her lips. No telling what Magnolia might do if she went off by herself.

She heard soft laughter. Magnolia must have spied on her thoughts.

The old town had changed since Crow and Arion made their last stand against the Singular Horde. At the same time, it wasn't as different as one might expect after a forty-year gap. The taller shells of burnt-out buildings had been dismantled to reduce the risk of collapse, but they'd left short crumbling walls in place. You could pick out the outlines where houses used to stand, and the ghosts of old streets.

No one knew exactly what alchemy led ashwort to flourish here. They'd only removed the bare minimum of rubble to let workers pass safely.

Ashwort grew from soil, and from dirty crumbling ruins, and from the silt that collected on narrow new roads. It didn't arrange itself in neat rows, and it had sparse competition from any other weeds or moss or grasses.

Laborers with woven baskets stooped to harvest leaves by hand. They paused when Crow and Magnolia passed, but the flicker of interest was brief, and quickly dulled.

Magnolia had stopped griping. "I wonder how long ashwort will grow here," she said. "Which will die out first—the harvest or the Dame? They've been disciplined about not plucking too much, but demand will always exceed supply."

Ashwort patches typically lasted a couple decades after their initial flush. In past times, people had used it as a rough guide to mark the return of the Horde. *Watch out for the Singular Horde*, they'd say, *when the ashwort bloom turns yellow and brown. That's when the Horde is sure to come. To the same place? Maybe. To a different place? Maybe. May the God of the End preserve us.*

Thick low-growing leaves still covered vast swathes of the old town, only ceding ground to thistle and clover near the walls. Almost forty years of continuous ashwort was an unprecedented run. That longevity, more than anything, might have convinced people that the Dame had a divine right to keep ruling. But it wouldn't last forever.

The sky was buttery yellow, with gauzy bluish clouds. That sensation of betrayal still trembled under Crow's skin, as fresh as ever, and yet daylight made it seem like a response to something that had happened a very long time ago. While her mind floundered about in a swamp of its own making, Magnolia took her hand again.

Her fingers were cool to the touch. Crow found herself holding them loosely, not at all with the same bone-breaking grip as last night.

Arion had died in—it was hard to tell now, actually. It was a yard in front of a house, or behind a house, scarred by the incursion of the Horde. There had been a chicken coop—a broken tangle—and the house lacked most of its roof. The smell of the Horde had gotten in their clothes, their eyes, their hair. They'd felt like hanks of meat hung up to smoke.

The spot where he'd died was unmarked. Not even a placard. The Dame had a strict policy of introducing as few foreign elements to the fields as possible. (She'd erected a statue for Arion elsewhere.) No one could stop the progression of time, but they could attempt not to change the old town any more than they had to. As if to trick all that ashwort into thinking no real time had passed at all.

"He stayed as bait," Crow said. No one was looking at them any-more. No one could hear her except Magnolia. "We studied the Horde's past awakenings. Once it starts moving towards a given settlement, it rarely changes direction. The only times it happened were when the entire settlement got advance warning to evacuate. If there isn't a single human left with a core—only then will the Horde change course."

"Arion was your single human with a core," said Magnolia. "He stayed after you got all the residents to leave. He volunteered for it, didn't he?"

"He was very young," Crow said, nonsensically. "He was—"

"Like your own child. Did you raise him from infancy?"

Crow didn't speak. His weight had never left her arms. She had held him at the end as she had held him at the beginning, when he was just a few months old. When his mother died.

To be more specific: when Crow killed his mother, as per their agreement, and swallowed her core.

After leaving the ashwort fields, they went to view Arion's statue. It was larger than life, cast in bronze, with glass eyes. Some details were very faithful. His long hair, for instance, and the medallion that hung from his neck, complete with a delicate relief of an acorn rendered in copper. Overall, though, it didn't look much like him. Partly because the artist had not known him, and would have struggled to find visual references. But mostly because it wasn't alive.

Nearby, children squatted on faded rugs. They peddled wooden charms whittled to resemble ashwort leaves, which had a rounded shape like bloated hearts. A substitute for those without access to the real thing—whether due to its price, or to rationing. One urchin also sold acorn pendants carved in imitation of Arion's medallion.

Magnolia looked at Crow. "Where's *your* statue?"

Forty years ago, Crow had made her wishes clear. Arion was the hero of this land. She wanted them to remember that. She wanted them to remember him alone.

She was the one who, despite Arion's sacrifice, had failed to kill the Singular Horde. She was the one who'd made a secret of her failure.

Given the Horde's ongoing silence, it seemed increasingly likely that some other immortal had pounced on the last fleeing survivor before Crow could catch up. She'd kept looking until there was no longer any hope of finding its trail.

"When I first seized control over you, I tried to taunt you," Magnolia said.

"You still taunt me."

"Just listen. I told you I'd never let you take another companion. I threatened your entire life purpose. You didn't find it threatening at all, did you? You'd abstained from magic for decades. You came to challenge me alone. You had your reasons—your excuses.

"But even if you'd slain me on the spot—you wouldn't have strolled into the village and put out a call for your next companion. You'd have kept subtly avoiding it, maybe for centuries, until you'd pushed yourself to the brink of starvation. That's why you were so torn up about Tamar."

Crow remained silent. She wasn't quick-witted enough to parry a stark thrust of truth. She glanced at the statue and then away again, with a pang like hot sunlight at the backs of her eyes.

In those forty years of magical fasting, she hadn't lingered in any one settlement for long. Sometimes she'd avoided settlements altogether. Still, she'd helped humans in passing; she couldn't ignore them. She'd accepted their heartfelt thanks. She'd left without turning back. She hadn't given out any feathers.

Yes—she'd shied away from taking another companion. It would have to happen someday. But she hadn't wanted to push Arion further into the past. She hadn't wanted to replace him.

They turned in their booklets and departed the city that afternoon. Magnolia didn't drag her feet: she was suspiciously docile. Maybe the miasma of ashwort was starting to get to her.

It was just as well that they got out quickly. It seemed highly unlikely that anyone would connect Magnolia with the death of a random man in an alley. But there were already whispers of Saint Crow being back in town. Either the Bureau of Saints or the Dame's household had leaked it. Whatever the case, Crow felt passers-by looking at her more intensely than the day before.

Magnolia breathed easier once they were upwind of the New City and its ashwort fields. She whistled for Dung, who joined them along a worn dirt path flanked by weed-choked ditches.

"Didn't you have a present for him?" Crow asked.

Magnolia duly produced a greasy paper package of candied locusts. Loot from the city market. She only had to open it partway. Dung's tongue plumbed the package as if scraping out an anthill.

"Bad news," she said afterward as she compressed the empty paper. "He didn't save any for the rest of us." She rolled the paper into a tube and whacked him. "You're so inconsiderate."

The land up north revealed itself to be a spectacular patchwork of farmland, all within the New City's sphere of protection. They walked alongside Dung, waving at families in the fields. Small children frequently forgot whatever job they were doing and ran closer to stare, dirt-smeared and bug-eyed. Dung pretended to take no notice of his audience.

But soon enough, the farms turned raggedy. Unused windmills and rotting silos stood like roadside temples to a neglected god. A feral cat with blazing green eyes glowered at them, then stalked deliberately away. No more children drifted out to trail in Dung's wake.

A traffic-tramped path still continued on ahead. The roadside ditches narrowed and petered out. Magnolia—deeming the potential for awkward encounters to now be much lower—jettisoned her body and latched on to Crow's shoulder.

"You could ride Dung," Crow pointed out.

"But I missed being here," Magnolia said in her ear.

"Already tired of urban life?"

"What a jokester you are, Carrie. We were only in the city for one night."

Still—Magnolia had scratched her itch enough, it seemed. She didn't veer off to find any folksier settlements between the city and her faraway hills.

The sky turned a weak watery shade of red, with a skein of dark gray clouds like a divine net cast out to catch aerials. Crow mounted Dung's back, and they aimed for a smear of richer red on the horizon. It looked as if the sky had started bleeding onto the edge of the earth.

It turned out to be a field of spider lilies much taller than Crow. They had livid green stems—trunks?—as thick as any sapling, and as sturdy as old bamboo.

"Well!" Magnolia sounded taken aback. "Doesn't feel at all like fall. But we must be near the equinox."

Dung pulled up short and refused to go further.

"They can't hurt you unless you chew on them," she told him. "They're extremely poisonous, this tree-sized kind," she added as an aside to Crow. "Lots of fables about pretty boys and maidens brushing up against one and then falling in a dead faint for the rest of their lives. But I doubt they have any effect on primevals."

"Don't force him," Crow said.

"You underestimate my finesse. If I force him to take us through, he won't mind it, and he won't be traumatized." From her current perch on his neck, she gave Crow a speculative look. "If you like, we can enjoy the scenery on our own. Give him a good pat for me. Meet us on the other side, Dung."

They dismounted. Crow gave him a good pat, and he gratefully reversed direction.

"I'm trying to remember the rest of the fables," Magnolia said. "There's more than just poison. Do they eat draft animals? Do they bleed when you cut them? Are they allegedly a land-bound monster? They don't seem to have cores, though. On we go."

There was an unearthly hush beneath the lilies. From far away, they had appeared as an unbroken block of crimson. Up close, the stems were spaced out enough to comfortably walk between them. Some of the flowers were more pink than scarlet, and some were a shade of cream or pale yellow. It could be surprisingly hard to discern their color from below—what with the brightness of the sky, and the interplay of shade and old daylight.

So long as they didn't look up, it felt like meandering through a venerable bamboo forest. The hefty stems were straight and smooth all the way from base to flower, without any extraneous offshoots. Crow held Magnolia's head in front of her to reduce the risk of accidentally grazing them. Just in case. Magnolia would probably find the poison delicious.

"I am sorry," Magnolia said, in a completely different tone from two minutes ago.

Anger flushed through Crow's veins. "For taming me?" she asked bitterly. "For ordering me around? For taking cores when you please? I can't imagine you being sorry for anything that matters—and if you say you are, you're only saying it. You don't even have lungs. Don't waste your breath."

"I am sorry," Magnolia said steadily, "that you didn't get a chance to see it on your own. Arion's statue. The ashwort fields. You're quite right. I'm not sorry about anything else, and I won't pretend I am. But that—I am sorry about that."

Crow looked blindly down at the top of her head. This field or forest, uncannily devoid of insects, felt like a world without any connection whatsoever to the reeking city. The sky had swiftly washed out to shades of gray and gold. The curly-petaled flowers and their numerous curved stamens cut down on much of the remaining daylight. At noon, the stamens would cast shadows like the bars of a fence.

"Did you know?" she demanded. How strange it was to hear her own voice shake. "Did you know when you spoke to me in his voice? Did you know when you said—"

"Listen," Magnolia said carefully. "I only scoop up surface-level thoughts. Only a small percentage of those, at that. The things you know and feel most deeply—those are the hardest to read, in a sense. Their true bulk lurks far below any place I can easily access. Without you noticing the intrusion, I mean. Without outright dissecting you. Anything I can detect noninvasively is only a fragment of its true shape, and I know better than to extrapolate."

Was she playing dumb?

But if she already knew, why wouldn't she use it? Why wouldn't she twist the knife?

"Crow," Magnolia said, "is there something you want to confess?"

It was not a command.

Crow had never told anyone. She had never planned on telling anyone. She couldn't explain it just by speaking about herself, or about Arion. She'd have to go further back.

She'd have to start with Arion's mother.

She flinched, startled, at the sight of her hand. Magnolia had wound a small green tendril in a curlicue around her finger, a spiraling ring. She'd done it with such finesse that Crow had barely known it was there.

"Then let me tell you something first," Magnolia said. "It's not because you're a saint that you turned the Devil down and refused your chance to escape me. Saints don't have any inherent love for humanity. Just like how scavengers don't harbor any greater love for their fellow animal than regular carnivores. All that marks a saint is a different pattern of consumption.

"There are plenty of saints who would have left me at the very first opportunity, without a second thought for who I might hurt in their absence, or what I might do to get them back. And there are plenty of saints, of course, who would have properly killed me in moments when you pulled your punches.

"Being a saint isn't what makes you grieve for Arion, or Tamar, or any of your other short-lived companions. Being a saint isn't why you harbor regrets about the man I left dead in the city. Being a saint isn't what makes you want to strangle me. It's you who cares, not the saint in you. It's only ever been you.

"When did it start? How long were you trapped on that altar in your past life, ninety-nine percent dead, mutely taking in all the entreaties and prayers and hopes and fears of your supplicants? Eight hundred years or so—that's my guess, from what the land told me. You could have hated them, those humans marching in and out of your shrine like an endless stream of ants paying homage. You could have ignored them. You outlived pretty much all of them, anyway.

"But you listened, when you were nothing but a withered lump of flesh without actual ears. You heard them, and you felt for them, and you carried that with you when you became a returner. There was already that seed in you. Maybe that's why you didn't start off as a monster. You listen to the likes of me, too, even on days when I'm not actively forcing you."

She stopped there, as if she would be satisfied without a reaction.

They had come deep into the forest of lilies. There was nothing visible in any direction except stems that rose up like load-bearing columns to stave off the dimming sky. They were the same color as the little green ring around Crow's finger.

Magnolia was the only immortal—the only one of their kind—who had seen Crow for what she was, who had perceived Crow with more deadly clarity and totality than she could ever hope to perceive herself. No other immortal (and no other being) would ever see her the same way. She felt this with such cold certainty that it broke out all over her like a sickening sweat.

Humans died too quickly. They had their own selves and their own lives to focus on in the time they were given. Other immortals simply lacked this profound interest in their peers. They might battle, they might kill each other, but it was distinctly impersonal: a predestined matter of instinct, competition, and gravitation. Like how two stars might smash together. Like how a planet might pull down a meteor and burn it to vapor.

The Horde had massacred Arion with the inevitability of a volcano erupting. It took no more pleasure in the act than any animal did in sating its hunger. It had borne no personal ill will towards him or Crow. It had barely acknowledged either of them, except as obstacles to be overcome. If, afterward, it had secretly burrowed underground for its next phase of compulsive dormancy—if it had survived all this time— upon digging free, it would not come after Crow to seek revenge. It would target the nearest large settlement, as it always did.

Magnolia had said and done things to Crow that were meant to hurt her. None of those cruelties could compare to the Horde killing Arion. But unlike the Singular Horde, she had been actually trying to hurt Crow, and not just in a physical sense. From the start, she had viewed Crow as a being capable of experiencing a broken heart.

"I do have to wonder." Magnolia wound subtle tendrils around her other fingers, too, each ring in a different style. "You always think of your companion before Arion as Arion's mother, and nothing else. She had a name, didn't she?"

"Her name was Leda," said Crow. Somehow this was all it took to break the dam.

50

Leda was only a teenager when she asked Crow to kill Calamity Bridge. Crow did it unaided—and then the Four Great Adversaries were down to three.

Calamity Bridge, for all its trickiness, had been a monster affixed to a single location. (Much like the Woman in the Hills.) Some people found its call irresistible. But on average, they could avoid its predations by keeping their distance.

Unlike land-bound monsters, the stampeding Singular Horde might blaze a path from coast to coast. It had one saving grace: its long stretches of dormancy gave humanity a chance to rebuild.

If scholars were to coldly rank the Adversaries, most would agree that the Beautiful Scourge was by far the worst. It was a monster that took the form of a magical plague. It couldn't have been more different from the simple physical pestilence that killed Crow's poet.

It made people beautiful—physically, yes, but it didn't stop there.

It lent a magnetic charm to their laughter, so that everyone else sounded wan in comparison. All in all, it made them a delight to be around, right up until the day it killed them. This helped the plague spread impossibly fast.

No one knew the exact mechanism of transmission, given that it was both a magical illness and a parasitic immortal being. Perhaps it had something to do with close contact, smiles, locked eyes, listening ears, friendly touches, friendly feelings. Naturally, it only infected people with cores. The coreless (as well as immortals, and very young human children) remained unaffected.

With the increasing prevalence of human cores, the Scourge had become more devastating each time it resurged. People of the past passed down painful lessons. Once the Scourge began spreading, once the situation grew desperate, mobs would lynch anyone they deemed suspiciously attractive. There was no logic to it: even people without cores might get stoned to death for standing out.

If it ran out of living victims, the Scourge could port up to a quarter-league from a fallen corpse to the next nearest person with a core. If it could no longer leap to anyone new within that range, it would perish, as if dealt a temporary death by human hunters. It would form cocoons and await its eventual revival. This cycle of instant starvation and surrender was what Magnolia might have called its compulsion.

During Leda's lifetime, the Beautiful Scourge emerged in a thriving town over in the western part of the continent. One that Leda had been eager to visit. She and Crow were already on their way there long before they heard any news of the Scourge.

They found their destination blockaded by an alliance of neighboring settlements. The alliance built a wall and hired coreless mercenaries to patrol the perimeter. Some coreless citizens of the quarantined town were eventually allowed to leave. When they went back to search for orphans, they got torn apart by anguished survivors. It was easier, in the end, not to let anyone out at all.

The surrounding settlements declared that no one would ever pass the wall again. But they couldn't afford to keep paying those mercenaries forever. A year or two later, no survivors remained. The Scourge burned out after claiming every available life within reach. Still, most people gave the dead town a wide berth.

Most, but not all. Without paid guards, there was no one to stop grave robbers from trying their luck. Wishful rumors of ashwort kept cropping up, too. Some claimed that it had begun growing all around the bodies on the other side of the wall. As far as Crow knew, no ashwort was ever actually found. But these stories served as an added incentive for more thieves and explorers to sneak back in, year after year.

Leda and Crow pursued other monsters. They hunted bounties all across the continent. But Leda never forgot about the horrors of the Beautiful Scourge: the walled-off town, the faraway voices screaming to be let out. Those voices merged into a wordless roar that came in irregular bursts like distant fireworks. Leda never forgot the blank-faced coreless kids who could neither cry nor speak. They were the lucky ones, the ones who got out.

When she and Crow had occasion to visit the automagi, Leda asked how long it would take the Beautiful Scourge to revive. They told her to make Crow take a look at its cocoons in person. All right, she said. Then she asked how to stop the Scourge after it reemerged—how to break its endless cycle.

The answer was simple. Let the Scourge revive. Let it infect new human prey. An immortal could defeat it by killing all the infected, every last one. Only then would it be possible to claim the Scourge's core.

The automagi liked Leda. She was a piece of living history, after all.

A human hero in her prime. At a very young age, she had arranged for the defeat of Calamity Bridge. The automagi were supposed to be neutral, but perhaps they couldn't help but give her extra encouragement.

They offered her a medallion that would slow the progression of the Beautiful Scourge. Only for the wearer, not for an entire populace, and only for a few extra years. *It's the last of our stock,* they said. *No need to return it. We used to give these out to our resident half-immortals—they're vulnerable to all sorts of illness—but lately, they haven't needed it.*

The next time Crow and Leda came west, they ported past the wall around the diseased town. No one sought to stop them. The bodies—in homes, in ditches, in mass graves, in temples, in schools, in the streets—all those bodies were just a collection of bones. Each had a cocoon growing somewhere on it: a cocoon so small that not even a silkworm would fit.

Crow examined several such cocoons. "Five more years," she said.

Leda explained her plan.

"You want to have children," Crow reminded her.

Leda laughed. "Carrie, I'm forty-two. I'm not saying it would take a miracle, but the odds aren't looking good. Well, we have five years to spare. Let's see what happens."

They returned five years later. It was still just the two of them. No family in tow, or waiting in a safer village; no young children.

Leda laughed again. "No one can say I didn't try. I must have slept with every brown-haired man south of the killer volcanoes."

"Not sure," Crow said. "I think you missed a few."

"Really? Damn. I'm losing my touch."

The next steps of the plan were relatively easy to execute. Much easier than doing battle with the spirit of Calamity Bridge. Crow performed a sweep of the ghost town and systematically chased away every last grave robber, treasure hunter, and vagrant, until there was no human left alive within the fatal walls except for Leda.

Then they waited for the Beautiful Scourge to emerge from its myriad cocoons.

Leda put on the medallion she'd gotten in Steppehaven. When the Scourge revived, it leapt to her, and her alone. Crow immediately ported her far, far away: to a cottage they'd built on an island off the west coast, an island where no one else had lived for a century.

Since the Scourge only infected humans, Crow could still make runs to the mainland for news and books and tools and supplies, though she tried to keep a low profile. There was always a lot to do on the island: laundry, sewing, repairs around the house, tilling, harvesting, cooking, preserving, fishing, cleaning ... no end of tasks, no matter how much Crow helped. Yet on some level, it felt as though Leda was just quietly whittling away at her remaining sliver of time, chiseling it down bit by bit, because what else was there to do when you were the world's last carrier of the Beautiful Scourge?

At this point, Crow stopped speaking. It felt as though her voice had reached the edge of a cliff. The spider lilies were dim in the gloaming.

"Did she become very beautiful?" Magnolia asked.

Crow was stumped. "Did she?"

"I wasn't there," Magnolia said tartly. "Did the medallion suppress her allure?"

"No," Crow said after some thought.

Leda had acquired a beauty that could not have been more exquisitely suited to the raging sunrises and sunsets over the island, the gleam of light in primordial ruins and on the carcasses of long-lost machina. Upon reflection, Leda had been more wildly beautiful than all the wild colors of the sea.

But Crow had not seen any of that. Crow had seen only her loneliness, her resignation, her uncomplaining labor, her private satisfaction, her unfilled hollows, and the keen edge of doubt that she would never face head-on. Leda would not ask herself if she had regrets—she would not leave any room for regrets to creep in—because however she felt, there was no going back.

Magnolia coughed. "Do saints take after their companions, or is it the other way around?"

"What?"

"Never mind. So what happened next? You stayed with her on that uninhabited island until the day she pronounced herself ready to die?"

"Yes," Crow said. "But first, she got pregnant."

"..................."

One long moment later, Magnolia said, "How?"

"Immaculately."

She'd figured Magnolia would mock her. Instead Magnolia asked, without so much as a smile: "Were you in love with her?"

"Leda was human."

"Is that an answer?"

"For as long as she was my companion," Crow said, feeling obscurely insulted, "we were a family. But I didn't love her like how she loved brown-haired men."

"Arion was your child, too."

"...Yes."

"Arion was half-immortal."

"Yes."

"Did you ever tell him?"

"Arion only ever had one mother."

"You mean—"

"Leda," Crow said. "His mother was Leda. That's what I told him. That was his truth."

"He could have lived with you longer than any of your other companions." A note of incredulity entered Magnolia's voice. "A half-immortal?

He could have accompanied you for generations. Instead he died at—what, the age of twenty?"

"Twenty-two."

"And he was your *son*. Your only offspring, I suppose? The only son you ever had?"

Crow shook her head harder and harder. "I raised him. I had to. But he wasn't my son. He was Leda's—always. I told him everything about her. I made sure he knew his mother."

Magnolia made a muffled noise that shared a couple syllables with a very old curse. Then she asked Crow to tell her the rest.

The Beautiful Scourge would not pass to infants. That was part of the reason Crow suggested pregnancy as an option. Between her magic and her previous career as a midwife's assistant, she was confident she could keep Leda safe.

Leda spent close to half a year thinking about it before she said yes.

She didn't die in childbirth. She was very weak afterward, and she never fully recovered her former strength. But it helped that Crow—who never needed to sleep or eat, and who could remain comparatively kempt even if she never bathed again—was always there to hold the baby.

"I'll hang on as long as I can," Leda said. "Stay with him for as long as you can, too. I know it won't be forever. Someday, someone else might offer you their core, and they might really mean it, and you might have to go where he can't follow. I understand. But please—hang in there. Until it becomes impossible. I'll do the same."

Crow asked, somewhat inanely, if she had any other requests.

"Other requests? Like what?"

"Would you like a statue?"

Leda found this hilarious. "I do deserve one, don't I? No, I don't care to have a statue. How embarrassing! But make sure Arion knows what I've done. Everything brilliant and stupid. Brave and wasteful. All of it."

"Should I tell him about your brown-haired men?"

"Maybe skip that part." Leda's expression turned thoughtful. "I like to think that Arion might get a statue. I hope he'll deserve it more than me. It's the heroes who live and go home who deserve all the praise and adulation, I think. We don't want our children to grow up and do stupid shit like—you know." She gestured at herself, mummified in winter blankets.

Arion was in the crook of Crow's elbow, momentarily placid. When he began to make little peeps of displeasure, Leda held her arms out, and Crow handed him back.

Leda kissed the fuzzy top of his head. "I couldn't have done it without you. Any of it," she said to Crow. She didn't glance up.

"I know."

Maybe, in that moment, Leda had mostly been thinking of Arion. But Crow was thinking of Leda's plan to lure the revived Scourge into her body, to give it nowhere else to go. Her plan to die, and to take another Great Adversary down with her. None of it could have been conceived of or accomplished alone.

Without Crow, that path would never have been an option.

Without Crow, she'd have lived a fuller life: less heroic, maybe, but also longer, and much less lonely.

With each new month after Arion's birth, Leda grew increasingly tired. The magic in her medallion had dimmed to the point of being almost impalpable. The Scourge would pose zero risk to Arion as a baby or a toddler, but her fears for him grew in tandem with her sickness.

A year passed. Arion turned one. He still had not spoken his first word or taken his first steps. Leda was bedridden, and too feeble to hold him.

She told Crow it was time. She didn't dare wait any longer. If she slipped into a coma, she wouldn't be able to willfully surrender her core. If she died of the Scourge in her sleep, it would perish and become a cocoon again. It might stay isolated on the island for many, many generations before finding anyone else to infect, but it wouldn't truly be over.

Arion was sleeping. Crow laid him on a blanket at the other end of the room, so his mother's blood wouldn't splash him.

She went back over to Leda, who had no energy left to speak. With a single fell blow, she took the life and core of her companion, and the life and core of the infectious monster inside her. In mechanical terms, it was a simple matter for Crow to give both of them a permanent death.

51

Without explanation, Magnolia took human form. She reached into Crow's pack and wordlessly pulled on a hip-length robe. She made it seem like a concession of sorts, although she was far from fully dressed.

She began walking. Crow followed, flexing her hand. It felt naked, now, without those cool tendrils around her fingers.

"Did he look like you?" Magnolia asked.

"He had black hair."

"So do a lot of people."

"He always looked more like Leda," Crow said. She'd been so relieved to see the resemblance. "He seemed human on the outside. In the same way as Tamar."

"And he never understood what he was?" Magnolia didn't wait for confirmation; she plucked it from Crow's mind. "You kept that from him, too. You could have told him he was half-immortal even if you didn't confess to being his other mother."

Crow had thought that one day she would tell him. Some of it, or all of it. She had thought she'd know when the right moment came. Arion would live far longer than any mortal humans around him. There would be more than enough time once he got older.

Half-immortals tended to grow up in lockstep with their mortal peers. Typically, it was in adulthood that the pace of their lives diverged. She'd planned to explain everything before it became clear that Arion was aging much more slowly than others.

"Good thing you didn't bring him to the archivists." Magnolia gave a harsh little laugh. The spider lilies seemed to dampen the sound of it.

Crow had never seriously considered leaving him with anyone else. But the automagi had more knowledge, and humans had more humanity. During the turbulence of adolescence, she'd despaired of ever teaching him how to be human. She felt like a fraud. All she could offer were memories of Leda.

Leda had stayed until shortly after his first birthday. One year, and it demanded from her the effort of a lifetime. No matter how Crow struggled, two decades spent raising Arion would amount to a smaller portion of her lifespan than that first year had for Leda.

They were nearing the edge of the field. The spider lilies had begun to thin out.

Magnolia touched a stem. Her hand only went halfway around it. She studied her palm for a moment, as though waiting to see if her skin would melt off. Then she licked it.

"Hm. The poison must be on the inside." She quirked her eyebrows at Crow. "Want a taste?"

Crow asked what had inspired her to put on her body.

Magnolia lifted her gaze to the waning moon, partially hidden by a host of stamens. They looked more like smooth curved whiskers than jointed spider legs.

"Why not?" she said. "I can wear a body whenever I want." Then: "It makes me more punchable. You find it difficult to lash out when I'm just a limbless head." A sudden look of horror crossed her face. "Please don't say that carrying me reminds you of holding a baby."

"Babies talk less."

"That isn't a no."

"Babies have simpler demands."

"Bards better add that to their songs of me. *More tyrannical than a baby.* Very frightening."

She stepped forward. The scent that came off her was reminiscent of a flower that Crow had never seen—not in living memory, anyhow. Perhaps she'd known it in another life.

The humor left Magnolia's voice. "Have you given up on finding out what became of the Horde?"

The moment she said this, Crow guessed the answer. It mired her in place. She had so little understanding of what she felt that she might as well have been back on the altar at Fellshore, only nominally alive—just alive enough to suffer for it.

"The lone survivor fled underground, as you'd feared," Magnolia said. "It burrowed deep—deeper than your ability to find it. It was far from my hills, too, but distances mean less to the land than they do to us. My roots spoke to the land. I learned what that scrap of the Horde was, and where it was, and I began calling it. Normally it would have lapsed into its usual fit of dormancy, but I worked diligently to break its compulsion. I made it come crawling to me through the ground, crawling below mountains and bogs and settlements that never knew it was there.

"The Horde came to me, diminished to a single body. It couldn't recover without going dormant. It was a bit like you, actually, in the sense of having no natural resistance to my commands. That's the downside of being a hive mind. But I digress. From there, I did the rest—I devoured its core. So you don't need to keep an eye out for signs of the Singular Horde. It won't ever come back."

She examined Crow's face and, dissatisfied by what she found there, resumed. "You should thank me. I achieved your vengeance. Or did I ruin it? The Singular Horde is in here." She touched her chest. "So is Arion, if you think about it. The Horde absorbed him, and I absorbed the Horde. There's nothing left of either of them but me. Might as well say that I stole Arion's core. *I* got your prize.

"Oh—but he was your child, too. Your only child. Maybe the Horde and I did you a favor. Wait long enough, and eventually it would have been time to kill him like his mother before him. At least you didn't have to do that."

The river of a thousand feelings churned past Crow's ankles. Her voice had dried up. She said something. It was something like: "I'm glad the Horde is gone."

Magnolia stared. "Excuse me?"

"Mm," said Crow, whose throat seemed to have been stoppered with a bundle of kindling.

"I assimilated your dead son by proxy," Magnolia said very clearly. "Now I'm taunting you about it. I waited until you opened your heart. I saved it for your rawest moment. That wasn't by accident."

"Better than letting the Horde run free," Crow said. "Better you than—"

She felt herself being shaken. For the first time, she glimpsed a narrow dark seam around Magnolia's embodied neck. Taut vines burst from that crack and caught furiously at Crow like hands trying to rattle sense into her.

"I don't want your saintly grace," Magnolia ground out. "I thought if I couldn't be anything else—and I can't, I'm a monster, and I'm glad of it—I thought I would at least become the one being in the world that you could never forgive."

The vines gripped harder, prepared to hurl Crow down like a vulture dropping prey to break it. Then they began to ease. The seam around Magnolia's neck erased itself.

Crow put a hand where that seam had been and kissed her.

Magnolia jackknifed backwards with such speed that maybe she did have the potential to learn how to magically port.

Her voice dropped. "You didn't hear a word I said."

"You're right. You're more punchable when you're attached to a body."

"That was a kiss," Magnolia said thickly, as if something irreplaceable had been besmirched.

Why act surprised? Crow thought. She had carried Magnolia—in her arms, on her back—through mud and stinking streets, across ponds crowded with giant spiky lily pads much wider than any stepping stone. She'd helped Magnolia hunt for fossilized shark teeth (and sometimes stranger teeth) on the banks of a tidal river. Magnolia had found a slate-colored tooth the size of her face, and a thin crimson one shaped like a stiletto blade. She'd arranged them in a silly display on the shore, and then she'd moved on.

In combat, Crow's body and magic would react with extreme efficiency even if she might later struggle to describe what she'd done. Similarly, she'd gained a feel for the best way to shock Magnolia in any given situation.

Much of the time, she didn't do it. She was cooperative—knowing that in the end, cooperation could be forced out of her anyway. She understood the value of being kept on a longer leash.

This time, she looked Magnolia in the eye and said, "You want me to explode? You want my fist in your face? You want a shattered nose?"

Too bad.

Crow kissed her again. She made it sickeningly gentle. The moonlight falling through spider lilies was harsher than her touch, and less loving. She had only ever done this at the behest of humans—curious humans, covetous humans, lustful humans, sadistic humans. It had never meant anything. But she knew what she was doing.

Magnolia didn't leap back. Rage vibrated through her, poorly contained. "What are you playing at?"

Crow had to laugh. "Why would I willingly give you anything you want or expect? If you're in the mood to throw punches, make me do it yourself. You can move me like a puppet. What's stopping you?"

Something unsaintly reared up in her at the sight of Magnolia rendered speechless. Truth be told, if Magnolia had sweetly requested kisses and cuddles, Crow would've socked her nose off. She would have wanted to, at least, if she were given the freedom to think it.

"I—" Magnolia's voice had gone very thin. The fragrance in the dark brought to mind their first meeting under her tree in full bloom. "I don't want..."

Crow tasted triumph. "Tell me."

"I don't want to touch your wings."

Crow removed her shirt. She sent her wings down to her back, to the place where they'd been rooted when Magnolia ordered her to tear them off. She'd dragged them out of herself as if pulling up weeds.

Now she shook them out to full size. The hands that stroked them were sometimes careful and sometimes fractionally cruel.

Unlike Magnolia's earrings, the feathers themselves had no more sensation than strands of hair. Crow felt her touch as an indirect pressure transmitted through the flesh that lay beneath.

There was a stripped look to Magnolia's face, empty of ridicule or levity or smiling superiority. In the city, people of every gender had let their eyes catch on that face—some startling once they realized she was an immortal, some too worldly to betray a reaction. Crow wondered if she had looked the same in her first life, dark beauty spots placed on her as if by the precise judgment of a jeweler. She imagined human hands dragging Magnolia toward a vorpal hole.

"You think I might've been handsome then, too?" Magnolia said derisively. "I was born to famine. We were not a beautiful people."

She knelt like a tailor taking measurements as her fingers trailed down to the ends of Crow's wings. By the time she got up again, she had—regrettably—recovered her composure. She faced Crow and moved closer. When the breeze plucked at the front of her messily tied robe, it billowed to tickle Crow's unclothed skin. A cold touch, like the edge of a cloud.

"I don't want your hands on my neck," she said. "I don't want to hurt you. I don't want to fight you."

Crow faltered.

"Fight me," Magnolia told her, discarding the ruse. There it was, that unholy red in her eyes, even in the shadows. "We're magical beings. We can afford to break a couple bones."

Crow found herself in the puzzling position of wondering if they were talking about the same thing. Where was the line between metaphorical desire and literal desire? Had she fantasized about dashing Magnolia's head open—over and over—out of thwarted hatred or secret bloodlust, or just to reassure herself that she still had some semblance of control over her own mind?

"I don't think that's how it's done," she managed.

"Who cares? We aren't mortal. We can make our own way. Fight me. Isn't that what feels right for us? We're rivals for the same prey."

She was still pondering this when Magnolia slapped her.

Magnolia didn't hold back. Her cheek felt like a hot jumble of coals.

She caught a blurry glimpse of Magnolia drinking in a ragged breath. As if she were the one who'd been hit.

The intense paradoxical calm of battle flooded Crow all the way to the tips of her wings. She hadn't received a magical order. No matter. Her retaliatory reflexes took over. Her body reacted with swift and total purpose, slipping into the steps of a predetermined dance.

Squirming roots scraped at her arms as she wrestled Magnolia to the ground beneath the lilies. There was a mix of outrage and rabid glee in Magnolia's face—and a hint of relief, and entreaty, and Crow could see her thoughts laid bare without any magic whatsoever. *More,* she cried. *More. More. More.*

52

LOOSE FEATHERS and flayed vines surrounded them. Spider lilies had dropped like chopped-down trees. Crow sat up—with considerable effort—but Magnolia flopped on her back, her token robe flung open.

They were both already heavily bruised. Mortal bruises would have taken longer to rise to the surface. Theirs coalesced faster and healed faster, changing color and shape like windblown clouds, soon to melt away.

"All that biting and growling. We're like young animals," Magnolia said.

"But far more destructive."

"I wonder—do wolves know why they play-fight?"

"I wasn't playing. Were you?"

Magnolia smirked.

"Whatever the case, that isn't how mortals copulate," Crow said.

"Oh, I don't know." Magnolia's voice came out fainter than usual, despite her closeness. "There are all kinds of people out there. Who appointed you the arbiter of human normalcy?"

"If you were human, you would have been dead five times over."

"Three times. At most."

The gentlest thing Crow had done—in a brief moment of total control—was when she'd caught at the base of Magnolia's neck with her teeth. She'd been gratified to taste the dark line that kept revealing itself like a fickle necklace, a seam in ordinarily seamless skin.

But for the most part, Magnolia gave as good as she got.

Now she pushed herself up on her elbows, wincing. Crow watched without comment and, through a haze of exhaustion, found herself running down a mental list of ways to make Magnolia wince harder.

Instead she leaned over and kissed one of those limpid earrings. Just for half a second. No teeth. She'd put a hand on Magnolia's side to balance herself. She felt Magnolia begin to shake again.

"You're allergic to tenderness." It was Crow's turn to be amused, for once.

Magnolia cringed away and touched her earring protectively. "Sometimes I am. What of it?"

"Release me from your spell of command," Crow said. "Then you'll be able to take anything without flinching."

"If I released you, you'd feel obligated to reap my core on the spot."

Crow could not think of any counterarguments other than the fact that she didn't want to do it. She could admit that much, here amid the carnage of lilies and purplish morning light. It was foolish. It was irrational. It was depraved and self-defeating. But it was true. She didn't want to give Magnolia a permanent death, to never again see those teardrop earrings shiver against her neck.

She hadn't necessarily wanted to kill any of her companions, either. She hadn't wanted to leave Arion motherless. The things she wanted did not always intersect with the things she had to do to survive, to be herself, to fulfill her role as a saint, to grant wishes that no one else had the power to grant.

"There you go." A smile touched the corners of Magnolia's mouth. "Do you wish you'd been around to kill me in my first life?"

"No," Crow said, startled. "You—your past self didn't deserve that."

"Such precise phrasing," Magnolia said slyly. "My past self may not have deserved to be sacrificed—and then cannibalized, may I remind you!—but who's to say that karmic justice works in a linear sense? What I am today might retroactively justify the ignominious suffering and death of a girl without food, magic, hope, or friendship.

"No need to shake your head at me. I don't think anyone ever truly gets what they deserve. Even we returners live consecutively, one century to the next. So does everyone. Except possibly the Devil," she added speculatively, "but that's her business, not ours.

"Sins and punishments might balance out like a grand equation across spans of time so vast as to make us seem no longer-lived than mere mortals. If that's true, though, we'll never see enough of the universe to prove it. Might as well consider it false. In our lived experience, the equation will never be balanced."

She patted the wet broken stem of a nearby lily, then wiped her hand off on Crow's naked back. Each short-lived bruise sang a different tune at her touch.

"How does it feel to be poisoned?" she asked.

"I think this poison is a myth."

Magnolia snorted. "Just don't go around feeding spider lilies—of any size, mind you—to pets or children."

Eventually they both got up. They hadn't leveled the entire field, thankfully—just one corner of it.

"You broke my wing." Crow turned to show her.

"Did I?" Magnolia sounded impressed. "Oh, it's already fixing itself. Shame."

She shrugged her robe off and draped it over Crow's arm, then switched to being a head. Crow caught her inside her own discarded robe. She was tempted to tie up the bundle of fabric and stuff it in her pack.

"Go on, try it," Magnolia said wryly. "See what happens."

Crow shifted Magnolia to her shoulder instead.

Shortly afterward, she heard a subdued voice in her ear. "All that aside ... I wish I could have been the one to kill your aerial self."

"You're still thinking about that?"

"The girl who rescued you did a great and heretical thing," Magnolia said. "She noticed the agony of a half-fossilized lump without any eyes to weep pitifully, and without a mouth to plead. You were a god to generations of locals, but she saw your individual soul. She killed you, even though she might later have paid a terrible cost. Yes—I still wish it had been me in her place. If I were her, I would deserve to feel this way. If I were her, I could at least claim to explain it."

She didn't elaborate further.

After approaching the edge of the field, Dung looked askance at all the toppled lilies. He refused to be touched—much less ridden—until they'd both bathed in a deafening waterfall. Even then, he only acted mollified once Magnolia offered him an extra helping of her glittering dew.

Crow recalled Magnolia's creamy roots wrapping her as if she were a pot-bound plant—and the immense catharsis of tearing those roots apart. She was very grateful that Dung couldn't read minds.

They circled back towards the radish village, crossing lands that Crow hadn't visited since her search for the last survivor of the Horde. They passed a couple silent settlements with grass-covered roofs. Some of these outposts were truly empty. Others were still inhabited. The residents—rightfully wary of strangers—had gone into hiding. Their cores lurked inside unlit buildings like traitorous lanterns.

Many humans possessed little or no magic perception; it was usually their weakest sense. They might not realize that an immortal could perceive their cores through walls and floors. Even if they did know—what else could they do? Retreating inside would feel better than waiting out in the open. It might afford them the opportunity to set a few rudimentary traps.

"You don't need to eat yet," Crow said when Magnolia urged Dung closer.

"What do you know of my appetites?" Magnolia demanded. She glared at the grassy roofs of the latest settlement, which was doing a good job of looking as though it had been recently abandoned. It spread out before them like a limp animal playing dead.

Then she sighed and sent Dung in the opposite direction. She grew a hefty root to pat him bracingly on the neck.

"You're so cold-hearted, Crow," she said. "At least Dung understands my woes. How he longs to gnaw on mortal bones! The two of us would make a great team, wouldn't we? All I want from humans are their cores, after all. He could make a real feast of the leftovers. It won't bother them if they're already dead. I might be the one former human being in the world who can state that with absolute confidence. In my first life, being cannibalized was the least of my troubles. They did me the courtesy of killing me first—after that, nothing mattered."

"You ordered Dung not to eat humans."

Magnolia fixed her with a gimlet eye. "Orders can be revoked."

They traveled on through the night, occasionally speculating about how the stars might shift ten thousand years from now. "If this world even exists in another ten thousand years," Magnolia interjected, "which—no matter how grudgingly it goes to its death—strikes me as doubtful. Humans seem fleeting to us, but I suppose everything seems fleeting if you're a star." She laughed at herself. "Wow, what an original thought!"

Later: "You come off as very wise and knowing, Crow, when you *mm* and *hm* at me. Silence always sounds wiser than a torrent of words. Silence can be laden with infinite shades of meaning. And yet—"

"I wasn't thinking about anything," Crow acknowledged.

She had been focused mainly on the sensation of time slipping past. It was a thing you could feel, sometimes, like a cool breeze on skin. When other concerns receded, you could sense yourself floating there, an invisible speck in the middle of a vast dark ocean of before and after, then and now, sooner and later. There was no seabed, and no shore. Time itself would not end when the world died.

"How existentially dreadful," Magnolia said mirthfully. "I'm glad you enjoy my company enough to wallow in the all-consuming sensation of your own temporal insignificance. Have you gotten too comfortable, Crow? I should do something to remind you how much you despise me."

Crow put a repressive hand on the back of her neck. "Please don't."

"Well, that just makes me want to do it more."

Dung snuffled loudly, as if he found them both ridiculous.

Magnolia had asked her, once, what she would do after humanity went extinct. Crow wondered how long immortals would be able to exist without any way to fulfill their deepest predatory drives. Perhaps they would wither until nothing remained but insubstantial parasitic leftovers like the automagi. With no humans to eat, they would kill one another until they reached a new equilibrium, a stalemate with barely any survivors.

She hoped humans would live good and fulfilling lives until the very last of them died. If humanity were already extinct, she might not mind being under Magnolia's thumb. They would have to fight off other saints and monsters, yes, but they could go anywhere. Every settlement would be uninhabited, with no candlelight glow of fearful cores. She wouldn't plead with Magnolia to restrain herself.

They could stay with Dung till he grew old, or release him to live out his days among fellow primevals. They could go visit every last long-lived crocodile and tortoise and shark, and perhaps even a couple of aerials. She wouldn't be against traveling the continent together forever. In the grand scheme of things, it'd be like taking idle walks around their own backyard, remarking on inconsequential changes—an anthill, rabbit droppings, a new patch of clover, animal tracks in fresh snow. Crow's poet would approve.

For the time being, they lived in a world with people. Fewer than in the past, but still too many to ignore. Even if nothing remained but a single village, eventually every last saint and monster would converge there.

Part Six

*The Scenic Route to the
End of the World*

53

After another week or so, they reached the fringe of Magnolia's old territory. Along the way, they witnessed a torrent of windblown butterflies migrating south. They looked like a bright blue explosion of confetti against a sulky orange sky.

Magnolia assumed bipedal form and stopped to probe the ground with questing roots. This time they grew from her hands and bare feet. More cream-colored vestigial roots crept out through the invisible seam of her neck, trying to join in. She told Crow to smack them like bugs to make them retreat.

"No other monsters have moved in yet," she said.

"Really? You were gone for months." Crow jabbed one of her neck roots. It fled like an eel whipping back inside a hole.

"I was a Great Adversary of all who entered my territory. Not just humans. If anything, monsters had even more reason to fear my reign of terror. I never went easy on competitors. But—it's odd to encounter zero opportunists." She straightened up, retracting her roots. "Hunters may have stamped them out."

"You sound tense."

Magnolia put a hand on one of Dung's huge dust-brown scales. "Stay close," she told him. "Don't want anyone mistaking you for a monster."

They both donned the green glasses that Magnolia had obtained in the city. They lent the world a subtler tint than Crow had expected. Within minutes, she could forget she was wearing them.

She removed them when a soft rain came through, just enough to spatter the lenses. When she put the glasses back on, she saw tents: multiple clusters in different colors and styles. Leather and canvas, tarred and painted, dyed and plain. Some structures appeared to be supported by full wooden frames. Others would have needed only a couple of strong poles. All were positioned downstream from the village.

It felt like treading backwards through time. She recalled army camps, mud, singing and infighting, the groans of the injured, the ritual songbirds that commanders brought for entertainment and eventually for slaughter. When it came time to kill and eat the birds—a tradition that was supposed to bring victory—they asked her to help. They'd thought that with magic, she could perform the sacrifice more elegantly and painlessly than any humans in the encampment.

Had it been painless? She couldn't guarantee that. Her own wings had seized up with a phantom cramp as she worked. The silver-tongued birds produced a pitifully small helping of meat.

"Too many hunters," Magnolia said grimly. "They must be itching for a challenge. I suppose they'll have a few core-bearers, but not nearly enough for my tastes. Well, none will see us unless we wish to be seen."

That last sentence seemed to infiltrate the ground beneath their feet.

Even so, Magnolia took Dung on a route that skirted around the farthest tents. A few hunters seemed to be busy doing maintenance on gear and weapons. Others hauled water and firewood, or sparred idly in open areas. At this time of day, perhaps most party members had gone scouting in the hills—or to the village, to requisition supplies.

The wind shifted. The air grew hazy and began to taste of smoke. Farmers were burning autumn grass and heaps of crop stubble in fields.

Magnolia's gait lengthened when the village came into view. It looked not so different from the day they'd left. No collapsed buildings; no screaming; no prisoners tied to stakes. And no one glanced their way. Even Dung went unnoticed.

"You always had the power to send them away without a fight," Crow said. "Every human hunter who ever came to you, coreless or otherwise, and every weeping sacrifice."

Magnolia shot her a baffled look. "Would a captive snake try to chase a mouse out of its cage? The thought wouldn't even occur to me."

She beckoned Crow and Dung over to the tea shop. It was very full, judging by the noise that came from within. No children in sight. Strings of golden fruit hung from the eaves to slowly shrivel and dry. Hunters had brought mancala boards outside and appeared to be placing outrageous bets on each game.

Dung curled up like a boulder in the shadow of the building and closed his eyes. Crow loitered nearby to make sure no one tried to climb him. Magnolia slipped into the tea shop and spoke for a long time with the owner and other locals. She said later that she'd made them think she was someone they'd known all their lives.

Upon emerging, she looked murderous.

"Predictable," she said. She didn't modulate her voice: she had ordered everyone in the vicinity not to listen. "Without me here to thin their ranks, hunters just keep coming. It wasn't so bad at first—most were prepared to pay with salt and sugar and spices, all the usual stuff.

"Stay long enough, and they start to think they've paid enough. They appropriate supplies. They demand accommodation in local homes. They ought to be delighted not to get decimated—and yet the lack of action makes them restless. Resentful, even. They blame the village for my failure to appear.

"When a lesser monster pops out of the woodwork, competing parties squabble to claim it. These are all hunters ambitious enough—or crazy enough—to come challenge the Woman in the Hills. They aren't just going to shrug their shoulders and depart the area because it's gotten quiet for a season. Not to worry: I'll give them exactly what they want."

Around the corner, out in front of the tea shop, pebbles and dried beans rattled in the carved-out pits of mancala boards. The smell of toasted beetles mingled with the distant scent of burning grass. Several men roared ferociously when they won a bet.

Magnolia sat down on Dung and crossed her legs. "A twelve-year-old boy came to blows with a hunter over an admittedly trivial insult. The hunter beat him to within an inch of his life. That boy still can't get out of bed. Wish you could see what his father's been thinking."

Crow said: "You would go after these hunters regardless of who did or didn't get beaten or insulted."

"But I wouldn't do it right here. If they were pure of heart and courageous, I'd call them to the hills, for old times' sake. Anyway, it's just as you think. The villagers have no formal justice system, and no enforcers capable of standing up to well-equipped bands of hunters. They've always counted on me to make their problems go away. With so much food getting seized, they would've starved if the later crews hadn't been trailed by enterprising merchants. Commerce saves the day—the silkworm nuns would rejoice if they knew.

"No, you can't stop me from cleaning house. Mull all you like over the justice of it, or the lack thereof. I'll leave some survivors to spread the news of my horrific resurgence. But let me tell you, I've peeked inside these hunters' heads, and it isn't pretty." She continued without giving Crow a chance to gather her thoughts. "Human civilizations have executed their own in grotesquely creative ways—for blasphemy and adultery, libel and arson, theft and corruption and rebellion, and for acts that people nowadays wouldn't even consider a crime.

"You've seen it. In some cases, you've been obligated to help. Do you find atrocities more acceptable so long as at least one human has a say in making it happen? This ought to pass muster, then. The villagers are desperate to see them gone. They're praying the sort of prayers that you might have heard on your altar, in darker times."

She got up to stretch. She petted Dung and called him a good boy. He shifted about with an air of mild offense.

"I'll spare you from agonizing," she said to Crow. "Don't interfere."

A very broad order—and nevertheless impossible to resist.

Magnolia barged back inside the tea shop. The mancala players shuddered as she passed, then glanced about in confusion. Crow didn't follow her. Whether she had gone in to chitchat or to immediately start cleaning house, Crow would not be capable of doing anything more than watching from a corner.

She began walking in the opposite direction. Dung didn't budge. Well, he was close enough to the tea shop. Magnolia could deal with it if he got himself in trouble.

The shopkeeper had felt some sort of culpability for all the hunters he'd served before they went off to face the Woman in the Hills. He knew they wouldn't stop at his urging, and he wouldn't offer his own life—or the lives of other villagers—as a sacrifice instead. But he'd asked Crow to take on the Woman in the Hills, even if it meant that their land relinquished all protection.

What about the rest of the village? Did they celebrate the first few hunting parties to make it back from the hills without casualties? Maybe they'd thrown another festival. Had they been relieved—or wary, confused, fearful of lost blessings?

Even the most congratulatory among them might have quieted down once more hunters returned safely, and more came looking for a place to stay. Enough hunters to overwhelm any number of minor monsters. And in all the hills, no one could locate their ultimate target. Nor could they find a telltale cocoon.

Would the shopkeeper have taken this as a sign of Crow's success? Would he have told anyone? Possibly not—as summer deepened, he might have questioned his own memory of events. The only evidence he had for her visit was a feather that could've fallen from any ordinary three-legged crow.

She strode through the grassy square where she'd seen young radish dancers rehearsing their steps. She could try to warn some hunters away before Magnolia got to them. She could test the boundaries of Magnolia's order.

Don't interfere.

The hunters might not hear her, or listen. They might turn on her and deem her a monster. But she could try. Should she start in the camp outside the village? Those who'd stayed there—rather than commandeer housing—might give more consideration to the words of a stranger.

She was about to port to the tents when a man's voice said: "Pick it up."

He was a hunter with a finely shaped head, recently shaved. He might have been considered handsome back in one of the old fallen empires. No core. He spoke with what would have seemed to the villagers like an indecipherably thick accent—difficult to penetrate even if they were used to communicating with travelers from faraway lands.

A woman at his feet—a local—used her bare hands to scrape millet back into a leaking sack.

Neither of them saw Crow.

A couple other hunters came over. One clapped the shaved man's shoulder. "Save that aggression for slaying monsters."

"What monsters?" demanded the shaved man. "Where are all the monsters? Show me. I came from a settlement much, much—"

"Yes, we've heard. You don't need to—"

"—much poorer than this fattened-up town. They've suckled the meat and bones of dying hunters for generations. Now we've finally got the upper hand in these hills, and they can't stand it. Wretched misers. We brought that millet to barter with—sweet and nutty, best quality in the continent—and look how she's treating it. Think of the sacrifices we made to carry that weight."

The other hunters said more soothing words, but they soon drifted off. Apparently they considered him a lost cause. They were gone when he turned on the woman again and chastised her for her clumsiness, for her carelessness, for plucking the millet too slowly, for getting dirt in the sack.

He lifted his boot. He had already stepped on the millet. Now he was going to step on her hand.

Crow slipped in to block him, supernaturally quick.

"You could help," she said.

He could not physically reach the woman—Crow stood in the way. Still, it seemed a struggle for him to notice her. Even after she removed her green-lensed glasses, his gaze roamed everywhere except for her face. Magnolia's magic lingered, turning his attention away.

Crow indicated her bared eyes. "I'm the Saint of ... the Saint of Millet." She wondered if he could hear her. "My promised companion wants every villager to be treated with the utmost respect."

Perhaps she was overdoing it. He seemed to be listening: he winced, one hand pressed to the side of his head. His face creased with resentment.

Behind Crow, the woman on the ground scrambled to leave. She'd grabbed more handfuls of dust than actual grain at the end. She staggered away, a trail of millet still trickling from the sack, which looked much too heavy for her frame. She'd hurt her back if she kept that up.

She must have recognized that any monster could claim to be a saint. Or maybe she remained blinded by Magnolia's magic, incapable of perceiving Crow right in front of her face. Maybe she'd seen a chance to get away and had seized it, without understanding why the hunter wouldn't chase her.

He wouldn't chase her because Crow had put a hand on his elbow in such a way as to suggest that if he moved, his arm might find itself divorced from his body. Even so, he may have wondered if she were joking, this so-called Saint of Millet. He may have wondered if she posed a serious threat. A no-name saint might be just as weak as a low-level monster.

"If my companion were here, you would already be dead," Crow said. "Soon this village will be empty of hunters. If you're smart, you'll run."

He startled when he looked sideways at her, as if he'd forgotten who was gripping his arm. Magnolia's magic seemed to wash her words from his awareness. She closed her fingers tighter and listened dispassionately as the first sounds of real pain escaped his throat. Maybe he would remember that.

When she let go, he stumbled away, crushing stray grains of millet underfoot. He didn't quite break into a run, but it was probably the best she could hope for. Keep going, and eventually he would reach the camp.

She warned off several other hunters, with varying success. One didn't hear a word she said. One tried to stab her. That was the risk she'd run if she intruded on the camp: they might rally to attack her. There weren't enough of them to do her any lasting harm, but it might be better not to get bogged down in—

Her veins quivered.

Villagers filed out of dwellings like animals crawling out of dens after winter. They were hollow-eyed, and they smelled, and their clothing was grubby. When had they last taken their laundry to the stream? Had they chosen not to bathe? In some situations, filthiness was its own sort of defense, though no more foolproof than rubbing herbal tinctures on your skin to ward off midges.

Disconnected thoughts paraded past her like shadows following the villagers, who were all headed in the same direction. They had no paid guards, no border walls, and hardly any fencing. She recalled their harvest festival: fresh salt-steeped cucumbers, the proud manic radish dance.

The villagers were going toward the tea shop. They formed a wide ring around it, as if the empty space before them was already filled with a mass of invisible bodies. Crow paused her step, too, although her veins tried to pull her forward like buried puppet strings.

The stench in the air was more than just unwashed flesh. It was a promise of violent deliverance, as distinct as the smell of rain. The villagers remained quiet, but something in their combined breath made it clear that this was a crowd that would throw stones at strangers.

There were no mancala players outside the tea shop. There were no hunters whatsoever in sight.

Then the door came open, and hunters flooded out like millet spilling from a too-full sack. They came out of side doors and upper-story windows, too, swinging down from balconies. There were far more of them than it seemed as though the building could have held. They milled about, ringed by villagers, just as silent as their audience.

The last hunter to leave the tea shop held Magnolia out in front of him. She was in the form of a head, though she still wore green glasses.

No trailing vines or roots. Crow's first thought, absurdly, was a flash of white-hot panic. As if they'd taken Magnolia hostage. Then she saw how the hunter lifted her up as though she were a crown about to get placed on the head of a new monarch. No skin touched her: her bearer wore gloves.

Ruby sap dripped from the base of her neck, slow and thick, coating his gloves, and of course it looked like human blood. She was probably doing that solely for dramatic effect.

Crow started to count the hunters and villagers, then gave up. Magnolia didn't need rescuing. If anyone needed rescuing, it was the hunters. But Crow had been forbidden to intervene. She'd gotten away with cautioning a few of them. Now the order took hold more deeply—in the way her legs turned to motionless trunks, the way her magic slowed within her like the heartbeat of a mortal creature entering hibernation.

The hunters' clothing was more varied than that of the villagers, who all wore similar trousers and tabards. Some hunters had sandals and bare legs. Some gleamed with bits of metal, as if they had been decorated soldiers in a far-off country. Even inside village borders, many went around visibly armed.

The tea shop owner sagged against a wall. He mopped his brow and jowls. He looked away.

Suddenly a voice exploded from beyond the ragged rows of watching villagers. The hunter with the close-shaved head charged in with a crossbow aimed at Magnolia.

"Fools!" he cried. "That's our target. That's the Woman in the Hills!"

No one roused to join him.

To his credit, he didn't falter. He trained his sight down the loaded bolt.

He would have pulled the trigger without hesitation. He would have fought the last Great Adversary even if he had to do it completely alone.

The bolt never left his bow. Another hunter ran him through with her sword. She came up from behind him, almost as fast as an immortal. Getting skewered threw his aim off, and maybe he had just enough self-control left to avoid randomly firing into the rest of the crowd.

He was not alive for much longer. He gurgled, and then he was on the ground. The hunter who'd killed him had skin the color of ironwood and a smooth, clear expression. She could have been thirty or fifty. She struggled to wrench her sword out of his back afterward; several others came over to help. The villagers observed with remote, drawn faces—men and women, old and young.

"The ability to resist me has no correlation with virtue." Magnolia's voice resonated as if they were all gathered in a cave. "It's just a trait. Like blue eyes, or curly hair, or long toes. That man could hold me off better than the rest of you—although not for much longer, naturally. I could have ground his will down in another twenty seconds. But there was no need, you see. I have so many people eager to protect me."

None of the hunters displayed any real sorrow. The woman with the bloody sword peered down at her blade as if she'd forgotten how or why to clean it. Disinterested tears ran from the corners of her eyes, unwiped.

"That body's for you," Magnolia told the villagers. "Water your fields with him, if you like. I'll take the rest as my due."

The arms of the man bearing her up had begun to tremble minutely. It was as though she'd forgotten that humans, unlike Crow, lacked the stamina to hold her aloft in the same position forever. Or maybe she didn't especially care.

54

"Come along," Magnolia said to the hunters. "No, Crow, you stay right where you are. First of all, you don't want to see this. Second—you need to watch over the village. If new slayers arrive in my absence, make sure they behave."

It was like watching a parade. The man holding Magnolia carried her away, trickling claret sap. Other hunters followed, winding through gaps in the wall of villagers, who shrank back to avoid them.

The hunters didn't look stiff or reluctant. Despite their mismatched garb, they had the air of holy warriors marching under the conviction that they were doing exactly as their god intended. More emerged from the woods to join them—some only half-dressed, some yawning.

When the last hunter had shuffled out of sight, the villagers closed in around the dead man. He lay awkwardly on top of his crossbow. Someone stooped to pull it free. Someone else warned them not to touch it. The bolt was still loaded and primed to fire.

A girl with a broken nose came up and spat on his beautifully shaped head. She had impeccable aim. She spat again, and again, until her mouth ran dry.

"It's him," murmured a hoarse voice. "He killed her lizard."

"Her lizard?"

"The one she kept as a pet. Said he mistook it for a snake. Cooked it back at their camp, didn't he? On a skewer. Like a roasted fish."

Crow cleared her throat. The villagers looked at her as if noticing her for the first time. The thorny air seemed poised to turn on her next: she was the only remaining stranger.

"You're a saint," said the tea master.

The villagers relaxed.

"There was a beetle leg in your tea."

She nodded.

"You gave me a feather. Did you ever give me your name?"

She gave it to him now. As soon as she spoke, Magnolia's voice blew through the crowd like a clean winter wind.

You can trust my Crow.

And they did, instantly. They turned to her and asked for advice on how to safely disentangle the body from the crossbow. Later she retrieved the bow and cleaned it of blood. It still seemed usable, although she would never use it herself.

Magnolia had assumed full control of every other hunter. She'd made it seem effortless. She must have been commanding the villagers, too. *Come and look. Just keep your distance.*

The other day, in a grassy plain, she'd used a woody root to whack at one of Dung's dry round droppings. She sent it flying. Then she made Crow pick up a stick and bat at a competing ball of dung. She wasn't satisfied until she'd hit hers much farther than any of Crow's attempts.

At such times, it was easy to forget about her being the last of the

Four Great Adversaries. Crow sometimes thought that although she was clearly a menace, she deserved her title considerably less than the Singular Horde and the Beautiful Scourge, which both ate and ate and ate without mercy, no different from locusts leveling cropland.

She arguably had more in common with Calamity Bridge—a land-bound monster that lured in victims. With each step across the Bridge, mortals lost years' worth of memories, and that was only the beginning of their misery. It had inspired many tragic love songs and ditties for children. The very concept of the Bridge fascinated and horrified people in faraway lands, who had nothing to fear from it. The Woman in the Hills was rather more obscure.

But the Beautiful Scourge might get cut off for generations via strict isolation. The Singular Horde was limited by its own need for periodic dormancy. Calamity Bridge lacked a calculating mind.

Magnolia did belong with the other three, now all gone. In her own way, she was capable of magic and terror on the scale of a natural disaster. She could subjugate all of human civilization, if she put her mind to it.

Compared to a creature like the Fellshore mimid, she was much better primed to make use of the nuances of mortal relationships and resentments and politics. Her magic might have geographical limitations—she couldn't physically be everywhere at once—but she could use nonmagical levers of power to manipulate faraway subjects, steering them with a dexterity and understanding that went far beyond mere mimicry.

Perhaps she had no interest in cultivating the entire world, converting it into a farm to harvest cores. If she really wanted that, she could have established her empire even while rooted in these rural hills. She could have nurtured her village until it became a great city. She could have wielded the structures of human society as a weapon—rewarding local warlords for governing in her name, incentivizing the eradication of rebellious elements.

Or she could say one word to the rebels and make them trail after her as loyal followers. Saints and their companions might try to attack her, but first they'd have to get through servants like Crow. Ultimately, they might find themselves just as easily tamed by the sound of her voice.

In terms of sheer potential, Magnolia was not the least of the Four Great Adversaries. She was the worst. Crow and Leda should have prioritized coming after her first.

Now Crow had fallen into the trap of knowing her. Magnolia would see no appeal in the hard work of crowning herself empress of a dying world. She was a predator to the bone, but she was more intrigued by small-scale affairs: landscapes traversed on foot or on the back of a primeval, strangely shaped rocks, the flight paths of aerials, fuzzy black bees weighing down wildflowers.

She perversely enjoyed making Crow want to throttle her. She would not find the same thrill, Crow suspected, in fending off armies of thousands.

That didn't mean she was safe. That didn't mean she was good. None of the hunters she'd led away would survive except by her will. Some had badly mistreated the villagers. Some had merely been rude.

And who could say that Magnolia would never change for the worse? She had only just been liberated from the compulsion tying her to this land. Her meeting with Crow had marked the beginning of a new phase of her immortal life. Like another rebirth. After she saw everything there was to see of the world, fresh ambitions might bud in her. One day she might decide to use her magic to its full extent. No one would be able to stop her then.

Something would have to be done.

Crow avoided becoming inextricably bogged down in such thoughts. Before anything else, the people of the radish village needed to reclaim the rhythm of their lives. Here Crow was in her element. If there was one thing she had experience with, it was helping humans deal with practical matters at hand. This had been the stuff of her daily routine for century after century.

Over the course of a human lifetime, days of glory or unforgivable massacre were quite rare compared to the number of times they had to wash clothes or air out bedding or cut their hair or pare their nails. Leaks needed to be sealed, fires needed to be banked, peppers needed to be dried in the sun, floors needed to be swept, fruit needed to be steeped in alcohol or stewed for jam, water needed to be hauled and boiled, wood needed to be chopped, fields needed to be cleared, and local forests—in their own way—required just as much tending as fields.

Crow was very good at all this. Moreover, she was patient. Given that she had no inherent desire to speed ahead, especially since she could keep working all night long without rest, she would only use magic when asked.

There was some indecision over how to handle the hunter with the shaved head. In the end, they burnt his body on a pyre located a good distance from both the village and the hills. Crow carried it there to spare them the trouble of hauling it atop a plank. Later she watched them—all of them, even children—trample his bones and ashes. Perhaps their ancestors had done the same to criminals and traitors in times past.

After Magnolia abducted the hunters, the village children had been the first to unbend stiff limbs and move in earnest. They'd gone over to the upturned mancala boards outside the tea shop. They'd started diligently collecting scattered beans.

No one spoke at length about anything the vanished hunters had done in their village—not then, and not later. Perhaps they whispered about it out of Crow's hearing.

Many of the slayers hailed from cultures with little in common with one another. They shared only their universal creed of mutual noninterference. A hunter would have needed to murder villagers in broad daylight, unprovoked, for their peers to even think about stepping in.

If it went that far, the shopkeeper would have used Crow's feather. The occupation would have come to an end very quickly. But he wasn't witness to everything that happened in hunter-hosting households. He would have struggled to decipher if this were a problem that could be solved by a saint. Saints were, after all, known more for protecting people from immortal monsters than from fellow humans.

On top of that, he might have been ashamed to appeal to Crow for help. It had all started when he asked her to take on the Woman in the Hills. Back then he had told her, on behalf of the village, that they would accept the ensuing loss of protection.

Crow checked to make sure he still had her feather. But she didn't ask why he hadn't snapped it in half to summon her.

The fog of frustration around the hunters had been exacerbated by the tall tales that drew them in. Made-up stories—spread at Magnolia's command—about some nonexistent reward that went far beyond the simple glory of giving a cocoon death to the last Great Adversary. With spare time to compare notes, multiple parties had grown suspicious. They'd accused the villagers of seeding rumors to lure them. But they wouldn't leave—and thus risk letting their competitors claim that illusory reward, uncontested.

The sky turned lavender, then filled with eerily solid clouds shaped like udders. Days of precipitation followed: pervasive enough to cause mildew, but not heavy enough for flooding. Crow borrowed a rain cape woven from straw and went foraging for meaty mushrooms that emitted musical squeaks when she cut them. She helped the villagers collect wild pomegranates, too, and rose hips the size and color of ripe persimmons. She picked autumn olives, red with speckles, and the tiny maroon fruit of hackberry trees.

From time to time, when she brought in her harvest, the villagers would feed her mulberry jam in return. She looked too human for them to accept the fact that she could get by without food.

Near the center of the village was a replica tree stump made of glazed stone, longer and wider than a rowboat. No one remembered the full story behind it: something about a sacred tree that had died long ago. Older villagers said it was the world tree, and that its felling by greedy men had led to the beginning of the end.

Crow didn't question it. That stony stump was realer to them than a human Devil they'd never met. Adolescents played with acorns and pebbles on its table-like surface. A few of their games had rules in common with ones that Arion had learned in towns along the western coast of the continent. Crow crouched down to join in.

No one made an offer to become her companion. Magnolia had probably left a secret order to preclude that. Or maybe, at the moment, none of them could imagine asking Crow for more than what she already did: endless fishing and hunting, oxen-driven milling, weaving straw into sandals, grating radishes, making detergent from plant ash. When the sun came out, she hauled their bedding outdoors and beat it like a drum.

She carried out every task with inhuman persistence. The excess population of hunters had dealt a mortal blow to the village's food stores. They would need all the help they could get to rebuild before winter.

Dung did not contribute in any meaningful way. On the other hand, he neither menaced the villagers nor dug up their graves. Magnolia must have ordered them to ignore him: they were fascinated by his fallen scales, and they collected dried droppings to use as kindling, but no one screamed when he came tromping past. Even the oxen seemed unalarmed.

One day, a three-legged crow landed on the roof of the tea shop and cawed raucously all morning. A new group of slayers arrived, led by a woman carrying a pike. She had a core, though her followers were mostly coreless. They looked around the village, visibly puzzled. Eventually they came to speak with the tea master.

The leader ordered enough beetle tea for her entire crew, although no one seemed enthused to drink it. In exchange she offered bamboo barrels filled with star anise and prickly ash peppercorns.

After some consideration, the shopkeeper gave her silver and copper coins along with a bonus round of tea. He wanted all the spices she had to offer. Later she pressed him to accept onion-shaped bottles of liquor as an additional gesture of friendship: sturdy blown glass, a deep somber green, designed to survive long journeys.

Crow, wearing her glasses and an apron, had retreated softly to the kitchen. She glanced at her feather, hanging on the wall as a ward against evil.

"Is this the off-season?" inquired the pike-wielder.

"It's a good season for round pears," the shopkeeper said. "And black apples—many different kinds of apples. Figs and chestnuts, too."

"Are we the only hunting party in town?"

"Indeed you are."

"I heard that…"

"Yes?" he prompted.

She seemed to think better of continuing. "Never mind. Must have been rumors. I hope we're not imposing."

Crow came to serve the rest of their tea. The woman with the pike smelled faintly of ashwort, as did the bulk of her followers. This alone suggested that her party was rather well-funded.

They had come a long way, too. They were most comfortable speaking a dialect from the far southern coast of the continent. They seemed thrilled for a chance to use it with Crow—the villagers couldn't understand a word. The woman with the pike made her sit down as if she too were a guest, and they talked all afternoon.

That whole time, no one else came in the tea shop. The owner brought out a platter of apples for them to taste: black apples (which had disappointingly light flesh) and cow-nose apples that looked like exotic elongated pears. This prompted a long discussion of how the trees near the village yielded differently colored fruit every year. Sometimes the black apples didn't turn out dark at all. Their flavor varied from year to year, and even from fruit to fruit.

Afterward, the pike-wielder's crew proceeded to question the shopkeeper and other residents about the Woman in the Hills. On their way north, they'd heard her described as a bloodthirsty monster with the martial skills of a legendary warrior and two human-looking heads— one silent, one chatty. From the villagers, they learned that she had either eradicated or driven off every other party of visiting slayers. They solemnly toured the abandoned tents still standing outside the village. Some said prayers in languages unknown to any locals.

The pike-wielder left the next day. She didn't say whether she was turning tail or taking her party deeper into the hills. Whatever the case, they were never seen at the radish village again.

Crow became an expert at collecting watercress during daylight and catching river eels at night. She also brought in a prodigious quantity of svelte autumn sweetfish.

She repeatedly suggested going into the empty camps to forage for gear and supplies. The villagers had taken some of the hunters' stranded pack animals and mounts. They released others into the wild, including a domesticated elk that sometimes stared in bewilderment at Dung from the fringes of the woods.

But they hadn't been willing to plunder anything else from the camps. Instead they burned herbs and built small cairns and did all sorts of spiritual rituals meant to drive away angry ghosts. The cairns, which were not especially stable, tended to collapse within a day or two of their construction. This was taken as proof that they had prevented disaster.

Magnolia came back on the night of a full moon. Crow was out fishing again, although she'd begun thinking that she'd better quit before she drove the local eels to extinction. She had just gotten started when the scent of magnolia blossoms drifted across the water, quite out of season.

Rod in hand, she looked at the opposite bank.

Magnolia wore soft black clothing from head to toe. Taken from one of the hunters she'd spirited away, of course. But at what point? Had she ordered them to strip naked before fighting their comrades to death? Had she sent them alone and unclothed into the northern wilderness? Had she made a survivor peel garments off the choicest corpses?

There should have been a terrible reek of blood following her, too, but all Crow breathed in was the essence of cup-shaped flowers at the peak of their bloom.

55

"YOU MAKE a good peasant," Magnolia said, once they were on the same side of the stream. (She'd refused to wade across, so Crow ported her over.)

Then, in a tone of surprise: "You're glad to see me."

Crow didn't contest this. "You were gone a long time."

"Less than a month. Did you miss me that much?"

"You could have stayed away longer," Crow said.

"Anything interesting happen? No troublesome visitors?"

"None at all. What were you doing?"

Magnolia hunkered down by the water, looking in vain for moonlit fish. "I led my parade to the far reaches of the hills. They did a thorough clean-up of all the monsters creeping in at the edges. Then they finished the job by getting rid of each other. The hills will be well fertilized, but it was a poor harvest for my stomach. That's the problem with hunters. Few of them come with cores."

"How many did you leave alive?" There was nothing Crow could do with this information, but she felt a compulsion to know.

"What number would please you?" Magnolia spread her hands. "More than one—I'll leave it at that. I made them bury their dead in the hills. No need to burden the townsfolk with rotting corpses. Mortal bodies are quite a handful, you know. The hunters who dug graves had to use their weapons as makeshift shovels. Inefficient, but poetic. I let them take their time with it. I even let them say prayers."

Half a year ago, Crow would have hit her upon hearing this. Her hand might have ground to an unwilling halt, trembling, her knuckles touching Magnolia's cheek as lightly as a kiss. Or Magnolia might have let her go through with it, might have laughed at her through a broken nose and blood-rimmed teeth.

Crow had misplaced that crucial impulse, the lightning charge that would bolt straight from her brain to her fist. It was gone from her, like a key fallen through a hole in an old pocket, and she had no idea where to find it.

She needed to get Magnolia to the end of the world before she forgot why they were going there in the first place. At the end, Magnolia would free her—or maybe she wouldn't. But it was all Crow had to cling to. She'd better hurl Magnolia off the edge of the world before she became fatally confused about her own deepest wishes.

"The same problem will happen again," Crow said, meaning the village, "as long as everyone thinks you still reign here."

"I know. But this ought to keep the villagers safe enough till—oh, around next spring. Better than nothing."

She made Crow carry her, claiming exhaustion. In exchange she held Crow's fishing rod (which was not especially helpful).

Many of the stars above were as green and blue as radiant fireflies. Crow thought that if she never put Magnolia down, then Magnolia would never go on another murder spree. She thought that if she were the one with the magical voice, then she could attach Magnolia to her like a mule on a rope.

What a bizarre thing for an immortal to crave. Companionship—simple and literal and nonmagical companionship—without any path to consumption. Was she sick in the head? Command after command had muddied her will and churned her brain like butter. Yet she knew—or thought she knew—when orders compelled her. This disorientation was all her own.

When daylight came, Magnolia told the villagers to loot the abandoned camps. "Use every last tent pole. Why wouldn't you?" She seemed amused. "Were you waiting for my permission?"

Crow moved to join them, but Magnolia tugged at her sleeve. She pointed out children drawing on Dung's scales with sticks of charcoal. His shed scales, yes, but also the ones right there on his body. He slept (or feigned sleep) while they decorated him as if he were a rock wall in a prehistoric cave.

"What a charming sight," Magnolia said.

To what extent did the villagers understand who Crow and Magnolia were? When commands moved them—to, say, disassemble the abandoned camps—did they know where those commands came from? At minimum, Magnolia seemed to be suppressing their awareness. No one reacted to her unless she addressed them directly, and when she asked casual questions, they answered as if she were a long-time friend.

"We should leave," Crow said in her ear.

"Now, now. The end of the world won't run away from us. Let's at least take a moment to collect your trunk."

Crow hadn't forgotten about it, but she hadn't intended on retrieving it. Not with Magnolia breathing down her neck. She was fairly certain she had never mentioned stashing luggage here, either.

Magnolia must have plucked it from her mind like a diving cormorant.

"Why do you want me to get it?" she asked.

Magnolia looked puzzled. "Well, if I could, I'd open you up like a suitcase and peer inside."

"*If* you could?"

"You overestimate me," Magnolia said amiably. "My fishing lines aren't weighted. I've said it before—I see little past the surface of the mind, and the outward seasons it reflects. I really have no idea what swims around in your depths."

"I don't have any valuables."

"Then you can scrounge up space to store my doll from the city. It's been stretching out your pockets."

Upon request, the tea shop owner brought Crow's trunk out of storage. It was made of dark wood, with protective brass corners. She could haul it about like an attaché case, or sling it from her back with sturdy ropes.

In a dusty corner room on the second floor of the tea shop, Crow laid the trunk flat. They'd gotten here by ascending a perilously steep flight of slippery wooden stairs. It had felt rather like going up a ladder. She hoped no elderly folk would attempt the same climb, but other multi-story buildings in the village must be built the same way. They probably did it every day.

She opened the trunk. "Behold," she said blandly. "A change of clothes."

Magnolia prodded her until she lifted out the first layer of garments. They needed a thorough airing, anyhow.

Sliding doors to a balcony, fitted with reed screens, had been pushed open. Magnolia lounged on the threshold between indoors and outdoors. Misty air at the fringes of the village concealed her hills. There wasn't much of a breeze.

Crow knelt beside the open trunk and resigned herself to performing an autopsy of her belongings. She no longer had anything from the young empress or the last mage, nor from most of her other companions, regardless of whether the archivists would have deemed them historically significant.

She showed Magnolia a sketch rendered on a very old, soft scrap of fabric—a drawing of a tree that someone had loved once. She'd paid that tree several visits, but now it was gone.

Magnolia started to say something, then closed her mouth.

"What?" Crow said.

"If you ever did manage to kill me, you'd be left without any trophies."

"I've never killed monsters in hopes of getting a trophy."

"Extermination is its own reward, is it? I could offer you my earrings. But they're part of me, too. You'd be left with nothing but pretty piles of ash."

"And your core," Crow said, "added to mine. And this." She wiggled the useless wooden doll, which wasn't even long enough to serve as a rolling pin. She made a show of placing it inside the trunk.

Magnolia put a hand on her heart. "True. What more could you want?"

Spare clothes aside, the newest artifacts were a letter from Leda and the acorn-carved medallion—now devoid of magic—that she had worn at the end. Arion had worn it all his life, too.

Magnolia looked without touching until Crow placed the medallion on her palm. She held it up to the white sky as if she could see through it like a spyglass. "Would Arion have liked me?"

"He was a slayer, and he had a core. You would have taken his core before he ever got a chance to know you."

"In other words, we would've gotten along grand."

"I didn't say that."

"If I didn't kill him first, I mean." She nudged Crow with her toe. "Are you going to read me that letter?"

"Read it yourself."

"I'd rather hear it in your voice." This lacked the strength of a full command, but there was enough pressure to make Crow's ears pop.

Leda had attempted to write letters to Arion, too. But by the time she worked out what she wanted to say, she'd found it difficult to hold a quill or a brush.

This letter was for Crow—written in Crow's own hand, a faithful transcription as Leda spoke. It began with apologies, and then a plea. She asked Crow not to make him a hero. To teach him other things—like how to navigate by the stars, and how to shell peas.

"I know you won't ever request his core," Crow read. "But if he promises it to you in the end—if he turns out like me—it's not your fault, Carrie. That's just who we are."

Sometimes Arion would ask about his father, and Crow would say she didn't know. Sometimes, even as an adult, he would turn to Crow and tell her: "I wish you were my mother."

He said it without bitterness. Seeing the stricken look on Crow's face, he'd add, "Don't worry. I respect my mother. She worked to permanently eliminate half of the Four Great Adversaries, and she never claimed credit." He brightened. "We'll take down the other two, won't we?"

Or else he would hug his knees and say: "You're here, and she isn't. I love her, even if I'll never meet her. I want to make her proud. But I wish she were alive. I wish she could've been you."

Magnolia leaned over Crow's shoulder and reread Leda's letter for herself. "Nowhere in here does she ask you to keep his origins secret."

"She would never have asked that."

"He had a living mother all along, and you never told him," Magnolia muttered. "There are times when I think to myself that you have all the makings of a very fine monster. Crow, how did this son of yours end up as your promised companion? Leda didn't want that for him. All you vowed to her was to stay with him for as long as you could."

Crow put the letter back. Something dry and tacky coated her fingertips, as if the aging paper had oozed secretions like human skin.

With Arion, she had tried to live as discreetly as possible. At times they avoided the company of other mortals, although she could hardly force him to grow up in total isolation. At times she covered her eyes and, as best she could, hid the fact that she was a saint.

At times she pretended that he was already her promised companion, despite his youth. *He asked me to save his mother,* she'd say. This was enough to make most people understand why a child might swear his life away. *I tried,* she'd say, *but in the end, I couldn't do it.* They understood this, too: even with magic, saints were not infallible against mortal death.

She'd wrestled again and again with how to explain herself to Arion. He had so many questions. What's an immortal? What's a monster? What's a saint? Do all saints have wings? What did saints *do* with their protracted lives, other than run around to stop little boys from petting flea-ridden feral dogs and cats?

She tried to be truthful about how Leda had died. He went through a phase in which he'd proudly tell every passing tinker that Crow had killed his mother with her bare hands.

As he grew older, he came to grasp the nuances of sainthood. This led to fresh difficulties, because now he understood the significance of the fact that Crow had no promised companion.

She assured him that she wasn't going anywhere. She had made a promise to his mother—and even without any such promise, she would've been glad to raise him.

He looked at her with troubled black eyes and asked what would happen if someone offered her their core.

Many people wished to secure the services of a saint, she told him. Most such offers would fail—even if made in desperation, even if they thought they meant it. And even if she did take on a promised companion, she would refuse to leave Arion behind.

"They might order you to leave me."

"I don't have to obey every order from a companion," Crow said. "Some orders are impossible."

"But that's how saints build power," he insisted. "By waiting, and obeying—by serving them. And leaving me wouldn't be impossible, anyway."

It began to feel as though he wanted her to leave. Not because he wished to be abandoned. His fear had become so palpable that he seemed driven to drag it into reality, to make it something factual enough to fight against. She was not sufficiently human—or eloquent, or loving, or maternal—to convince him that she would fight just as hard to stay. She knew how to butcher dangerous beasts, but she was helpless when it came to dismantling the absolute conviction of an intelligent child.

That was why Arion promised her his core.

He was so terrified to lose her that he would have died to prevent it. He really would have died on the spot—that was how much he meant it. She never got a chance to persuade him otherwise. He made her a sincere offer: it closed around her like the jaws of a trap.

They remained companions bound by a promise until he died to the Horde. She told him over and over that she would have stayed with him no matter what, but he had no reason to believe her, and she had no way to prove it.

She hadn't meant to tell Magnolia any of this. She gazed down at the trunk as if it were a window onto the immutable past.

"If I were truly his mother," she said, "in even the smallest of ways, then I failed every possible test."

"Could've been worse," Magnolia said after a long moment. "It could've been me attempting to raise him."

"...Are you trying to comfort me?"

"Am I not comforting? Imagine me in your place. I would have given up the first time he threw a tantrum. At least you didn't murder your own child and gobble down his core."

"I hold myself to a higher standard of conduct," Crow said, caustic.

"That's where all your trouble comes from." Magnolia reached past her and softly lowered the wooden lid of the trunk.

Windows were open on the floor below, too. They could hear metal and ceramic clinking, along with liquid pouring and splashing and simmering. Sweeping sounds came from somewhere outside. Fallen seed pods and pine needles would need to be collected in every season, not merely at the tail end of fall. Just another one of those neverending tasks. From further away came a thumping that might have been hammering, and the airy whistle of children blowing on leaves.

"Something broke when they sacrificed me, or when I returned," Magnolia said thoughtfully. "I'll never be a being that cares much for the sanctity of life. Human or otherwise. Guilty or innocent. On occasion, I can go through the motions. I can follow certain rules, even if they strike me as arbitrary. I can hold myself to what you might call a slightly higher standard of conduct. Still, I'll never actually care. But I like that you're the opposite. It would be a boring world if there were no one but me in it."

"You would be very bored if you had no one to torment."

Magnolia grinned.

"Slaughtering hunters out of my sight—was that your idea of compromise?" Crow asked.

"I have a reputation to maintain." She was no longer smirking. "I sent the survivors out to seed terrifying new stories. Now people in other lands will hear that vanquishing the Woman in the Hills will lead to no special reward except glory."

Crow understood her logic. For some heroic types, glory alone might be good enough. Traffic would thin out, but no one wanted the flow of hunters to stop completely. The villagers would be in dire straits with zero chances for trade, and other monsters would annex their rivers and fields.

When they took one last stroll through the village, the air was filled with the scent of someone stewing a vast quantity of lentils. Magnolia showed off a thriving herb garden with proprietary pride, as if she'd tilled it herself. Dung's fallen scales had been stuck in the soil as plant markers.

"Let's plant a tree," she said. She did it in the open area near the replica stump—a stony grave for a sacred tree of forgotten provenance.

It grew much faster than the one she'd planted at Fellshore. Granted, the ground around the shrine had been barren. This land, in contrast, was the heart of Magnolia's original territory. And although most of her recent victims had been coreless, she was nevertheless flush with at least a couple of freshly consumed cores. It was as if those dead hunters had been directly transmuted into the flesh of her tree.

She didn't make it bloom out of season. The stone-carved stump rested in its shade like a graciously placed bench.

She held Crow's hand for no reason, as though the magnolia tree were something they had accomplished together. No one noticed them, because she'd forbidden it, and no one saw them leave.

56

IT TOOK SOME trial and error for Crow to figure out what to do with her trunk. She could hold it one-handed, but she would inevitably have to set it down during spats with roaming monsters. She tried roping it to her back, but it became unwieldy when Magnolia climbed up there, too.

Now that they were out of the village, Magnolia spent most of her time as a head. While riding Dung, she sent roots out to help secure Crow's trunk. Eventually Crow used lengths of rope to sling it around the front of Dung's chest, between his rows of forearms. He objected less to that than to having it rattling on his withers.

Magnolia mentioned what she knew of the land beyond her hills—gleaned partly from human minds, and partly from her talks with the earth. Crow was fuzzy on the geography of it all, but this gave her some idea of what to expect.

Take their entire meandering journey from the hills to Fellshore to

Steppehaven to the New City, and back to the hills. Straighten it out like a piece of string. Place the end of that string where they stood now, and stretch it out to the north. The supposed end of the world would lie farther away than the sum total of all their travels to date.

But Magnolia wanted to savor the scenery. Crow was in no rush, either. Shortly after skirting around the hills, they spent one night in a cave. They had no need to spend nights anywhere, but it was storming. Sometimes even immortals prefer not to get soaked to the bone.

On the way in, Magnolia kept insisting that they were being watched. Crow told her not to be paranoid. They were both right, as it turned out: the cave was settled with birds instead of bats. Pale white birds, moist-looking, like the flesh of cooked fish. They gave Dung, Crow, and Magnolia a wide berth—which was just as well, considering how much work it took to find a part of the cavern not already painted over with centuries of droppings.

"Do stars exist?" Magnolia asked while they waited for the storm to pass.

"We met a star," Crow said.

"Huh?"

"The Devil."

"She doesn't count. She just looked like one. Or was that your point? The stars look like stars, but are they really *stars*? The same as before the end began?"

"I don't follow," Crow said mildly.

"There are places down on the ground where the world just stops. A physical border to mark the end of existence. Who's to say there aren't more borders of nonexistence above us, higher than any aerial will ever fly? If the world is a dying flame—why would anything around it be real?"

"I guess faraway stars could be an illusion."

"Or ghosts and memories," said Magnolia.

"But you're in for a headache if you want to argue that the sun and moon are fake. The seas still have tides."

Magnolia's expression turned mulish, but she let Crow have the last word.

Some days after the storm, they came across a valley of travertine terraces: flat limestone plateaus filled with shallow clear water, limpid green and blue. From the mountains around the valley came the whisper of myriad waterfalls.

Magnolia's eyes gleamed. "Look!" she said to Crow, who was already looking. She sprang off Dung's back, manifesting the rest of her body as she went. She was naked and, evidently, dead set on splashing barefoot in that transparent water.

Magic flickered in the air. It was so weak that it could have been the trail left by a passing aerial, too high to see.

Crow moved without thinking, and an arrow meant for Magnolia struck her in the back instead.

Magnolia started to speak. Crow grabbed her. There was no time to waste on pain. The long arrow still protruded foolishly from her back.

"Don't tell me to kill them," she said.

"Then protect me with your whole self," Magnolia replied.

She turned into a head, falling, erased from the neck below. Crow caught her. And then Crow became an aerial.

From the sky over the valley, those travertine terraces looked like a genteel swimming pool. Nothing could strike an aerial up here, not even arrows fletched with magical feathers or anointed with sacred oil. The day was as clear as the water below, and Magnolia couldn't stop laughing.

"You just flew away! I was hoping to see a fight."

It would have been a very one-sided fight, thought Crow, who did not currently have a human voice box.

"They'll think you're the Woman in the Hills."

They'll think we're the Woman in the Hills.

Indeed, they bore a curious resemblance to the Fellshore mimid: a vast sky serpent with Magnolia's human head attached up front, bolted on with vines, as if she were the part that did all the thinking. It did feel that way, sometimes, when she gave orders.

Magnolia wanted a closer look at the arrow, but it was nowhere to be found. Crow must have shed it—together with her clothes—when she shifted into the body of an aerial.

I'll be fine. The wound didn't carry over. What about Dung?

"He'll lie low," Magnolia said dismissively. "They won't notice him. Even if they do, they'll know he's not a monster. Probably."

He has my trunk.

"He'll take good care of it."

Some corners of the continent know primevals only as man-eating mythical beasts.

"Let's hope that no intrepid heroes find him."

They spent several days and nights aloft, watching the moon wane until it went dark. The mountains below looked like moss-covered rocks, smaller than Magnolia's hills.

Crow found the time river that they'd forded near the beginning of their journey. She coasted above the gold ribbon of sunset-reflecting water while inquisitive minor aerials bobbed around Magnolia's head. Some made the air very hot or cold. Some were no more substantial than soap bubbles, and glowed as if with memories of another day's light.

Magnolia kept wanting to know what they were called. Crow offered her a few words in defunct languages. Many of these aerials were so small and shy that it was quite possible no human had noticed or named them in generations. To observe them, you'd need access to an extremely high-quality spyglass, the sort that the automagi might jealously protect as evidence of fallen technology.

When they flew alone, flocks of birds crossed below them, as dense as clouds of gnats. Another time, the ground rippled with movement, and Crow swooped lower to inspect colossal herds of a nameless ungulate. A single branching antler grew from its forehead, forming rebellious asymmetrical shapes. Magnolia claimed the creature was a type of monoceros.

The mass of the herd reminded Crow uncomfortably of the Singular Horde, and of foot soldiers and cavalry in imperial armies, and of legends about cities that would make the one run by the Dame look like a backwards hamlet.

This was a diminished world, a waning world, but not a lifeless world. There was more than enough to make up for a sparser human presence. Streams choked with iridescent fish, forests draped with fungi curtains, isopods churning in soil, marshland flies like living smoke. And aerials—Crow among them—painting every level of the sky with a filigree of faint shadows.

After they whiled away time until the new moon, Magnolia ordered her back to the travertine terraces.

Why not go north? Crow asked. *We'd travel faster in the air than on ground.*

"And ditch Dung?" Magnolia said, sardonic. "Weren't you feigning worry for him just a few days ago? I didn't get to properly enjoy the terraces. We didn't even go find any waterfalls. Anyway, it's much more of a risk for you than it is for me. You're the one who's trying to avoid cutting a swathe through human heroes."

The watery terraces had a shape reminiscent of overlapping scales, although you couldn't see it as well from ground level. Crow stalled for another half a day, then reluctantly descended. Dung refused to come out until she left aerial form.

She sat naked on a lip of yellow limestone. Magnolia roosted on her shoulder, fresh roots trailing down her spine to taste the water in the pool behind her. She'd swept those roots all over Crow's back before declaring—with evident disappointment—that she could find no trace of any injury left by that one mildly magical arrow.

Even now, her roots were not motionless. They quivered at irregular intervals, tickling Crow like fingers grasping gently in the throes of sleep.

As sun filled the valley, Dung condescended to show himself. The wooden trunk (and the ropes fixing it to him) were intact, albeit crusted with a mysterious mud.

Crow searched the area until she found her dropped clothes—only partially drenched—and her pack. She dressed in what she could and hung a few other things to dry.

"I'm surprised our slayers didn't steal your underwear," Magnolia said snidely.

"They were looking for big game," Crow said, "not wet rags."

She scouted out the remainder of the travertine terraces and the wild mountains around them. She returned to report that—as far as she could tell—whoever had shot at them had promptly departed.

"In fairness," Magnolia said, "they might not have been professional hunters. They might have been robbers, or frightened refugees from a displaced settlement. If they were hunters, they wouldn't expect us to come back. You put on a very good show of running away. Humiliating, but effective. What kind of pathetic monster flees humans without a fight? They must think we're halfway across the continent."

Crow removed her trunk from Dung so he could wallow in the wide natural pools without soaking it. She'd rolled her pants up, but her clothes just seemed to be getting damper and damper. She stripped everything off again and draped it from tree branches, although it was already close to evening. Only a few lost-looking speckles of sunlight lay scattered across the water.

Magnolia expressed an interest in communing with the earth.

"We aren't far from the hills," Crow said. "You won't learn anything new."

Magnolia laughed. "If you'll be lonely while I speak with the land, you can just say so."

Irritated, Crow turned and saw her resting on a pile of roots: this kept her from gurgling underwater. The terraces were at least deep enough to drown a severed head. She regarded Crow with open appreciation.

"Stop ogling," Crow said. She transformed her lower half into a serpent again—now that would give Magnolia something to look at.

Her serpent tail thrashed. It swept water out of half the terraces and sent waves over Magnolia. She squawked almost as loudly as Dung, who had rocketed away into the forest.

"Now you really are just like the mimid," Magnolia said, spitting water. There was no more sunlight left in the evening air.

"That's not a compliment."

"If it's any consolation, you're much more attractive. I wonder ... after another thousand-something years of moonlight, maybe I could learn to take aerial form, too. Seems worth a try."

Crow opened her wings. They were anchored in her lower back, near where her waist became serpentine. The human part of her was laughably small compared to the serpent part. Her tail bulged and coiled and doubled back on itself in wall-like loops. Magnolia would no longer be able to see anything of the terraces sloping behind her, all that faded gold and white limestone glistening under early stars.

New white roots reached for Crow, hundreds of them. They jerked and pulled back before touching her, as if they hadn't realized they were reaching for anything at all.

A moment later, Magnolia was in human shape, a defiant look on her face, her hair wet and slicked down. As if to announce that she was the same thing as Crow, even if her body looked like a perfect whole. Her head was as alien to the rest of her form as Crow's torso was to the serpent tail that swelled large enough to loom over both of them.

It was easy to see what she wanted. It lay reflected in the twist of her lips. Crow, half-aerial and half-humanoid and fully immortal, lowered herself like a snake. She felt her heart as a series of silent thumps. She didn't think about anything important. She didn't think about a single second in the future or the past. There was nothing outside the overwhelming present.

She touched Magnolia's damp neck, and then the bead of her earring. Magnolia's head tilted into her head. There was a scent of orange blossom and tea olive, of flowers that had no name in human language. She kissed Magnolia roughly, drawing blood, and felt answering hands on her throat, shutting the valve of her breath. There was no real threat in that, just as there was no real threat in the prospect of drowning. Quite a bit more determination would be needed to destroy either of them.

She took advantage of her superior mass to bear Magnolia down on her back, making her lie there as if the limestone plateau was a pastel bed. She held both of Magnolia's earrings with crushing fingers and glimpsed an arrested expression in her eyes—consumed, entranced, almost trusting.

But her fingers still bit at the front of Crow's neck as if she couldn't let up—as if she were doing it to pay off a debt. Crow, choking, spread her wings like a roof above them. There was a weight on her back, and she just had to ignore it.

She kissed Magnolia again, longer and more lightly. She tasted blood like springtime sap.

When she pulled back, that heaviness on her shoulders lunged into motion. A pike came down past her, right into the center of Magnolia's face, mutilating all her immortal beauty in a single hideous pile-driving blow.

57

THE WAITING HUNTERS sprang out of the shadows of Crow's coils.

They were thorough. They didn't just settle for spearing Magnolia's face with a pike. Someone used a black blade made from one of Crow's feathers. Someone loosed another arrow fletched with Crow's feathers, too; as promised, it flew true. Someone else shot Magnolia point-blank with the crossbow from the village. Crow had let them take it, as she'd had no use for it herself.

They exclusively attacked Magnolia's head and neck, all at once, with swift ferocity. It was a wonder that none of them fell to friendly fire. Crow didn't emerge unscathed, but she'd told them they could treat her like a stray bush on the battlefield. They could stab straight through her if it might help preserve the element of surprise.

It all happened so quickly that Magnolia only had time for a single command. She had no eyes left to look with. She had no mouth left to speak with.

DIE, she told them—a geyser of fury, a booming thought like the sound of a landslide.

That order was meant as much for Crow as for the hunters. But it rolled off her out of sheer impossibility. You could order a human to use magic, in this era without mages—but even under threats of torture or death, they wouldn't be able to meet expectations. Telling an immortal to self-destruct would be just as infeasible.

DIE.

Crow, paralyzed by her inability to act on it, felt a phantom of Magnolia's seeking hands at her throat. Magnolia should have looped a wooden root around her neck to wring it—that would have been much surer, more dangerous.

Her serpent self dissolved. She landed on her knees on wet copper-colored rock.

Magnolia was already turning to a pile of muddy ash—sugary-sweet blood and bones and all. She had no more orders to give. Barely any time had passed. But her last magic still reverberated in the air, as if the worst of the landslide was rumbling closer with each fractured fragment of each chopped-up second.

The hunting party had begun killing themselves, and Crow was much too slow to react. One man had a heart attack from the strength of his obedience. She heard him collapse; he never opened his eyes again. If she were mortal, she would have been right there with him.

Magnolia's ashes had a fragrance like incense, although nothing was burning. Waves of nausea radiated from Crow's gut to her head.

She rocked into motion just in time to stop the pike-wielder—who had abandoned her pike—from disemboweling herself with a knife. Crow wrenched the knife away and hurled it off into the mountains. The woman didn't argue. She started groping around for other weapons, other ways to slit her belly, and she kept this up for hours to come.

Meanwhile: Dung hurtled out of the woods with an unearthly scream. He slammed into Crow, who nearly failed to hold her ground. Her wings went tense with magic. He had another go at biting her arm off while she grappled frantically with the suicidal pike-wielder.

It took all Crow's strength to keep from getting bowled over and trampled. She blasted Dung backwards with crude magic, too strained to avoid hurting him. At last he gave up on dismembering her. He screamed even more shrilly and began to furiously attack the nearest corpses.

No earrings glinted in Magnolia's muck.

By dawn, the pike-wielder had stopped actively trying to kill herself. She sat on a gray-white terrace, catatonic. Crow had managed to save one other hunter, packing their self-inflicted wounds with magic. She hadn't been quick enough to reach the rest.

Dung dragged the corpses into the woods where the terraced valley met the rising slope of mountains. He snarled whenever Crow looked his way. He was dark all over with human blood and stinking shreds of solid gore, as if he'd rolled in it like mud. In a detached way, she found herself glad she'd taken her trunk off him, although she couldn't remember where she'd put it. Her mind had become a wasteland.

Soiled pools reflected a cold red sunrise. Crow watched impassively as the faceless dregs of Magnolia's corpse gave way to an irksome shimmer in the air. She had been defeated, but only at the hands of humans. One day, somewhere in these lands, a cocoon would form.

Crow found the clothes she'd hung on the other side of the valley. She found her wooden trunk, no worse for wear, and still impressively dry. She dressed slowly before going back to the two human survivors. She had promises to keep.

It was the worst kind of victory. She felt no personal triumph, and besides, it wouldn't last. Neither Arion nor Leda had aspired to give the Four Great Adversaries a temporary death. On top of that, in her dying moments, Magnolia had immediately gotten revenge on her attackers. The only saving grace was that the potency of her final command appeared to be fading with time.

Crow felt very little, in fact, except the weight of the years ahead. And a maudlin desire to apologize to Dung, who'd loved Magnolia much more than he'd ever let on.

Although that love, too, might have been forced. She might have commanded him to avenge her with the full force of his latent bone-chomping bloodlust. She might have whispered it to him every morning. *If anything happens to me, you'd better raise hell.* The more Crow listened to his ragged nightly screams, the more likely this began to seem. He was ravenous, and inconsolable. She couldn't recover a single bone from any of the pike-wielder's comrades without driving him into another frenzy of violence.

The dazed survivors had no choice but to leave their dead in the tooth-gnashing care of a primordial beast. They would be hard-pressed to understand why Crow couldn't just slaughter Dung as if he were a monster or a man-eating tiger. It wasn't something she could explain in words. For the rest of their mortal lives, she would work to pay off this debt.

58

Sixty years passed.

It was late fall when Crow returned to the radish village. Spotted toad lilies grew all along the banks of nearby streams. Soon it would be time for the second season of long radishes.

The population seemed smaller, but that was true of most settlements she'd seen along the way. The current tea master was a young woman who had been born after Magnolia's death. The shop itself had burned down in a lightning strike about a decade ago, and had been completely rebuilt.

Crow paid for her tea with southern spices. She helped repair several dozen roofs, and dispatched a couple circling monsters.

Like her predecessor, the shopkeeper asked, "Don't you have a companion?"

"My companion just died," Crow said, and the shopkeeper shyly murmured condolences.

In winter, Crow bade the villagers farewell and hiked out to the travertine terraces beyond Magnolia's hills. Snow dusted the mountains around the valley.

Sixty years ago, she hadn't dwelt much on the temperature of the pools—they weren't scalding, but certainly warm enough to qualify as a type of hot spring. The crystalline water remained unfrozen. On the iciest days at the beginning of the year, steam rose like a mirage.

No bloodstains marred the pastel-toned rock. At least not in any way distinguishable from ordinary discoloration. She searched the black-branched woods for some time, but failed to find any hidden cache of human bones. Dung might have masticated them all to pebble-sized shards in his fury.

By this point, most wild isopods had gone into hibernation. Every so often, three-legged crows swooped down to mock her. She had always found crows to be less helpful than humble pill bugs. But she wasn't worried: by her reckoning, she still had plenty of time.

She located Magnolia's cocoon in a mountainside bower surrounded by the noise of countless thread-thin waterfalls. She wrapped her trunk in a woolen blanket to keep snow out, and she settled down to keep vigil until spring.

Blizzards aside, the most notable event of that winter was a night when the sky rippled with blazing curtains of purple aurora.

Once the last of the snow melted, she had to admit that she'd arrived over a year early. She waited for the usual springtime dust to blow past. Day after day of hazy silver air and skies. On the worst days, the dust turned violet and tasted irredeemably acrid. Everyone back in the village must have been coughing from morning to night.

Human explorers claimed to have discovered this cocoon some decades ago. But none of their weapons or explosives or borrowed magic could make much of a dent in it. Cocoons were impervious to mortals.

Immortals had their own fundamental taboo against attacking cocoons, too. A taboo so strong that Crow had never considered breaking it, even when doing so might have spared Leda from infecting herself with the Beautiful Scourge.

She considered it now, if only as a gruesome thought experiment. She could destroy Magnolia's core and all the regenerating goop inside it. She could stamp out the last of the Great Adversaries without a fight. There would be no final conversation, no core to claim, nothing but brutal one-sided eradication.

She didn't do that.

Instead, she began planting a garden.

A year or two was not long enough, in her estimation, to create anything truly impressive. She did it mainly to fill time. She'd brought a handful of small brown bulbs packed in dry moss; after winter, she buried them in soil.

That summer, only a few egret orchids grew from her bulbs. Given that they were by now close to extinct, she chose to count this as a victory. Especially since she hadn't relied on magic to increase her odds of success.

Her magical fast would by necessity be much shorter than prior to her first meeting with Magnolia. Even so, she was at the height of her powers. Before revisiting the radish village and the mysterious hills and the little-known limestone valley, she'd taken a core from her twenty-fifth companion. (Twenty-five companions, yes, including Tamar—but this last time had only been her eighth successful reaping.)

On humid summer nights, those fringed egret flowers lifted off their stems and danced capriciously around the drab cocoon. They looked as if they wanted to find a way to sneak inside.

Crow stretched out on the woolly blanket that she'd previously used to protect her trunk. She spoke to the silent cocoon all through those white fluttering nights, and all through the following days. She spoke even when a chorus of cicadas buzzed so loud that she had trouble remembering what she was trying to say.

It felt like quite a role reversal to talk on and on at Magnolia. Crow found that she, too, relished having a captive audience.

She told the cocoon how she'd begun paying more attention to the quirks of other immortals. In doing so, she'd been forced to concede that saints—not just monsters—could also have inborn compulsions.

She'd met a saint who took companions only from among the descendants of a single matrilineal bloodline. Would they be automatically released from that compulsion, she wondered, if the bloodline died out?

She'd heard from bards about a saint who was compelled to sing for hours whenever they reaped a core. By human standards, their voice was quite terrible. An apocryphal story, exaggerated to entertain? Perhaps.

She'd personally dealt with a saint whose compulsion made him murder an extra coreless human each time he lost a companion. As if balancing a set of scales that no one else could see or understand.

Once she started observing immortals with more of an analytical eye, she realized that such compulsions were like an iron cage to the one obliged to enact them. Seen from outside, though, they appeared as fragile as spider-silk—magical cobwebs that could be torn away by a friendly stranger.

It was just as Magnolia had always claimed. Immortals could easily break one another's compulsions—no expertise required. The reason they rarely did so was a lack of interest and motivation, and maybe an inherent struggle to comprehend the point of it all. Immortals were not social creatures, at least not with each other. It had been the same for Crow. She would stop to help mortals in distress, but it wouldn't have occurred to her to stop for a fellow saint.

She perceived more now than she had before. She could have freed that murderous saint from his compulsion, but her companion ordered her to put him down. She didn't feel strongly enough to object. To those coreless humans he'd strangled in passing, he might as well have been a monster.

She encountered monsters whose particular compulsion made them lie low most of the time, all but harmless. They would only rise up and devour mortals during sun showers, or during an eclipse, or beneath the arc of a rainbow, or in the space between thunderclaps.

"We all start off with compulsions," Crow said. "I'll give you that. They're everywhere, once you start looking. But I still don't know mine."

Had a generous saint—or an idiosyncratic monster—freed her many years ago, without her knowing it? She didn't remember anything of the sort. But then, she hadn't committed to remembering every single day of her life. If, in the moment, she hadn't grasped the significance of what was happening....

In autumn, after all the orchid leaves died back, she dug them up and sorted old bulbs from new. There were more new bulbs than she'd expected, enough that she could replant some in the ground and pack others to keep. The egrets seemed too finicky to survive here on their own, but perhaps they'd prove her wrong.

She'd just about finished when the cocoon cracked open. Smoke and darkness came pouring out.

A head followed moments later, tumbling free as if freshly decapitated, landing ignominiously on its face in the middle of Crow's garden.

The drifting smoke smelled of burning leaves. Crow's hands formed fists on her knees. She would not reach for that head—it would probably bite her fingers off, anyway.

Hidden birds voiced loud complaints from tree to tree. The noise of the nearby waterfalls—so constant that she hadn't consciously heard it in months—began to intensify. She couldn't be sure if that noise came from the waterfalls or from something inside her. A frisson went through her wings: just little bat-style scraps of skin right now, no wider than a human hand, folded down against the backs of her shoulders like crumpled paper umbrellas.

Fragile white roots hung from Magnolia's shorn neck like the veil of a mushroom. They looked too floppy to be of much use, but somehow she succeeded in turning herself. She faced Crow, her head lying sideways in a patch of dying sorrel. The broken cocoon behind her bubbled and shook and then collapsed into a pile of mud flakes like an empty anthill. Her hair was mussed, and her eyes were the bright hard red of winter berries.

"Who are you?" she said.

59

CROW WAITED.

Twenty seconds later, Magnolia burst out laughing. She laughed hard enough to push her head around in the crushed patch of sorrel. Given time, she could have laughed herself all the way across the clearing and over the edge of a waterfall.

Her cackling died out. "I should've kept you in suspense," she said, expressionless. "Oh, well. So much for that. Carrion Crow. My faithful servant."

My faithful servant.

Those words, all on their own, already had the magical tone of a command.

"I was hoping to forget you, too," Crow confessed.

"Are you stupid?" Magnolia asked. "Or just incredibly arrogant? You had—I assume!—all the time in the world to prepare, and once again you show up alone."

"My companion died two years ago," said Crow.

"Died?" Magnolia said sharply. "All on her own?"

"I killed her and took her core."

"You should've gotten another."

"The timing didn't work out."

If Magnolia were any stronger, she would undoubtedly have started ripping up Crow's plants. "Isn't this wonderful. You've taken another step up the endless staircase of power. Look at me in comparison, a worm in the dust.

"You got your revenge for when I made you tear off your wings. You paid me back a thousand times worse. It's all gone now—my years of moonlight, every human core I ever swallowed, every scrap of gathered magic—all ruined. Now I really am just a head with a voice. Who knows how long it'll take before I can form a decorative body, or speak with the depths of the land, or plant trees?"

"It wasn't personal," Crow said. "I gave humanity a chance for vengeance."

Magnolia made a sound like the reverse of laughter, a hysterical gasp. "I wish it could have been personal. I wish you'd done it yourself."

"If I'd done it myself, you would never have revived."

"And you would be devastated, without knowing why. Sounds good to me."

Crow disregarded this. She spoke logically. "More to the point—I couldn't have done it myself. You would have ordered me to stop. No matter how I addled you by pinching your earrings, you would have noticed me gearing up to kill you."

"I wonder," Magnolia said bitterly. "I got sloppy, obviously. I didn't think you would let anyone else kill me. Not after learning that I'd defeated the last of the Horde. The Horde integrated Arion's core, and then I integrated the Horde's core, and some tiny splinter of your Arion might have lived on in me forever. Well, not anymore. Didn't think you had it in you."

"I expected more rage," Crow said, wondering if these would be the words that set her off.

Magnolia's lips curved. It was difficult to read her expression, what with her lying sideways in a bed of sorrel. "I can perceive just how undignified it would be to roll around on the ground as a severed head, throwing screeching impotent tantrums, my roots as floppy as wet string. So let's fix that. Pick me up."

Her voice remained light and controlled, but the command hit like the lash of a whip.

Crow's thoughts stopped, as if her mind had been struck. Then she found herself standing, holding Magnolia up like a piece of ancient treasure, slender roots tangled around her fingers. There had not been any opportunity to resist. Confused pain darted from one nerve to the next, trying to figure out where in her body it belonged.

"See?" said Magnolia. "I've lost all my silken finesse. Ugh—will you get that ant off my neck?"

Crow brushed it away. "It was a beetle."

"Whatever. All I have left is my voice, and it's so diminished that I can't even keep insects from crawling on me. Not without serious effort. I would have to exert myself to command a single lowly human, too. If they came equipped with a good solid stick, they could bash my head in before I finished wresting control.

"And yet my magic still works perfectly well on you. Astonishing, really. You manage to snare yourself in my clutches even when I'm at my absolute weakest. I truly don't understand what madness brought you here, except maybe idiotic pride. Did you think your willpower would finally be enough to get the best of me? You aren't built like that, Crow, and you know it."

She made Crow turn so she could look about the bower. All the trees had black bark. Knobs of hardened sap caught the light like raw gems.

Her eyes went back to Crow. "What is that you're wearing, some sort of cassock? Tell me, what kind of saint makes humans fight their battles for them?"

"An effective one," said Crow.

"Hah. Not so effective now, are you?"

She ordered Crow to take her down to the terraces. To the spot where she'd died.

"How long has it been?" she asked.

"A little over sixty years."

"Goodness."

They contemplated the pearly stone ridges, the scalloped pools, the reflections of branches and wispy brush-stroke clouds.

"You did a very good job of not betraying your plans," Magnolia said at last. "Or your hopes, I should say. I don't suppose you had any concrete plans at all. That would make it easier—no details to obsess over. I knew something was on your mind, truth be told, but I figured you were just profoundly disturbed by the culling of all those hunters. Disgusted with me, and perhaps with yourself."

"That was part of it," Crow agreed.

She'd told the woman with the pike that she and Magnolia would venture north of the hills. They would wander, take their time. She'd described the sort of situation in which Magnolia might be caught unawares. She said she would create opportunities around the next new moon—and the next one after that, and the next.

She hadn't offered further specifics. Nor did she receive many in return. The pike-wielder didn't guarantee that her crew would cooperate. They definitely weren't prepared to trek up to the northern rim of the world. At some point they would have to drop away.

But Crow swore she would serve them for the rest of their lives if they killed Magnolia—the Woman in the Hills. She could no longer afford to be squeamish about new companions. Whether or not she ever took another, time would work inexorably to erase Arion's presence off the face of the earth.

"Lady Pike signed her core over to you after killing me. And thus she lived happily ever after, she and her merry band of slayers."

"You told them to die," Crow said, "and most of them did. Right here in these pools. It was a scene like human paintings of hell. Are you proud?"

"I'm not remorseful, that's for sure. If you waited six decades to nag me, then you've wasted your time."

"I waited because we agreed that I would bring you to the end of the world," Crow said evenly.

"I didn't agree on a sixty-year detour to the land of the dead!"

"You weren't in any rush, either. Now we can get going."

"Have you arranged for bandits to ambush us?"

"Maybe I have."

"Who's going to attack me this time? An army of grandchildren with heirloom pikes?"

"That wouldn't be much of a surprise, would it?" said Crow.

"I was joking. Does Lady Pike have a bunch of descendants?"

"Two sons."

"Neither of them yours, I hope."

"...................."

"I give up," Magnolia declared. "You make no sense. You thought my revived self would be feeble enough to defeat on your own. You thought you'd take my core and be done with it. Or perhaps you planned to make a misguided show of mercy. Perhaps you would've blackmailed me into good behavior with threats of permanent death. I can't imagine that you came strolling back with every intention of falling straight under my spell again."

Well, no. But Magnolia did seem to pose less of a threat than ever before. She already had a late-season mosquito bite swelling on the side of her neck. Crow was the only living being she could still control with ease. Unlike in the early years after her genesis as an immortal, no villagers would come bearing sacrifices. It would take her an unfathomably long time to rebuild her strength.

"I don't see why I shouldn't make you my sacrifice-bearer instead," Magnolia said coldly. "You're all I've got. You'll lurk like a two-headed wolf at the edge of settlements, always keeping me on your shoulder—I'll have to stay close. I'll make you pick out easy victims—starving children, the elderly, invalids. You'll loathe every second of it. But it won't be the worst thing you've ever done."

The livid stress of existing in a human-shaped body had not coursed through Crow so potently in decades. Not since she'd watched Magnolia's face cave in beneath the blade of a pike. She dug her fingertips into the wounded end of Magnolia's neck. The flesh yielded like old honey. Magnolia winced—but, bewilderingly, did nothing to stop her.

"I missed you," Crow said. It came out sounding like *I'm going to kill you.* With Magnolia, those two phrases were more or less interchangeable.

"You wished to forget me," Magnolia said, her voice much smaller than before.

"I couldn't. Sixty years isn't a very long time."

"You can say that because you weren't trapped in a cocoon."

"What was it like?"

"I'm tempted to play it up," Magnolia admitted. "Would you feel sorry for me? But no—it wasn't torturous. I had some awareness of time passing. I heard you speaking to me, towards the end."

"Do you remember what I said?"

"I remember everything you've ever said. Being cocooned wasn't especially tedious, at any rate. Do you ever go dormant? I used to, out of sheer boredom. It's like that—or like how sleeping is for mortals. Whether you're dreaming or totally oblivious, or drifting in and out—it takes as long as it takes. Time becomes this soft cottony thing. Beyond the lantern-light of your awareness, the world in all its dimensions ceases to exist. Do you understand what I'm saying?"

"Not at all."

"We should put you in a cocoon next. You can find out for yourself."

Crow eventually settled on holding her trunk in her arms, and balancing Magnolia on top of the trunk like a drinking glass on a tray. She crossed the valley of travertine terraces, listening to Magnolia make ironic comments whenever crows cried mockingly from the treetops. At one point, Magnolia opened her mouth and let out an impeccable series of answering caws. She hadn't assented to continue onward. Nor, however, did she give orders to turn back. So Crow kept going.

"Sixty years," Magnolia repeated under her breath. "How's my village?"

Crow described her last few visits. The radish village was smaller, and poorer, and saw fewer visitors than it used to. But they got by. Each time Crow passed through, she helped wipe out a new collection of monsters. The hills weren't safe for noncombatants.

Still, even the most intrepid monsters rarely encroached on the village. Locals theorized that Magnolia's tree offered some form of mystical protection. Pilgrims and ascetics came from distant parts of the continent to pray at its roots.

"They call it a miracle of the God of the End," Crow said.

"Are you kidding me?"

"If you wanted credit, you should have left them with a placard. Or a memorable myth about its origins. A lot of people think that tree helped defeat you."

"If I cared what people think, I would start screaming, and I might never stop," Magnolia said through her teeth.

"Screaming won't get much attention here in the mountains."

"The ghosts of past civilizations might sympathize. Unlike you, you…"

Crow held her tongue while Magnolia cast about for insults.

Later, she related other stories of the village as they occurred to her. Like about the time when a helpful trader brought an invasive beetle as a gift. It bore a close resemblance to the tea beetle, but it couldn't be used the same way. It tasted terrible, and besides, it was deadly to all but the halest of humans. For fabric, it only produced a brown stinking dye.

The invasive species immediately outcompeted local tea beetles in the wild. It kept mixing with farmed stock, too. For a time, the original tea beetle had been in serious danger of extinction. This was part of the reason that the village had declined.

"If I still possessed my old power, I could've ordered the invaders to leave," Magnolia commented. "Every last one of them. Which is why nothing of the sort ever happened before. Thanks to me. Ah—that's what I should do to you!" she said in a tone of madcap inspiration. "You were waiting around by my cocoon. For twisted reasons of your own, you want to be here with me, self-righteously judging my natural monstrosity. Yes, you want this. You're a pest. I ought to order you away."

"Can you keep me gone for long?" Crow asked.

Magnolia glowered. "Don't test me."

"Could you survive an attack by lower-tier monsters without my protection?"

"……………"

Recognizing a rhetorical dead end, Magnolia changed the subject. She had no end of questions about past acquaintances.

Crow answered to the best of her ability.

Dung had never forgiven Crow. Eventually she'd taken him back to live with his brethren. It was hard to tell how well he fit in. But the last time she went to see him (from a respectful distance), he showed no greater interest in her than any of the other slavering beasts.

They had been forced together for less than a year—not a hefty percentage of his life. Time had purged every last molecule of Magnolia's magic, and maybe it had weathered his memories, too. Crow watched him bask in hot glaring sunlight; he was larger and creakier than most primevals. A senior beast, now. A survivor. The same intense sun heated her wings until she soundlessly stole away.

Haida, much to his own disappointment, had lived—in improbably excellent health—for nearly a decade after the slaying of the mimid. This perverse run of good fortune lasted until he caught a chance infection through a trivial wound. As his fever worsened, Rinlin panicked. She broke Crow's feather. Haida had told Rinlin how and when to use that feather, and he'd specifically warned her not to break it till he died.

The moment he saw Crow port in, he turned to the wall and passed away, as if out of sheer stubborn spite. At least he let Rinlin hold his hand.

Crow took Rinlin and her latest generation of chickens to a quiet settlement south of Fellshore. As it turned out, her birds were the last of a lost regal breed. She cultivated a magnificent flock and did very well for herself, despite her lack of relatives and her curious accent. She married a trapper and raised four daughters, all with a boundless love for fluffy chicks.

"If she's still alive, she must be crawling with grandchildren," Magnolia said dryly. "If not great-grandchildren."

"Or grand-chickens."

Rinlin had done her best to propagate those fussy egret orchids, too, but they refused to grow in the land she'd come to call home. She'd asked Crow to plant them in other settlements and wild places all over the continent. Rinlin herself might never see them bloom again—but she would rest better, she said, if she could believe that they wouldn't die out.

The automagi of Steppehaven were the same as ever, albeit sleepier and more subdued. Over the past few centuries, they had already started to fade from human memory. One day, they might even fade from their own memory. But they had no real capacity for horror or dread.

Pothos still came back to check on Tamar's jar. As the years passed, she seemed to range further and further afield. Crow had glimpsed her in some very unexpected places, though never this far north. She thought Pothos might be searching for other half-immortals, or other dire foxes. She didn't know which would be more readily found.

"How about that stinking city?" Magnolia asked.

"A lawless ruin."

"Typical. What happened to Arion's statue?"

"Still there. But half-forgotten."

The New City government had imploded in the wake of the Dame's death from old age, and the subsequent departure of her saint in the sky. Ashwort harvests had already dropped precipitously in the years before she died. Monsters flooded in once the aerial saint left, and residents scattered like fleeing rats.

"As for me," Crow said, "I'm your servant again."

Magnolia scoffed. "Servant to a crippled king. I don't dare let you more than twenty paces from my side. No idea what my magical range is now that I've been reduced to all the power of a newborn babe. You hear me admitting that? No deception, no clever ruses, just piercing complaints. That's how far I've fallen."

"You were always prone to complaining."

"Oh, shut up."

"You'll discover your range as we go," Crow told her. "There's a long way to travel before the end of the world."

"You've got to know that there's no way I'm keeping my original promise."

"Don't you want to see the end?"

"I want to rip your throat out with my teeth," Magnolia said pleasantly, "but I need to conserve my energy."

60

After a couple days, Magnolia seemed to tire of muttering darkly about plans for bloody recrimination. Sometimes her grandiose plots focused on Crow, and sometimes on any hypothetical human who carried a pike or a bow, or who aspired to fight monsters.

She made Crow scratch the mosquito bites clustered on the side and back of her neck. "It won't help," Crow said.

"Just keep scratching."

"You'll bleed."

"Are you my servant, or my grand vizier?"

Crow stopped scratching. She marked the bites with her nails, forming starbursts of intersecting lines. Leda used to do that. Crow had taught Arion to do the same, back when he was young enough to believe it was a cure.

"If you hadn't been there when I revived, I would have gone crawling to find you," Magnolia said.

"To wreak vengeance?"

"Doesn't matter why, does it? You were enough of a chump to show up and save me the trouble." She perked up a little. "In a way, I've already achieved retribution. I made you mine all over again, in an instant."

It had been frighteningly easy to fall into the rhythm of sixty years ago. Before the cocoon opened, Crow had not been sure if she could remember the exact location of Magnolia's moles, or the shape of the scar that marked her forehead like a brand.

But there they all were, right where they belonged. Her lush eyebrows, one split by another scar. Her sparkling teardrop earrings. The self-aggrandizing lilt to her voice. Nothing about her was unfamiliar.

Maybe—and this went both ways—there was just no point in feeling awkward around someone who already had every reason to think the worst of you. No matter what Crow said or did, no matter who she pretended to be, she could not possibly lower Magnolia's opinion of her any further. There was nothing left to lose.

It was very freeing, actually, after spending over half a century bogged down in mortal society. Her old haunt. All the while, she'd made a good-faith effort not to hurt anyone she didn't have to. It got rather tiring to show constant compassion to sinners and victims alike—to the strong and the weak, to those who saw her as a tool and those who saw her as a beast.

Maybe Magnolia had felt this exhilarating knife's-edge freedom from the moment they'd met. When she'd taunted Crow with Arion's voice. No need to fear shameful missteps or wounded feelings or a loss of respect when the baseline state of their relationship had always been coerced obedience and murderous wrath.

"I'm not as angry as you'd like to think," Magnolia said philosophically.

"You keep threatening to bite my fingers off."

"Put another way—I bring extra excitement to your everyday life. No need to thank me."

"I won't."

She waved frail roots about in a gesture that might have been the equivalent of a shrug. "You played your hand better than I gave you credit for. But it hurt to die. I can be furious about *that*. I've never hated or admired anyone as much as I did when that pike blade smashed the bones of my face. It's a wondrous thing, you know, to be simultaneously impressed to your core—and to boil over with all the violent loathing of an exploding star. You make me remember emotions I haven't felt since I was human."

"If getting stabbed in the face inspires admiration, you should admire my pike-wielder. She did all the work."

"Your twenty-fifth companion," said Magnolia. "Shall we visit her grave?"

"It's in the opposite direction of the northern end of the world."

"Maybe some other time, then. Keep going."

They stumbled across hints of old settlements, and even older civilizations. The wreckage of pontoon bridges. Lonely standing stones blotched with lichen. Cubbyholes bored in cliffs—most were empty, looted, but one or two had bones at the very back.

The only humans they saw were nomads living on a plain carved out, long ago, by the passage of a particularly restless volcano.

Magnolia had a weirdly flat reaction to the smell of corn cakes, the threads of smoke curling up out of autumn grass, the silhouetted figures unaware that immortals stalked them from afar. Crow had been prepared for a grand confrontation.

"What?" said Magnolia.

"I thought you would tell me to bring you dinner."

"And what do you mean by that, Your Righteousness?"

Crow deemed it unwise to continue.

"I am hungry," Magnolia said. There were shadows as thick as thumbprints under her eyes. "I'm always hungry. But I find myself somewhat preoccupied with memories of human weapons cracking my skull. Mashing me like walnuts in a mortar and pestle. Believe it or not, those memories do turn my appetite. I'm not indifferent to my own pain and suffering."

Crow bore her away from the nomads before she had a chance to change her mind.

On a dry day without too much wind, they inventoried the contents of Crow's trunk. She no longer had Magnolia's pair of green glasses, although she'd succeeded in keeping her own. She still had the wooden doll from the now-vanquished city, too.

Magnolia gave the doll a critical look and said: "If you kept it to remember me by, you should have chopped off its head."

She seemed disappointed that Crow carried no artifacts from her most recent companion. She displayed an unflagging morbid curiosity about the woman with the pike, so much so that Crow wanted to thwart her by lying. But Magnolia would dig the truth out eventually.

Crow explained that the pike-wielder hadn't brought her crew to the radish village in hopes of taking down the Woman in the Hills. They had no interest in any rumored rewards. They'd traveled from the distant southern half of the continent on a recruiting mission. They'd heard that many famed hunters had gathered in an obscure land known to host the last of the Four Great Adversaries.

"I'm insulted," Magnolia said. "Thoroughly insulted! They weren't even planning to slay me?"

Down south, an abominable monster had swallowed entire seaside settlements. Some were already calling it another Great Adversary. Perhaps the greatest.

"Lady Pike promised you her soul to defeat it?"

"I didn't defeat it. I bought time for them to recruit the saint in the sky."

"Ah. So that's where it went after the city's leader died."

The Maw from the Sea was unique in that something about its presence inflamed other monsters. It brought them crawling out of the ocean, dropping fearless from the sky. It felt like facing a grotesque pastiche of the Singular Horde.

The resemblance was superficial—on a fundamental level, the Maw was no more like the Horde than the Fellshore mimid had been like a true serpentine aerial. The Maw incited a frenzy among smaller monsters, but it didn't share a mind with them; they came rushing along as opportunistic scavengers, not as extensions of its ship-sized sluggish body. The end effect, however, was akin to facing an allied army. Less single-minded than the Horde, but every bit as avaricious. It had been all Crow could do to fend them off while refugees fled further inland.

The saint in the sky had pushed the lines of battle back to the shore—where, as far as Crow knew, the decades-long war continued to this day. With the exception of a few reckless holdouts, humanity had abandoned the entirety of the southern coast.

"You just left?" Magnolia said, eyebrows raised. "Before anything was concluded?"

"My companion was ready to die, and I had an appointment to keep," Crow replied.

"If you crushed me the moment I came out of my cocoon, you might still have succeeded in taking my core. I was rather dazed for those first few seconds. Why are you always so slow?"

"If I had it in me to crush you like a fly in my palms, I wouldn't have resorted to asking humans for help."

Magnolia went silent. She was on Crow's shoulder, but her roots were too weak to hold her there like the claws of an eagle. Instead, Crow kept a constant hand in Magnolia's hair to balance her. Over time her raised arm grew stiff, but never tired.

They stopped to marvel at a grove of evergreens whose meaty branches bent at fastidious right angles, squaring off again and again on their way towards the sky. These were not native to the continent, Magnolia claimed—they must have been brought over from some other faraway land.

"Always wanted to see an angle tree with my own eyes," she said. "All right, Crow—I forgive your transgressions."

"If it's that easy to forgive, then maybe I let you die too quickly."

"Didn't have much choice, did you?"

This was true. Anything but a swift, decisive death would have given Magnolia a chance to turn the tables. A single tossed-off syllable had been enough for her to annihilate nearly all of her slayers. If she went to hell, she would drag as many souls as possible with her.

The bark of angle trees was allegedly a hallucinogen. They chewed it, and found it pleasantly spicy, but of course it had no other effect on them. They spent several languid days watching the sharp, uncompromising shadows those branches made on the spongy ground.

"Angle wood is extraordinarily beautiful," Crow said.

"You would know, I suppose."

"It's difficult to work with, and difficult to source."

Partway through the grove, they found a number of old ropes dangling from high branches. In the not-so-distant past, there must have been a settlement nearby.

"They hung their criminals and outcasts," Magnolia said cynically. "Or tied them up to get pecked to death."

"Don't think this is the right kind of rope for that. Or the right length."

"What were these, then?"

"Swings for children," Crow guessed.

"You might be onto something. Give it a try."

The branch creaked in protest. Crow hastily jumped down from the rope she'd started climbing. Magnolia dissolved into a puddle of squeaky laughter.

Every once in a while they heard distant music, as if from unseen bands of wandering mortals. Up north, humans were like the mystical beings in fairy stories of old. Cautious hidden creatures, shy and unpredictable, making furtive sounds of merriment as they crept about the wild world.

Further north, all signs of humanity vanished as snow started falling. At first it came lightly, stopping and starting, glazing spruce needles like sugary frosting but leaving much of the ground gray and bald.

At the summit of one semi-powdered mountain, they found a rock formation shaped like a half-buried human foot.

"The Hallowed Toes," Magnolia said.

"The what?"

"The Toes of the God of the End. Hey—I didn't name them. The automagi mentioned this. Means we're on the right path."

The god's toes were grand indeed. Crow balanced Magnolia in the slight cleft between two of them. This didn't last long: Magnolia complained that the rocks were freezing.

"No divine aura?" Crow asked.

"Alas, no. Nothing."

They moved from one mountain to the next. Eventually the snow came down in sufficient quantities to bend heavily-laden trees in half.

"That's right," Magnolia said. "Bow down to me, you stupid trees. You're in the presence of the last Great Adversary."

"Unless we count the Maw from the Sea."

"Hmph. I've still got seniority."

"Are your teeth chattering?" Crow asked.

"I can't be cold," Magnolia pronounced with frigid dignity. "I'm a terrifying immortal. I'm a decapitated avatar of human folly."

Crow cradled her in a woolen blanket, despite her objections. "Did it snow in your village?"

"Which village?"

"Either one."

"Not this much, that's for sure."

Crow found the cold bracing—far from unpleasant. An immortal in good health might live comfortably anywhere. The thinnest air at the top of the highest peaks, the pulverizing pressure at the bottom of the sea ... if they failed to frequent such places, it was only because their prey had settled down in more temperate climes.

Magnolia's jaw wouldn't be shivering if she still had her old hoard of consumed magic. Revival had left her with nothing but her original naked core—the most basic of equipment, which might ensure survival, but not comfort.

A haunting quiet surrounded them. The stars looked so piercing. It was as though layer upon layer of translucent old skin had been peeled away from the night. Crow patted melting snowflakes off Magnolia's cheeks.

"Can't you make it stop snowing?" Magnolia said. "Oh, right—you've sworn off weather magic. Guess I'll just have to suffer."

"You'll live."

Another mountain. Here the fir trees did not stoop: instead, they formed the core of misshapen columns of rock-textured snow, no longer recognizable as anything remotely alive. Dawn cast long turquoise shadows across the untouched snowy fields beneath. It looked like a forest of white standing stones.

Crow hoisted Magnolia up high overhead for a better view. The daytime sky was a clear watery green. She used magic to walk softly atop the snow, wings growing from her ankles. No footprints; no danger of plunging down into a hidden void and getting buried.

When the wind came back, it blew already-fallen snow upwards, a blizzard going the wrong direction. She held Magnolia closer. It was in the midst of this that Arion's voice said, like a tiny insect in her ear: *I knew you were my mother all along.*

Her arms tightened around Magnolia's bundled-up head.

I knew you were my mother, but I wanted you to tell me. I wanted you to be the one to say it. I waited and waited, but you never admitted it. I waited all my life.

"Mag—"

"It's not me," Magnolia said harshly. "Whatever it says—don't answer."

A land-bound monster, then. Why else would it be stuck in a snowy realm without any human presence? But this voice went much deeper than the reedy echoes on other mountains.

Why do you think the Devil let me go?

"It's using your voice now," Crow said.

"Stop walking. Get this blanket off me."

Crow obeyed. Magic dripped from the bottom of Magnolia's neck like blood from a never-healing wound. She was incandescent with— something. Outrage, or possibly humiliation. Crow stood there for twelve hours while voices swirled around them and Magnolia slowly, slowly talked the monster into becoming tangible enough to rip to pieces.

Crow did the ripping; Magnolia's vines lacked the strength. Afterward, Magnolia drank down the little sun of the monster's core. At last it was silent, the whiteness around them riddled with black holes from ethereal acid. Powdered ash blew away, mingling with microscopic needles of snow, and then the wind died down once more.

Magnolia licked her lips. "This is like a starving human eating shoe leather to survive."

"That bad?"

"Victory is always scrumptious. But mortal cores are much more nutritious. I'm not as cold anymore, so at least something good came out of it."

"What did the voices say to you?"

Magnolia ignored her.

"What'd they say?"

"A whole lot of gibberish. Keep going, Crow. Get us across those mountains."

61

CROW COULD HAVE taken aerial form. Barring that, she could have spread her wings. There were all sorts of ways to travel faster with magic. But speed had never been the point of the journey. Magnolia wanted to see things up close. Those trees transformed into monstrous hulks of snow. Rocky alien landscapes pockmarked by now-vanished vorpal holes.

They didn't encounter any living giant tardigrades. Just old husks on the far side of the mountains, large enough to use for shelter like a cave. Later the snow gave way to a hot oasis of white sand, strangely lifeless except for shimmering bugs that hung about in the still air, only moving when Crow walked straight into them.

Crow rested her ankles in a pond surrounded by sterile sand. Beside her, Magnolia said: "Do you miss my legs? Do you miss my hands? It'll be a long time before you ever see them again."

"I missed your voice."

"You really do enjoy pain, don't you?"

As evidence, Crow said: "I came back to witness your revival. Without being ordered."

"There we go," said Magnolia. "Perhaps you're a masochist. Perhaps you view me as a charity case, now that you've cut me down to size. Perhaps you're wary of the threat I might pose after another thousand years of moonlight—no one would call me a Great Adversary in my current state, but you feel a duty to keep an eye on me. I guess it's some perverted combination of all three."

"Also," Crow said, "I enjoy your company."

Magnolia chuckled. "You enjoy being ordered around."

She couldn't deny that. While Magnolia cajoled the immortal voices in the mountains, Crow had held her aloft—becoming a living pedestal, as still as the snowed-in firs. The waxing moon tracked a path across the sky, hour after hour, and her mind had felt like a wide-holed net cast in clear barren water, catching nothing. The cold edge of an abrasive wind touched her face. She'd steeped in the long-lost sensation of having no other purpose, nothing to run towards or away from, no subtle choices that might go terribly wrong, no mortal lives in the balance. *Stop moving. Hold me up higher.*

Wouldn't anyone else—mortal or immortal—feel the same? Wasn't that simply part and parcel of Magnolia's magic?

"I've decided to be truthful, for a change," Magnolia said.

Crow blinked.

"I'm serious. I have no pretensions to goodness. But I'm quite literally a changed woman."

"Because you were dead?"

"Because dying stripped me of every last crumb of hard-earned power I'd ever gained. I have nothing left to protect except my core. It's quite pathetic now, a squishy bit of magical larva. Won't taste very good, but it's all I've got." She dipped slow-growing roots in the oasis water. They were the color and shape of bleached coral. A couple of those odd hovering flies took up a position in the air near her temple, like decorative attendants.

"You know what I want?" she asked.

"To consume enough mortal cores to make up for all the magic you lost?"

"That goes without saying. Along the way, I want to see everything there is left to see in the world. But I don't want to see it alone. Which makes me fundamentally flawed, as far as immortals go. I could blame it on being a returner, but I'd rather blame it on meeting you."

"You forced me to stay and serve you," said Crow, struck by the unfairness of this. "If you got used to having me around, it's entirely your own fault."

A new confusion rose in her. "It's easy to break the compulsions of other immortals. You could have made any passing saint or monster free you much earlier. Why wait so long—why wait for me?"

"It's easy to break compulsions voluntarily," Magnolia said sourly. "It takes a miracle when done under command. Under duress. Because then it's like attempting to break your own compulsion yourself. A victim operating under total control becomes a tool—an extension of my will.

"How many times do you think I tried to leave that land before you came? I did have some hope when I called over the last survivor of the Singular Horde—but that too was all for naught. The famous Horde isn't worth much once you whittle it down to just one body. The only reason you failed to take it out was bad timing, and bad luck."

She told Crow to dig at the edge of the oasis in search of isopods. For her part, Magnolia used white fleshy roots to probe the silt at the bottom of the preternaturally calm lake. They reconvened at twilight beneath gray strangling trees that looked neither dead nor alive.

The whole point of this exercise had been to map a path around any upcoming volcanoes. But upon conferring with buried crustaceans and with the earth itself, they separately reached the same grim conclusion. The migratory volcanoes were gone. In fact, the physical end of the world was much closer than the automagi had told them. They'd expected to spend several more months traversing the rest of the harsh wintery north.

"Well," Magnolia said. "If the automagi knew of any big changes over the past half-century, I suppose they wouldn't have told you for free."

"Their information may already have been out of date when we first got it," Crow pointed out.

"True. No more moving volcanoes … I'm sad to have missed them. This must be devastating for the supply of ashwort, though. No wonder that new city thrived."

"Until it ran out."

"I, for one, won't shed any tears if ashwort vanishes from the continent." Magnolia raised her eyes. "Crow, how long have we loitered here? Is that a full moon?"

"Looks full enough to me."

A fuzz of short silken roots sprouted from the bottom of her neck, stirring like agitated cilia against Crow's palms.

"What?" Crow prompted.

"Have you figured out your own compulsion yet?"

"I—"

"It's not complicated," Magnolia said wearily. "It's just harder to perceive when you're all caught up in it. You have a compulsion to obey your promised companions. I'm not your promised companion—never have been, never will be—but that compulsion is like a structural weakness in you, a vulnerability tailored to the particular shape of my magic. Your compulsion is a keyhole. My magic just so happens to be a set of lock picks."

Crow took a breath and started to object, mostly on reflex.

Magnolia overrode her. "You're going to say that you obey your companions by choice. Within reason. You serve them faithfully because that's how saints till their fields for greater magic, more glorious cores, an all-surpassing reward at the end.

"That's all very well. The saint in the sky served that godforsaken city for decades, for much the same reason. This is what you tell yourself. And, sure, your companions can't force you to do the impossible. You couldn't kill yourself when I ordered my murderers to die."

"There's no special distinction between me and the saint in the sky," Crow said. "Service takes different forms in different times, and with different companions."

"The young empress." Magnolia was adamant. "She ordered you not to save her. You let her die to a mob. You lost her, and you lost your chance to claim her core. You told yourself afterward that you let her die because it was the right choice—for various reasons that no longer matter—or because you valued above all else *her* right to choose how to end her short bloody life. You told yourself that your final obedience was the ultimate sign of respect. You told yourself this because there was no other way to explain it. No other saint would have let a precious companion throw away their life and their core like that."

Crow's voice came out scratchy. "When did I tell you about the empress?"

"You and I did nothing but talk. When you weren't trying to kill me, that is. You told me about all your companions, at one point or another. Maybe you've forgotten what you've said to me, and what you haven't. Understandable. You've been off living your life. I was in a cocoon—I wasn't busy.

"You agreed to be caned instead of your human companion—even though he was a traitor and a murderer, and fully deserved it. He told you to take all the blame, and you took it. Not because you really felt it was right, or smart, but because you couldn't *not* take it. Want another example, Crow? Here's a good one. Your poet, Snowberry. Faced with plague, he ordered you to go treat the poor of the city before you treated him. You left, *and you never came back*."

"I came back," Crow said, stung.

"Years later! He was dead! You waited till the plague had swept its way in and out of every slum. Another lost chance to reap a core. You explained it away in your usual fashion. Yes, you did save a couple extra people, although who knows what kind of lives they lived afterward. Yes, you devoted yourself to helping the forgotten and abandoned. Very noble. No, I don't suppose Snowberry's life was worth all that much more than the life of a beggar.

"You made yourself believe it had been your choice to follow his orders to the end—to follow his orders so literally that you let him suffer and die alone. You found this more bearable than believing that you never had any choice at all."

"You can't tell me I had no choice," Crow snapped. "You can't—you weren't there. You were never there."

"I know precisely how your compulsion works," Magnolia said with finality. "I feel it every time I take advantage of it to give you orders. Like a thief caressing the tumblers of a well-loved lock.

"Say, what's the other reason they call you the Saint of the Carrion Crow? Generations ago, you fought in wars between tribes and wars between kingdoms. You fought brutal wars of annexation. You made human corpses—at least as many corpses as I have!—and flocks of crows and vultures followed you around like loyal pilgrims. Afterward you remembered these as good battles, just battles, or at least as marginally better than the alternative. You had to think you bought into it. You had to shore yourself up. But don't tell me you wanted to be a part of it—shredded limbs and innards, muddy carnage, screamed-out prayers, devouring fire. You aren't me. You wouldn't want that for anyone. You wouldn't have slaughtered soldiers without a compulsion to obey."

Crow gathered herself to say—to say how wrong this was, all of it.

Her voice ran headlong into a dead end. The right words were hiding inside a labyrinth. She couldn't find them.

"It could have been much worse," Magnolia continued, relentless. "You never realized how defenseless you were against the whims of your human companions. This ignorance, in a way, turned out to be the best defense of all. You always picked out some tortured justification after the fact, even when following commands you found abhorrent. Or you skewed your interpretation of orders, bending them to become just barely within the realm of acceptable.

"Your companions never understood the full extent of their power over you, either. None of them expected to be able to issue absolute commands to a saint. They thought there would be limits, some degree of ongoing negotiation. At times, if you acted reluctant, they would modify their directives before you even asked. If you readily did things for them that other people might find disturbing—well, who expects the morality of immortals to align with human beings?"

Crow glanced down. The black pond looked like a sea of broken glass, brimming with stars. A fine skein of roots had crept up her arms while Magnolia spoke. Sleeves of living lace, freshly formed, the same hue as pallid cave birds.

She felt as though that lace had already reached her throat. She choked on her hard certainty that Magnolia was right. She had not changed very much, after all, since her previous life as a passive lump of fallen flesh. A relic forced to listen to an endless litany of mortal woes.

"This should be easy," Magnolia said conversationally, "but it isn't. Not for me. In part because I've lost nearly all the magic I ever had, no thanks to you. And in part because immortals are really, really bad at giving things up. We can't use our cores as a bargaining chip, the way humans do. We're physiologically incapable of killing ourselves.

"Ah ... I've delayed long enough. I'll stop putting it off. I'm the lowest of the low now, as far as monsters go, but I'll break your compulsion anyway."

The roots tightened, fizzling with magic. Crow's body wanted to struggle like a fish in a net. Something in her slipped, dislocated. Magnolia looked at her with a face like a statue found among ruins. The vision of an unknown sculptor, now bare of paint, and bare of mortal or immortal emotion.

62

"Now reach forward," Magnolia said, "and rip out my earrings."

Her voice was rife with magic. Crow almost reached out of habit. But—she realized this with dreamlike slowness—Magnolia's magic hadn't gone all the way inside her. It felt more like an ocean current urging her body along. She could push in a different direction. She could strain herself to resist.

"Of course you would wait till now to give me that command," she said.

"Well, I don't actually want you to do it," Magnolia said, unabashed.

"I don't need orders to bully you."

Magnolia gave her a sharp-edged smile. "Oh, but you do. In this one respect, we're very similar. You relished hurting me when I was in a position of power. You won't have much fun with it now that I'm a weak and hapless head. As for me, I'll take what I can get, but that's why I like eating hunters. The reversal makes it thrilling. Arrogant humans laying their arms down at the sound of my voice. Or—one of the world's most accomplished saints bleeding from self-inflicted wounds, deprived of her wings."

Crow thwapped her on the side of the head.

"Ow! Stop that!"

She did it once more, for good measure.

She stood up, and found suddenly that she needed to sit down again. She rested against a rock that jutted from the sand, twisting and writhing in a battle with gravity. The ground felt warm, as if a humongous mammal slept beneath it. She rested Magnolia on bent knees, one hand held out to steady her.

"You broke my compulsion," she said.

"So?"

"You gave up the secret to your power over me."

"I can still command you."

"It won't be as effective as before."

Somewhere beyond the hot oasis, it was storming—snow piling up to new heights, blind whiteness clogging the night in every direction. Everything here remained quiet and placid—the flat water of the pond, the reflections of stars, and Magnolia. Broom-shaped pines cast a legion of confusing shadows.

"Why?" Crow said. "Why would you do that?" Then, when Magnolia failed to reply: "Why did the Devil let you go? What did you say to her?"

"I already—"

"Don't pretend you told me all of it."

Magnolia had wrapped strangling vines around the backs of Crow's knees. "We're close to the end of the world," she said abruptly. "Much closer than we'd thought. Would you like to know my original plan?"

"You said you would free me."

"And now I have. In a manner of speaking. Ahead of schedule, even."

"But that wasn't your original plan."

"Not quite. At first, I was going to make you throw me off the edge."

"Of the world?" Crow said blankly.

"Of the world."

"Would that work? Using me to kill yourself—"

"Who knows what lies beyond the edge? Maybe I would be annihilated—a head dropped in the equivalent of a vorpal hole. Maybe I'd land elsewhere, or become a returner in a different realm. Sounds like an adventure."

Crow shut her mouth. She didn't want to ask why.

"So my first plan," Magnolia said blithely, "was to give you a single clear command. Hurl me off the edge. Hurl me into oblivion. I might have miscalculated—perhaps this couldn't result in any outcome other than suicide—but I was pretty sure you'd be forced to go through with it. I wouldn't even have been lying. You'd get rid of me, and you'd free yourself, and you'd be nicely traumatized in the process. Then I reconsidered."

"Because you didn't want to risk dying at the end of the world?"

"No, no. I didn't want to make it too easy for you. My next plan was to break your compulsion. I would free you, and then I'd suggest tossing me into the abyss—or whatever lies beyond the end. Just a suggestion. Not a command."

"I might have gladly done it," Crow said.

"You could get up and go do it right now," said Magnolia. "Will you? Circumstances have changed. I've been thoroughly hobbled. But in my original vision of our confrontation at the end of the world—in that vision, I was still at the height of my magic. I was still very much a threat. I would have lost some measure of control over you, after releasing you from your compulsion, but I would have remained a Great Adversary all the same. I didn't want you to be able to say that I'd forced you. I figured it would leave a deeper scar if you had to do it yourself.

"Whatever became of me at the end of the world, I quite liked the idea of haunting you for the rest of your interminable life. You would think of all the mortals whose cores I'd steal in years to come. You would think of all the lands I might plague. You would make the right moral choice. Then you'd look back and know, always, that you could have chosen differently. I wanted you to be tormented forever by thoughts of a future in which you'd spared me."

"Forever?" Crow said, incredulous.

"You came back for me after sixty years."

"That's nothing."

"True. However, time has yet to prove me wrong. I've haunted you for sixty years. Not a bad start. All that aside, I changed my mind."

"What, again?"

"My plans are ever-evolving. Why not try something new? I decided that I'd offer you my core at the end of the world. I'd become your promised companion."

The hints of dawn light looked all wrong. Too gray, too tired. Dizziness swamped Crow as she said: "Immortals can't—"

"Immortals can't kill themselves. Immortals can't surrender their cores. Immortals never give up power of their own volition. But I broke your compulsion, didn't I? I gave up the key to commanding you. A promising first step. Besides, a half-immortal can swear away their core. Tamar did it. So did Arion."

"You're not half-immortal."

"I was human in another life. Perhaps that's enough. Won't know unless I try. You, on the other hand, have never turned down a genuine offer from a potential companion. You couldn't even turn down Arion. If I offered from the bottom of my heart, you'd have to take it. That's got nothing to do with your broken compulsion. That's just part of being a saint."

"You would make a big production of breaking my compulsion," Crow said slowly, "and then you'd immediately turn around and use a different tactic to imprison me."

"You'd be trapped with me in a whole new way. You would hate me for it all over again. I can hear it in your voice already. I've always treasured how much you hate me."

It took every last granule of Crow's self-restraint not to crawl over to the pond and drown her. "You're selfish. You're sadistic. And you never know when to shut up."

"No one has ever known me as well as you," Magnolia agreed.

"If that's still your objective—"

"I'll confess to being tempted. I'd like to try it, if only to see what would happen. Is there still a ghost of humanity in me—enough, at least, for me to become your promised companion? No other way to find out. Stop glaring at me like that, Crow. If I were going to go through with it, I wouldn't have told you."

"What's your plan now?" Crow said heavily. Ordinary conversations with Magnolia were sometimes more exhausting than a life-or-death battle with any of the other Great Adversaries.

"Look at me." Magnolia put on a sunny grin. "I'm here with you now, and I've got nothing. Perhaps *this* is the plan, if only by process of elimination. If you want to know for sure—better take me to the end of the world, no?"

"You already freed me," said Crow. "The deal is off."

"But I want to see it," Magnolia said plaintively. "We've come so far already."

Crow pictured herself pressing that grinning face into pond silt, as if making a mold for a mask. It would be immensely satisfying. She would hold Magnolia's head under like those villagers forcing her into the vacuum of a vorpal hole. In another time—in another life. Magnolia had lost all meaningful power except, apparently, the power to annoy her.

She got up. The vines around her knees tore apart. Magnolia mewled piteously. Crow, heedless, plunked Magnolia's head on her shoulder and trusted her to hang on for dear life.

63

MORE CEASELESS SNOW, more steaming oases. Then the landscape became stranger. They reached a stretch of dry scrubland sprinkled with cloud-soft bushes, which tore off in globs at the lightest touch. The globs stuck to Crow's clothes and skin like a mist made of spicy needles. Stifled laughter emanated from the extra head on her shoulder.

Every so often, she locked eyes with a rabbit covered in large warty growths. When those rabbits went still, they could pass for chunks of wood festooned with mushrooms. When they moved, they looked like diseased ambrosia hares.

"Nothing seems familiar?" Crow asked.

"Not at all. The climate, the land—utterly unrecognizable. Maybe the village of my first life existed way beyond the current edge of the world. Maybe you're walking on what's left of it right now. No way to tell."

The sky had turned the same stark, uncompromising blue as the sky above Steppehaven. It held only a few isolated black vultures.

"There must be a reason that aerials avoid this place," Magnolia remarked. "Good thing you didn't fly us over."

Crow didn't feel much different without her compulsion. Perhaps that was only to be expected. She'd spent most of her immortal life unaware of it. Beneath the unending blue sky, she attempted to catalog all the orders she'd regretted obeying—from Magnolia, and from her twenty-five past companions.

When it came to her companions, she'd thought she had a choice. She'd thought none had ever pushed her past the point of refusal. If she could've said no, what would she have been unwilling to do? Where would she have stopped?

Magnolia, true to form, didn't give her much time to ponder in silence. "I have a pet theory that all worlds go through cycles of more magic and less magic. Unfortunately, no civilization will ever last long enough to measure these cycles in full."

Crow had a theory that Magnolia ought to close her mouth for once.

"Can you still read my mind?" she asked.

"I can, but it's muddier, and takes more concentration. More effort than I can afford to spare, for the most part. Why? I'm sorry if I missed out on a cutting retort."

"It was an ordinary retort," Crow said.

"Not worth repeating?"

"No."

Hours blurred together in the totality of their aloneness. It felt as though they had been traveling forever, and as though they were only just getting started. No matter how Crow scanned the horizon, she could no longer see snow-capped mountains anywhere behind them. They'd come far, but those mountains should still have been visible. If she were mortal, she would have been thoroughly disoriented.

She'd expected Magnolia to slip up, to toss out careless commands and then start grumbling when her one-time servant no longer leapt to obey. Magnolia did still make a lot of demands, but none of them came with any extra thrust of magic. Maybe she had too much pride to issue haughty orders that might devolve into a magical wrestling match and, in the end, go pathetically unheeded.

Trees dotted the scrubland. They were uniformly short, stuck in the ground like swords buried to the hilt—trunks all hidden, only their tops spreading out. It was as though they had been submerged by an unusually gentle landslide.

The air didn't feel as hot and arid as the scenery looked. Still, it was jarring to encounter huge snowdrifts as tall as sand dunes. They refused to melt even in blazing sunlight. Magnolia, enthralled, asked Crow to put her down on one.

"I'm like a fresh fish on ice!" she said.

"A true gourmet dish," Crow muttered.

Since Magnolia could no longer casually skim the surface of her mind, she would have to voice anything she wished to share. How galling.

She lifted Magnolia off her bed of snow, and patted her dry. She moved ahead, walking on and on and on. All the while, the sun barely shifted in the sky.

"You claimed we were close to the end," Crow said.

"Time moves slower here, and so do we."

It took so long that even Magnolia began to grow quiet. Yet this rare respite wasn't enough to purge her voice from Crow's head. There was really no escape: remembered words sidled down into her mind, one drip at a time, as if coming through a leaky window on a rainy night.

Perhaps this *is the plan.*

A throwaway comment; a tone of jest.

It was not difficult to pull up memories from sixty years ago. Ever since her first meeting with the pike-wielder—every moment from then until Magnolia's death—Crow had been on high alert. All sorts of minor details became indelibly imprinted on her brain. The shape of the low-branching tree that Magnolia had planted as a guardian. The curse-absorbing straw ornaments that people wove to hang near windows and doors.

Outside the village, Magnolia had said they were being watched. Crow went through the motions of checking for pursuers, and reported none to be found. She'd implied that Magnolia had been misled by skulking cave birds.

Magnolia let the issue drop, even though she was right. The pike-wielder's party had been trailing after them all along.

On that note—Magnolia had displayed a distinctly muted reaction when they first attacked. When Crow unthinkingly took an arrow for her. She hadn't argued when Crow grabbed her and flew away without fighting. She hadn't sounded especially angry. Was that her usual response to a threat?

And why, days later, had Magnolia demanded to revisit the scene of the ambush? Granted, Crow herself hadn't thought the hunters would make another attempt there. (She did figure it would give the party a chance to collect themselves and start catching up.)

Magnolia had shown a genuine interest in the beauty of the travertine terraces. Was it really worth the risk of returning? Crow herself hadn't proposed going back—she hadn't even endorsed it. She'd feigned reluctance. Once they did return, though, she'd devoted herself to keeping Magnolia distracted.

And Magnolia threw caution to the wind. She let Crow beguile her.

The scrubland had become sprinkled with round puddles. In their regularity and spacing, they resembled an inverted version of Magnolia's hills. Each pool was stuffed to the brim with motionless algae, like an overgenerous serving of seaweed soup.

"Is there rosemary growing from that rabbit?" Crow asked.

"It's certainly something herbish."

"You knew my humans were coming to kill you," Crow said, without any change in tone.

"Not exactly." Magnolia didn't miss a beat. "Don't discredit yourself—you did pull one over on me. But there may have been some element of mutual effort. I may have attempted to meet you in the middle—just a little bit. You tried very hard not to think about it. I, in turn, tried very hard not to make any obvious deductions."

She laughed without rancor. "Come on, now. Lady Pike had a core. I could sense her sniffing around no matter what, even if I valiantly disregarded her coreless teammates. Sometimes it takes a lot of work to be ignorant."

"Why?" Crow said, stupefied. And irrationally angry. "You told them to die. If you knew—"

"Knowing it's coming is something entirely separate from the actual experience of having your one precious head shot and bashed and stabbed until nothing identifiable remains. Did I have a face at the end—a nose, a mouth, eyes, unbroken bones? Surely not. The contents of my broken shell came dribbling out like a half-cooked yolk. I hope you never forget the look and the smell of it. I was a vital collaborator—unbeknownst to any of you!—but that doesn't mean I liked dying such a savage and degrading death. Of course I was mad with fury. Of course I felt vindictive. Who do you think I am?"

Crow halted. She'd been on the verge of stepping in one of those algae-choked puddles. They went much deeper than they appeared at first glance. She pulled Magnolia off her shoulder and held her up at eye level.

"Then why did you play along?" she said. "Why did you give them an opening?"

Wild thoughts ran through her; few made any sense. Had Magnolia handed this victory to her solely for the sake of tainting it? Had Magnolia accepted death and given up her thousand-year stash of magic just so she could claim that Crow had not really defeated her after all—that it had only been possible because she went along with it? Ridiculous. The cost was so much greater than whatever tiny bragging rights she might—

"You wanted to know about my last conversation with the Devil." Magnolia's lip curled. She glanced at a spot over Crow's shoulder. There couldn't have been anything to see except more mindless blue sky. Truncated roots curled around the sides of Crow's hands.

"It's easy to be honest with someone you'll never see again." Her gaze shifted to Crow's other shoulder, though her voice never wavered. "I let the Devil know that I found myself in the unusual position of caring for you—as much as anyone can care for a prisoner dead set on killing them. This was a strategic choice, of course—the Devil's own troubles all stem from true love. Thought she might find it persuasive. How did she react? With a trace—I swear—of pity. That woman is devilish to the bone."

"Pity," Crow echoed blindly. Her wings twinged as if every feather shaft had become a piercing needle.

"She told me that with the power I held over you, you would never really be mine. Simply freeing you wouldn't suffice. The problem with the Devil is that she knows exactly what she's talking about. At first I hoped to prove her wrong. Upon reflection, I realized how very right she was. Infuriating, really."

She caught Crow's eye, briefly, and said—as steady as ever—"We immortals excel at clinging to life, and clinging to power. We aren't made to surrender. I knew I couldn't do it alone. Lucky for me—there you were, a righteous saint. Trapped with me and hating it. Hating me. Which was all I needed."

"You rounded up the hunters at the village. You led them into the hills to be slaughtered." Crow's voice sounded detached, but her thoughts jostled and stumbled. "You reminded me of your cruelty, and then you left me behind. You left me alone. You took your time on purpose. You gave me space to plot against you."

"You can't reduce anything I've done to only one motive," Magnolia corrected. "I did want you to keep an eye on the village while I went on my murder spree. And, yes, I reckoned it would give you a chance to recruit allies. To concoct some sort of half-baked plot to fell me.

"I killed the hunters because I wanted to, and because a few of them had cores. And, yes, to force you to recall that I was the last Great Adversary for a reason. Your sworn foe. You're used to sympathizing with unsympathetic companions. You might deny it, but over the course of our travels, you'd become dangerously inclined to give me the benefit of the doubt.

"In conclusion—I had fallback plans for the end of the world, but I wanted you to get the better of me. I wanted you to make me give everything up. The Devil got me thinking—and eventually I came to agree. I had to lose it all. I could see no other way to meet you as anything but your final adversary.

"I'll build up more magic over time. Like how you regrew your wings. But it'll take me much longer. Cocoon death is a far less forgiving setback. The world might end before I once again become worthy of being called a Great Adversary. The border has already moved far enough to eat up most fleeing volcanoes.

"Even if I do regain my former glory—with your compulsion gone, you won't be uniquely weak to me."

"A devious scheme to lay yourself low," Crow said, "and to become utterly vulnerable."

"Not too impressive, as far as nefarious plots go. It was the only strategy that had any chance of working. Still no guarantee, though."

Bits of those woolly bushes blew into Crow's ankles, stinging her. "You could have forced me to love you," she said. "You could have given me some kind of excuse."

"I could have forced anyone in the world to love me. Where's the value in that?" She'd tilted her head just a bit to the side. More roots braided their way through Crow's fingers to brace her. She wore a dreamy look, a nostalgic smile. "When we first met, you know, I had the time of my life."

She'd spoken to Crow in an imitation of Arion's voice. She'd attached herself to a corpse and crawled around on the ground below her tree. She'd made Crow pluck parasites off the bottom of her neck. She'd forced Crow to behead a brave young swordsman to defend her.

"I should hire slayers to off you a couple more times," Crow said frostily. "We can keep going until you learn some semblance of remorse."

"You'll never change me that much." Magnolia was no longer smiling. She contemplated Crow with a deep, deep calm that verged on sorrow.

"But you never did anything like that again."

"Like what? Do you mean your wings?"

"You maneuvered me into killing a human hunter."

Magnolia blinked as though she'd forgotten. "Oh, right. That's true. Early on, I loved trying to shock you. Disgust, hard-knotted rage—you gave such good reactions. When revulsion burned in you, I felt it like the heat from a fireplace.

"But I soon lost the element of surprise. Your reaction solidified. That implacable, cauterized hatred is nice in its own way, sure, but it leaves you too protected. The more I hurt you, the less capable I am of *really* hurting you—does that make sense? Your enmity becomes a shining shield. My knife turns blunt. Now, if you like me, if I make you laugh, if you want to think the best of me..."

She looked at Crow expectantly.

"Your logic is too twisted to follow," Crow said. "You'll have to explain to the end."

She heaved a sigh. Her voice remained relaxed, but her roots clutched Crow's wrists for dear life. "I was struck by the way you looked at me when I told you to tear off your wings. I was mesmerized. I wanted to be able to do that again, to shock and wound you in ways you've never even dreamed of being wounded. I wanted to plant seeds of immeasurable pain in parts of you that no one else could ever reach. The thing is, I wouldn't actually do it. If I won you over, and then betrayed you—it would only ever work once. I want eternity."

Despite her aptitude with languages, Crow struggled to translate this. A current of deranged joy kept trying to overtake her—or was it just sheer mind-wrecking exasperation? Above all, there came the magnificent relief of hearing in words everything that she already knew without proof.

She opened her mouth to speak like a sane and rational human being. But she wasn't human; she had never been human. Whatever her feelings were, she could have expressed them more purely by screaming like her namesake bird, the three-legged corpse-picker. She could have shown her heart more definitively by taking aerial form and conquering the empty sky at the end of the world.

"You wished I would trust you, against all reason," she said at last. "You wished for the ability to crush my whole heart in your hand. You would hold it carefully, because once you crushed it, you would never be able to destroy it again. You would lovingly cultivate your potential to ruin me—and you would strive to preserve that potential for some unfathomable length of time. Till everything ends."

Magnolia beamed. "I'm surprised! You understand perfectly."

Crow was sorely tempted to wring her neck. "That's a very roundabout way of saying you want me to love you."

"I never said *that*."

"If you don't want to end up at the bottom of an algae pool, you'd better start speaking plainly."

"I have been nothing but plain and truthful," Magnolia protested. "It's not my fault if none of the languages we speak can adequately capture all my profoundest depths of immortal emotion. The only love I've ever heard of lasts—at most—for the length of a human life. Maybe a few centuries beyond that, if we believe romantic ballads about half-immortals. I'm talking about something on a much broader scale."

"We've known each other less than a century," Crow said crisply.

"Time will prove me right."

"If I don't chuck you off the edge of the world first."

"Better make up your mind," Magnolia said. "It's right over there. But what about you, Crow?"

"What do you mean, what about me?"

"Do you love me? Do you adore me? Am I perfect with or without a body?"

Crow went rigid, outraged to the point of paralysis. Magnolia was not quite smiling. Sunlight twinkled in her earrings and glanced off the scar that split her eyebrow.

"I came back for you," Crow said. "I've stopped trying to kill you. Even though you're constantly goading me. I have every intention of staying by your side until the world breathes out its last exhausted breath. I'll stick with you like a curse cast by the Devil—I'll make you sick of it. Is that not good enough? It had better be good enough."

"It's more than I ever knew to hope for," Magnolia said quietly.

64

STRICTLY SPEAKING, nothing lay beyond the cliff at the edge of the world.

Crow shook her wings out. She put her trunk (and Magnolia) on a natural plinth of weather-eroded sandstone. Wind riffled the tips of her feathers, and the ends of Magnolia's tendrils: unruly creepers that spiraled from the edge of her neck like summer vines. Tiny leaves unfurled on green shoots that reached out as if tasting the air.

"Is it like looking into a vorpal hole?" Crow asked.

"No. This is gentler. Or maybe," Magnolia said, reconsidering, "maybe it's exactly like a vorpal hole, and it only seems different because we're immortals. We don't have a visceral dread of the void."

They knew they were gazing at nothingness. Their eyes and their magic perception failed to fully take it in. They saw instead a misty sea of shapes that swam about like ghostly elder aerials. A phenomenon akin to patterns of light glimpsed inside closed eyelids in a pitch-black cave. Their minds invented vague movement and cloudy scenery to fill in the dead space outside the end of the world.

"You haven't thrown me in yet," Magnolia observed.

Crow picked up a head-sized rock and lobbed it like a cannonball. Somewhere near the peak of its arc, it disappeared. Her brain seemed unable to register the precise moment when it stopped existing. Her heart beat very slowly, as if ponderously grinding to a halt.

They had not encountered any saints or monsters since the land-bound voices that Magnolia had devoured during a blizzard. The white mountains and the shimmering winter oases and the hot scrubland were all equally devoid of human beings. Ordinarily, no immortals would come here by choice. Magnolia was the first to point that out. "It's very unnatural for us to linger in a place with no human population."

"It's unnatural for immortals to have long conversations," Crow said.

"Or to do anything other than efficiently kill one another."

In response, Crow delicately scratched the back of Magnolia's neck. She was rewarded with a soft pulse of honeysuckle fragrance: the closest Magnolia would ever get to outright purring.

"I didn't have high expectations," Magnolia murmured.

"For what?"

"For you not killing me. This time for good."

"If you just wanted the pleasure of my company, there would have been no need to forfeit all your years of moonlight."

"I wanted you to be more than my servant, and more than my pet."

"A risky bet."

"Did I win the bet?" asked Magnolia.

"Do you think you won?"

"I haven't lost." She gave a modest nod. A more vigorous gesture would have been wont to topple her over. "I do think I'm very attractive, as far as severed heads go."

"It's true that I've never met a handsomer severed head."

"I'm sure you've seen plenty to compare me with. And you know we'll never run out of things to talk about, no matter how much time goes by. But the simple fact is that I'm better equipped for being a villain than for being anyone's suitor. I keep thinking wistfully of how I could have tied you down with magic. I could have forbidden you to conspire against me. I could have kept everything I'd gained from my long centuries rooted hopelessly in the hills."

"You're greedy," Crow said. "You wanted me, and you wanted me to choose you. You fixated on the one thing you couldn't take by force."

"You know what settled it for me? Hearing about the way Arion became your companion." One of her green runners twirled around Crow's forearm like an elaborate bracelet. "You never had a chance to prove you wouldn't leave him. He needed a guarantee, and he got it. But he lost the ability to know for sure that you would have stayed with him of your own accord, without a promise of binding magic.

"Any day, or any night, you could change your mind and leave me. If you don't punt me over that cliff, and if you don't take my core yourself, you could leave me right here to soak up moonlight. The edge of the world might rumble closer—but my roots can probably crab-walk quick enough to escape it. You could turn your back on me with a clear conscience. Another thousand-something years from now, if we're still around, if the continent is still around, if I start wreaking havoc further south—I'm sure you'll hear of it. I'm sure you'll stop me."

"I never thought about abandoning you at the end of the world," Crow said. "That would've been an elegant form of revenge."

"I haven't influenced you all that much, have I? You still find it difficult to think like a villain."

"Your obsession with me hasn't made you saintly."

"Point taken."

Crow was still a saint. One day she would take another human companion, and she would keep taking companions until the day when no more humans remained. She'd have to find a way to explain Magnolia's presence—whether riding her back, or attached to the end of an ostentatious wooden staff.

Magnolia was still a monster. She would keep eating human cores—frequently or infrequently—until the day when no more humans remained. Crow had never aspired to be an arbiter of mortal life and death—but she would rather pick and choose than let Magnolia kill on a whim.

They spoke of uncomfortable compromises, and the tenacity of mortal society, and the bone-deep peace at the end of the world. It should have been disturbing, this abrupt sheared-off land where reality rotted like a gangrenous limb. But their voices filled the morbid silence, and gradually they got used to how the edge of that plain blue sky melted away into nothingness.

"We can't travel further north," Magnolia said practically, on a night without any moon in sight. "Where did you want to go next?"

"Your radish village could do with some help."

"And after that? You went all over the southern edge of the continent, didn't you? During your dallying with the Maw from the Sea."

"If you want to go south, just tell me," Crow said, amused. "I'll take you to see my pike-wielder's grave."

"Oh, great."

"Don't spit on it."

"I would never. She brought me down, after all. She must've been one of the most illustrious heroes of this dying age. All right, so we'll pay our respects. And then?"

Crow picked Magnolia up with one hand and her trunk with the other. "We can watch the Cat Comet together."

"That's got to be at least two or three centuries away."

"It's something to look forward to," Crow said.

Magnolia mumbled under her breath.

"What?"

"This has nothing to do with any profound discussions about our philosophical differences," she stated, this time with clear dignity.

"Well, what is it?"

"Even as a disembodied head, I would enjoy being kissed."

Crow shot her a look. Then she raised Magnolia's head to her lips and kissed her hair, her ear, her mouth.

"That's the gentlest you've ever been," Magnolia said afterward. She sounded dizzy.

"I can't be rough when you're just a head."

"Oh, you'll learn. It'll be a while until I can generate so much as the ghost of a human body. But I feel my roots getting stronger. In the meantime—"

"Let's talk about that a little further away from the physical end of the world."

"What kind of throes of passion are you envisioning here? Do you think we'll roll around so much that we go flying off the edge?"

"You're much more prone to rolling than I am."

Crow turned her back on the edge of the world. Magnolia settled down as a warm, grouchy weight in the crook of her arm.

"Wait," Magnolia said. "Get my doll out. The one from the New City."

"It's a vanished city now." Crow produced the limbless doll from her trunk. It made no noise whatsoever, but it seemed as if it ought to rattle—or offer some other form of musical contribution—when she shook it. "Should I throw it past the border?"

"No. Although that would make a certain amount of sense. Like dying in effigy." She pointed a tendril at the natural plinth that Crow had used as a pedestal. "Leave it. Next time we come back, we can see if it's still there."

"You want to measure how quickly the end of the world advances?"

"That's part of it."

"The rock already serves as a landmark."

"You say that now, but there could be a thousand other rocks with the same shape. Immortal navigation won't work so well in a place like this. My doll will let us know we're in the right spot. As long as it doesn't get swallowed."

Crow conceded the point. She half-buried the doll in sandy soil at the base of the plinth. It felt like placing a stake for a tent.

"What was the real reason you wanted to come here?" she asked as she dug.

"I wanted to go as far as possible, and I wanted to go there with you. The end of the world sounded like it would take a while to reach."

"That's it?"

"No." Magnolia's voice slowed. "No, that's not entirely true. I wanted to see if this world really is just a larger version of my first village—the village where I was human. Surrounded by inescapable nothingness. Steadily shrinking. I wanted to see if the end of the world would feel familiar.

"You know, if I'd made it here on my own, I might have decided to become the God of the End myself. A god to help bring an end to it all. Why drag things out? Extra time breeds more mortal and immortal agony—that's a fact, a guarantee. Whether it also breeds an equal amount of joy and pleasure and glory is, quite frankly, a matter of eternal debate."

"For all your haughty talk about the Devil—"

"Oh, I'd happily become a world-ending devil too. The difference between me and her is that I wouldn't be horrified. I'd embrace it. But things are different now. I lost so many years of magic to that cocoon of mine. I couldn't possibly play-act at being a deity. And I didn't end up facing down the border of the living world alone."

Crow balanced Magnolia's neck on the tip of a finger. Somewhere along the way, she'd learned to do this without a single wobble.

"Is it the same?" she asked.

"The world as a whole, and my old village? It should feel the same, shouldn't it? Is it strange that I don't feel trapped? The only difference is the size of the fish tank. And—this greater world has you in it. No, I don't feel trapped at all."

"You got your answer," Crow said. "One way or another."

"Maybe. I did think there would be more answers. I thought I'd peer over the edge of the world and understand why I became a returner. But there were no revelations to be had outside ourselves, were there? No one stood waiting for us at the border between existence and death.

"There is no God of the End, or anything else of that nature. No one to define which appetites are righteous and which deserve suppression. No one who can prove that either cruelty or compassion make any difference whatsoever in the long run. It's all grains of sand crumbling off the edge of a bottomless cliff. There is no given reason in the world for any immortal to try to be good or bad—whatever that means—or to follow anything other than the promptings of their inner nature. There is no special reason for anyone's suffering, no grand plan, nothing but a fading land creeping through the final stages before total oblivion."

Crow glanced at the nothingness where the land stopped, then back at Magnolia—who, despite the sepulchral tone of her sermon, looked quite serene.

"Not even the end of the world has a deeper meaning," she continued, "or hidden secrets potent enough to change the tenor of our lives. I can't alter my inherent self, and nothing here—or anywhere else—will do it for me. But I find myself wanting to behave a few shades differently than I otherwise would. For you, if you'll believe me."

Crow considered the practical aspects of this claim. "So it won't be a constant battle to stop you from devouring entire settlements?"

"Not constant," Magnolia hedged.

"Only once in a while, then."

"I've got to keep your interest somehow."

Magnolia's eyes were as red as ever in the slothful light from the lifeless sky. Almost vermilion. They were as hungry as ever, too. But also—for the first time since Crow had known her—strangely sated.

Crow jogged Magnolia's neck on the tip of her finger, feinting, ready to toss her into the void. Magnolia returned her gaze without fear. The dead air crackled as if with the promise of a storm. They both laughed, dry and deep and spontaneous.

Then they left, this time without second thoughts. She carried Magnolia through night and day, through unrelenting blizzards and sunlight. It was a relief when the blueness above gave way to a sumptuous peacock sky.

Magnolia collected magic like rain in a barrel, drop by drop, but she never tried to use it on Crow.

On the opposite side of the snowy mountains, they ran across a shrunken patch of old ashwort. They spied a haze far on the western horizon. Wildfire smoke? Or perhaps the breath of one last distant volcano.

Silent scrubland, and everlasting snowdrifts, and deathly algae pools, and the decapitated rim of the continent—all of it began to feel like scenes witnessed in another long-ago life. There was so much more for them to see and remember. Their future together would dwarf the months and years since they'd met.

Every last living human might forget about the Woman in the Hills, as eventually they would forget about Calamity Bridge. And the Beautiful Scourge. And the Singular Horde. And the Maw from the Sea. And the reason that massive armies had called a winged woman the Saint of the Carrion Crow—cursing her power, and cursing her name.

Subsequent generations might begin to hear of new legends. A two-headed saint, perhaps. Or an immortal sky serpent with an extremely bewitching and talkative face. Or a bodiless monster who would seek out the cruelest of humans to steal from their beds with dark vines. She would select those who had shown they could match her for savagery. She would do each victim the honor of splitting them open, and swallowing their core, and cleaving it to her own.

There would not be many stories of a saint and a monster together. Who would believe or understand it? But they didn't need mortal stories, or binding promises, or magical servitude, or anything except the repetition of a daily choice to stay close, and to refrain from killing one another; to live together in defiance of nature. They made this same choice for themselves again and again.

Human companions died one by one. The continent shrank. Old languages blurred and dwindled. Ear-shaped pasta became a lost art. An earthquake made a giant crevasse open in the middle of Magnolia's hills.

Magnolia learned to form a temporary translucent body to go with her head: human-shaped, albeit with about as much heft as a jellyfish. (Real solidity would come later.) Once embodied, the first thing she did was to reach up and yank at Crow's hair. This didn't go well—she was too ethereal—but she seemed proud of the attempt.

Later the Cat Comet returned, with its four brilliant tails. They saw it together, night after night. A flare to herald another apocalypse, or so people claimed. Much to Magnolia's sorrow, it didn't make her invincible: her cocoon death had reset all her progress.

Crow flew the two of them up to the peak of an icy sky.

"See you next time," Magnolia said to the comet.

Perhaps they would meet it again. Perhaps they wouldn't. Even now, there was plenty of time left for immortals to keep nibbling away at the corpse of the world. They weren't meant to need anyone, but they had learned to need each other. So long as they were still together, they would be content no matter when the end arrived.

A Note from the Author

I HAD A BLAST writing this. Hopefully you had fun reading it, too! Whatever your feelings, I'm grateful to everyone who spent time with *Carrion Saints*. As always, thanks so much for your ratings & reviews, which are extremely helpful to fellow readers—and to me as well.

I don't know what it says about me that I've always wanted to write a book about a talking severed head. At least I'm not the only one. Over the years I've encountered multiple stories, particularly in anime, with a living head serving as either a major character or a plot point.

Speaking of anime—but not of severed heads—a fantasy series called *Frieren: Beyond Journey's End* has become renowned for its depiction of relationships between characters of varying longevity. *Frieren* wasn't a direct inspiration for *Carrion Saints* (I didn't watch it until I had mostly finished writing), but it's definitely a go-to story for anyone interested in a gently melancholy exploration of immortality.

I should also add that the Devil who appears in this book is one of the main characters of my Clem & Wist series. Start with *The Lowest Healer and the Highest Mage* to discover more about her origins ... and keep going further along in the series to learn how she came to the world of *Carrion Saints*.

I'm currently planning another standalone novel. I want to try writing something more compact—if only to prove I still can!

Follow my Author Page for future updates if you'd like to see more: **https://amazon.com/author/hiyodori**

Hope to see you again next time!

– Hiyodori

Novels by Hiyodori

The Clem & Wist Series

Prequel: No One Else Could Heal Her

Book 1: The Lowest Healer and the Highest Mage

Book 2: The Reverse Healer Case Files

Book 3: Clematis and the Queen of the Void

Book 4: Three Murdered Mages, Two Broken Bonds

Set in the World of Clem & Wist

The First and Last Demon (Standalone)

The Forest at the Heart of Her Mage (Standalone)

Carrion Saints (Standalone)